MW01105438

TAUT STRINGS
OF CALICO

TAUT STRINGS
OF CALICO

Dorothy Flowers

To order additional copies of this book, contact:
Xlibris Corporation
1-888-795-4274
www.Xlibris.com
Orders@Xlibris.com
32853

This book is dedicated to
the memory of my mother,
Mrs. Ruby Mae Harvey,
a strong woman who fought against the odds
for the good of the family.

ACKNOWLEDGMENTS

I would like to thank my husband, Frazier for his sincere efforts to give me space while I lost myself in a world of dedication to these writings.

PREFACE

This writing is an imaginary account of the possibility that the rhythm of life's ardor can be handed down from generation to generation. It most likely repeats itself over and over again, by strings of words spoken in whispers. When cool breezes blow, the strings tighten to form musical chimes that can cause hormones to rage, sparks to fly and relationships to take root in the unsuspecting hearts and minds of men, women and even innocent children. Chords of love, hate, friendship, courtship and marriage may change suddenly. Strings of Passion presented as a gift and beautifully decorated by bows with ends waving in the wind are oftentimes unattached to anything. Some people are meant to be together and some are not; or knot.

"Let there be light. Let there be light. Let there be light." The rhythm of the force of nature must have been in God's mind when He spoke the words that created the world and brought the heart of mankind into existence. The creator and conductor of the ultimate symphony has the power to change the rhythm of resounding words to synchronize at will. Thus, a tale of a secret has power to fine tune chords of life. If one will listen closely, harmony can be heard as taut strings loop around the imagination where stolen moments and sweet dreams hide. Tales handed down from one generation to another are capable of binding the hearts of the innocent and tantalizing the minds of the wise.

PART ONE

Young Thera heard that before she was conceived, her father was on the run from a mob lynching. She questioned her mother about the meaning of the word, "lynching," and her mother drew a picture. A man was hanging from a string and had no shoes on his feet. Thera looked at the string that was tied to the man. She inspected the picture with interest and wondered why the man was just there, he and the string. She had many questions in mind but when she sought her mother's attention, her mom whispered, "Shhh," and held a finger against her lips. Some time later, meaning years, Thera learned that they had been riding on a train. She went to sleep longing to know more than she had ever known before but she had been told to keep silent.

For years to come, she remembered the train ride. She also remembered hearing the sounds of hissing steam and of metals that clinked, clanked and screeched. From the window of the train the child saw other trains in the rail yard that had large wheels rolling on greasy iron rails. The boxcars started moving and rocked with a jerking motion like a crippled swan that she and her mother had once found and tried to nourish back to perfect health. Thera wanted to be in a quiet place like in her home where her mom and dad laughed and talked. Things were very different on that particular day of travel. Her parents sat with their faces appearing to be bland and drawn. The way that she felt about her immediate situation had been displayed in her mother's drawing. Thera imagined that she was hanging on a string separated from the world as she had known it. The reverberating sounds of the train relaxed her when its rhythm caught her attention. She began to look around the passenger car. Other people were seated and talking. They had whispering lips that appeared to harmonize their voices. She gave her full attention to them in an effort to hear what they talked about. Somewhere a tale had been told of slave ships that transported human cargo. At her tender age she imagined one of the people on that ship to have been her. What she had heard was probably her dad speaking of his dilemma when he had thought it best to leave the south. Thera began to question her thoughts. She wanted answers to the many questions that crowded her mind. The rhythm of the moving train again captivated her as she looked through the window in time to get a glimpse of the locomotive that followed the tracks around a bend. Thera began to move her feet to the rhythm and sat watching people talk while her parents slept. She did not remember falling asleep but was awakened by her dad when he lifted her from her seat. It was cold and in the dark of the winter's night when they left warmth of the train. After a long ride in a taxi cab the family of three again exited their mode of travel into darkness and icy winds that blew debris from its hiding places along the gutters of the city's street. After a short journey from the curb to a cemented walkway that led to a building, Thera with her mother and father entered a house. She found warmth and comfort in a darken parlor that smelled of cinder and ashes. An old and rusted stove stood in the corner of the room. The stove displayed a bright red glow and was blazing hot. It warmed the parlor. Thera snuggled down in a soft, plush overstuffed chair and watched dancing shadows on the painted wall of the room. The hot stove made popping sounds when a big lump of black coal was added to the fire that roared within its round belly.

She, her Dad and Mom had arrived at a strange house in the middle of the night. Thera was chilled to the bone before she had snuggled in the chair. A woman called Chick opened the door. She had her hair standing tall and it looked matted upon her head. When they'd arrived Thera was in her mother's arms and must have fallen asleep because her mother was not in the room when she woke up. She had been covered with a blanket. No matter how hard she tried, the child could not remember when her mother had left her alone. Surprisingly, she was not afraid because it was morning and she felt as if she snuggled in the arms of a trusted friend. Warm inviting sunlight was filtering in through colorful homemade curtains like God had sent a special welcome. The old stove in the corner did not have a colorful glow anymore. It stood looking cold and uninviting. The smell of ashes still lingered in the air. Thera was comforted by the scent of those ashes because it was confirmation of their arrival to the house the night before. It seemed that out of no where several small children came running through the room. There came three or four boys and three little girls with wild looking hair like Chick, the woman who had let them into the house at night. The children's bare feet pounding against the wood floor made the sound of beaten drums that echoed. Squeals of delight rang out when one of the children would outrun the other. They ran from room to room while Thera sat as still as a mouse in the chair. Bumping noises and the booming sounds of running feet caused Thera to cover her ears and wonder when someone would get spanked for playing indoors. The children began to plead and whine to go out and play. A man they all called daddy had walked into the parlor. Suddenly the begging of the children to go outside subsided. In its place a rush and rummage from room to room began. The children were searching for warm shoes and clothing to wear out of doors. The temperature had fallen during the night. Big and white fluffy snowflakes were falling. Thera could see from the window that the ground was covered with billowing white foam and glistening. To Thera, the long tracks where cars had plowed through looked like ribbons. She had never seen snow before that day. The snow covered the ground like a white and sweet sugary frosting on a cake. Thera's mother walked into the room where she had slept all night and took her into a small bedroom where a large galvanized tin tub of warm bath water sat in the middle of the floor. Her mother waited until Thera undressed and stepped into the tub before she left her alone again. The warm bath reminded Thera of home. She sat down in the tub and splashed the warm soapy water all over her body. The warmth felt good and it chased away her chills while she bathed in the drafty room. Her Mother returned to the room again carrying warm clothing for her to wear. With chattering teeth Thera stepped from the tub and welcomed the warm towel that was wrapped around her small body. After eating a bowl of hot oatmeal, Thera was sent outside to play with the other children. She wore a new navy blue wool sweater beneath her coat, mittens on her hands, heavily woven cotton stockings to warm her legs and rubber boots that covered her shoes to keep her feet warm and dry. Before she went out of the door, a wool scarf was tied around Thera's neck and her mother put a heavy cap on her head that covered her ears. Thera could hardly walk and could barely hear. Never in her life could she have imagined the need for so many god-awful, ridiculously heavy clothing. The first thing she did when her booted feet touched the ground was to take a scoop of the falling white stuff on the ground to place on her tongue. To the child's chagrin, as sweet and tasty as it looked, the snow did not taste sweet at all. To make it worst, the snow had no taste at all. Her butt felt the freezing cold wind chill her to the bone when she had bent to gather the snow. In spite of all that she wore, a gust of icy cold wind had blown through her layers of clothing and became trapped under her armpits. She shivered until her body warmed up again. The other children continued to play as if it were springtime.

It taught her a good lesson that she decided to remember forever. When it's cold outside and the cold winds blow, never bend over. Always squat to protect your ass from the elements. Later in life she was to find that it meant more than protecting ones self against the weather. The fact that the snow had melted on her tongue coupled with her discomfort saddened her. She went to stand in a corner by the steps of the house until she fully recovered from the chill. Thera stood huddled up and looked around to see what the rest of the outside world looked like. Cars and big buses crept down the street following trucks loaded with ashes and cinders. The trucks carried men armed with shovels who pitched the black, rocky mess onto the pavement. The heavier it snowed the more black, mushy, frozen gook was thrown onto the streets causing dark and dirty slush to fly from the curbs when buses passed by. The intensity of the games that the children played became too much for Thera. She went inside and told her mother that she needed to warm her hands. From a window, she watched the rough and ready kids that could brave the cold weather continue to play and have fun. The throwing of icy balls made from snow created fights among the older boys. Pandemonium sent the younger children scampering to get themselves out of the line of fire. She also observed children on home made sleds zipping past each other as they glided fiercely down the cement sidewalks. Heavy shoe boots called clod-hoppers protected their feet with iron cleats attached to the thick soles. The cleats could be heard cutting through the ice that had formed beneath the snow. A few of the children wore mittens but most of them wore nothing on their hands. They stuffed their freezing fingers into their coat pockets for warmth.

It was the winter of 1945. Thera had just turned four years old. Her folks migrated from the south to a small town in Indiana where they hoped to make a better life for themselves. Pete Jones and his wife, Chick had a brood of children. Thera's dad met Pete while in the army. From what she'd heard her parents say, the south was not a kind or profitable place to try and raise a family. The appearance of their surroundings she saw the first night in the north, prompted Thera to figure that they would be on the move again before too long.

She noticed that her mother was not smiling much anymore. There were too many things and familiar faces missing from her life for reasons that weren't clear. Besides her parents, Thera found comfort in the warm, overstuffed chair in the parlor. From the parlor she could almost hear sounds from every corner of the house. That first Friday night Pete and his wife, Chick put their children in a back bedroom to play while they opened their house up to gambling games. Thera had heard Pete talking earlier in the day and saw how displeased her mother looked when people began to fill the house. Thera was heard years later to say that Pete had a house cut of 5% on each game that helped him to feed his family. It was not long before Thera began to love and look forward to the sounds that the gambling action created. The environment of enjoyment and spontaneity was all that the child found to like about the place where they lived. Each time she heard the bass of a guitar strike up a rhythm, she would sway to the beat. Her daddy looked charming and smooth with the guitar pick held by his fingers while he strummed the low down blues. She just could not help herself. She missed the green grass, flowers and tall trees. The mourning lyrics of the blues allowed her to hear her true feelings within. When she looked outside the next day there was no snow, only clouds of gray. Dismayed, she started to reminisce and compare one habitat to another. There had been chickens laying eggs that she helped her mother to collect. Out in their pasture had been cows that swished their tails and horses that her father would ride. The same streets that were covered with snow now looked dirty from the grit and grime left over from the cinders and ashes the men on the big trucks had shoveled onto the streets during the heavy snowfall. Pete and Chick's gambling games brought to her ears the sounds of a live rhythm that she would liken to sunshine and flowers. The harmony of chickens clucking and horses braying and neighing were being created by the melodious tone of every voice in the big room. She learned to couple those tones with the peals of laughter; and it turned into a joyous night of jive. Thera's imagination added charm and passion to musical notes in the pitch of people's voices that seemed to bounce through the walls into the bedroom to tickle her ears. When the liquor flowed freely she would rise early the next morning and find the glasses to sniff the aroma of the alcohol. Old Grand Dad whiskey and Gordon's gin bottles were left on the table empty. Johnny Walker Red scotch was put on a high shelf above the kitchen sink that was attached to the wall near a window. She liked the smell of apple wine and peach brandy. The fruity aromas reminded her of the apple and peach trees down south. Some of the voices threw the notes of rhythm and jive talk slightly off key when people drank too much. Women would walk into the house grinding their hips and winking their eyes. Thera heard things like, "They call you coffee because you grind so fine", or "it must be jelly because jam don't shake like that." Wanting to soak up every word and action, Thera would try to stay hidden somewhere so that she could stay up late into the night like they did. She would snuggle down in the warm chair in the parlor and secretly vow to be like those women with the red lips and swinging hips when she became old enough. Later in life she told someone that time was not long before she swung her hips more than she should have. She also found that every rhyming word she'd heard during the gambling games had a few adverse meanings somewhere down the line. When the time came that she could no longer stay awake, Thera would scamper undetected into the bedroom, lie in bed and jiggle her toes to the beat of the many sounds of laughter she'd heard in the dark of night when the moon was shining bright and everything was right. Oh, baby. That's what the words to one of the songs were about. Without a doubt, her mother was on a mission. In less than a week's time after the second gambling game, Thera and her folks moved a mile down the road in the right direction. They moved into a home with a much larger bedroom with the understanding that they would only be there a short period of time. The family of three shared the bathroom and kitchen with other members of the household. Well, there were the four children who were too young to cook. Those four were Thera, a girl her age by the name of Abby, her sister Lettie and brother, Hank. Taut strings of harmony began to play a tune and Thera listened to the blended chords and responded in more ways than one. It was as if the young child had heard a feeling that somehow had become tangible. Her yearning for rhythm and rhyme was set in motion. The leaves on the trees, sun, moon and stars became something about love. A casual walk through a field of grass, myrtle and clover warmed the young heart of Thera and became a glorious love story.

Eli Benson had a religious household. His family went to church every Sunday morning. They would rise early and turn on the radio to listen to songs with words like, "heaven" and "glory," while they ate breakfast around the big table in the kitchen, which was the largest room in the house. I would lie in bed and move my toes to the beat of the music. Quartets with blended voices sung, "O Lord, stand by me" and "Just a closer walk with thee." I began going to the Church with them so that I could dress up and get my hair fixed pretty with ribbons on my twisted braids. At church we prayed that the Lord would protect us and we thanked God for everything that we had. Life for the Benson family seemed to be perfect until one day the preacher, Reverend Jack Benson; Eli's brother was told that the congregation no longer wanted him to pastor the church. I had noticed that many people had joined up with us to worship on Sunday mornings. Most were relatives or kinfolk to the Bensons. Two prominent families of the congregation saw that they were outnumbered and thought that they had smelled a rat. They proceeded to falsely accuse Reverend Jack and his brother, Eli of devising a plan to bring their kinfolk from the Mississippi Delta to Indiana. During that time, the deacons were in charge of collecting church dues. The neighborhood was only so big with five streets and alleys running east and west and five running north and south. The school stood in the middle of the community. The surrounding property featured a park complete with a picnic area and a playground. Saturday was collection day so each of the member's houses were visited by a deacon, their names listed and their dues written beside their names. On Sunday mornings during the time between Sunday school and the beginning of morning service, the money was tallied up. The deacons laid it aside until the offering trays were passed through the congregation for more donations. The church congregation accused the Reverend of skimming money from the bank deposit and using it to buy train fares from the southern states to Indiana. His first relative to arrive had been his brother Eli, who became one of the deacons of the Community Church. From the prominent family by the name of Harrell, there was Deacon Judson and Deacon Brady who claimed to have found discrepancies in the bank deposits and reports. They began to spread rumors throughout the congregation. As a result Reverend Jack was voted out of the church as pastor. His brother Eli had been working on a plan of his own. He went into the grocery business and helped his brother to land on his feet. The two of them simply built another church. The building went up as nothing fancy, but their families and others who felt snubbed by the Harrell family stuck together and worshiped. As Deacon Benson's business flourished the church did also. Its choir became popular as did the manner that services were conducted by Reverend Jack. The older Benson siblings were vivacious, rip, roaring teenagers who played music all day during the summer months while their father worked. They played slow and sultry sounding gospel music that placed the melody in your spirit. They also worked in the grocery store. After dinner on most evenings they busied themselves washing and repairing clothes to wear on Friday and Saturday nights. There was a lot of fun in listening to the jive talk and seeing older boys and girls practice new dance steps. When the house became too quiet for me I would go out on the porch and stay long enough to sneak to the park and play. If I saw Abby, I would play nearby until I became bored. I didn't feel the need to be around anyone in particular. I just happened to like wandering around and hearing idle talk. I enjoyed seeing birds fly from tree to tree and hearing bees buzzing in and out of morning glory blossoms that covered the fences. I tried hard to keep up with the teenagers in the house in order to find out where they went when they would leave home, but they seemed able to lose me no matter how hard I'd try to watch them. It was on one of those kinds of inquisitively somber summer days that I broke the radio. I sat alone in the living room while my mother was busily hanging out the laundry to dry. The only reason I sat in the living room was so that I could tail one of the older kids. They all somehow ditched me again. The knobs of the radio looked inviting enough. I had seen the big kids of the Benson family turn those knobs so I proceeded to do the same things that I had watched them do. Only, I got no sound. I twisted and turned the knob until the indicator no longer moved. Instinctively, I knew to get away from the mess I had made. I also knew better than to go by my mother, because she would have remembered that I'd come from an empty room. She would be able to tie me to the evidence later, I thought. So, I left the house by way of a side door that was rarely used. It led to the sidewalk on a side street. Making sure that the coast was clear, I walked around to the front of the house. That was the day that I met a girl by the name of Janie Mae Bass. We played until my mother came looking for me. A few moments later, her aunt Nolia called her inside to eat dinner. For dinner I only wanted a baloney sandwich. The other children of the household thought it very strange. Abby said, "Your mother cooks pork chops and gravy while we scrounge around for meat and you only want baloney?" It just happened to be my favorite food of choice. I made a few silly gyrations and licked my lips to make them laugh. All I wanted was for them to hurry and be done with teasing me so that I could enjoy my meal and sneak outside again. The older boy, Bill, came in and went into the bathroom. When he came out he walked over to the stove and looked into a pot and yelled to the top of his voice, "Who took my ham hock out of this pot?" There were melodious echoes of, "I didn't . . . . I didn't . . . Not me . . . . It wasn't me." Bill began to search those who stood around and when he came to the youngest boy, the child whispered, "Uh oh, Look what's done jumped into my pocket." He ran over to the stove juggling the hot meat in his hands to place it back into the pot. The house came alive with laughter again and the incident was recalled repeatedly throughout the evening. In spite of the teasing, Yul took it all in stride. His personality stood out as one with logic who kept everyone in stitches. The summer jubilation came to a close. One day I was surrounded by plenty of folk that had helped to make my life fun and interesting. The new season brought with it another way of life. Fun shopping for new shoes and sweaters filled the house with excitement. Early one morning I awoke and the kids were gone. Poof! I was alone. The other children all went back to school. Daddy and Deacon Benson were working and Mrs. Benson was not in the best of health so she mostly stayed in her room. Normally she was one who enjoyed her children and husband. On Saturdays she and Deacon Eli would shop and return with goodies that put a smile on everyone's face. One Saturday morning they went shopping and the clerk had given Mrs. Benson too much change back. Her husband thought that she should have given the money back. She countered, "I did. I never brought it out of the store," she said. "I stood right there and spent it." I found out when I was older that she had been pregnant and that the condition made her sleep more than usual. When my dad came in from work that day, I talked about how everyone had left me and gone somewhere and that I did not like the house anymore. Being a man of few words when he was sober, daddy gave me a pat on the head and walked into the house. We could enter our bedroom from the back porch, so he went inside and returned with what I believed to be one hundred dollars in a shoebox. The new coins were only copper pennies but they made me feel rich. Shortly thereafter, the children all came home chattering away about their first day back to school. I felt so relieved that they were home that I relaxed and went to sleep at the dinner table shortly after finishing my meal of baloney. Early the next morning I heard such a commotion that I peeked out of our bedroom to see what it was about. Somebody had taken a pair of clean socks that one of the boys had washed and hung to dry the night before. Joel was twin to a girl named Joan. He was in the process of checking everyone's feet before they left for school because he wanted to see if they were wearing his clean socks. Joel was the last one to leave the house and I could see his disappointment at having to wear dirty socks to school. He was very meticulous. Whenever I saw him around the house, he was preparing for some event or washing dishes or offering to do something for his mother. I was saddened by his disappointment. For some reason Miss Nolia had kept Janie Mae home that day so she and I mimicked each other from across the fence while the women hung their wet laundry on the clothesline to dry. Janie was a very friendly girl with a bright smile but sad looking eyes. Miss Nolia kept her nice and clean but would look at her with distaste when she thought nobody was paying attention. We both went into the house after the clothes were all hung out to dry. I went with my mother and she went with her aunt. After lunch, I used a portion of the day to watch Miss Ida who lived directly across the street and a lady named Lizzie hang out clothes to dry. Lizzie lived down the street and had a girl about my size. Her daughter played in the dirt while she and Miss Ida went back and forth into the house for more wet clothes to hang on the clothesline. Lizzie went inside and did not return for a long time and I became bored. Miss Ida began taking in the first linens that they had hung out to dry. I had resorted to counting her doilies with crochet ruffles around the edges. When the school bell rang I knew that it was time for everyone to come home from school. Joel was first to get home from school that afternoon and he sat where he could check everyone's socks as they entered the door. By then I, too was sitting quietly in the living room. When Joan walked in the house he spied his socks on her feet and confronted her. She left the room and returned holding in her hand the socks that she had gone into the bedroom wearing. She had removed from her feet. With scorn she threw the worn socks in her brother, Joel's face. I saw her turn quickly and run through the back door. She jumped over the banister with Joel following close behind. Joel seemed to throw punches at her back. We all ran out on the back porch and witnessed how he would reach for her with one hand and swing at her with the other hand as if he was trying to catch on to her clothing. Joan ran like quicksilver down the block. All of us children began to jump up and down and cheer for her to duck or cut to the right or left while the neighbors watched. We joked and laughed each time she would manage to out maneuver him. A neighbor finally caught Joel by the tail of his shirt to make them stop. His sister's face was streaked with tears while he was yet showing rage. Mr. Mann, the neighbor, held on to his shoulders, and walked home with Joel while he continued to bristle with anger. In the neighbor's hand was a meat cleaver. Joel had tried to kill his sister. I don't remember realizing the magnitude of what had transpired on that day until we were much older. The world seemed to have stopped the music and I lost my harmony. On that following Sunday morning the radio was silent. I had broken it. I lay in bed between my parents and listened to the uproar and accusations that were batted back and forth between the children like a game of Ping-Pong. "You DID, I DIDN'T" Finally the all went to church. I missed going to church that day and stayed close to my mother. It was a bit unusual for me to have done so, but no one else seemed to notice that I held my breath. I'm sure my lungs appreciated the deep breath I took when the family decided to take the radio back to the store. On that Monday morning the new radio was put in place and I pledged to myself to leave it alone. Carrying guilt around had been awful but the fear of being caught was sickening. I stayed in the house until the radio was put into place. After I heard it begin play I sneaked outside until lunchtime. In the cool of the evening I sashayed next door when I saw Deacon Benson talking with Mr. George, Janie's uncle. Janie sat on the front steps leading into their living room so I sat beside her. The more the two men talked the faster the words spewed out of their mouths. Deacon Benson was trying to convince George to come to Sunday morning service. Janie leaned over and whispered, "He just wants money, because they pay dues on Saturday and they give in the offering on Sunday. Half of the members of the church, (Janie paused.) Nolia, Janie's aunt had come to the door and Janie had to stop talking. When Nolia left, Janie continued, "Half of the members are gone." Deacon Benson didn't seem to make any progress because we heard George say, "You cannot control me like that, now. Y'all go on with the nickels and dimes. Control that." Janie laughed after her uncle George went back into the house. What she told me next made me want her to never stop talking. The things she said, I could not relate to but they caused my curiosity to peak. When she had begun talking, the sun was shining bright and the air was sweet with the fragrance of honeysuckle. By the time she finished, my senses were saturated with a substance that couldn't be washed away with the Mother Goose Rhymes at bedtime. Janie told me that she, her sister and their mother, Carrie had come into town on the train and was picked up by her mother's boyfriend, who was her sister's father. Just then, at the crucial time of finding out what all of the things she'd said meant, I heard my name being called. I ran around to the back door so that it would seem as if I had been playing in the back yard. I don't recall what made me want to hide myself from the world. I was only one little person who saw many people who said many things. All that I had in my mind were questions; and if I had asked someone to explain everything that they told me, I would have had to explain why I didn't know anything. I just tried to listen and watch. There were plenty of interesting things going on all around me and I would put a rhythm to it so that I would not forget how funny or enjoyable the event or happenings were. I went into the house and mother sent me to get washed up for dinner. I rushed to eat so that I could hear more from Janie. Janie was not sitting out front when I went outside again so I had to sleep on a hard pillow of confusion that night. The next day I saw her but would not try to steer her back to our previous conversation.

Somehow I had come to believe that by letting people know that you are anxious to hear about a certain something causes them to consider keeping the words to themselves. Instead of talking so much, we played with our dolls on Janie's screened in back porch. Miss Nolia was a short, plump-looking lady who walked really slowly. Her weight would make the floor boards creak when she walked across the room. I had noticed how slowly she walked but I had never equated it with whether or not she was capable of sneaking up on us. Evidently, Janie had. We used our little blankets to put our dolls to bed in pretense of them taking a nap. Janie, who wore a dress that was way too small for her, began to do things with her doll that made me laugh. She licked it from head to toe. Her panties were showing while she bent over and when I told her about it, I found myself laughing so hard that I could barely talk. She pulled her panties off and the more she showed her behind, the harder I laughed. We could hear Miss Nolia heading in our direction. Janie hurried to put her pants on and we pretended to be sleeping with our babies. Her aunt came in and looked. We giggled and got up. Without saying a word, she turned and walked back to the front of the house. Janie whispered, "Now it's your turn." Out of curiosity, I let her make all of the rules. It was a game that her uncle would play with her when she cried for her mother, she said. Aunt Nolia would go to bed and would tell her uncle to go and shut her up when she cried. She said that she cried because she was afraid, but she could hear Aunt Nolia say, "George we don't have no children, so why did you let your sister drop this child off on us?" Janis said that her mother didn't have anywhere else to take her to and that her boyfriend only had one bed. Janie wished aunt Nolia would leave so that her mother and sister could live in the house. Anyway, she liked the way that Uncle George would come into her room and get into bed with her. "Let me show you. It's your turn," she repeated. Out of curiosity, I followed her instructions. With her tongue, she opened up a world of sensuality and planted a greater understanding of vulnerability in me. Mind you, I did not feel like I was any less for it. It was just strange to me that her uncle did things like that to her. When she lifted her head, she smiled and said, "Now! It's your turn." I shook my head and rose to my feet to quickly pull up my pants. My mind was made up that my mouth would never do or touch such a thing. Janie left the room and came back with something that looked like chocolate in her hand. She bit a piece and offered me a bite. It tasted horrible and bitter, but she stood there chewing so I chewed the bitter, dark, burning stuff. Janie scooted herself down in a corner and whispered, "Come on! You'd better or I'm going to get you!" I don't know why I became frightened. Maybe it was because I had never felt threatened before. Janie pulled down her panties and tugged at me until I was kneeling before her. I put my head down while she held her tiny self opened, but I had to spit. So I did, right where she held herself. She let out a scream and jumped up. I ran to Miss Nolia who was struggling to get out of the overstuffed chair in the living room. She was moving as fast as she could and yelling, "What's the matter with that gal?" Startled out of my mind, I just kept running because I could not tell her why

Janie was yelling and screaming. My mouth was burning and I had to go home. I raced to the back door and didn't see my mother only to find myself looking down at her feet. I was crying and trying to tell her that Janie had given me something poison and that I thought I was dying. All of the people in the house broke into laughter while my mother washed tobacco from my mouth. Miss Nolia came in while we were in the bathroom and I could hear the Bensons telling her what I had told my mother. Miss Nolia said that she could not get Janie to come out of the bathroom. We could hear Miss Nolia's voice through the window after she went back home yelling, "Gal, you'd better bring your ass out of that toilet 'cause I'm going to tear you up. I'm going to bust your ass wider than a lot gate!" The next time I saw Janie, which was a few days later, she was with another girl and I was afraid that she had told other people what we had done. She held my new doll that I had left at her house and I just wanted her to keep it and disappear into thin air. She wanted to fight and I had never done that either. I remained in safety on our back porch. Later that evening Uncle George heard Janie tell other children that she was going to keep my doll. As far as I was concerned, I just wanted their whole family to disappear. I cared nothing about the doll and I was afraid that she was going to get me, whatever that meant. Her aunt Nolia thought otherwise. She took the doll from Janie and returned it to my mother. When my mother invited her to sit down, I almost yelled, "Let her go!" Miss Nolia had a lot to talk about that night. It seemed that George and Carrie were ten years apart in age. George was the oldest and claimed to Nolia that Carrie had always been bad luck to him. She would carry trouble and bad luck around in her bosom, he once said. George in their younger days had lied for her so much that he was ashamed of himself. He told Nolia that he would always get caught and paying dearly for it. When he married and thought that he had gotten rid of her for good she would write and beg to come where he was. Now here she was again, Nolia said, "Now here she is again with her wanton children with her." Nolia had heard George in the night trying to stop the child from crying, but she knew that there was a reason why he would come back to bed and ravish her like a mad man too. I didn't know what Miss Nolia meant when she told my mother, "Child, since that child been there he's got the nerve to know how to make me come." I thought that she meant that she could walk a little faster. It wasn't long before we moved into a larger place and we lived alone as a family in a house by ourselves. I kept going to church with the Benson family each Sunday morning and I continued through the week to roam around the neighborhood to watch and listen to people who talked and sometimes jived with rhythm. There was an alley behind our new place that ran from our end of the block clear across the neighborhood. Many of the back yards had some interesting characters hanging out in them, but I want to tell you about a few more of the Benson neighbors, such as Wilbur and Ida Avery. In the house directly across the street from the Benson family was the Avery family. Wilbur and Ida had an adult son named Rufus and a niece by the name of Myrtle who was a year or two older than I was. From the time that we moved into the community I had watched the people of the Avery household come and go. Rufus seemed to be going no place special and Myrtle was kept in the yard. I came to believe that Ida washed and hung clothes on the outside clothesline every single day except Sunday. Her husband Wilbur went to work in the middle of the night and mostly worked on cars every day until lunchtime. Myrtle said that Ida would fuss if he did that kind of work on Sunday so he just stayed in bed while the two of them went to church. Anyway, whenever I would see Myrtle sitting alone, I'd walk over to the front gate and speak to her. I learned that she was from down south and that she wished that she were still there. She said, "Now how is she going to keep me in this house when nobody could keep her in the house. Let me tell you about Miss Ida, baby." Here are some of the things Myrtle told me over the years. I will try to unravel the time frame of Myrtle's historical views as the tales were shared with her by family members who lived in the southern states.

There was a woman named Jubielha who was sold into slavery by her father. She was believed to be bearing the child of a rival tribesman who was not of the Bantus. Because of the warrior's height her father believed him to be of Watusi origin. It was in innocence that the child had been conceived but the couple's engagement proved to be an unacceptable excuse and her father ruled it unforgivable. There were seventeen persons expelled and sold from the village where Jubielha had lived. She was from a place across the ocean called Africa, a continent with the second largest mass of land that makes up the earth. She and the others of the Bantu tribe were herded onto a big ship one evening at sundown. There were countless others from the Swazi, Sudanese and Ndebele tribes that crowded the hold of the sailing vessel beyond its capacity. She described the cries in the night as the ship sailed away from the shores of the deep sea waters. A man by the name of Nathaniel LeGish, who had looked at Jubielha as she was being led down the steep stairs of the ship's hold, yelled for the shipmates to release her to him. In his cabin, he washed her with cold water mixed with vinegar until her body was sore. Vinegar and oil was poured over her head while she cringed with a burning scalp. He pulled her hair while trying to comb it and finally gave up. He then put the comb into her hands. There was a bucket of water sitting at his feet. Faint from hunger, Jubielha got down on her knees and stuck her head into the bucket to cool her irritated scalp and to rest. She was able to comb her hair with ease as long as she held it under water. Nathaniel stood over her and held a large piece of gray fabric that she grabbed to cover her body with. When it was handed over to her, Jubielha dried herself and wrapped the damp material around her body to hide her nakedness. Nathaniel LeGish reached down and tore a piece of the cloth from the gray fabric's bottom that was dragging the floor and tied it around her head. He said to her, "I'm your Master." Jubielha backed herself into the nearest corner and stayed there repeating the words to herself that he had spoken. During sundown, Nathaniel LeGish handed her a chunk of hard bread, ate a meal himself and went to bed. It was a long time before the weary travelers saw land for a second time. Jubielha kept the cabin clean and was given food daily. She used the corner of the cabin as her place and he never bothered her. The only time he looked at her was to give her daily rations. It seemed to take forever to become accustomed to the tossing of the angry waves that caused Jubielha to cry in misery out of fear that the vessel would sink. On the day that Jubielha felt she could no longer survive the ordeal, the rocking of the vessel lessened and she was able to sleep without fear. She could not tell how long she'd slept but when she heard voices yelling "Land Ho! Land! Ho!" She stood up feeling better than she had felt for many days. Nathaniel LeGish had placed two helpings of bread near the place where she slept so she gathered that she had slept for at least two days. Jubielha hurried to straighten his bunk and she folded his clothes after she'd eaten the bread and drank her fill of water. She said her morning prayer to the gods and returned to her corner. They unbounded the ship after traveling for what had seemed like forever. Jubielha had a hard time finding her legs well enough to walk down the ramp. She did as well as she could and was able to lean on the rails for support. She then was tied to the back of a wagon by someone she did not recognize. She stood alone, while countless others were taken to another place. The hot sun beamed down on her head but it felt good and refreshing. She had spent many hours in a cold, dark and lonesome place. She was no longer sailing on the sea without seeing daylight and the light was blinding. It was hard for her eyes to adjust to the sunlight but she could see enough to tell that someone moved in her direction. It was a man that walked in her direction and stepped up to the wagon. Jubielha was afraid to lift her eyes from the ground. The man grabbed her wrists and found them shackled. He then looked for a place bound by ropes where he could untie her. She felt her garments being lifted. A finger poked her in the stomach before Master LeGish rushed over and angrily talked to the man. She heard the man called "I am your Master" speak roughly and was relieved to hear the sound of the other man's footsteps and the smell of his body beginning to fade. From a distance she was able to get a glimpse of other men who pushed and shoved the ragged, tired and filthy bodies of the living dead around. That was what she imagined of those who had been kept in the hold of the ship. They were broken in body and spirit. The stories that they later shared of misery and violence prompted her to keep silent. The gods had protected her from the hurt, harm and danger. Her heart cried for them so much that she made a promise to her gods to show kindness towards whomsoever she chanced to meet so as not to mistakenly add to suffering of others. Persons she came to know as white men who sailed and black men and women who were cargo crowded the grounds. Jubielha cried and wailed when she realized their plight. She was unable to look at the deplorable conditions that surrounded the shipyard without crying out to the heavens for mercy upon minds of humanity. Most of the weary human cargo looked too weak to walk. More men who came from only God knows where, herded them into wagons where they sat with their legs open for another to sit between them until they were all in there except for four to six big men who walked with her behind the wagon. When they would pass the shade of a tree, she longed for her homeland. The wagon came to a stop at the Nate Plantation and the wagon loads of shackled folks were weeping and wailing. Men rushed to the crowded wagons to round them up like cattle and to lead them to a big barn. The tired and hungry were given precious bread and water. They were allowed to eat until their bellies were full and drink until their thirst was gone. Jubielha saw women who favored her features carrying bread and water for them to eat and drink. Long troughs of water were put around the walls of the building and the suffering imprisoned black people were able to wash themselves. Three men bade them to sit on bales of soft straw and a few of them went to sleep. Master LeGish stood at the door and watched the free men unloose the shackles from first the bounded hands and then feet of those that had rode in wagons. Not one of them ran. They were too weak to run and besides that, they knew nowhere to run. Late in the evening someone built a fire. LeGish had heard of how the natives loved to congregate and he wanted them to be mentally prepared so that he could work them to make his crops flourish. He promised his father that he would teach them to build houses on the land so that they could live like people, and that he also planned for them to build a mansion on the estate. Every landowner they knew wanted to steal what belonged to others of considerable wealth. The many efforts he'd made to work with his father had failed. Young Nathaniel LeGish found that it proved impossible to both govern the land and work the fields alone. The older his father got the sicker he became. They owned hundreds of acres of land and so far as the landowners were concerned, it was every man for their own selves. In his head and in his heart, LeGish believed that if he would allow the chattel to live decently, that they would protect him and his property. The Nate Plantation already owned a few slaves who were good workers but someone else had worked them and abused them by selling off their children to make ends meet. When young Nathaniel had bought them, he had to work extra hard to build them up enough to get a decent day's work out of them. He knew that it would be foolish to trust anyone who had been mistreated. In his heart, he believed that if he'd had to live the life of a slave, his first instinct would be to kill the oppressor. Of course, the slaves were rumored to be animals. Their desire to survive was considered a threat to the oppressor both socially and economically. Most of the landowners had lost young Nathaniel's respect by beating and killing slaves. They were afraid to let the bold ones live and pretended to not know what drove them. In consideration of the evident facts Nathaniel spent his last money in the world to buy his own slaves and give them the liberty within the confines of his property. It had taken years of planning to hire a good Ship's captain with loyal shipmates and to travel to Africa. He decided that if things didn't work out to his satisfaction, he would sell his holdings and move on.

While they were housed in the big barn, the battered men and women were allowed to move around but they were locked in. Early the next morning, they were fed big bowls of steaming mush laced with cane syrup and chunks of dry bread. They drank water until they could hold no more. It took a few days for the look of fatigue and worry to fall from their faces and be replaced with melancholy. They communicated well with one another in whispers until three over seers came and led them into the yard where they walked and stretched themselves. The women stood in huddles and Master LeGish took note of it. There were about ten huddles of about seven or eight women each. Jubielha stood alone. He had about one hundred and twenty men. The ones that walked and stretched, he decided to keep together. He needed to build houses. With a figure in his head, he ordered several trees to be chopped down that surrounded the corn fields. The twenty or so flexing men were taken out and given axes after his overseers chopped a tree down for an example. They worked until sundown with skills that he never would have imagined they had. He had to leave and set up more teams of workers so he gave orders for the overseers to spread themselves out towards the border of the wooded area to guard his property. Each overseer carried a shotgun and a machete for defense. They not only had to worry about themselves but they were subject to poachers who roamed the roads of the countryside looking to steal the valuable human chattel at any and every opportunity. Successful poachers would then sell the property to another landowner who had connections with auctioneers in other counties. The evening meal for the slaves consisted of Hog's maws, chitterlings, potatoes and gruel from hominy. Each day they grew stronger and became more responsive to commands. The tree cutters were separated from the others to sleep in a shack located closer to the woods. The women were put to work pulling weeds and briars to clear the land for the new quarters to go up. That night, there was another big fire before they again were locked in the barn. The heat from the fire had felt good to them and lifted their spirits. Master took Jubielha inside of the big house and gave her to the women who cooked in the big kitchen. They washed her with warm soapy water and gave her a clean frock of muslin to put on. Jubielha refused to let go of her wraps, so they put the pieces of fabric into the water and washed them. The heat from the big fireplace dried them before they took her to their lady, Miss Nervy. Mrs. LeGish's name was Minerva but they called her Miss Nervy. Each morning Jubielha made the fire to heat Miss Nervy's room. She bathed her, dressed her and cleaned her bedroom. It was a while before the two women could communicate properly but it happened rather easily after Minerva saw that Jubielha learned quickly by watching her closely. Jubielha became the mother of eighteen children fathered by Ushra, the yardman who made the morning fires in the mansion fireplaces and Master LeGish who fathered seven of them. There were two sets of twins, Rudy & Roger and Jude and Jubella. There was a set of triplets who were named by him. They were named Joseph, Joshua and Nadien, the only girl. The civil war started and was cold and brutal. The Nate Plantation sought to continue as it were. To keep from becoming a target, Old Master LeGish left the states and went to England leaving his son to do whatever he could to support the south. His son gathered the enslaved families together and entreated them to remember the life that they now lived. The land was flourishing with crops, the cattle were healthy and their children were safe as long as they stayed within the boundaries if his land. They slaughtered many hogs and cured the meat. Beef was salted dried and stored in log cabins. Dried beans, corn and peas were also stored. The Nate plantation waited for the war but it never came their way. Several slave families who were freed migrated from nearby plantations and were given help and a place to stay. Landowners who sought to punish them by sending them away empty handed, gave the Nate plantation more than they needed in labor. Nobody made them work. The released slaves were glad to live and work in peace. There were two cabins of women who sewed. They worked from sun up to sun down making clothes. Small babies and children too small to work were kept by fifteen nannies in three cabins during the daytime. They were bathed, dressed and kept clean. Food was given to them twice daily. Down in the bottom lands of the plantation were planters of herbs and around their fruitfulness, living quarters were built. Behind the community were stables and barns with carriages and quarter horses. The plantation was able to supply many areas in the state with medicinal herbs and salves. Gallon jars and quart jars filled the storage shelters almost to capacity during harvest time. Field hands and cooks and maids all stayed across the fields or were sheltered in small cabins near the big mansion.

Out of the shadows rose the Moore family who migrated from the Patrick Moore Plantation during the time of the serfs. During the middle ages in Europe farmers were called serfs who belonged to the land they worked on. They could not be bought or sold but if the land was sold, they had to work for the landowners. Patrick Moore released his people to the land and went back to Europe. He was careful to give them deeds and bound them to notes payable for fifty years until such time that the land was paid for. It was set up to pass through generations until paid in full. Johnny Moore and his family by the third generation owned one hundred acres free and clear. He and his wife had one son who married a descendent from the LeGish Plantation. His wife Mable traveled across the bayou of Louisiana to get to the banks of the Mississippi River. Her father was a Frenchman who fell in love with her mother, a Cherokee Indian squaw. Together, John Jr and his family raised two daughters and a son. Mable still had a sister living in France and a brother who lived in London. Her mother and father were deceased before she left France. Mable, the grandmother of the family, met Johnny Moore, the grandfather of the Moore family, on a loading dock in the State of Mississippi which was a long way from home. He had crossed the Mississippi River on a ferry to buy oil and kerosene. He, while standing in the shadows of a wagon, saw a golden goddess standing on the dock in Gulfport watching a barge go by. Johnny had traveled through Mobile Alabama to the Gulf of Mississippi. The wind caught Mable's scarf and her long curly hair glistened in the sunlight. He noted the bags sitting at her feet and asked if she wanted him to carry them. She looked into his eyes as if she could tell his fortune. The bags that she wanted him to carry were not as heavy as they were awkward. She lifted and gave them to him. The rest of the bags, she gathered to keep close by her side. In the course of their chopped up conversation, he learned that she needed lodging, so he loaded her bags onto the ferry and took her home with him. His carriage and horses had been left at the banks of the river awaiting his return. He knew that it was the hand of God working things out for him. His mother, Belle, greeted them at the door with dinner waiting. Mable Francis Cordone' was delighted that she had been able to cross the ocean alone and had not been molested. It had been the only fear that she'd had. She had kept herself hidden from the world while on the ship. In France her family had been farmers with vineyards as far as the eyes could see. Now the land was barren with disease that had wiped them out financially. Before her father died, he sold the land and divided the small family fortune. As long as her father had been strong and in good health, they had friends and many workers who worked faithfully. Their mother did not know the business. Mr. Cordone' made sure that his wife could continue to live well, but after he died, she quietly grieved herself to death. Mable told her siblings of her plans to go to America and farm. They wished her well, but not without laughter. Her sister was a tiny, beautiful and petite person who loved parties and adornment. Mable was tall and bone heavy with abundantly firm hips. Her breasts stood at attention and she spent a great deal of time trying to make them less evident. Mable could cut patterns and sew without instructions. She carefully packed her clothes along with some of her father's old work clothes that she had washed and patched up. Seeing his work boots gave her many happy memories. So she took them along with her mother's jewelry, fine dresses and laced handkerchiefs. The day before she left for America her and her sister spent the evening crying and promising to write one another. The woodlands and fields of Mississippi caused the robust traveler to wonder if she could ever settle down in such a place. By the time the wagon came to a rest they had crossed the border into Alabama. Mable looked at the woman standing in the doorway that greeted Johnny when they arrived after the long ride and smiled. It had been some hours since they'd left the banks of the river and she was worn out. Many of her mother's beautiful dresses were packed in her bags and she now believed that she knew just who to give them to. Mother Moore, Johnny's mother directed the young lady into the largest bedroom in the house. It had been built on to the house so that sewing would be comfortable because that was what Mother Moore had always done. That night, Johnny woke up and found Mable in his arms and never let her go. When she had looked into his eyes on the banks of the Mississippi River, she could feel a certain comfort from the sense of masculinity that she saw in them. Mable had always desired a strong man to give herself to. Johnny stood straight and had no slump in his posture. He had removed his warm Jacket to wrap around her shoulders during the long ride. She saw the strong hard muscles of Samson of the bible days and had shuttered. A bit of mischief lay in his eyes that seemed to say, "I dare you to love me." Mable climbed in the bed and breathed a sigh of relief that she had traveled safely to America. She thanked God for sending a strong man in the midst of the hustle and bustle to bring her the last mile to a place of comfort and care. When she heard the sounds of snoring come from the old lady's room, Mable had tipped into Johnny's room and slid between the sheets to lie beside him. He did not flinch, but wrapped her in his arms and kissed her forehead. They made love throughout the night without regard to his Mother in the other room smiling. Of course they thought she was sleeping. His mother had prayed that some young woman would find and desire her son who had something to give back. Mother Moore had not wanted him to mess around in slave quarters. God answered her prayers in a big way. She studied Mable from head to toe and watched how she'd handled her personal belongings. She watched her eat the meal that was set before her and the way that she would strut across the room. Mother Moore saw a new twinkle in her son's eyes and knew then that she could begin to rest. Mother Moore slept better that night than she had slept in a long time. When Mable tipped back into her room that next morning she was surprised to find dainty perfumed soaps with soft brushed cotton towels lying on her bed. A tub of warm water had been placed in the middle of the bedroom floor. The icing was put on the cake later on in the day when Mable gave the beautiful clothes to Mother Moore, her husband's mother, who had never before seen the fabric with gold and silver threads running through it. They quickly bonded as mother and daughter in law without as much as a preacher.

Mable learned to work the farm with her husband and followed instructions well. She loved feeding hogs and milking cows. She planted a small vineyard of wild grapes and taught Mother Moore how to make wine. They spent time together like mother and daughter and began sewing baby clothes before Mable knew whether she was pregnant or not. With the kind of love her and Johnny were making, they both knew better than to wait. One could hear their cries of passion way across the fields. When he was spent, she would mount him and show her body, which he delighted in. Johnny could not believe his luck.

He met freemen who hired themselves out by the day to build fences and to dig trenches. A pump was sunk behind his house by a skillful stranger who had needed water and shelter. The man offered to find water on the land and held a branch from a peach tree in his hand. Johnny Moore stood and watched the stranger follow a quivering stick to the corner of his house. They dug in the spot where the branch relaxed and was able to sink a pipe into it. The stranger dwelled with them for two months and slept in the barn. Before he left, a pump sat in the yard and made it convenient for Mable and Mother Moore to have water without going down into the lower lands to a spring. Mable never messed around where men worked and would stay in her husband's line of vision. She never would show as much as an arm. Johnny could tell that she enjoyed his delight in her hair and body. She was built like a stallion and would preen and prance for him. She knew how to position her breast to find his mouth during their lovemaking in such a way that he would forget to take the next breath. Johnny Jr. was born during the winter. He was a big baby and Mable was told to not have any more children again or it could very well kill her. Mother Moore went out and found some elm leaves that were not dried, crushed them and packed them around the mouth of Mable's uterus. Mable never bore another child. After the birth of their son, Johnny made a few changes so that his wife could give her full attention to their home and child. With the help of Mother Moore, Mable was able to learn new sewing skills and before too long, she could create patterns for men and boy's clothing. Life was good. Her sister and brother continued to live abroad for the next twenty years. Finally the time came that their lives and livelihoods changed so Mable's siblings chose to venture across the waters to America. They both settled in South Carolina near the city of Charleston. Johnny Moore had so completed Mable's life that as much as she had missed France and her siblings, she was satisfied in her marriage and with the life of harmony that she lived. On John Jr's eighteenth birthday he went to his mother with a request for her to make a dress for the girl that he planned to marry. There was a creek that ran behind the house of a farmer down the road and across the pasture so John Jr was able to fish. He would fish to his heart's content during hot summer days when work was slow around the farm. After a good rain, the soil would become its own magician and draw the plant's roots deep into itself for the precious moisture. On such mornings, John Jr. would let the earth rest and go fishing early in the morning and he did not return home until bedtime. Through the dark pines, he would often walk carrying his lantern. Its light helped him to follow the creek down to the Calico bottom Community to sell some of his catch. The low lands of Calico situated on the LeGish plantation had been given to Jubielha and her children. This was done after the death of Old Master LeGish, Nathaniel's father. Many of the original field hands and builders had gotten old and could no longer work in the hot sun. Housing was provided for them in Calico Bottom where they could work in the herb gardens and in the stables. Some of the younger ones ran the shipping operations out of the storage barns. In Calico there was a cattle ranch and a hog farm that workers attended to. On higher ground, Master LeGish built a school with enough classrooms to educate the young people on how to read, write, learn agricultural skills, and sew. The first teachers were his children by Jubielha. Her first child, Ushason, whom the yardman thought was his offspring was sent abroad for higher learning as was Nate Jr. and Paul, Nathaniel LeGish's children by his wife, Minerva. Usha had claimed Jubielha as his wife shortly after she was given to Minerva. Jubielha's first born child that she sired in Africa was the yardman's pride and he never considered her condition prior to meeting her on the plantation. The only Caucasus workers on the Nate plantation ran a dairy farm near the old serf properties. Nate LeGish had sought to buy that property but found that the former owners had already sold it to the ex-slaves and their families. Anyway, John Jr met Effie in school. Most of the children thought that Effie could not talk. She could talk, but her mind was too muddled with questions to talk. Her problem was finding someone who could answer her many questions. John watched her closely from the first day that he saw her beautiful teeth. The entrances in and out of the bottom lands were pretty much hidden. Every chance he got to go down there with a classmate, John would go just to see if he could see Effie. There was an old lady named Miss Tenzy who sat on her porch everyday and stitched handmade quilts. Effie would sit with her for the peace and quiet. Miss Tenzy had wise looking eyes that would comfort Effie without her having to utter a word about her troubles. Her father was an unstable person who had moved them from one farm to another as he hired himself out. Every time their family moved to a different place everything was lost and they had to scrounge around to start over again. By the time they came to Calico, the older children had learned to carry their own bundles of belongings. Effie learned to carry her bundle and took care of the younger children whose mothers were her older sisters. Her mentoring cut out a lot of verbal and physical abuse that the younger children would have otherwise suffered. She kept them clean and well fed. Sometimes she would return home from school to feed them, wash them up and change their clothing. They often went to sleep while she combed their hair. Miss Tenzy told her the story of Jubielha and taught her to sew. Miss Minerva and others would send Miss Tenzy clothes that the sewing women of the plantation made. They were given to the families of Calico by the season. No one worked for free and on Sunday mornings they gathered for worship. John Jr learned to follow the creek to a certain tree and to cut through the thick pines to go down a slope into the Calico bottom lands. He was in love with Effie and wanted to bring her to church but she'd told him that she had nothing nice enough to wear to church. He went home and inquired of his mother about her dressmaking skills and patterns. Mable sat down in her sewing room to explain to her son the standard procedure for taking proper body measurements for the cutting of a pattern. He left home armed with a tape measure, a pencil and a piece of paper and headed towards Calico. He and Effie measured more than enough of everything that she had. Effie followed him to the back of the schoolyard and neither of them could hold back the flood of emotions that engulfed them. Afterwards, she stood naked while John Jr measured her and wrote the results on paper. Again, they did what came naturally. At sundown, they managed to get themselves together enough to return home. They managed to walk around to the front of the building, but had to sit on the steps to gather strength. Their knees wobbled so much that they had to lean against one another to continue walking. They chided each other by imitating the sounds of their lovemaking. John Jr looked into her sparkling eyes and radiant smiling face and knew in his heart that Effie was the one. He kissed her softly at her door and with a steady gait headed home to give his mother Effie's measurements. Mable made Effie a dress of light blue cotton. When John Jr stepped inside of the church door with Effie, heads turned, for he had never shown any sign of any involvement with the opposite sex. Mable took one look at them and knew that she had to hurry and make another dress. Effie was simply radiant and made John Jr's proud look usher him into a higher stature of maturity. He was now, a man. Later that evening, Johnny looked at Mable and asked, "Didn't you make that dress?" "What dress are you talking about?" Mable asked with a glint in her eye. Johnny laughed and said, "If I were you, I'd get started on another one tonight. I saw your trademark all over it." After Effie ate dinner with the Moore family, John Jr walked her home and hated to leave her there but he had no choice. He was so lovesick that his appetite had left him with a longing that only being with Effie could satisfy. By the following Wednesday, he had counted up his savings so that he could purchase a ring for the time that he would ask for her hand in marriage. Meanwhile, Effie was sitting at the feet of Miss Tenzy as much as she could to listen to a story of Jubielha. She loved to hear about how out of more than a hundred people; Jubielha was rescued from harm. In the tale, she could imagine herself with another chance to live a different life. Late Sunday evening when Effie returned home she'd hung her new dress up for just a moment and then she quickly packed it away so that none of the others in her family would be tempted to wear it. As a young girl Effie's mother had worked in a field with her family down in a place called Rittman, Arkansas. She told Effie that one early morning a man walked up behind her at the end of a row of cotton situated near a grove of young saplings and in the shadows of those thickets, he had his way with her. No body in her family had said a word so she dried her tears and worked the rest of the day in spite of her hurts and fears. The man continued to come back daily until one day, he had a short talk with her father who sent her with him. It had happened during a time when there were no moral boundaries which was most unfortunate because her mother simply accepted inbreeding as a way of life. In John Jr, Effie saw hope and prayed that things would work out between them. John Jr made her feel new and special. When she gave him her body he gave her his soul. When she looked at her mother she saw resignation and gloom.

After working around the farm with his father and living in agony another week, John Jr went to his parents and stated his case. His father took him to Effie's house in Calico where he asked for her hand in marriage. Her daddy sat drunk in a chair at the table and if there was one person, there were twenty people in that house. Young'uns were everywhere. The house had to be clean because there was no room for even dust to settle. John Jr stated his case to her mother and Effie walked into the room carrying a baby on her hip. Her mother looked at Effie who stood with her eyes cast down and said, "Effie, If you jest promise to come from time to time and help me with these Young'uns, I'll say yes." He wanted to put the ring on her finger but Effie told him to wait until they married. Johnny sat on pins and needles waiting to hear something while his son was inside. It took Effie a while to convince John Jr to let her stay with her parents and finish some things up for the children's sake. When he walked out alone, Johnny exhaled. They had walked down into the valley from the upper road and the walk back took longer that their entry. Miss Tenzy heard the news and sent for her brother Farmer Wilson, who owned property adjoining that of Johnny Moore. After their conversation, he got in touch with the cooks at the Nate plantation who began to pilfer smokehouse scraps and take up some of their chickens from the ground to corn feed them. The scraps were for the fresh seasoned vegetables they would cook and the chickens were for roasting. Many preparations were made for the wedding and celebration. Miss Tenzy reminded as many people as she could, while using her own interpretation, of what Calico stood for. In memory of generations past, the occasion was meant to be a grand celebration. They jumped the broom and said vows beneath the magnolia trees that grew beyond the pasture on the Moore property. The weather was warm; the air balmy and the ground were dry enough to enjoy walking and dancing. Long covered tables held loads of food. Cold lemonade from gallon jugs that sat in the cool creek overnight along with the sour mash and home made wines were there for the asking. Other foods were loaded on a wagon and driven in by Farmer Wilson and his wife, Dora. Miss Tenzy had rounded up the best cooks in Calico to fix their special dishes of corn pudding, Fried mullet, camp stew and gumbo. At sundown, after eating and drinking and dancing to the fiddle and washboard rhythms, the last food and drinks were served. Families parted and returned to their several abodes rejoicing and sometimes singing together. The best stories had been heard at the feet of the aged patriarchs and everyone heard the same things at the same time. The young were reminded of the true legacy of Calico. Effie went with her husband to spend time alone at a special place prepared by the women of Calico. She lay in bed after satisfying her new husband and drew a conclusion that Jubielha had done alright for herself, but questioned the reason for the suffering of others. Miss Tenzy had said, "Though we were born during the time of slavery, we are not enslaved." She envisioned a whirlpool sucking the life out of the earth filled with human remains. Her heart became fearful and she wondered if God was angry at her will to have such thoughts. She felt herself being kissed on the lips and opened her eyes to see her husband smiling. Callie, their baby girl was born seven months later during the month of May. Mable and Effie had some precious time together. The men would work the farm with their crews while the women spoiled Callie and talked while they did their chores and made clothing for the coming season. Mable told Effie about the pussy paper that John Jr had given her for her measurements and made her blush. Mable quipped, "Come on now, you must draw pretty well on paper. I need to be sewing baby clothes again." It went right over Effie's head. Ida, another baby girl was born two years later in the month of June. Their son, Johnny III was born the following June. They called him Lil' John to keep down confusion between the first names of the three generations. So there was Johnny, John Jr and Lil' John. The farm prospered and the children were healthy and mischievous. As the children got older, Effie began to work the farm with her husband so that she could better understand the operation. Her father in law spent more time planning and steering his son in business matters. Before long the children were in school and times were continuing to be good and abundant. Farmer Wilson and his wife, Dora were good neighbors who helped to oversee the Moore properties and the children. After John Jr married three more rooms were added to the already five-room farmhouse. The Moore family got together with their neighbor, Farmer Wilson. He gladly helped them to build beds and dressers for the children's bedrooms. Mother Moore, Johnny's mother passed away two years after John Jr was born. The children had loved to sit at her feet and play while she twisted shiny ribbons between her fingers. After her passing Effie would catch the children looking for their great grand mother so Mable suggested that she sit them on Mother Moore's bed, give them each a ribbon and tell a good story. Her small bedroom was filled with sweet memories of her. Mable kept her jewelry and special linens trimmed in lace, in a cedar chest containing homemade quilts of satin hoping to one day share them with her grand daughters.

While Myrtle talked, I could almost smell food and my heartbeat danced to melodies unknown to me. My rhythm band had come together again. I got a glimpse of what I imagined Calico Bottom to be like when the golden leaves began to fall to the ground later in the season. Red, yellow, brown and green leaves blew into my imagination the dry sounds of rushing feet that hurried towards a table covered with people, places and piano keys that played melodies unknown into the minds of man, but to life's appetite it sounded and tasted sweet, tantalizing and delicious. I kept my questions to myself and continued to listen.

The Clifton Nate family was headed by a grandson of four generations. His great-great-grandfather was Ushra, the yardman whose children were given birth by Jubielha. The house in Calico was his inheritance. After settling in, his son Roger was lured into a relationship with Effie and John Jr's daughter, Callie. During their teen years, Roger found it hard to move out of adolescence. Callie befriended him and as she continued to mature, he became suitable for athletics. He grew muscular and more confident while Callie became voluptuous and charismatic. Callie's best friend, Verta would most often be left out of the equation even though she had walked home from school with them for years. On a day nearing Callie's sixteenth birthday, Callie made it plain to Roger that she was ready to begin a sexual relationship. A quarter of a mile from the Moore farm was a bend in the road. When the children were toddlers they would play in the tall grass and force the grownups to look for them when they wanted to play a while longer. Farmer Wilson and his wife Dora would keep their eyes on the creek area out of fear that the children would wander too far across the pasture. Callie and Roger stopped in the tall grass around the bend in the road leading to her home and Callie removed her underpants and began to fondle Roger's manhood. When his jockstrap prevented her from proceeding, she convinced him to take part in releasing himself. Callie had him to lie on his back because she saw that he was awkward. His massive manhood excited her so much that she sat on it and satisfied her lust. Her climax was more than she could take emotionally. Roger was perplexed for his father had not told him a thing about that part of doing things with girls. He had only seen a few animals mate. He stood up to gather himself and she wrapped her legs around his waist pulling him into her again. From out in his pasture, Farmer Wilson saw them go into the brush. A month later, he positioned himself in the bushes to watch them make love again. Farmer Wilson buried his hanky in the pasture so that his wife Dora would not have to wash it when she did the laundry.

Cliff Nate noticed the change in his son, Roger who had always been shy. Suddenly, he was losing time by more than two hours in getting home from school. His twin brother, Rudy would dodge questions that their father would ask and it made bad matters worst. The final straw came when Roger went home and sneaked into the barn late one evening. He had planned to sneak into the house later on hoping to avoid a confrontation with his father. Only he fell asleep in the barn and had to face his father early the next morning. Roger had managed to stand up like a man and take his father's tongue lashing. It was his character that was shattered when his father called him a "pussy-whipped-son-of a so-and-so." He now found Callie demanding and her antics were draining him. A classmate let it slip that he had missed a few baseball practices. It rendered Roger speechless. Callie was killing his relationship with his dad. Roger decided that he was headed in the wrong direction with Callie, so he cleaned up his act and began to ignore her. Verta ultimately found others to walk to and from school with after Rudy told her some of the things that Roger went through. Callie now had more time on her hands than she needed. Roger decided to travel yet another route with Callie and to see her even less. Verta's father had seen Callie and Roger in action one day when she'd met him behind the school building. He was disgusted. Callie had cut her visit with

Verta short on one particular evening and instead of going back the way that she had come into Calico, she took the other trail leading to the big stables for a cut through around the tail end of Farmer Wilson's property. She doubled back to the schoolyard with no idea that she was being watched. His daughter, Verta did not know about it so he chose not to tell her. It just made him more aware of a few things.

There were two trails in Calico. One led in and one led out. The paths were designed to protect the school and outer boundaries. Callie's association with her long time friend and classmate Verta was indeed out of bounds. Roger Nate went to visit Verta as often as he could. He liked the way that she listened to him. He taught her about the sports that he played and she gave him her undivided attention. Her questions, though petty, made him feel good about himself. She admired his muscles and she knew how to let him know it by the look in her eyes. Verta's father would frown and sometimes sit within earshot of their conversations but Roger would not allow it to discourage him. The old man could have listened all evening and never know that Verta's spoke without her having to say a word. She thrilled Roger to the bone and made his heart sing. Meanwhile Callie was contented with seeing Roger every now and then because they really had nothing but their sexual prowess in common. She enjoyed making him beg to meet her around the bend of the road in the tall grass. Farmer Wilson equally enjoyed himself. If they had ventured further towards his property line there were times that his peeping would have been discovered. His spree certainly made a new woman out of his wife, Dora Mae. He had only to recall the ploys of Roger and Callie to rejuvenate his libido. He would go home to tease and taunt Dora's body in ways that she had never experienced before to bring her to a climax. Farmer Wilson began to walk proudly throughout the community and Dora once again allowed her hair and nails to grow. Her lips would pout for him and he learned to come running to turn them into a smile after his own satisfaction. Over the course of time Lil' John, Callie's younger brother kept trying but could not find the right time to tell Callie what he knew about Verta and Roger. Once he discovered her and Roger's special place, he too would look in on them from time to time. One day he headed Old Farmer Wilson off and started a conversation to deter him from going into the grass where Roger and Callie were. It had caused the old man to walk in another direction and Lil' John stuck with him until he saw Callie out on the road again. When he walked home and went into the parlor, Callie was sitting there smiling and looking like an angel. She simply looked too happy for him to burst her bubble. Lil' John kept quiet and promised himself to remember to mind his own business.

Myrtle broke away from her story and turned to watch her Aunt Ida stroll across the yard towards the postman. She said, "Look! I would not be a bit surprised if she ain't fuckin' him." Lizzie and her little girl named Alice headed down the street to their house. We sat and watched them pass by before Myrtle spoke again. Her next words were, "I bet you I gotta go inside. The bitch got finished washing." I left and cut across the park towards home. People were milling around out in the park while laughing and talking. I heard the young at heart and the old with wisdom sending out a sound of soul signals that were as refreshing as an orchestra playing in springtime. The watermelon man sang his lingo saying, "Hey little children playing in the sand, go tell your mama here comes the watermelon man." At the same time I heard a tenor croon, "Hot tamales, hot tamale man! Hot tamale man is here! Come 'n get your hot tamale!" Coming down the next street was the roaring sound of a huge truck with a rickety sounding clutch. A man was yelling, "RAG MAN, RAG MAN RAG MAN RAGMAN. GIT RID 'O YORE'S TODAY!" There were enough variations in the sounds to entertain me for hours. I could see that there were women coming with their bundles of rags to throw upon the back of the truck. Doors were swinging open by people that rushed to get a melon while others waited nearby to make their purchase or taste a plug of the sweet fruit. The hot tamale man had his own crowd too. Still to come was the vegetable truck, the ice truck and Seafood, the fisherman. I was privileged to sit and listen to all of those words and tales of woe. I think that it may have been the day that I no longer wanted to hear a story from Mother Goose Rhymes. The very next time I sat to talk with Myrtle, I asked her a question. I got no answer to it immediately but she had something else to tell me. "Lizzie," she said, is going to have a baby and Rufus is the daddy." My question had not been answered. I asked again. "Myrtle, why do you hate your Aunt Ida?" Her conversation concerning Lizzie did not interest me until she began talking about sex that sizzled. She watched me closely while she described in detail where the man's thing was and where he put it when he did it to the woman. I guess I must have looked too enthralled because she took a shortcut and began to tell me about Lizzie's wedding. "She and Rufus were in love," is the way that she started to tell the story. "When he went into the service, Lizzie did it with Nash Cole who had always loved her. She got pregnant. The wedding was so beautiful that their picture was in the newspaper." Her facial expression changed at the point where she told me that Aunt Ida had made Lizzie's dress and was so proud of it that her head was up in the air for a long time. Myrtles looked me in the eye and asked suddenly, "And guess who had to clean up her mess she made in that back room?" Before I realized that she expected me to answer, she shouted, "ME!" So I guessed that to be her reason for hating her Aunt Ida. Surprisingly, she opened up the subject of what I really wanted to hear about.

Ida was Rufus' stepmother. His mother had been Ida's teacher from her fourth grade class in elementary school. Back then they kept the same teacher until the teacher would quit teaching or the student would quit school. When Ida was in the seventh grade, she saw Wilbur and sparks flew. On her way to school that morning, she met her friend, Melinda by the bend of the road as usual. They both timed themselves to try and get to the bend of the road to meet one another on school days. It was situated at the property line between the Wilson and Moore farms. Callie had her own friends to walk to school with every morning. After Ida's first day of school, she walked with her own classmate, Melinda. Ida had long curly hair like her Grandmother Mable and liked to keep it tied back with ribbon. On that particular morning, she made herself a special style in front called a pompadour. Her grandmother had made for her a cute pink skirt set with the matching blouse. Ida had gotten dressed early and felt special. The blouse was a perfect fit for her itchy budding breasts that were beginning to get larger by the day. Along the roadside wildflowers grew tall and emitted an intoxicating fragrance that was beginning to fade away like the summer's wilting blossoms. Before the frost came, grass grew tall willows that surrounded the meadows. It had been a fun place to hide and romp around in until Ida's itchy breasts started slowing down her upper body movements. Now Ida and Melinda visited one another to sit and talk with a little music playing on the radio. Playing jacks was still a nice challenge for them too. After a refreshing walk to school the two girls walked into the classroom laughing. There sat a man who sent Ida into a dream world. He looked about 18 years old and had a thin mustache above his luscious lips. It was Wilbur with skin so smooth that Ida likened his complexion to that of a red heifer. The sparks began to fly between them when their eyes met and she tripped over her own feet. Her stomach fluttered. Her face began to burn with embarrassment. Ida was sure that it had to be the worst moment of her life. When she realized her good fortune to still be standing, Ida hurried to slide a slip of paper from her book to the floor so that she could pick it up and recover. That little feat gave her time to bend down to pick it up and check out her classmates to see if they had noticed anything. She whispered between her teeth, "Thank God, they are not looking." She took a small breath and walked to her seat. Their teacher Mrs. Avery introduced her husband to the class. He and his wife walked to the door and said a few words. A short time later, he left, taking a child's heart with him. Her attention returned to her textbook but her stomach continued to flutter whenever she remembered the sparks that flew between them. He had truly taken her breath away.

Wilbur Avery was used to women and young girls swooning over him but he would ignore it. Luella his wife was used to it also, but did not like to introduce him to her female acquaintances. She knew that he loved her but when her women associates found out that he was married to her, their dispositions more often than not, would change. During her high school years, her popularity had been average. After high school she attended Houston County training school because she wanted to teach. Wilbur had swept her off of her feet in record time and caused her father much grief. Wilbur liked to work with his hands and he loved being free and creative. He loved to build and repair fences. Her family thought that she should hold out for a more ambitious husband that had more to offer. Wilbur's gentle nature and fine brown muscular body was irresistible. She simply had to have him. Luella did not take Ida's reaction to Wilbur seriously because she knew the feeling. She did not realize that a raging fire lay smoldering between the child's budding breasts. Ida with her sparks in tow began to practice Mrs. Avery's mannerisms. Three weeks later, after saying their good byes and so longs, Ida stood near bend in the road to watch Melinda head home. As she rounded the bend, she saw Wilbur. The two of them stepped into the tall grass as if it were a dance step. She felt time stand still when their eyes met. His eyes were smiling. He was overcome by the look of her eyes. She looked down and grabbed a sheet of paper from her notebook. He watched with interest while she slid it to the ground and reached down to pick it up. Wilbur beat her to the punch and picked it up for her. It gave her time to compose herself. Wilbur remembered the move and chuckled. Ida thanked him smiled and scooted out of the tall grass back onto the road. After dinner, she walked to Melinda's for a game of jacks. She was dying to tell her friend what had happened but decided that she should keep it to herself. She spent the evening playing jacks and trying to keep her stomach from melting inside. Her emotions played a melody of grunts and groans. Ida struggled to calm her imagination down by sewing and cutting patterns for her grandmother. When her stomach fluttered, Ida would whisper, "Oh, I pricked my finger." Grandma never saw a needle and made a mental note of it. Ida's creativity also flourished. She used her passion to enhance her skills while sewing and it helped her to focus on the present. Whenever Ida was not sewing or cutting patterns for Mable she walked around swooning and forgetting to eat. She would often conjure up the possibilities of what could have happened when Wilbur had pulled her into the tall grass at the bend of the road. Daydreaming would cause her to stare into space.

Ida went through the winter months in a daydream. Wilbur saw her from a distance a week before Thanksgiving while working on a fence across the field. He could tell that she had matured by the way she walked. He lost sight of her and pulled his mind back to the task of mending the fence. At each season's end, Wilbur had more work than he wanted. Farmers needed him for several reasons. His skills were not limited to fence repairs. He was known for his ability to make recommendations and drafts. Each contract brought him three or four more. Small rural communities needed someone to watch their backs. They needed someone who knew how to scratch it. They needed Wilbur. Wilbur thought nothing of knocking on a landowner's door to warn of a pending problem he'd noticed while repairing a fence for his neighbor. Mending fences was a lucrative hustle without the burden of being bothered by women. When women chased him he found it hard to concentrate on his work. Sometimes the subtle remarks made by women made him become paranoid. Wilbur was a hard working man and a faithful husband. He shook his head in memory of the sparks that flew between him and Ida. The little girl had a hold on his imagination that made his heart skip. The thought of her made him sing the blues for days. The words of a song seemed to swell his memory like flood waters saying, "Oh Baby, don't do me this way, I came to tell you I love you and all you want to do is play." Wilbur dug deep into the earth with his shovel and forced himself to concentrate on the work at hand. It was hard to do.

The bend of the road became Ida's special place to daydream. She became obsessed with the idea that Wilbur would one day be there to pull her into paradise. When she heard that he was mending Farmer Wilson's fence over by Melinda's house, she devised a plan to visit her classmate more often. Unfortunately the fall rains started and it rained heavily for three days straight. It continued to drizzle another two days before the sun broke through the clouds again. Ida suffered and pined for want of seeing Wilbur. By Friday the rainy weather took a back seat and allowed the sunshine to drive the clouds away that fueled her heartache. The world started to flourish in the splendor of brilliant colorful falling leaves that covered the meadows. Trilling birds sang songs to the heavens and filled the vineyards. The bend of the road hosted grasshoppers and butterflies that glided through the air in a merry waltz. Grandma Moore and Effie were glad for the rain to stop also. They had ironed clothes, cleaned the house, cooked and created new recipes while they were cooped up in the house. Callie and Ida busied themselves planning for the holidays. The fellows, Grandpa Moore, John Jr and Lil' John were all out in the barn. Lil' John prided himself in being called one of the fellows too. He loved rainy weather for it was the time that he would get together with his father and grandpa in the barn to catch up on things that happened in the area. Neighboring farmers sometimes came to sit inside the Moore's barn when the ground was soggy and wet out of doors. The men seemed to tell the best stories on rainy days. Lil' John loved going to the barns and stables because it allowed him to hear things that were never talked about in the house while females were present. Ida and Callie joined their mother and grandmother in the kitchen to prepare lunch. Effie told Ida to wash and season the pork chops while Callie peeled the potatoes. Effie shelled green peas and grandma made lemonade. When the cooking was done, the women sat down to eat. When they finished eating Ida announced that she planned to walk over to Melinda's house for a visit.

She had patiently waited until Callie went into her bedroom to take a nap, but had not mentioned it earlier for fear that Callie would want to go with her. As Callie started towards the bedroom Ida offered to see if the men folk were ready to eat lunch. She did not want to get sidetracked by Lil' John either. She wanted to leave the house while he was eating. Ida wondered how many people could see her from their windows if she went with Wilbur into the tall grass. She needed to consider the possibility that people who gazed out into the pasture might see her. Her creative mind tried to create a balance of logical thinking in order to force her to calm down. She was ready to give her yearning heart to Wilbur. Before going out of the door to call the men to lunch, she decided to put on her old garden shoes for her walk to the barn. She then reached down between her legs and grabbed the hem of her long skirt from the back and brought it up between her legs and pulled it upwards until it reached her waistband. She then tucked it under the waistband in front so that it would not sweep the ground or touch debris from the barn floor when she walked. It made her skirt look like wide legged britches. Ida meant to be well prepared when she saw the men. She loved to clown around and decided to give them something to laugh about. She pulled on her old straw hat and was out of the door. On her way to the barn she took giant steps and swung her arms to the beat of grown folks' music. She found the men folk inside the barn stacking fence posts and wire behind a truck that was parked by the wide back door. For the fun of it Ida tried to carry a post and her grandfather, father and brother cheered her on. Their loud laughter caused her to miss the sound of the truck's door being slammed. Wilbur walked around the truck just as she straightened up. Ida stood dumbfounded and embarrassed with her mouth wide open. She ran to her father and hid her face in his jacket. She held on to him in order to still her trembling legs. The men were so busy laughing that they had not seen the sparks fly and the swell of Wilbur's trousers. Ida opened her mouth to speak and could barely tell them to come into the house for lunch. The men began to tease Wilbur about the effect that he had on women. Wilbur blushed. The sparks from Ida's eyes had once again landed in his heart. He readily accepted the invitation to eat lunch with them. His heart began to sing and he wondered if the others could hear it. He sat at the table between her Grandpa Moore and her father looking as cool as a cucumber. Wilbur managed to digest his plate of lust that he had carried around with him all season along with the delicious meal that was set before him. Grandma Moore asked Ida to serve the iced tea and she served it with a smile and with the elegance of a swan. Ida had rushed in from the barn and laughed at her excitement. She rushed to undo her skirt and styled her hair. When she reached over the plate to fill Wilbur's glass she let a napkin drop to the floor. Mable saw the move and smiled. "Oh hell!" she thought. She knew that move. Mable left the room to try to keep her drawers dry. She wondered if her observation had been correct. She saw Wilbur pick the napkin up and watched Ida's eyes as she scoped out the family around the table. They were too busy eating their food to notice Ida flirting with a grown man. Ida gave him a quick smile and moved on. Mable did not witness the sparks flying between her grand daughter and Wilbur, but she felt them. "Lord," she whispered. "Thy will be done." Her mind went back to her first night on the banks of the Mississippi River. She called it "Joy Night." By the end of the meal, Wilbur knew that he was smitten and had to do something somehow in some way. He took a look at Ida's father and decided that it would be better to go home to his wife whom he loved dearly. He didn't want to deceive John Moore Jr, his client who was willing to pay a decent price for his fence to be mended. Ida left while the men were in deep conversation about the remaining work to be done. It surprised Mable that Wilbur sat until the conversation and strategy planning was over. If she had truly known Wilbur she would not have troubled herself with all of that thinking. His passion was tempered. His wife, Luella was more than enough for him but that little girl held a piece of a puzzle that must have been in the shape of a hook because it tugged at his heartstrings. The men gathered themselves and walked back to the barn to finish loading Wilbur's truck. He spent as much time as he needed to place the posts and wire along the sites to be repaired on the Moore property. He had recently finished the work for Farmer Wilson so he drove over to Farmer Wilson's place to collect his money before beginning the contract with the Moore family. After her visit with Melinda Ida walked towards home and chose a spot in the thickets of tall grass to sneak into to wait for Wilbur. Her heart sang and the whole world felt like a soft pillow to her pounding heart. She innocently followed her heart to a place of no return. Wilbur left his truck on the Wilson property and followed the fence around the property line until he found a place to enter the foliage. He saw where the ground seemed to tell a story of secrets but hoped that he would find a treasure that belonged to him. He almost laughed at his foolish heart. A wish that Ida would be waiting for him set his soul on fire. Ida stood waiting for him as if they had planned it. Wilbur gently pulled her into his arms and held her until she relaxed. The rainy days had left dampness upon the grass so Wilbur removed his wool lined jacket and made a pallet to give them a place to sit. Ida did what came naturally before Wilbur began to talk. The script for what happened next made her daydream a reality. She laid her head on his shoulder and kissed him. When his tongue found hers, she felt herself open up and a tiny drop of moisture released itself and made her panties damp. Wilbur felt the fire in his loins and opened his eyes to look into hers. Ida's eyes were closed so he lightly rubbed his nose against hers until she opened them. She started to unbutton her blouse and smiled up into his eyes again. Her tiny nipples were scorching hot to the tip of his tongue. While he nipped and kissed her breasts, Ida slid her panties down and stepped out of them. His knees wobbled when she reached into his fly and removed his manhood. "Oh shit! I'm hanging by a shoe string," Wilbur moaned. He was impressed by her brazen action and slightly dismayed. He silently prayed that he could contain himself and decided to ask questions later. He was on fire with lust. They fell back ever so gently and with their bodies moving in the harmony of a song, he guided himself into a tiny, wet bud waiting to be opened and watered. He whispered in a hushed voice, "Baby, please don't move." Wilbur knew that any movement of her hips would cause him to ejaculate. He eased himself out of her to rub her clitoris with the tip of his penis. When Ida began to cry out in ecstasy he re-entered her and gave her everything that he had of his being.

Her body drew him in deeply and pulsated for all of five minutes while her legs lay propped upon his shoulders. Wilbur tried to pull out of her but his member became swollen again. Ida became fearful because of the pain she felt. She began to cry but Wilbur couldn't stop himself. The soreness took a turn for the better when Wilbur finished and used his hanky to clean her up. They lay still until she stopped crying. Wilbur sat up and kissed her eyelids. She felt his breath on her stomach and giggled when he began to tickle her with his tongue. The sound of her laughter was like a love song. He made Ida climax again. Quietly, they each gained their composure enough to get sit up. Wilbur wanted to stay there forever and a day. Ida, though bewildered, was glad that her dream had finally come true. Wilbur used his fingers to rearrange her hair and to tie her ribbon again. He turned her around first one way and then the other to fix her clothes the way that they should have been. When Ida faced him again, she stood on her tipped toes and kissed him long and deep enough to embed her dreams in his memory. Wilbur continued to sit in the grass until he was sure she had made it home. Her maturity was way beyond his imagination. He felt like she had dipped him into a cool spring and taught him how to swim. Ida had satisfied the deep longing fire set by the flying sparks. Ida walked home and headed straight to her grandmother's garden. She gathered the ripened tomatoes in her skirt tail and walked into the house. She intentionally dropped one of the tomatoes on the living room floor. While the family watched the tomato roll, Ida scampered into the kitchen to take the remaining tomatoes out of her skirt. Only her grandmother saw the glow on her face when she made an announcement after her bath. Ida had called her sister Callie into the bedroom and said, "I'm bleeding down there." Callie helped her fix herself up and put on her nightgown. She said proudly, like a big sister, "Now go tell mama." Effie and grandma rejoiced and laughed when she said, "now, I'm a woman." If they had only known how much of a woman she truly was, they would have hung Wilbur's ass up by a rope and slung it over a pot of boiling water.

Roger met with Callie every now and then to keep his raging hormones in check. Verta's father had not given an inch towards letting his daughter out of his sight. Roger would meet Callie at school outings or small parties that Verta could never attend. Though Callie would invite him often, he never came to her home to visit. He saw that Callie was a selfish lover who knew how to take pleasure away from him by playing mental games. Sometimes, just for the hell of it she would whisper something demeaning to make Roger's manhood shrivel up. Afterwards, she'd set his loins on fire for her pleasure and drive him mad. While she enjoyed herself and wore him out, the fear of being left without an ejaculation plagued him. She would make him stop and beg her to allow him to finish. Callie learned how to make Roger cry like a baby in both joy and sorrow. The last straw had come when she asked him a question about his organ failing to grow to full size. When it responded to her innuendo and shriveled up, he had zipped his pants and left her lying in the grass. Callie got up and dusted herself off while she laughed. Her panties were in her coat pocket so she slipped them on and said, "Well, you're the one who didn't finish, dummy." Roger had kept walking until he was out of her life. She saw him in town three weeks later and invited him over for Christmas but he had not shown up. The way that Ida and Melinda danced around during the season had kicked the celebration into high gear so Callie had not taken the time to wonder about Roger much. Lil' John stayed on the dance floor too. He had also invited some of his friends over. Callie did not see Roger again until the first of the year. He ignored her so she did him likewise. On their first day back to school Ida and Melinda met by the bend in the road and one could not talk for the other. Melinda laughed and talked about her family members who had shown up to visit during the holidays. Melinda said that her mother's sister had come into town and was a friend to their teacher, Mrs. Avery. Ida took a deep breath and swallowed hard.

Ida could feel the hair on her neck rise and her ears perk up. Melinda said, "She's going to have a baby." Ida doubled over and grabbed her stomach. A painful cramp had hit her in the pit of her stomach and she could not straighten herself up. There was an image in her mind that ebbed away. She hated that Wilbur had held his wife in his arms and made love to her. She stood up and whispered to Melinda, "I stared menstruating." Melinda said softly, "Me too." They both broke into laughter and hugged one another. After dancing around and giggling the girls ran the rest of the way to school. Mrs. Avery was not in the classroom when they arrived. The school had hired a new teacher to take Mrs. Avery's place. The pressure was off and Ida was able to settle down and pay better attention to her school work. Her passion shifted gears that changed love to envy of her former teacher, Mrs. Avery. During school hours Ida had to work extra hard to keep thoughts in a child's frame of mind. Her body tormented her with a longing that she began to fear. She was as lovesick as a new bride and was only thirteen years old. During the evenings, she began to roam the countryside looking for Wilbur's truck after getting permission from Effie to visit Melinda. As often as she could find him their lovemaking kept Wilbur's truck rocking all over the wooded marshlands where nobody was likely to find them. It was a miracle that they didn't get caught. Wilbur was becoming burnt out. He loved his wife. He found that he loved the way that Ida thrilled his soul. When he did not see her, he found it hard to concentrate. By Luella being a mild mannered person and not feeling energetic during her pregnancy, she was content with Wilbur sitting with his arms wrapped around her. They had spent their holidays in Athens, Georgia with their families. When school started in January and she decided not to go back to her job, Wilbur was happy. The baby was due in June and he loved seeing Luella radiant and relaxed. His tender loving arms were enough for her but she had learned how to match his passion. She liked to sit gently on his manhood and exercise her vulva until he exploded. He loved it. Wilbur had nothing that presented itself as a problem but began to doubt his ability to keep Ida's hot box of infatuation a secret. Luella had the baby in June after school had closed for the summer. Wilbur was the proud father of a baby boy whom they named Rufus Wilbur Avery. When the Moore family went to see the baby and to take gifts, Ida stayed home. While her family was at Wilbur's home making a big fuss over the baby, Wilbur made his way to their house. He and Ida did not come up for air until someone knocked on the front door. Ida peeked through the draperies and saw Farmer Wilson. She was a little slow answering the door but after she told Wilbur who it was she opened the door and stood talking with Farmer Wilson to give Wilbur time to climb out of her bedroom window. He circled around to his truck as Farmer Wilson headed towards home. When Farmer Wilson looked across the pasture he saw Wilbur working hard on a fence. Satisfied that Farmer Wilson saw him, he got into his truck and hurried home. Wilbur told Luella that he had to buy a few supplies before the lumber store closed. Judging from his nails she could tell that he had been working. Other visitors arrived so the Moore Family headed home. Callie and Lil' John had returned from town a little ahead of their parents. Ida had scrubbed the house in every corner. She knew that her grandmother and other females in the house could detect pussy a mile away. A pair of panties lying anywhere besides in a dresser drawer would cause Effie and Grandma Mable to sniff around. One evening Ida and Wilbur had ravished each other so passionately that she had come home too exhausted to think. She had undressed, slipped into her nightgown and crawled into bed. Her grandmother had sat on the side of her bed the next morning and said, "Ida, if you are going to be grown, act like it." She then held up a pair of Ida's soiled panties. A shocked and embarrassed Ida reached up and grabbed them, rolled over in embarrassment and covered her head. Mable didn't tell Ida what she knew and Ida didn't ask her grandmother anything. She figured that keeping silent about it was acting grown enough. In hot pursuit of Wilbur Ida hid in the back of his truck one evening. He was almost home before he saw her head in his rearview mirror. Wilbur almost turned the truck over trying to stop. If there was ever a time that he wanted to hit a woman, it was then. His eyes were blazing with anger. Her smiling eyes turned his anger into mush. The mush went straight to his loins. Wilbur drove into the woods and had it not been for her passion, the way that he ravaged her would have been rape. Afterwards he had cried. She, a mere child, had kissed his tears away. When he could think clearly, he drove her as near to the bend in the road as he dared and went home to his wife. Wilbur knew that he had landed on a bolder in the middle of a shitty creek and he had no paddle. He lay in bed with his wife, Luella and relived his anger and fright over and over again. He kept seeing Ida in the back of his truck only in his mind he'd parked in front of his house and had gone inside. He wondered if he could talk Luella in to going to visit her relatives because he feared the worst repercussions. He recounted his old days of freedom. The burden of infidelity was great and began to eat away at his pride . . . The thought of giving up his relationship with Ida made his chest tighten up. Wilbur loved Ida. He looked at Luella and saw love personified. She was nice and soft and breakable. Rather than hurt his wife he chose to hurt himself. He visualized him sitting at Johnny Moore's table. Wilbur shook his head as if to clear it. He realized that God had sent an angel to let him know that at John Jr's table lay his safety. Wilbur needed to take a step back from his lust and breathe new life into his marriage. Early the next morning Wilbur went to talk to John Jr about the fencing job and to collect his money. Ida's father, like a good client, had referrals for three more contracts waiting for Wilbur. There was an area on the fence where Wilbur had used a different clamp on the post and he wanted John Jr to take a look at it. Wilbur caught him with his head down and casually mentioned that he'd been teased about one of his daughters hanging around his truck. John Jr laughed and said, "Man, you just put a son in the cradle and now you trying to rob mine." Wilbur ran his finger across his lips and countered, "Hell, just be glad as hell I wasn't in the truck." John said, "Man, what have you been up to? If you dance on your shoe string, you'll trip yourself up". "Shoe string?" Wilbur asked. "All depends on how far I got to fall." Wilbur and John doubled over with laughter. They parted with John Jr promising to have Effie talk to which ever one of his girls it was that had hung around Wilbur's truck. He had an idea but chose not to think about it. Wilbur drove his truck away from the fence holding a taut expression on his face. He whispered, "Thank you Lordy, but please forgive me for loving her." All he wanted was a little time to gain control of the situation. A mere child was toying around with his emotions and he had to put an end to allowing her to make the rules. Effie listened while her husband talked. None of what he said had surprised her. Her daughters were swift and she couldn't keep up with them. Ida popped around all day long. Her stride was one of, "Get the world ready, y'all, here I come!" She was just like her grandmother. If she wanted something, she usually got it. Effie remembered the time Ida saw a dress and wanted her grandmother to make but it. The dress was too mature for her. Ida took brown paper and a pair of scissors and turned the pattern backwards before she cut it out. She ended up with a dress to die for. Effie knew that if Ida had guts to go after a man like Wilbur, her little ass was TOO hot. Effie sighed when she thought about Callie. Callie was listless and talked very little that summer. She was waiting for her to snap out of what ever it was that had caused her to change. Callie had gone from being controlling to being an introvert in a matter of a few months. After dinner, Effie sat both girls down stating that they needed to talk. She looked Ida in the eye and said, "Young Lady! You will NOT be going out of this house alone to visit Melinda and no body else until you turn 18 years old." Ida didn't blink. Innocence was written all over her face. Effie stared her down until she broke her gaze. Ida was sent to her room. Effie saw too much wisdom in that little heifer's eyes and knew she had to break her little ass in like a mule. Mable sat in her rocker and rocked back and forth in silence. She had prayed for her family and was thankful that the day had finally come that her grand-daughters would be held in check or accountable for their actions. Effie then sat and folded her arms and watched Callie cry. She put her hand on Callie's shoulder and said, "Child, somebody must have hurt the hell out of you." Lil' John sat in the parlor and yelled, "Roger did it!" Callie cried harder. "Callie, who is Roger?" her mother queried. "He is a square from school and Callie made him look good and he dumped her," 'Lil' John blurted out in one breath like a lullaby. The household had a good laugh on Callie. She reached under the table and threw her shoe at her brother. It missed him because Lil' John threw himself from the seat of the couch down onto the floor. Grandma Mable strolled into the room and gave Callie a big hug and laughed so hard that it was catching. She and Callie laughed together because her shaking shoulders shook Callie's shoulders too. Grandpa Moore yelled from the kitchen, "Now you know how God feels when we turn the other way." Johnny Jr sat staring into space. He could not believe that it had been his baby girl that had the desire for Wilbur's attention.

He still saw little girls when he looked at his daughters. He wondered if he would have had the strength to run from a box of cherries. He was glad it had been Wilbur who thought enough of him to say something. The questions that Effie really wanted an answer to, she was afraid to ask. Her little Ida had become a "red-peppered-hot-heifer" with the nerve of a brass assed monkey. She decided that time would tell the whole story. Fortunately, both girls had independently concluded that they needed to stop having sex before they got caught. The realized that it was time to be thankful that they were not pregnant. At mid winter, Callie started going to training school so that she could begin to teach elementary school. Ida decided to totally ignore Wilbur and his truck. She gave up on chasing Wilbur because it had been a close call. She wondered what her parents knew. Her mother had not called his name. Well they hadn't killed her so she began to look for another way to enjoy the privileges she still had. Before the next holiday season, Wilbur who had missed Ida terribly managed to find a way to pull Ida into their love nest around the bend. She gave herself to him while he talked shit in her ear. It had sounded rather comical and she struggled to keep the words he spoke out of her heart while he pumped away to satisfy his loins. She had matured and found that passion held on to you tightly. Ida felt complete in his arms but she refused to let him rule in her head. He only made her body feel good. He thrilled her soul but she tried not to let it show. But, Wilbur did know it. Wilbur could feel her intentions and he enjoyed her defiance. When Ida's feet hit the soil at the bend of the road again, she headed home making a promise to herself. She was going to hold the magic within herself and leave the bend of the road to Mother Nature. Ida snickered at the way that she had learned to make a grown man holler. The smile was still on her face when she walked into the house and greeted Effie.

Rufus grew by leaps and bounds. Because of his appetite and energy Luella had another full time job on her hands. Wilbur was more than enough inspiration for her and their lovemaking was superb. She learned to rest while the baby slept so that her energy level would be up when her husband came home every evening. She made Wilbur blush by telling him how good he looked and how his rippling muscles sent her body a signal to crawl into his arms. She'd never imagined a life so perfect. Her girlfriends told her thousands of times that she needed to get out of the house sometimes but Wilbur had made everything so comfortable for her that she loved being home. In spite of her family's disapproval, she knew she had chosen the right man to spend the rest of her life with. Luella went back to each one of her friends who had tried to talk her out of their marriage to hear them admit that their advice to her had been wrong. Wilbur took his family to Athens for Christmas. He had his freedom again. His longing to be with Ida was confined to the hours that he worked in pastures mending fences. On his way home to Luella and Rufus, he would conjure up a time clock and punch out his lust for her as if he were hitting a time clock in a factory. Wilbur would struggle for the will to leave thoughts of Ida in the pasture. That Christmas, Luella was the Belle of the Ball and each day Wilbur made her realize it. Everyday they were in Athens he gave her a gift. It had started with a red carnation. The next day he gave her a ruby ring. Day three she received a pearl necklace from Wilbur. The gifts kept coming. Wilbur ended it by taking her to Atlanta on a shopping spree in case she decided to return to her teaching job. Simultaneously, Ida's thoughts were on the upcoming Christmas pageant. Everybody in the community planned to be there. She and Melinda had some dance steps waiting for them. Her stomach would flutter when Wilbur crossed her mind but by then, she knew that even if she couldn't see him, she would live. Ida looked across the living room at her mother and father. John Jr sat reading a book and Effie was darning socks. She could never remember a time when they weren't there when she needed them. Ida cultivated a maturing adoration for Wilbur in the place where her budding sexual appetite had mellowed. She discovered all sorts of fun things to do. While she had fun with people her age, she knew that Wilbur was where he needed to be. She wanted him to raise his son. "Oh Well," she sighed. "The wife comes with the damn package." A sassy voice in her mind said, "I will open the package when I'm good and damned ready." Ida's eyes still welled with tears at the thought of Wilbur being with Luella. She sniffed and pinched her nose between her finger and thumb to make the tears go away. Ida learned how to muddy her imagination when the thought of him being with Miss Avery crept into her mind. She had laughed at the sounds that Wilbur made during their lovemaking, and she hoped that she was the power behind the passion. Someday, she wanted someone to be devoted to her. In her innermost being, Ida wanted it to be Wilbur. Her fluttering stomach chased the thoughts away. Ida wrapped her arms around her body and whispered, "Oh! God!" Just then, her friend Melinda came through the door and asked, "Girl, what's taking you so long?" Melinda had looked for Ida along the way so they would meet at the bend of the road. Ida had forgotten what time it was because Wilbur had been on her mind. The girls went to tell Ida's parents who sat in Mother Moore's old bedroom that they were leaving for the pageant. Christmas carols were being sung while the women sat and reminisced. Callie and Lil' John had left the house earlier in the day to help with the decorations at the town hall. Callie secretly longed to see Roger. She continued to long for him throughout the holiday season and until

Warm and gentle spring rolled around again. The world woke up to the sounds of noisy tractors and the smell of manure. The sounds of songbirds were given to the hearts wistful lovers. Children arose early in the mornings to sit on porches and breathe life's sweet aroma. Grown ups knew that when a tree filled with birds that sang it meant to run for cover unless you wanted shit in your hair. Life for the Moore's took on a dexterous tone. There was work to be done and somebody had to do it. The winter had been unusually wet and cold which meant that repairs needed to be done quickly before the hot summer's sun dried the already molded planks of wood. The sun had been known to chase them inside again if they kept the work waiting too long. John and Effie went to walk the land over to see if the repairs that were done the year before and livestock feed bins had held up and fared well. They checked the fields and the pasture. John Jr saw that trenches had to be dug out and feed bins needed to be replaced or patched up. The barn also needed a new roof. They finished the long walk by way of the fence around the pasture. The posts were standing firm. John Jr wondered how Wilbur was getting along and reminded himself to check on the neighbors that he had referred Wilbur to. He and Effie returned to the house where Mable had cooked a hearty breakfast. Grandpa Moore and Mable ate and listened to Effie and John Jr's report. Johnny Senior reminded his son of a few other structures that needed attention. The Moore family knew they made a good team because the farm remained profitable each year. Grandma Mable wouldn't reveal the thousands of dollars that she had stashed away from her dressmaking business. When Easter and Mother's Day came around, people came to Mable with money in their hands to pick up their clothes she'd made for them during the winter months. Ida loved to help her grandmother cut out patterns. She was quick and smart enough to save her grandmother time and money. Ida could hold pattern variations in her mind and could stitch a style into a design outright without making a pattern adjustment. For instance, if she knew that a woman was heavy in the breasts and the dress was low cut, she would give her the same style with a higher cut right on the fabric without stopping to adjust the pattern. If two women wanted the same dress she would make a noticeable difference in the style. Somehow she knew how to make clothes fit people just right. A big heavy woman with heavy hips would gain a longer skirt in the back to make the dress fall even all the way around. Any adjustment she needed to make was made in the hem. She and Mable could whip those orders for dresses and skirts out quickly while they talked about attitudes and adding twos. That's what Mable would call their conversations. Ida loved to feed her grandmother a bit of gossip and say, "Add that up, grandma." Mable would chide, "Anybody ought to be able to put two and two together." The two of them would roar with laughter. Sometimes Effie would hear the laughter and go into the room to run Ida out of her chair so that she could enjoy the gossip with her mother in law. She hated it when Ida crowded her out.

Wilbur and Luella spent another Christmas with her family. Wilbur was at his wife's beck and call. He made it hard on his in laws who were served by their women, but Wilbur enjoyed spoiling his wife. They had a wonderful trip to Athens, Georgia and back. Luella returned home to spoil Wilbur rotten. It was his turn to be pampered because he had earned it. They cuddled a lot after putting Rufus to bed. Wilbur continued to be extremely busy soliciting contracts. It depended on how far he traveled to work but Wilbur would repeatedly spread himself pretty thin the majority of the time. It was during the month of March, that Wilbur began working later in the evening. To compensate for his late arrival Luella would put the baby to bed a little later than usual. Wilbur would play with his son before dinner and afterwards he would enjoy talking things over with his wife. On one particular night, he pulled Luella onto his lap so that she could relax and cuddle as she often did. She went to sleep on his lap and he noticed a short time later that she didn't respond to him. He got a strange feeling when Luella failed to answer when he called her name. Wilbur thought that she was just exhausted, so he carried her into the bedroom and laid her on the bed. She never opened her eyes again. Wilbur remembered being weak in his body and he remembered that suddenly the house had filled with people. When he came to himself, cool breezes of the March winds were blowing tears that ran down his cheeks and lapped beneath his chin. He felt the movement of someone. Whoever it was placed a blanket around his shoulders and urged him to go inside. He'd felt a tiredness sinking down, down into a pit of blackness. Someone said that Luella was dead. Her family must have taken care of things from there because his mind would not function. At the sound of her name, his thoughts broke into tiny pieces. While he grieved Wilbur could not stand the sight of Rufus because he seemed to represent lost hopes and dreams. Each time he looked at the child he saw the image of his mother and he envisioned her turning into stone. Why hadn't he known that she was ill? In years to come the mystery was solved but when Luella had suffered the ruptured blood vessel there were no answers to the cause of her death that Wilbur could comprehend. The question of her demise repeated over and over again in his mind. When Wilbur was not wondering that, his mind was blank. He continued to mend fences with his hands having a mind of their own. He remembered driving or riding with someone, maybe his sister holding the baby. People who knew Luella wept with him while he totally gave in to the burden of grief. When he could, he went and deposited several checks into his bank account. Some of the jobs he didn't remember doing. The referrals kept coming so he kept working.

It did not take him long to rebuild his clientele base. He continued to work as much as he possibly could. A lucrative contract took him to Atlanta so he made sure that Rufus was situated and found a room to rent near the job site. Wilbur would work until his body refused to function. He then would drink beer and sleep for two days straight. He sent money to his sister Mae Alice for the baby. Aside from what Wilbur paid for room and board, he saved his money. It was six months before his sisters in Athens saw him again. Mae Alice and Ruthie knew that Wilbur was in Atlanta from the information on the money orders. The day that he showed up at their door looking refreshed they were elated. He had returned without notifying them. In reality he didn't quite remember planning the return to Athens. He simply did it. A check in his pocket told him that he had finished a lucrative contract three days earlier. Someone placed his son in his arms and led him to an overstuffed chair. Wilbur held his son and wept. Ruthie and Mae Alice wept with him. It took a while for the tears to stop flowing and he could cry no more. Wilbur did not remember who had taken the baby from his arms. It was late at night when he awakened from a heavy sleep. His sisters, Mae Alice and Ruthie were asleep on the sofa. They had covered him with a blanket and removed his shoes before they had bedded down for the night. He eased to his feet and went into the bathroom to undress and go to bed. They woke up determined to help their brother however they could. It did not take long for the news of his return to Athens to spread. Single women began to show up at his sisters' door. Wilbur was not ready to engage his frayed emotions in a new relationship. He was cordial and allowed the women to make a fuss over him as they had done for years. The gathering of old friends must have allowed him to nurture his mind enough for him to somehow set his grief aside for a time. His home boys and classmates gathered at the house more than once. It had been soothing to his conscience to think about his carefree years. The day came for him to decide what he wanted to do with the rest of his life. That's when he shook off the cobwebs and wondered what Ida was doing. At the mere thought of her Wilbur started packing his clothes as if he were driven. He asked Mae Alice and Ruthie

Lee if they would take care of Rufus until he finished the contracts in Atlanta. His sisters agreed to keep Rufus for another six months and to take him to see Luella's parents as much as possible so that when he came back for his son, they wouldn't feel that they had been slighted. He left Athens, Georgia looking for the road that led to the border between Mississippi and Alabama. The burden of grief had lifted and felt somewhat lighter. There was comfort in remembering that he had given Luella the best of life that he could have given her during their short moment together. To him, that was what it all had come to be . . . a moment. His thoughts afforded him the strength to mend his conscience. He wondered what the world had been doing without him. He felt like a man who had been on a long journey and had struggled to find a way to return home. Wilbur drew a mental map of how to get where he needed to go. There was another fencing contract he wanted to secure. He believed that if he could complete the task at hand, everything else would fall into place for the rest of his life. Wilbur put his petal to the metal. He drove until he felt tiredness sweep over his body. He reluctantly stopped to rest along the highway in a cove filled with the scent of honeysuckle.

Around noon the next day Wilbur stood at Johnny Moore's door holding a bouquet of red roses. When Ida saw the smile on his face and the twinkle in his eyes, she got up from the table where she had sat talking with her mother, went to her room and pulled her luggage from the closet. She began to pack her clothes after deciding what she was going wear. There was cursing and loud shouts coming from the parlor but she refused to concern herself with it because there were things that she had to remember to pack. Ida figured that packing alone was enough for her to think about. She could have cared less than a damn about whose voice it was or who it was that shouted at whom. All she knew was that when Wilbur left the house that afternoon or evening, she was going to be with him. Wilbur believed that he had been through too much to be afraid of what the future held for him. Life was fleeting and if there was something more for him to have, he wanted it that day. He looked down at his feet to make sure that his shoestrings were tied. They were. It was no time for laughter but he felt giddy at the thought of John Jr trying to hang his ass on a string. Wilbur had walked into the Moore family's parlor and removed his hat in an effort to be the gentleman that they all knew him to be. After a proper greeting he asked for Ida's hand in marriage. Grandpa Moore and John Jr were in a rage. They stuttered and spat and sputtered and sent curses flying. Grandma Mable and Effie were cool and calm. They kept their eyes on John Jr and Grandpa. John Jr tried to ease his way into the bedroom for his shotgun,

but he would have had to move his mother out of the way. She stood like a
soldier and wondered what that girl child of John Jr and Effie's had done to
impress someone of Wilbur's stature. John Jr's father grabbed his hand to
prevent him from taking his jackknife from his pocket. He had totally
forgotten how strong his father was. Tears rolled down Ida's father's face. He
frowned and asked Wilbur in a whisper, "Man, what business do you have
knowing a child of mine?" The words had the sound of a whine and implications
of him having taken advantage of Ida. In his mind, he saw Wilbur holding his
baby in his strong arms in secret. He wanted to kill him. Just then, Ida strutted
out of her bedroom wearing a powder blue swing coat ensemble. The dress
was a perfect fit with a Nehru collar. Her pumps and purse were a matched set
of blue brocade. Effie had made the outfit for Ida's birthday. She had seen it in
a book and asked Mable to draw the pattern. Ida looked stunning. She ignored
everyone else in the room and smiled at her father. John Jr let out a sentence
that sounded like the stammer of a cartoon character. Effie gently touched
him on the shoulder. He sat down and held his head between his hands. Ida
was a baby. She was his baby girl. He wondered how much had gone on
between her and Wilbur. Then he remembered how long it had been since
Wilbur was anywhere nearby. He saw that her bags were packed and ready to
be loaded into Wilbur's truck. Ida had fit every stitch of clothing she owned
into her suitcases. Callie began crying her eyes out as if her sister was going to
jail. John Jr wanted Effie to say something and pleaded to her with his eyes.
Effie spoke up in a tone of reasoning saying; "Now Wilbur, we can't let our
daughter leave home without being married." Wilbur pulled a beautiful set of
rings from his pocket and dropped to his knees. Even Ida's grandpa and father
had to smile at the boldness of the grand rascal. John Jr looked at Wilbur and
Ida and shook his head. He looked from one family member to the next and
whispered a question as if it were his dying breath, "Can you believe this shit?"
Lil' John yelled, "I can." He was the only one truly smiling because he was
happy. Someone went and came back with the preacher. Wilbur kept his eyes
on the men of the house because he was ready to die for love of Ida. If they had
known that he'd talked to the preacher before coming to the house it would
have been World War Three down on the farm. His love for Ida was
overwhelming. They were married while tears were shed by her family. Lil'
John had heard rumors that his sister had been infatuated with Wilbur. They
all turned out to be wrong. He now reasoned that whatever Ida had done
must have been right. He was thrilled that Wilbur really loved his sister and
wanted to marry her. When the preacher said, "You may kiss the bride," Wilbur

put as much love into that kiss as he could. Ida wrinkled her smiling face with embarrassment. Effie thought, "Whatever she has, I'm glad someone like Wilbur is getting it, 'cause a younger man probably can't handle it." Only Callie and her sobbing made Ida sad. This was the first separation they'd had. Effie was trying hard to calm her down before Ida started to cry. Lil' John shook his brother in law's hand and helped him to load up the truck. Ida held tears back and promised her sister that she would write often. She appeared to be strong until the truck reached the edge of town. Wilbur had to pull over so that he could hold her close while she cried. He made her sobbing change to laughter when he described how she walked out of the room with her bags packed. He said, "Ida Baby, rather than leave there without you, I would have lay down my life." Deep within her heart, she believed him. He covered her face with tiny kisses until she giggled. Wilbur pulled slowly away from the curb to continue their journey. It was a long ride to Atlanta and Ida was tired and hungry before Wilbur stopped. Wilbur drove and checked from time to time to see if she was still there beside him or if he was dreaming. He'd have climbed the highest mountain for her. She looked grown up with that expensive ring on her finger.

Just as Ida had promised herself, she had kept Wilbur out of her head. In his place she had put dancing and its many steps and rhythms. There was a café near town where the teens that worked in the bean fields frequented at dusk during the summer. They would finish working and go home to eat, bathe and dress for a good time of dancing. Ida and Melinda took their fancy steps to the café on Friday evenings. There were many steps they learned and would practice during the week if the weather wasn't too hot. Sometimes Ida, Melinda, Callie and Lil' John would go behind the barn with their friends to socialize and drink cold lemonade. Lil' John was the key element during the sessions because he coordinated the male's role. He invited a few of his friends to join him after the girls had worn him out. His popularity catapulted. John, Rudy and David from Calico, Frank and a guy called Champ became known as the "squad". Ida and Melinda took pride in the fact that they'd taught them to dance. Wilbur knew of a boarding house near the place where he'd worked. Behind the boarding house was a Jazz club. It was a fun place where the elite would meet, dine and party. He checked in for the night. It allowed Ida to relax a little and to freshen up before dinner. An awning covered the walkway leading into the club. It gave the club a certain charm. A young girl was indeed living in a daydream and was fascinated as reality unfolded. What a wonderful experience it was for Ida who had never traveled anywhere before. She looked up at the sky and saw stars twinkling. Ida was glad that she knew how to dance. She and Melinda would practice in high heels to make their feet look pretty. She and Wilbur walked through the door in style and drew the attention of the other patrons. Ida had walked to the beat of her favorite dance tune and swung her hips in stride. They were a striking couple. She was unaware that eyes were on her. Wilbur led her to the dining room where she ordered smothered pork chops and mashed potatoes. For himself he ordered chicken livers with rice and a beer. While Ida ate, Wilbur could not stop his arousal. The band began to play and he watched his wife move to the beat. He didn't know what a dancer she was. She finished her meal and looked into his eyes. When she said "Let's dance" he led her to the dance floor and held her close. Ida felt his swollen member and with laughing eyes she looked into his smiling face that reminded her that it had been two years since they had made love. It was Joy night. They rushed to the room. Ida made Wilbur wait until she took a bath. The smell of Honeysuckle filled the room. Wilbur turned on the radio and found a station that played the blues. Ida walked from the bathroom wearing a towel. "You're the one. You're the only one I'll ever love." The melodious words and sweet bass sound gripped her emotions and sent her running into Wilbur's arms. They clung to one another as the song continued to play. "You're the only one I'm thinking of, so hold me and thrill me and fill me with your love." Their lovemaking became so passionate that Wilbur began to plead saying, "Ida, Baby, don't let me hurt you. Ida had locked her legs around the arch of his back. Wilbur stopped moving for her good. He felt her body release its hold on him and pull him deeper where he exploded. It took his breath away. Wilbur was surprised that Ida was able to walk the next morning. When he attempted to talk about her passion she enticed him again and again giving her body to him with abandonment. Afterwards Ida kissed him from head to toe and said, "Wilbur, I've waited all of my life for you and I intend to keep you satisfied." She gave him a long kiss and drew his arms around her shoulders. His organ stood up again. Ida straddled him saying, "You are fine and now you are mine." Wilbur was powerless. He yelled, "Baby, Please!" Ida smiled and shook her hips like a rabbit. She said, "I will."

Callie was alone and felt disgruntled. Ida was gone away and was happily married to the love of her life. Callie realized that she had been completely self centered and Ida had left behind without her having as much as a friend to tell her troubles to. She wondered how she had come to know so little about Wilbur's interest in Ida. The town was buzzing with activity and there was plenty to do only Callie did not feel needed by anyone. Grandma Mable knew the signs of depression. She had grappled with it herself after her parents passed away. Mable began to compare her grand daughter's and their differences. After her mother in law passed away Effie would give them bits of ribbon to twist while she told them a story or two. Mable noted each of their reactions. Callie would sit and hold her ribbon as a matter of routine and give Effie her undivided attention. Ida would take her piece of ribbon and look all around her great grandmother's room as if she expected to find her sitting and twisting ribbons. Her tiny fingers would to try and make something out of her ribbon. While Effie talked Ida would twist the ribbon. Finally one day she stuck it into her mouth and wet it. It took her a while but before the story ended, Ida held a ribbon tied in knots. Callie saw what her sister had done and broke up the session when she tried to snatch it from Ida's hand. Callie had been closer to Ida than she realized. Once again, Ida had fashioned something that Callie wanted. Mable decided to give Callie her undivided attention until she could make a comeback. Callie helped her to wash windows clean the house and sew aprons while John Jr and Effie attended to the farm. One sunny day she decided to take a break and get out of the house into the warm sunshine. When Lil' John went to the fields to help his father sign up the workers Callie tagged along with him wearing Ida's old garden boots and a straw hat. It surprised her to see how much she and her sister looked alike. She soon found out that she was dressed wrong for her walk through the fields when the cool air of the morning went north. The hot sun beamed down on her head and simply paid her straw hat no attention. She never could have dreamed the magnitude of work that went into securing their modest lifestyle. Callie and her brother left the fields and walked another mile to find Farmer Wilson who needed Lil" John to take and repair a gear from his tractor. Callie saw Miss Dora sitting on the porch before they located Farmer Wilson. She sat down in a cool shady spot on the porch and felt too exhausted to move so Callie told Lil' John to go on without her. The shade where Miss Dora sat had looked too good to pass up the chance sit with her. Miss Dora was glad to have company and invited Callie to stay for a bite to eat and to refresh her self. Callie said, "So this is where the cool breezes come after leaving the fields." Dora threw back her head and laughed showing a set of pearly white teeth. She said, "When we got ready to build this house, Farmer and I walked this land over and every time we came to this spot, there was a cool breeze. After we built the house to catch the breeze we noticed something else. Any time we don't get a breeze, we know that there is a storm coming because the wind has changed." Farmer Wilson walked around the house carrying a jug of cool water from the creek.

Every evening just before dark, he and Dora walked down to the creek to lower a jug of water down into it. The creek made the tepid jug of water ice cold. The small bite to eat that Dora prepared turned into a feast. Callie talked about how Wilbur had come to ask the family for Ida. At one point, Farmer Wilson excused himself and walked to his barn to take out a hanky. When he finished using it, he headed out to the pasture. Time moved swiftly around the chattering of Callie and Dora. It was getting late. The sounds of horses braying, chickens clucking and wagon wheels turning signified the end of another workday because the hens were roosting and the wagons headed towards the barns. Callie took her time and walked home. She felt calm and serene. She began to think of what she desired to accomplish in the future. The first thing she wanted was a husband. The second thing she decided was that she needed to move away from home. Finally, she wanted Roger any way that she could have him. It was not long before she saw him again. The next afternoon after helping her mother with the chores, Callie went to Calico Bottom. She followed the creek to the clump of pine trees that were now full grown. She wondered how the entrance to Calico was going to look after the trees were cut down for the lumber. It had been so long since Callie saw the place that it now looked like a miniature village. Women and men alike were working in the herb fields and harvesting roots from the winter plantings. Roger was standing on an ornamented porch of potted tropical plants. The porch looked like a tropical paradise. Callie walked past his house without looking in his direction. She could feel his eyes on her while she headed towards the schoolyard. School was still in session. The sun was hot but the school yard was a cool and shady place. She knew Lena Nathanson who taught the children and found her and the students out back rehearsing for the May Day pageant. When Lena saw Callie she stopped and recruited her on the spot to take half of the children and rehearse them for the dance troupe. Farmer Wilson was constructing the annual May Pole and Callie allowed some of the children to cut strips of colorful streamers for him to attach to the top of the pole. As she watched the crowd of kids practice the dance Callie remembered how many of her classmates were saddened when all of the streamers around the pole were taken by anyone who reached them first. It meant that others could not participate in that particular part of the ceremony. The ones that had been fortunate enough to have a streamer would dance around the pole weaving the streamers in and out until the pole was covered. A multicolored design was displayed from the pole's top to the bottom. Callie had been one of the children that had not gotten a streamer. She became one of the members that did a dance but had longed to weave the May pole. She spent the afternoon teaching the young girls a secret to the dance steps that would make their skirt tails sway. Back in her day it had made May Pole weavers want to exchange the streamers for a chance to dance the "Calico Rock." She took time to show the boys how to give the sway a macho stance. The dancers cheered and became energetic. They began turning cartwheels and tumbling. Callie had to explain to Lena what the excitement was about. Lena laughed and said to Callie, "Oh yes. I remember when you got us all in trouble." Lena agreed to allow the children to do the swaying because she'd never seen anything wrong with the dance either. Callie rode back home with Farmer Wilson after the class went inside to finish their studies. She was happy to have seen Roger. The only problem was the fact that Callie made herself believe that Roger was in love with her. She told her self that he would have followed her except the children were on the playground. In reality, Roger was glad to finally be in full control of his life. He wanted no parts of Callie and had acquired a tremendous dislike for her. She had severely bruised his male ego and had looked down on him as a person as if he had no pride. In another week, Roger planned to go to Florida where he would make money working in the orchards. He wanted to save all that he could for the future. He and Verta were beginning to talk over some serious matters and Roger wanted to prepare himself for a life with her.

When May Day came around, the area stood in readiness for the annual parade. Callie helped Mable to finish making skirts for the girls who most likely would not have been prepared. She went to the school and took proper measurements of every child on the list to be a dancer. She, Effie and Mable got them fixed up. Miss Tenzy who was up in age and moved slow had been the person who had taken on the task years earlier. Some of the plantation residents that sewed helped with the boy's apparel. The parade had become a phenomenal event. It proved to be the best one that the community ever remembered. When the dancers did the "rock" and their skirt tails swayed in unison, the crowed cheered. Every dancer had a smile on their face until they saw Callie. They changed their facial expressions to appear monumental and serious. Lena, their teacher taught the children a secret step to surprise and thank Callie for what she had taught them. They turned in unison towards her and did the "rock" one-two-turn back-step-curtsey to continue on down the lane. Callie's former classmates were thrilled that the dance step had been passed to the next generation. When the disappointed dancers of Callie's class had first presented the dance steps during the May Day parade it had angered their teacher. Nobody seemed to understand that, as children, they had been insulted too. If there were not enough colorful streamers for all of the children, the class thought there should have been another pole; Callie told her mother that her and her classmates had felt slighted when they were scolded for doing the "rock." It hadn't done any good to express their feelings at the time. She was happy that times had changed enough for the message to be understood. The scolded children of the past were now the teachers. The crowd had joined in to dance the rock long after the parade ended. Callie headed home from the pageant with Miss Dora and her husband, Farmer Wilson. She saw Verta walking with her mother and father but they each turned their heads as if they did not see her. Dora invited Callie to stop and sit with them a while because the night was still young. Callie was perplexed and wanted to demand that Verta give her a reason for the snub. Farmer Wilson saw the hurt on Callie's facial expression and started an exciting topic of conversation. He laughed and began to compliment the children's performance. Dora joined in to tell of how she and Farmer Wilson would stand near the creek until Callie, Ida and Lil' John was safely home after each annual May Day festival. They had feared that the children would accidentally fall into the creek on their way home after the May Day celebration that lasted until dark. It warmed Callie's heart making her feel special. Calico Bottom was alive with excited children and proud families. Each year Miss Tenzy baked cookies and recruited cooks from the quarters to make treats for the children. Every child went home on May Day with a colorful streamer and something sweet to eat. Miss Tenzy was determined to keep traditions going on in the name Jubielha. It was getting late and Callie wanted to get home to talk about the pageant before grandma Mable went to bed. Dora suggested to Farmer Wilson that he see her home. As he walked with Callie, Farmer Wilson hated for the walk to end. He bade her good night at the property line and went home to Dora. Grandma Moore opened the door for Callie and made her skirt tail sway before she sat down. After they had a good laugh about it she said, "Child if I had known why you wanted that extra little swing in those skirts, I would have made them pop." Effie got out of her seat and did the "rock" and her husband John Jr beckoned for her to come to bed. She said, "Wait 'til we learn this new step."

Callie woke up the next morning feeling so depressed that she didn't want to get out of bed. Right away the memory of Verta rushed in and took a front seat to drive her thoughts farther than she needed them to go. She made herself get up and make her bed before getting washed and dressed for breakfast. Her appetite was just not there. Callie choked down an egg and a piece of buttered toast. She thought about writing a letter to Ida but there was nothing new to write about. Callie grabbed the old straw hat that she'd worn the day before and set out for Melinda's house. She only made it as far as the bend in the road. Surprisingly, it was not as wet as it usually was in May. When she got to the place where she and Roger met, tears began to flow. Callie looked up and saw birds soaring overhead. They were free enough to soar, she thought. Her ability to soar had been taken away. She was so unhappy. Farmer Wilson walked into the grass and sat down. He said, "I heard you crying, but the boy ain't worth it. He didn't know what to do for a girl like you anyway." Out of sheer frustration, Callie continued to cry. He said, "When you get yourself straightened out, why don't you come by the house and sit with Dora. She enjoys your company". He turned and left the way that he had come. His little speech was what Callie needed to lift her morale. She dried her eyes and walked back to the house to write a letter to Ida. By dusk, Callie was spiraling downward again. She felt lonely and rejected. Lil' John talked her into going with him to a ball game. She really did not feel up to it but she went anyway. Some of her old acquaintances were in the crowd so she sat and cheered hoping to feel as happy as she pretended to be. Lil' John was with a girl when the game ended so Callie told him that she had found someone else to walk home with. She had not seen Farmer Wilson at the game but he showed up to walk beside her. They cut around the pasture across from Melinda's house. It enabled them to see the bend in the road from either side. Before then, Callie never knew that she could be seen going into the thickets. It angered her to realize that Farmer Wilson probably knew more than she wanted anyone to know about the things that she and Roger had done. Her anger changed into a force to be dealt with. She first smiled seductively at Farmer Wilson. It was a smile that caused him to become aroused. They were still on the path so he knew not to be callous. Her heart and self esteem was shattered and Callie wanted someone to pay dearly. Callie quickened her pace and whispered, "Follow me." They walked into the darkness where there was only the light of the moon shining like a halo above the willowy grass. Surprised by Callie's touch, Farmer Wilson said," Now, wait a minute here, girl." Callie stood on the tips of her toes and kissed him full on the lips. His breath was surprisingly sweet. She kissed him for all of the kisses she had missed with Roger. She felt his face grow hot as if he had a raging fever. Farmer Wilson lost control of his passion. While Callie's sweet lips were glued to his, he reached under Callie's skirt and pulled her panties to the side. His fingers were big. He used them to manipulate her body. Callie was ready to come but he stopped to lift her up and into his arms so that he could lay her on the grass. Callie hastily lifted her hips to remove her panties while Farmer Wilson undid his coveralls. He knelt down to lay between thighs that felt hot to his touch. Callie helped Farmer Wilson to guide his throbbing manhood. He entered her like a hot piston. They both cried, "Lord, have mercy!" Callie salivated uncontrollably. She arched her back to swallow everything he offered as deeply as she could into her body. Farmer Wilson took his time and tried to make his hot volcanic-like eruption last forever. He spewed fire from within his loins while her body pulled him deep into paradise; so deep into her silky cavern that his energy was depleted. Surprised Callie became ashamed that her youthful body had completely surrendered to an old man like Farmer Wilson. She grabbed her panties and scampered from beneath him. Out of sheer embarrassment, Callie ran home like a small frightened animal while her body continued to throb between her sticky thighs. Farmer Wilson stood in the grass and laughed until he cried. Never in his wildest dream would he have been so lucky. Young Roger Nate had completely missed the cherry. "Whew!" The old man eased his breath out slowly because he had just gotten a cherry and the damn box that it came in too. He did not bury his hanky that night because Callie had drained him dry. He used his hanky to dry his eyes and headed home to Dora.

The next letter that Effie received from Ida had an Indiana post mark on the envelope. Two Weeks prior to the mailing of Ida's letter, Wilbur had been referred to a small shipping company for a fencing job. The company had ties to the Nickel Line Railroad that made Wilbur a job offer. It was an offer too good to be true. There had been a business in Indiana that needed a position to be filled by a man with logistical skills. Wilbur, while finishing a job in Atlanta had worked around the company's incoming and outgoing shipments. In order for him to be skillful and work in a timely manner, he kept a mental record of the shipping and receiving schedules. He would go to lunch or take breaks when the workers used the dock. Wilbur noticed their use of heavy equipment and was mindful that accidents often happened to people who miss signals and codes between workers that worked close together. Wilbur kept himself out of harm's way. The company's manager became aware of his other skills when Wilbur went to get his check after he'd finished the contract. He overheard the shift manager's conversation. The man was trying to cover his ass because of discrepancies in the shipment log. The tally was bungled in a big way. Wilbur sat and waited patiently until the manager was almost in tears and had started to pull his hair out. After receiving his money, Wilbur whispered to the owner, "Man, you need to check what came in at ten yesterday morning and at two thirty in the afternoon." The owner yelled the information to the manager and asked Wilbur how he had come to any conclusion since his fencing skills had nothing to do with shipments. Wilbur explained that he had almost finished his fencing job but had to wait until that two thirty train pulled out. He had no intentions of working near moving trains. While he waited, he decided to help the workmen who unloaded the cars. They had an interesting conversation about the materials, weights and how being short a worker affected the handling. Wilbur said to the manager, "Those are the same numbers that you are missing." When it was checked out, other wheels besides the iron wheels on the rails began to roll. A call was made to Chicago, Illinois. A job offered Wilbur more money than he would have made if he'd continued to work alone. Wilbur needed to finish contracts in Atlanta before he left town. He also needed to talk to Ida. She was flattered. She wondered why he hadn't known that she would have followed him anywhere. Nickel Rail Road did not baulk or blink. They found land in the state of Indiana for a house to be built for Wilbur. Its location was near the Coal Yard Station where Wilbur would work. A lucrative benefit package came with the position. Ida loved Atlanta, but she loved her husband more. The city was satisfying enough for her to not get homesick. It was a friendly city with enough fine men to make women leave Wilbur alone. She and Wilbur enjoyed six glorious months alone before it was time to go to Athens for Rufus. The job offer sealed their fate. She and Rufus bonded quickly. Caring for a small child gave Ida a double dose of love. Wilbur adored her and Rufus needed a mother who would love him back. She did. When Ida and Wilbur arrived, the house that Ida had asked for was finished but needed a few final touches. Wilbur would work during the night and after sleeping a little; work on the house until dinnertime. After dinner he slept until time to go to work. The house sat on a corner lot. Wilbur had purchased two parcels of land. He was used to seeing land that surrounded a house. Each parcel was one half acre. He left twenty feet at the front and side for the entrances and lawns. The foundation was laid and built up to form a basement that could to be entered from the front and side of the house. When the builders finished, it was a house two stories high. From the front steps they entered the parlor which then led to the living room where a large gas heater stood. Ida marveled at the way that it kept the house warm. The master bedroom sat on the right wall of the living room. Next was the hall closet and linen closet. The bathroom sat across from it and the hallway continued into the huge kitchen where another heater warmed the bathroom and rear bedrooms. On the kitchen wall next to the bathroom was Rufus' bedroom and the back wall housed a third bedroom and the door leading down the stairs and out. Each room had windows and every bedroom had a closet. Nickel Railroad paid for their belongings to be shipped from Atlanta. Wilbur chose to drive his own vehicle. It was new and he did not want to sell it.

Callie read her sister's letter and was happy for her. To fight boredom she began to help more with the running of the farm. Callie was amazed when she saw the profits. It had never occurred to her to turn the value of the harvest into dollars and cents. She believed that her mother and grandmother kept better books than the bankers did. Grandma Mable even had her books for the profit and loss of her dressmaking ventures. Every once in a while she would sew up a bunch of children's clothes and send them to Effie's people in Calico. Her records showed it as gifts. Most of her entries for gifts were offset by a very profitable venture like baptismal gowns for some prosperous church with a large congregation. The left over scraps of material would often be enough material for three or four children's blouses. Store bought patterns called for more material than was necessary but Mable would trim the pattern before pinning it to the material and reap yards of extra fabric. People who didn't know better followed the instructions to a "T" and purchased more than enough material for the items Mable made." Callie was beginning to feel good about life again. The air was refreshing because the spring flowers seasoned it with fragrances that constantly changed. She enjoyed taking time to relate to things happening in the household among the family members. Herself, Ida and Lil' John had been very confident and independent youngsters who each loved to bring new ideas and challenges home to be considered by the family. They independently took pride in making decisions that enhanced their abilities to take their medicine, so to speak. The three children rarely got into trouble at the same time because they had each gone their separate ways. John Jr and Effie had breathing room because while they worked the children were taken care of by grandparents. Morals and family values was a mainstay that was not to be overlooked. Callie hugged her shoulders at the thought of how much support she had known all of her life. Right when she thought that she had pulled it all together, Verta messed up her head again. Verta mailed what looked like a wedding invitation to "Mr. and Mrs. Johnny Moore, Sr." Callie took the mail to her grandmother who handed it to Effie. It was indeed a wedding invitation. Verta and Roger were getting married on June 1st. Callie left the room and sat down to write a letter to her sister. She tried not to show any signs of painful agony, but her heart was breaking into sharp jagged pieces of dismay. She remembered the snub that Verta and her parents gave her and was tempted to go to Calico Bottom to kick Verta's sneaky and deceitful ass. Disheartened Callie didn't write down any of that. She managed to mask her feelings with a bland script. What she did was send the invitation to Ida with her nice letter that simply read: Dear Ida:

> I trust this letter will find you and your family well. We are doing fine, but I wish you were here. Tell your family, hello for me. Don't forget to write and tell me more about your new house. Pray for me, your sister, Callie.

Ida read the letter and burst into tears. The invitation lay folded neatly beside it. She saw the hurt in Callie's handwriting and went crying to Wilbur. If Callie could just come to Indiana so that she would not have to tolerate the humiliation of being there on Rogers wedding day, it would surely lessen the pain she felt. To Wilbur, nothing was too good for his wife, Ida. He agreed to let Callie come. He held Ida in his tired arms until she stopped crying. On May 26, 1939, she arrived. Ida, Wilbur and Rufus met Callie at the train station. She too had Mable's strut. She also was big boned like her grandmother and stood almost a head taller than Ida. When Wilbur saw those legs strutting, he wanted to whistle, but he caught himself. Callie and Ida sent a telegram to Effie from the train station. It read: "Arrived safely. Ida is here." The Moore family of Alabama broke out the moonshine. It was a rare occasion for the Moore family to drink but they were tired. They had helped Callie to pack every stitch of clothing she owned while she had been walking around as if she were in a daze. Mable whispered to Effie when she could no longer keep quiet, "That boy's thang must have a wart on it." Effie said, "I don't know if she's upset because Verta took him or what." Effie hated for Mable to imply that Callie had already had a sexual relationship. After Ida's marriage, Effie treated Callie like a child again. Callie could not conceal her hurt but she never spoke about it. Every hope of living happily ever after with Roger had been squashed by Verta, the only person she had ever called "friend." Before Callie left for Indiana, Lil' John introduced her to his special friend, Patricia. She thought to herself, "Lil' John is going to have the bend of the road for him and his friend." Lil' John and Callie were both guilty of thinking the same thing at the same time.

By the time she reached the Chicago train station Callie was exhausted. There had been some good looking men on the train, but Callie's mind was on starting all over again without having to hear anything about the wedding

of Roger Nate. She wanted to say good bye to Miss Dora but she was ashamed
to face Farmer Wilson after what they had done. Her body still "blinked" at
the thought of how long he had made her come. She vowed to put it all
behind her and treat her heartstrings to a new life of excitement. Ida's house
was lovely. With that thought in mind, Callie crawled into bed and slept like
there was no tomorrow. Callie's tomorrow began the evening of the next day.
For hours she lay awake in bed and recalled the events that led to her leaving
home. A breeze blew through the bedroom window. She took it to be an
omen and whispered to her self, "That's what I must do. I must cool myself
down." Ida kept Rufus quiet and played with him in the parlor so that Callie
would not be disturbed. Wilbur busied himself building a cabinet down stairs
for Ida's sewing machine. They had eaten breakfast and lunch before Callie
began to stir. She did not leave the bedroom until she smelled turnip greens
cooking. It was almost time for dinner so Wilbur came inside and took his
bath. Callie waited until she heard the bathroom door open and peeked to see
who came out. It was Wilbur dressed in his pajamas and bathrobe walking
towards the parlor. With clothes in hand, she slipped into the bathroom to use
the toilet and to bathe her tired body. Ida waited until she came out of the
bathroom before setting the table. They sat and ate dinner in silence. Poor Ida
was trying not to talk for fear of asking the wrong questions or saying the
wrong thing. Callie did not look well to her. All of their lives Callie's
complexion had a natural glow. Sitting at the dinner table Callie's skin looked
pale and ashen. Finally Ida had to say something. She said, "Girl, you must
have stayed awake during your whole trip." Callie began to laugh and describe
some of the comical things that happened on the train. There described a
couple that had an air about them. They were exquisitely dressed. The couple
went into the dining car for every meal and to the bar for cocktails. They did
things to deliberately make an impression upon the other passengers of the
train. "Well," Callie said, "before the train passed through southern Indiana,
the couple had a fist fight. The lady had marked her money before leaving
home and she caught her husband paying for their drinks with one of her
marked bills. The lady went into a rage and slapped her husband off the barstool.
Her man had been spending her money all along." Ida laughed and said, "It
must have been hard to sleep after that." Wilbur had finished eating so he got
up and went to bed. Once in bed, he fell asleep with ease. Ida wanted to sit and
talk but she felt that it was best for her to not make any changes to her daily
routine. After all, Wilbur had allowed Callie to come just for her. Ida cleaned
off the table and did the dishes while Callie talked. Rufus had two hours to

play before bedtime, so they took him to the playground across the street from the house. A guy whose name was Ennis Nelson sat and watched Callie Moore walk across the street with Ida Avery noting that a new girl had come to town. When they strolled past the bench, he just had to say something. He was in the middle of a card game, but he decided that the other three guys would have to wait for him to play his card before continuing the game. Ennis' gaze went from Callie's legs to her eyes. He played a card and greeted her saying, "Hey, cool breeze, what's shaking?" Callie smiled and said, "Ain't nothing shaking but the leaves on the trees." The guys at the table sat with their mouths watering. They figured on Ennis being star struck like they were. Ennis turned himself into the character he had always portrayed. They all knew him by his nickname, "Dude." He countered, "And they wouldn't be shaking if it wasn't for the breeze." He had played his trump card. Callie winked at him and strutted in long strides to catch up with Ida and Rufus. The card table turned into the place to be when the game ended. There were shouts of, "Boy, Dude came THROUGH!" And, "Didn't he?" Dude was smiling but he could have sworn that he saw a spark in her eyes. The game was over. All of the guys but Dude had to go home to ready themselves for the night shift at the steel mills. Ennis was on a two weeks vacation and was off for the next five days. He had no idea that Callie liked the looks of him but he was greatly impressed by her.

Dude was a popular fellow in the community. His family lived down the block from Wilbur and Ida. His mother's name was Iris. She was a fair skinned robust lady with silver hair. His four sisters' Gerta, Marie, Alma and Rose spoiled him rotten. Their father was deceased. He walked home to spend the evening with his family who enjoyed telling tales of better times and gossiping about the neighbors. For the next five days, Dude made a trail as he walked back and forth through the park looking to catch sight of Callie. She sat and watched him walk and enjoyed his swagger. She watched from her kitchen window how the guys would laugh and joke around while they played. That's the way life is, she thought. You get serious enough to laugh and joke around while playing games. Dude left the park and headed home on the fifth and last day of his vacation. Callie ran and stood by the front gate to say Hello. He responded, "Say Hey, Sweetness. I thought you had left town." He swaggered over to the gate to give her his best smile and accidentally tripped over his feet. When Callie could stop laughing at the way he made a cool looking dance step out of it, she told him her name. The two of them sat and talked until Wilbur went to work that night. Ida put Rufus to bed and was sewing in the back room when the winds off of Lake Michigan sent a stream of cool air. Callie invited him inside when the wind began to grow colder. Neither of them had eaten so she served him sandwiches and homemade wine. They talked about families, friends and foe. Both of them had a nourishing childhood and a supportive family. She talked about the farm life and he talked about city life. It all came together when he asked her one simple question. "Do you like to dance?" He watched her face light up and quickly said, "Let's go." Callie grabbed her sweater and asked Ida for a key to the side door. They were off to the dance that was down the block. They could hear the musical beat of a bee bop tune. "Drinking wine spo-di-ody drinking wine, mop, mop", or straighten up and fly right, swoop down mama don't cha' blow yo' top." They walked into the dance hall and hit the floor with steps that Callie had wanted to show but had no place to show them or anyone to show them to. Dude was a smooth dancer. His dance was the icing on the cake of his personality. He could feel all eyes on them because they looked good together. At one o'clock in the morning, Callie was ready to go home. Dude's friends wanted to start a card game, but he couldn't keep his eyes off of Callie long enough to sit and play. They walked back to her house holding hands and did some heavy petting at the door. She let him feel her wetness but would not allow him to go any further. His hot breath warmed the air. Callie walked away, unlocked the door and went upstairs to bed. She slept hard that night. Wilbur came home to a sleeping house. Ida had sat and waited for Callie to come in. She crawled into bed at midnight. Wilbur eased into bed for his usual short nap and eased himself into Ida. The idea of stealing her goodies excited him. He pushed himself into her as slowly and deeply as he dared and felt her constrict and draw him deeper. In his state of euphoria the words of a song came into his mind and he cried," My, my, oh, oh, I love you so." They all slept until noon. By the end of June, Dude and Callie were seriously courting.

Ida took Rufus to a circle meeting with her one Friday evening because Callie was not feeling well. Wilbur had eaten his dinner and gone to bed. He went to use the bathroom and saw Callie sitting on the side of her bed with her dress hiked up to her hips. He was drawn to her door crying," Lawd, have mercy." Callie's presence was overpowering. She stood up and looked into his eyes and smiled. He wrapped his arms around her and didn't stop making love to her until he had nothing left to give. Callie walked him back to his room and tucked him in. Before Rufus and Ida returned home, she had unpacked her clothes and took her empty bags to the basement storage room. Callie then went to bed and was out like a light. She didn't hear Wilbur leave for work nor did she hear Ida and Rufus come home. Wilbur loved his job because he loved calculating figures and the camaraderie in the workplace. It was his job to confirm shipments by weights and measures that the other shifts recorded. Some materials went into production so the scales had to balance throughout the complete process. If a ton went in, a ton had to come out even if some of it became scrap metal. It had to balance. He loved it the way he had loved mending fences. It was hard to describe how he felt about losing the mother of his child so he didn't try. Grief dulled his senses. The love that he and Ida shared together was a miracle. Wilbur was close to his destination and liked to check in early, but he pulled his car over to the curb. Aloud, he asked himself, "Wilbur, what in the hell have you done?" There he sat with the nerve to listen for an answer to his question. He wanted someone to tell him, but he did not get an answer until he said sorrowfully, "I'm dancing on a damn shoestring and my ass is gonna TRIP!" He didn't know Callie well enough to call her a name, but if he did, he thought, he would call her a whore. His inner voice asked him what he'd call himself. He covered his face with his hands and answered, "Call me sorry!" Wilbur looked at his watch and had to get his mind together. It was time for him to hurry. The railroad business was a tangled web of stocks and bonds funded and owned by both government and private citizens. They knew how to keep tabs on everything. He reasoned that as well as he did on his job, he should be able use the same principles concerning his home. He concluded that anything was worth a try. When Wilbur walked into the house the next morning, Ida was cooking breakfast. Rufus was out of bed and playing in his pajamas on the floor. Callie's bedroom door was closed. Ida preferred to let her sleep.

Wilbur decided to take a bath and go directly to bed after breakfast. Ida dressed Rufus and sent him to the back yard to play. Dude rang the front door bell looking for Callie who simultaneously walked out of her bedroom. Ida served him coffee and donuts while Callie bathed and got dressed. When Callie came and joined them, Ida excused herself to go downstairs and do the laundry. When she came back, they were nowhere to be found. Callie came home with a pair of gorgeous ivory colored heels and a soft peach colored suit. Dude had taken her shopping and dropped her off on his way to work. Ida wanted to ask questions but Callie was a grown woman. She did ask where she had shopped though. There was a store that Ida loved to frequent that sold dresses. The owner, Mack Nickles owned a building in the heart of the business district. The first floor was a dress shop that he operated himself. His family consisted of his wonderful parents who owned a number of business locations in the

Chicago Loop Area across the Indiana line. He could have operated any one of their businesses but he did not care for the fast pace that he encountered in Downtown Chicago. Mack thought he wanted to be an architect, then a draftsman but he found fashion design more fun. The personalities that he encountered in fashion design did not agree with his way of seeing things so he bought a building of his own and opened a dress shop. He loved to see Ida walk through his door. He smelled honeysuckle in her hair. He watched her check stitching and the cut of the material of items before she purchased anything. They started talking a little here and a little there, and became fascinated by one another. She ordered gifts from his store and he would sometimes sneak something in the bag for her. She shopped often and would leave a bag lie for days at a time in her closet. His gifts would surprise her and make her smile. The smile gathered momentum and changed into the joy of seeing each other again. Things got out of hand in more ways than one. The more she saw Mack, the more Wilbur and Callie carried on. On one particular morning Ida and Rufus went shopping and left Callie and Wilbur. Callie went into Ida's room and had him yelling for her to get out of Ida's room. She stuck out her tongue and lowered her head to his lap while he cried, "Baby, Pleeeaaassseee, and Oooouucch!" Dude came to the door and rang the bell while they were well into their act. He heard what he thought was a cat and looked over the fence into the back yard. He walked back to the door see if anyone had come to answer the door. "Well," he thought, "the car is gone." Dude then went and sat on a park bench and was joined by two other guys a few minutes later. They started a game of dominoes. Wilbur's car drove up. Ida was driving. Dude expected to see Callie climb out of the car with Ida but she didn't. Rufus got out of the car and helped Ida carry her grocery bags into the house. Dude had fallen head over heels in love with Callie and was at a heightened stage of desire to see her daily. Since their little shopping spree, knowing her dress size, he'd gone by himself and bought Callie an Ivory colored chiffon dress to match the shoes that he'd bought her earlier. The set of wedding rings he carried in his pocket intending to propose that day would have to wait. When the game of dominoes ended, Dude left the park and went home to prepare for the evening shift on his job. From the parlor, Callie saw him enter his house and wondered if it had been him at the side door earlier in the day. Ida cooked liver and smothered onions for dinner. She steamed some spinach for a vegetable. Callie wanted rice and gravy with the Liver and Ida invited her to cook it. She cooked it but Wilbur and Rufus refused to eat any of it. Callie sat at the table and without any conversation, she ate all of the rice.

It angered Ida to see that she had cooked enough for herself and nobody else. Wilbur walked with Ida and Rufus to the playground because he wanted to get away from the likeness of Callie. She was getting a little too bold and it was beginning to unravel his nerves. After they returned from the playground he took a short nap while Ida sat in the living room and hand stitched something. Callie decided to walk to the corner store so that she could get a little fresh air. She was flattered by the whoops; cat calls and whistles that came from the men in the park. She purchased soft drinks for her and Ida and returned home to sit in the parlor. There was a cool breeze blowing through the screened parlor windows that she enjoyed. When night fell she was still sitting in the same spot. Callie found that she suddenly had plenty to think about. She heard Wilbur talking with Ida before he left for work and had a hard time getting his voice out of her head. His words to his wife had told a story of his love for her. Ida was on his lap with her face buried under his neck. The darkness of the parlor hid her envious eyes. Shortly after Wilbur's car pulled off, Dude rang the doorbell. Ida was glad Callie had company so that she wouldn't have to talk to her before going to bed. She spoke to Dude and went to bed, leaving the two of them in the parlor. Callie waited for him to speak but instead he covered her mouth and face with soft kisses and held her in his arms. They sat in silence until Callie went to see if Ida was asleep. They both eased themselves down to the floor between the front of the sofa and the wall and made sweet love. When it was over and when they were seated again on the sofa, Dude bowed to one knee and asked Callie to be his wife. She answered, "Yes." He slipped the ring on her finger and kissed her hand. Their melodious sounds of lovemaking were carried away on the wings of the night's cool breeze. Neither of them wanted the night to end. Dude swaggered home like the coolest man that had ever walked on the face of the earth, and he was. His countenance was cooling, calm and collected. When he got home he headed straight to his bedroom but tripped on his shoestring that had come loose. He muttered, "Damn! Everything was perfect until I had to dance on this mutha fucka!"

Callie broke the good news to Ida as soon as she heard her walk into the kitchen early the next morning. The sisters hugged and cried together. Dude was sitting on his screened in front porch having coffee with his mother when he saw Wilbur heading home. Iris, his mother, was chattering away about the things that hadn't gotten done like, painting the porch," she was saying. She noticed that he was half way listening and asked why he was up so early. He said, "Mama, I'm getting married." She just knew he wasn't going to marry the girl that she knew he dated for so long. Iris couldn't stand her. Dude said to his mother, "Put your clothes on and come with me." Iris stood up and shouted, "Hey! Gerta! Marie! Alma! Y'all better come here and see about your brother." She said, "He's talking some shit in here I don't understand." The girls jumped out of bed and come running with their head rags on and they each wore nightgowns. Marie was first to get there. Rose did not budge. Her best rest was during the morning. Marie looked at Dude who held his head in his hands, laughing like hell. By the time Gerta and Alma made it to the porch, Marie was laughing and trying to get their mother to sit down. In the end, around noon, they all went down to Wilbur and Ida's house to meet Callie. Callie was dressed like a 'bride to be' on a mission. The girl was so pretty that it made Iris proud that her son had chosen a beautiful girl to fall for. Ida had such a poised personality that people did not realize how young she was. Iris saw for the first time that she was just a baby on a fast track. She couldn't have been any more than seventeen years old. She was eighteen at the most, Gerta figured. To them, Callie looked to be about twenty or twenty-one years old. They watched Dude give her a box and when she opened it, he had to catch her before she slipped to the floor. She and Ida had been getting ready to try and find the same dress. She had seen it when Dude took her shopping but never in her wildest dreams did she think he could pick a dress for her. Ida bustled around in the kitchen and made lunch for the ladies while Callie and Dude stayed busy trying to pick the date for their wedding. Dude was so popular that six bridesmaids and groomsmen were easy to recruit. What made it so special was that they were all good friends.

The wedding was scheduled for the second Saturday in August. It was only a month away. Time began to fly. The night before the wedding, the bridesmaids came over to help Callie pack for her honeymoon. The groomsmen came later and turned it into a swinging party. Ida made Callie's veil and cooked most of the food for the reception with the help of her women's church group. When the dancing started, Ida went to bed. Wilbur sat up until the party ended at 6 in the morning. The wedding was at 4pm in the afternoon. Callie walked Dude down the stairs and gave him a quick kiss. She came back and went into her room to get into bed. Wilbur watched Dude go home and talked Callie out of her drawers for old time's sake. They lay between the bed and the wall in her bedroom on the floor to avoid the creak of the bed's springs. Wilbur whispered, "Baby, it feels kind of sour with a little grit in it." She whispered back, "My name ain't baby! Say my name!" He went, "Mew! OoooooowwwwwwwwwwCallie!" Ida was so tired that she rolled over and said to herself, "Those damn cats!" and went back to sleep.

The community rallied around the new couple. Dude stood proudly at the Altar. The carpet was rolled out and flowers spread when Rufus appeared with the rings. He walked down the isle like a butler in charge of all operations. Wilbur walked Callie down the isle as if she was truly his. No body knew how much she was his. He was so fine that the church mothers started fanning. It tickled Ida to the bones. The wedding was beautiful and Callie was glad for it to be over with. She was nauseated and needed sleep. She sat through the reception and ate very little while everyone else had a good time. Dude was so in love that he wanted to hurry and get her away from the crowd. The bridesmaids finally took her into a room and helped her change into her suit. She had one more dance to go wearing her suit and Dude wore his drakes and pocket watch with the chain hanging. All eyes were on Callie. Young women came to see the girl who came to town and swept Dude off of his feet. Old women looked carefully and spoke in hushed tones carefully stifling their thoughts. Old men fantasized and the young men were envious of the prize that went with Dude out of the door towards a honeymoon. Joan Benson, one of the twins from across the street caught the bouquet. The happy couple left as Mr. and Mrs. Ennis Nelson Jr and headed to the windy city of Chicago. They partied the night away at Club DeLeesa doing the Bop and dancing the Hucklebuck. Dude stayed on his feet and was suave and debonair until he reached their hotel room. Callie undressed him and tried to kiss him awake. He was snug in bed when she removed her clothes and examined her naked body. She didn't see any signs of pregnancy but she had the symptoms. She lay down beside her new husband and went to sleep.

The Moore's were not able to leave their farm and go to where their daughters were. They were happy for Callie. They all had worked hard to give their children good lives. John Jr and Effie lay in bed that night and talked themselves to sleep. It was harvest time and they needed each other to make everything run smoothly. They sent gifts and well wishes to Callie and her new husband. The girls promised to send pictures of the wedding.

Wilbur left the wedding reception looking like the happiest man alive. He decided that since Callie knew how to cover her ass so well, dancing on a shoestring wasn't so bad. All he had wanted was the pussy. Dude had her and he was elated that his tracks had all but disappeared. Wilbur had begun to worry like hell when Callie started sleeping so much. He had a sneaky suspicion about her the last time she hung him out to dry. The girl's pussy was too hot for her not to be pregnant, he said to himself. It was hot and throbbing like the beat of a drum. He thought he chuckled to himself but Ida heard him and

asked, "What's so funny?" He laughed again and said;" Baby, besides us, them
two were the best looking couple I ever saw." Ida said, "I was just thinking the
same thing." "What about me?" Rufus asked. He looked into his father's face and
said, "Me, you and Mama is the only best couple and we married a long time ago."
When they went to bed, Rufus slept between them. Wilbur and Ida left him
sleeping and made love in the parlor by the light of a full August moon.

Dude woke up in the darkened room and reached for Mrs. Ennis Nelson
Jr who lay beside him. She was now his to have and to hold, he recalled.
Slowly, Dude repositioned her body and entered Callie while she slept. She
remembered that Ida was home. She whispered in her sleep, "Shhh." She didn't
say another word, but gave of herself freely while Dude enjoyed himself. His
release was one of the sweetest moments of his life. When she felt him put her
breast between his lips, she knew it was Dude and not Wilbur, because Wilbur
would have cried out. Callie was glad that the room was dark. She forced
herself to stay awake to respond to her husband's lovemaking. He moved his
body down, down, down, to her belly button and when it became clear to her
that he was going to go further with his tongue, she grabbed his manhood and
scooted her body down to allow him to enter her again. Callie wanted to save
her body from the climax that his tongue would have forced her to have.
When he came the second time, and had given all that he could; she lay cradled
in his arms and went back to sleep. Sleep was what she needed most. She
dreamed of Calico Bottom and the May Day pageant. The children were
doing the "rock" and the crowd saw her in her wedding gown and cheered.
Her brother walked up and handed her a string of fish but Farmer Wilson
took them instead to give them to her mother. Callie tried to wake herself up
but kept walking until she reached the May Pole to add enough colorful
streamers for all of the children. Dude stood holding the streamers for Farmer
Wilson to put on the pole. The dream was so vivid that Callie heard herself
ask Dude, "When did you get here," in her sleep and the sound of it woke her
up. She opened her eyes and Dude was not beside her. She heard water splashing
so she eased out of bed and after she relieved her bladder, Callie joined her
husband in the bathtub. When he lowered his head the next time, she responded
in a mighty way. While they dressed themselves, the lovebirds marveled at one
another's physique. They walked out of the hotel room proud of how they
looked and as hungry as hell. Soul Food cafeteria was on the corner near the
Regal Theatre and it was only a short walk from where they were. They had a
wonderful meal. Afterwards, they went to the Regal to relax and enjoy a show.
Heaven and all of nature seemed to bless the union of the young couple's new

life together. They watched the setting sun go down over Lake Michigan before returning to the hotel.

Dude had not taken the time to say good bye to Shirley, the girl whom everyone in the community had expected him to marry. She had always been a friend that he could count on. There were times that he would make dates with other women that somehow fell through. At the last minute, Shirley would get dressed and take it upon herself to fulfill his desire for enjoyment. She loved Dude and ignored the obvious signs of his infidelity. He would stand her up and she often found him out on a date with another woman on the same night. Shirley would walk over to him and casually speak to both he and his date. Before the night was over, he would end up at her door. She had ways of watching his date watch her. His friends were her friends too. They watched her back. This was the one and only time that Shirley lost out. Dude was gone. Their friends never said a word to her about Callie Moore. He'd spent almost every night in her bed until two weeks before the wedding. The last night he'd spent with her, Dude mentioned something about working overtime, and then he vanished into thin air. Shirley worked at the Indiana Hotel across the tracks of the next community. One day while on the job, someone showed her an invitation to the wedding. It was unbelievable. Her and Dude would sit and talk for hours and had done so since the fifth grade of elementary school. He was her soul mate. A pair of his shoes stayed beneath her bed. She was ready to die for him. Three days later, he was married to another woman. The shock of what the invitation said left her without the ability to react. While Dude and their friends celebrated, Shirley went to bed and stayed for a whole week. Her mind went on a roller coaster ride and she had no idea when it would stop. She could see them dancing together. Shirley remembered how Dude would step back and watch her own shapely hips swing to the music. One night he matched her steps and pulled her close enough to whisper, "Girl, you look like your thing is so good, it's keeping a smile on your face." His compliments were thirst quenching. There was no other man in the world that she admired more than she admired Dude. Finally, she just sat up and crawled out of bed and took a shower. She stripped the bed and did a load or two of laundry and fixed herself something to eat. It was August 29th she surmised, and Dude had been married two weeks. It was time for her to try and get her life back. Shirley called her job to thank them for the get-well card they sent and asked to be put back on the schedule. She found herself in need of a doctor's release slip. It was a long walk to the bus stop. Shirley's neighbors who had missed seeing she at Dude and Callie's wedding barely spoke to her when she said, "Hello." She could hardly hear them and began to feel betrayed again. Shirley felt like going back home to crawl under her bed covers again, but she kept walking and spoke to each neighbor she met. Their bland expressions told her that it was not her imagination that made her feel betrayed. She felt deceived by someone she loved dearly while the entire community got news of her beloved Dude marrying another woman. The wind took on a life of its own to blow a harsh storm into her life. The doctor's office wasn't very busy. Shirley was examined and given a prescription for her elevated blood pressure and the release form for her supervisor. She then went into the nearest drug store where she encountered Dude. He swaggered up to her and said in a honey dripping voice, "Hey little girl, what do you know?" She matched his tone and said, "Dude, you need to pay for this prescription. I know that." He asked, "How much is it, Baby?" Dude reached into his pocket and gave her money before she could answer. He then whispered, "See you tonight, alright?" Shirley was back to square one. She was over powered with affection for him. She wished that she could swallow him whole. His voice was as sweet sounding as honey and his eyes consumed every bit of good she desired to be. Shirley shivered and hugged herself. All the way home she recalled his voice saying, "How much is it, Baby. See you tonight, alright?" SHIT! Her heart turned into glitter covering up the shit that she knew he was talking.

Dude made himself contented to live with the Avery Family. After his father passed away some years earlier, Dude became man of the house and protected his mother and sisters. He now realized that Wilbur was man of his house and he resided under Wilbur's roof. It was not a good feeling. He and Callie had a plan. It was a sure way of being able one day to own property. Dude asked Wilbur if he would agree to let them keep Callie's room and pay monthly rent while they saved enough money for a down payment on their own home. Wilbur and Ida both agreed that it would be good for them to do so.

Callie was sitting at the kitchen table about to eat a bowl of hot soup when Dude walked into the house. In another hour he was scheduled to leave for work. Ida invited him to sit and have a good hot lunch with her and Callie. Ida was the youngest woman he knew who could whip out a meal at the drop of a hat. Callie was not handy at anything in particular, he noted soon after their short honeymoon. He was anxious to get into a home of his own. Dude was so in love, he felt that whatever her shortcomings were, he would pick up the slack. Shirley ran across his mind while he sat at the table and ate his soup.

He was glad that she couldn't see his knees when he walked up to her. She was like his favorite pair of shoestrings. No matter which pair of shoes he wore, Dude liked to replace his strings often. Old strings broke and tired ones came loosed. The favorite pair of shoestrings was worn with any pair of shoes. When they become untied, walk on them. To his self he said, "Tonight, I'm going to keep my word and go to her house. I might go for some leg," Dude finished his soup and gave Callie a smile. She knew what it meant and got up from the kitchen table. Dude went into their room and waited for her to come in. She walked in with her shoes in her hand. He lifted her dress and salivated when he saw she had no panties on. Ida had caught the amorous look when he moved his chair back to get up from the table. She took Rufus to the park. Wilbur, who was asleep, heard their sounds of lovemaking and covered his head with a pillow. Dude had stolen his goodies, he thought, and he just had to deal with it.

Shirley regained some of her lost energy during her bus ride home. When she exited the bus, there was pep in her step. After resting and daydreaming a little while, she took two thick T-bone steaks out of the refrigerator to marinate. She measured ingredients for homemade dinner rolls and washed the vegetables that she was going to steam. Next she scrubbed and oiled her potatoes that she planned to bake. It was Dude's favorite meal and she was going to have it ready for him when he came over. He knew that everything about Shirley was the opposite of how Callie was built and her personality was more outgoing. Shirley planned her social life around being constant at making good impressions. She was short, dark and wore her hair in a pixie styled hair cut. Her face was round. Her lips were thick and she had slanted eyes. Her body was made to fit everything that Dude desired. She had beautiful feet and legs, wide hips and a tiny waist. It was known throughout the community that she stopped traffic whenever she walked down a busy street. Dude, for the hell of it, would ask her to walk around naked when they were alone, and he would whistle. Everything was ready when the knock on the door came. Shirley opened the door to a tired and weary traveler who gathered her in his arms and kissed her tenderly. Dude smiled on the inside and thought to himself, "This is nice, but it ain't quite right." While he ate the steak dinner, Shirley went into her bedroom and changed into something sexy. Dude finished his meal and responded to her efforts. It was a totally selfish act and he knew it. What really set him on fire was the thought of how much she wanted him. There was no limit to her actions that night and when she had done what she could to please him, Shirley lay in his arms and cried. Her tears began to run silent, so Dude eased his arms from around Shirley, got up, cleared the table and washed her dishes. She saw his act of kindness as a jester of his love towards her. When he left a short time later, she kept her memory set on how good she felt in his arms. Shirley went to bed and slept peacefully. At 5 o'clock in the morning, Dude unlocked the back door and eased into the house as quietly as he could. Ida's bedroom light was on. She had just come in herself, but nobody knew it except the one she had been out with.

Mack Nickles waited patiently down the block for Ida to unlock the front door to her house. Little by little they had learned the names of one another's family members. They talked about likes and dislikes, business ventures, habits and love. Ida realized that like babies sometimes did, she had walked before crawling. Mack put singing in her heart. He knew how to transpose the singing into rapture that overtook her body when he made love to her. Every Monday night, she saw Wilbur off to work and after Dude came in and went to bed, she would go to Mack. Rufus was sent to bed at 8, awakened and taken to the bathroom at midnight just before Dude came in so he would sleep the rest of the night. On Tuesday mornings, Wilbur came home to a nice breakfast just as he did any other morning. Like most jobs, Monday was a hard and long night for him. On Tuesday mornings, there was something about how his woman moved around in the kitchen that made him want to holler. He would pull her into his lap and make Rufus blush. She would smile and rub noses with him to cool down Wilbur's swollen member and tease him by winking her sparkling eyes. Tuesday was her wash day. Wilbur would wait for her like he had an addiction. In the downstairs laundry room Ida had to set her wash aside to please her husband while Rufus played in the back yard. He would finish where Mack left off with his yearning for more. That morning though, while Ida was grinding her hips and kissing Wilbur she was wondering where Dude had been during the night. She'd thought he was home when she'd left the house. She also knew it was time for her to be more careful. Her husband cried, "Oh, girl!" and it cut her thoughts off. Ida then made her move to squeeze her hips together. She wanted to drain Wilbur so that she could get on with her day. He held her tightly while he gathered enough strength to move his legs. She smiled when Wilbur talked so much shit in her ear that she wanted to laugh out loud and tell him he was telling a lie. When he pulled out of her, she washed him with warm soapy water. Ida then rinsed and dried him off. She watched him zip his pants before heading towards the stairs. Considering that Ida had much to do, she carried him and Mack around until she filled the washing machine with water to do her first load of laundry.

While the clothes washed, she checked on Rufus and went to soak in the bathtub. The warm scented water and the lull of the washing machine relaxed Ida so much that she dozed off to sleep. If Callie had not knocked on the door, she may have slept until noon. Callie sat and waited while Ida dried herself and hurried to get back to her housework. Before washing another load of clothes she checked on Rufus who had three other children playing in the yard with him. To help Rufus retain his playmates Ida invited them to stay for lunch. They went to ask for their mother's permission while Rufus put his toys away. Ida loved a happy family. That was all she had known her whole life. Rufus was a loving child who was now hers. She loved him enough to share everything she had with him. Ida had decided at the spur of the moment to make lunch for him and his friends. Callie came out of the bathroom and Dude went in. Dude bathed and got dressed in time to sit with the boys for lunch. They had a good time. Callie and Ida watched Dude turn into a kid. Rufus was determined to not let him carry the conversation because the boys were his company. Dude, a homey from way back, was skillful in taking a back seat to the crowd so he let Rufus have it. Rufus said, "Uncle Dude, now tell us again why the cowboys always win." The two women laughed. Dude got his chance to talk, and Rufus ran the show as the perfect host. After lunch, Callie and her husband went into the parlor while Ida finished her wash. As soon as she hung out the first load of clothes, Mack's car moved slowly down the street. She said to herself, "Damn! I got to be more careful with this shit!" Ida enjoyed playing around with Mack. Wilbur had been her only relationship. He was her prince in shining amour. Mack was her toy. Callie fixed a thick sandwich for Dude to carry to work. He left to visit his mother for a few minutes before heading to the job. What he really wanted to do was get to a telephone to talk to Shirley. He missed her conversation and ideas. For years they planned parties and kept the neighborhood party goers on their toes. Most of his popularity was connected to the way that Shirley made him look good. He was beginning to miss his spot on the bench in the park, the crowd and he missed his own bed at his mother's house. As soon as Dude walked into his mother's house he called Shirley on her job. Callie was glad to see him leave home and she went back to bed.

That next Tuesday morning, Shirley felt like she had the world on a string. Dude had spent Monday night in her bed. She sang all the way to work that morning. When her co-worker called her to the phone, she was overjoyed that it was Dude on the other end of the line. Callie had gone shopping with Ida and Rufus. He gave Shirley a little food for thought, and told her that he loved her before he hung up. Dude didn't know that Wilbur was in the bedroom. When Wilbur heard the things that Dude promised Shirley, he snickered. Some of his guilt dissipated. Dude was not quite finished moving his clothes from down the street so he took a couple of boxes from downstairs and headed to his mother's house. Wilbur heard the door close and tipped to the back bedroom to find Callie. When he saw that the room was empty, he gloated like a kid. Dude and his sisters had a good time folding and packing his clothes. They had plans for his old bedroom. Iris heard all of the chatter and yelled, "If y'all think you're going to put my baby out, you'd better' find somewhere to go yo' damn selves." Dude stuck out his chest and strutted saying; "Did y'all hear what your mama said? Put my winter shit right back in there." He was unpacking his clothes when Callie returned. Rufus asked Uncle Dude if he had gone shopping when he saw him hanging up the clothes from his mother's house. Before Dude could answer Rufus, Callie took his hand and rubbed it against her belly and said, save closet space for the baby." If the bed hadn't been there Dude would have fallen. Callie's eyes began to tear. He had never wanted to see Callie cry. Dude held her close and whispered, "You are the best thing that ever happened to me." Ida offered her a sandwich and a glass of milk. Dude, out of kindness asked if she wanted him to take the night off. It warmed Callie's heart but all she wanted was more sleep. She assured him that she would be fine. He was greatly relieved. He made it to work in record time and surprised his co-workers. Dude was busy wracking his brain trying to figure out just how pregnant Callie could be. They were engaged on August first or sometime during the first week, he thought. That had been a wild night of lovemaking. He began to feel a tiny bit of pride about becoming a father. At the end of his shift, he hurried to get to Shirley's house so that he could leave early enough to go home at a reasonable hour. Wilbur listened while the two ladies talked and planned Callie's Maternity wardrobe. He was as nervous as a cat. He silently counted the months, June, July, August, September and almost October. He thought, "If I tapped her in June, I should start counting at July, August and September." He moaned. It was time for dinner but he wasn't hungry. He stayed in bed until time for work. Ida packed his dinner to go. Each day after the announcement of Callie's pregnancy, Ida would sew. In a week's time, she had fashioned four maternity tops for her sister. For her daily exercise, Callie walked Rufus to the park twice a day and walked around the block, twice a day. Wilbur and Ida began to use that time for their lovemaking. It was so sweet because the moments were stolen. Dude was working overtime, or that's what he told Callie. He would wake up at

Shirley's house and feel free. Shirley did not know that Callie was pregnant but her co-workers had found it out through someone who knew her doctor's receptionist. They would make sly comments to try and coax Shirley into conversation about her love life but Shirley would use wit to steer clear of their discussions. Systematically the staff prodded and posed leading questions like an investigative reporter. First they would compliment her. Their next move would be to tell her that maybe Dude's marriage to Callie was best for her because she had been too good for him. Shirley secretly became as happy as a lark. Lately, Dude was in her bed almost every night, but she refused to put her business in the streets. She said on one occasion, "Girl, you know how it is. Sometimes you laugh on the outside and cry on the inside." Shirley wondered if Callie thought that she had Dude to her self. "Oh well," she'd said when they told her of the pregnancy. "He belonged to me first." Dude's next payday rolled around and he told Callie that he'd loaned money to his mother. In reality he had taken Shirley shopping.

Wilbur heard that his in laws were coming for a visit. They were done with the harvest and saw where they could get away for a week or two. He rarely went shopping with Ida because they had plenty of room for storage. He only went when Ida wanted large sacks of sugar or flour. Fresh vegetables and milk was what she liked to shop for maybe three or four times a week. She made her own breads. Canned goods were stocked downstairs as were potatoes, onions and spices. On Saturday morning, Ida needed Wilbur to take her shopping. The couple turned so many heads that Rufus asked, "Mama, why is that man looking at you like that?" It was Mack. She waved and Mack waved back. Rufus then asked, "Why are all these people looking at daddy?" Ida looked up and saw Alma, Dude's sister staring at Wilbur. She hunched him with her elbow and asked, "Wilbur Honey, aren't you going to speak?" He bent and kissed her on the lips and said, "I just did. I said I love my wife." A younger lady walked up to him and made him laugh. She strutted towards Wilbur and dropped her scarf. Wilbur picked it up and handed it to Ida who smiled and asked her in a tender voice, "Is this yours, dear?" Rufus knew when his mother was being sarcastic because she often used sarcasm to make him giggle. He kept his eyes on her. Ida smiled and continued saying, "I asked because he's mine." She handed the scarf back to Wilbur who gave it to the girl. The three of them walked down the street laughing. Ida asked Wilbur why he had done that. He said, "Because I knew you could handle it. Remember when?" She blushed and doubled over with laughter. She remembered. She loved old silly Wilbur to death. He was referring to the way she would drop something to recover from her stumbling around at the sight of him. She had fired off some lethal sparks during puberty. He shook his head and whispered a prayer of thanksgiving that he was blessed to marry her. The possibilities of what might have happened otherwise, gave Wilbur chills. Wilbur carried the groceries into the house and went to bed. Ida made Callie help put the food away and remembered a cake at the bakery that she'd ordered and forgot to pick up. Callie waited until Ida drove off. She then woke Wilbur up and asked him to listen to what she had on her mind. She told him that she loved her sister but she was envious. He asked her to please leave Ida's bedroom. If he had waited another ten seconds to ask her to leave, Dude would have caught her coming from the room. Dude came in whistling and took Callie to a movie. She proved to be the perfect date. He just wished that he didn't love her so much. She didn't even realize that she held his heart in the palm of her hand. When they returned home Dude sat and rubbed her swollen legs and feet until she fell asleep. On his way to the parlor Dude saw Rufus lying awake in his bed and asked if he wanted to use the bathroom. Rufus answered no, but Dude told him to use it anyway and he could stay up with him and eat ice cream. They sat in the parlor and talked about how ice cream was made. Rufus talked about the people watching them while they shopped and the cake that mama forgot to pick up. A man that his mama had waved at carried it to the car for them. Rufus finished talking so him and Dude sneaked to the kitchen and washed their spoons and bowls. Dude told Rufus to bring his favorite book to the kitchen table. They put their heads together and while Dude read the book word for word, Rufus was telling the story in his own words. They had a good time laughing together. After the story was over Dude tucked Rufus in for the night. He gave him time to go to sleep before he went and straddled his wife and kissed her awake.

Mable and Effie called the men from the barn as soon as they received the news of Callie's pregnancy. Lil' John, his father and grandpa had worked much of the day doing repairs before winter set in. His wife to be had sat with Effie and Grandma Mable while the men worked. Lil' John's greatest desire was that she would fit in with the family. So far, it seemed to be working in his favor. Bennie Mae did not like to plant gardens or sew but she could cook and turn heads as she walked down the road. He loved her sweet smelling breath that smelled like baby's formula. It thrilled him when he remembered watching her breasts grow. Her nipples were the size of a dime. When they were much younger, Lil' John played with her brothers and she was always around because their mother would make her brothers watch her while they worked their crops. She was a tomboy. Her brothers, Sam and Ivan would run off and leave her. Lil' John would keep her safe while they played because all he knew about girls. He knew that they were cute and nice like his sisters. He often teased her of how she would cry from a window when her mother would not let her out to play. He was glad to hear that his parents were going north to visit Ida and Callie. Grandma Moore started pulling out patterns to look for ones that could be used to make a special maternity style for Callie. Grandpa shook his head and began to whittle away on a new block of wood to turn it into something fantastic for Rufus. They both had friends who traveled north to visit their families but they had no desire to travel. Alabama was as far north as they desired to go. They loved mild winters where one didn't need to leave off planting but for two or three months of the year. Ida had written and told them of the snowy winters and that around Good Friday was the earliest they could begin to plant a garden each year. The young couple left and headed down the road towards the bend. John Jr. and Effie went to check the grounds and lock the barn doors. Mable sat at her machine with the motor whirring and caused a stir in her husband when he looked at her stature. Within his loins lay a smoldering passion. He walked over to her and took the scarf from her head and watched her silky platinum colored curls fall about her shoulders. Mable knew what to do.

From the window Mable saw John Jr. and Effie closing the barn. She knew that they would not be returning until they checked the grounds. She reached for her husband's crotch and the two of them instinctively exchanged positions. He sat on the chair and she eased her body over and down on his rock hard penis. Their passion had mellowed into having a mind of its own. Johnny Sr placed his hot lips on her nipples and drew hard while massaging her clitoris. A soft moan escaped Mable's lips when she contracted her pelvic muscles to pull him inside her body as far as nature allowed. Grandpa Moore exploded. Mable lifted herself when he let her go. He slipped into the bathroom as she hurriedly brushed her skirt down and began sewing again. Mable had barely tied her scarf on her head when in walked Effie and John Jr. Effie saw the sparkle and wished she could have let Mable know that she knew, but John Jr. was standing there in the way. She couldn't imagine telling Mable's little boy that his mother had just finished fucking. Mable sat until they left the room. Her ass was wet. Effie laughingly talked John Jr into the bedroom. She sensed that Mable had wanted to get up from her chair to do some grooming.

John Jr. and Effie had a hard time deciding what clothes to pack for their trip to the north. He and Effie were filled with wonder and excitement. Since Callie left home they had continued to receive only good news from their daughters. The pictures of the wedding and of Ida's family warmed their hearts. As far as John Jr was concerned, he preferred to stay and find something to do around the farm. His father said that nothing was pending but there was always something to do on that many acres of land. He had never traveled more than seventy-five miles away from home in his life. Effie, on the other hand, was ready for anything. She was ready to become a grandmother and would travel anywhere she had to if it meant seeing her precious girls. They finished packing and went to bed.

The northbound train left the station at exactly 7am on Tuesday morning. At the exact time that the train was leaving the station, Ida was trying to beat Wilbur home. She had run a little behind her schedule when Mack had not been able to get enough of her. She was in the process of getting dressed while he watched. Ida lifted her leg to put her laced panties on causing Mack to pull her into his arms again. Ida tried to make Mack stop by pushing him away but her resisting excited him more. All she could do was be patient and hope for him to release her. It was time for Wilbur to return from work. For the first time in her life, Ida's best efforts failed. Her bed was unmade when Wilbur looked into the room. Rufus was asleep. Her towels were dry so he knew she had not bathed that morning. He searched the house for a clue as to where she could be. When Wilbur heard her footsteps at the door, he whispered a prayer of thanksgiving. She was nearly out of breath while she explained that she had spent the night with a sick member of the women's circle. A neighbor stayed with Mother Brown until time for her to go to work. She explained that Mother Brown's daughter lived across town and had small children to care for. Ida stayed until the daughter came. Wilbur went to take his bath. Ida busied herself fixing breakfast and brewing coffee. She got Rufus up, dressed, fed breakfast and off to school. Ida walked him across the street and watched him join his classmates for the rest of the walk. She rushed back up the stairs and served Wilbur his ham and eggs. He was already sitting at the table waiting. She popped two slices of bread into the toaster and darted into the bathroom to take a pee and quickly wash her ass. With a seductive smile on her face, Ida come slinking out of the bathroom, lifted her skirt and flounced it at Wilbur who howled with laughter. She buttered his toast and quipped, "Wilbur, y'all are working the piss out of me. I almost wet my drawers. He continued to laugh while she gave him his toast and a glass of orange juice. As she poured his coffee and he reached his hand beneath her skirt but only got as far as her thigh because Callie ran out of her room heading to the bathroom. Ida was relieved. She was still carrying Mack around. Wilbur had almost touched him.

Wilbur was tired of Callie. If she had came to town and looked for a job like most people who left the south and came north, by now, he reasoned, she would have been out of her sister's house and on her own. He began to consider her heart break issues as a selfish scheme to follow Ida. He also had noticed how she had rolled her eyes at Ida when she came from the bathroom. The reason he put up with her now, was because he was in a bind. If he even thought that Callie would squeal on him, he figured that he would push her down the stairs. Dude was a good cover because she was now sleeping with a husband and the baby could be his, he summarized. The only thing about that was that he knew Callie had to be farther along in her pregnancy than the time of her and her husband's relationship. Wilbur wiped his face just to feel the pressure somewhere else besides in the woven web of deceit that plagued his heart and mind. His mind wandered back to he and Callie's beginning pleasures. Those stolen moments had been as sweet as a honeycomb. He didn't realize that a grunt had escaped his mouth until Ida ran to his side, and asked, "Wilbur, what's wrong, are you sick?" She had been standing at the sink washing vegetables. He stood up to hide the bulge in his pants and said, "Just thinking about you, baby." Callie walked into the kitchen and fixed herself a bowl of cereal. Wilbur retreated to the parlor where he sat read the morning newspaper. Ida called him to come and lower a big smoked ham into the oven and afterwards joined him in the parlor. Callie was left in the kitchen alone. Dude walked from the bedroom and kissed her on the lips. She opened her lips and darted her tongue into his mouth. Dude lifted her body from the chair and headed back towards the bedroom before Callie could protest. Her body was hot on the inside and made him sizzle with delight. She matched his thrusts by slowly grinding her hips to make her husband slow his pace. He waited for her to catch the flow of rhythm that built his flood of desire as high as the heavens. He cried, "Wait, baby. Baby, waaaiiiiitt! Oh! Shit! Girl, look what you made me do!" He lay and sucked her breast until they both fell asleep again. Later, when Callie walked from their bedroom, she looked bright eyed and contented. Ida invited her to walk to the school with her meet Rufus. When they left, Dude made up the bed and walked down the street to visit his mother. The two of them sat on the front porch and talked about old times. They both missed the original man of the house who taught and protected them, but had learned many things the hard way for him self. Dude's father had given his children's lives excitement with a twist. He loved to drink and would fix his children fruit flavored icy drinks during hot summer nights when he'd wanted to tie one on. He'd taught them to take a drink whenever he turned his glass up. He'd say to them, "That way, I can look at y'all and see myself. Then I know how much I'm drinking." Iris would leave him to baby sit the children while she went to the beauty shop. It kept them sitting right beside him until she returned. It also had kept a crazy lady named Daisy from sneaking around his house. Dude wondered how his father would have handled his current situation. He left his mother sitting there and promised to bring his in-laws over before they returned to their home in the south. As he neared the corner, he had to stop and tie his shoestrings. He saw Callie and Ida returning home from the schoolyard with Rufus between them. After crossing the street, Rufus ran to show him his drawings of the family. There stood Ida and Callie holding hands. Wilbur and Dude were the same height and were placed away from the ladies with a little boy in the middle. The three of them also held hands. The house was drawn above the people. It had a big door and many windows. Wilbur watched the four of them from the window and whispered a prayer. He said, "Lord, please sir, have mercy." Wilbur and Ida put their heads together after dinner and decided to give their room to her parents. They thought it wise to sleep down in the basement. While they planned Dude had left to sit on the park bench and Rufus went with him so that he could play on the swings. Wilbur and Ida had a plush sofa that reclined into a comfortable bed so Ida and Wilbur Used comforters to pad it down the middle. They then covered the whole bed with fresh sheets, blankets, and soft pillows. They lacked one item and that was a bedside lamp. While Wilbur continued to make the room more comfortable, Ida jumped in the car to go and shop for a cheap lamp. She couldn't make her self pass by the dress shop and not stop to see Mack. He had no customers at the time so he locked the doors and put a sign in the window that read, "Closed." Ida tucked her chin pretending to blush and ran into the storage room. His emotions overwhelmed her. While he made love to her, she was trying to tell him that she needed a lamp. Mack caught his breath and cried out while using her breasts to muzzle the sound that escaped from his lips. He kissed her over and over again and tried to help her to straighten out her clothes and fix her hair at the same time. Ida used the bathroom while he ran upstairs for a lamp. His mother had given him a set of lamps as a gift when he decided to move from the city of Chicago. Mack handed it to her and asked, "Did you hear me calling your name, Ida? I whispered your name to the heavens and you came." Ida laughed and he tried to lighten up his conversation until she answered, "Shit! Mack, you made me come in more ways than one." He said, "Oh! God! I wish you could stay. What else do you need?" Ida untangled herself from his arms and picked up the boxed lamp. They had forgotten that the door remained locked. Mack would have gathered her in his arms again but quickly grabbed the box when he noticed a customer peeking in the window. He unlocked the door and said to Ida, "Could you help her, please? I'll be right back." The lady looked surprised and said to Ida, "If I had known that he needed help in here I would have applied for a job." Ida walked her over to the white blouses and asked what she was in need of. It was Saturday evening and she thought about standard dress for ushers and choir members during Sunday services. The customer chose a blouse. Mack came back as they were walking towards the register. It was a good thing that he did because Ida knew absolutely nothing about ringing sales. He showed Ida how to ring the sale while she placed the blouse into a bag for the customer. Ida was glad that the customer had not been someone she knew. To be sure that the customer witnessed her leaving the store, Ida left with her. She had no idea how much had been seen through the window of the store. Ida walked out with draperies, two large boxes and a bedspread. Mack loaded them into the car for her and said, "I want you to think of me when you rise in the morning and when you go to bed at night like I think of you. I love you, Ida." She pulled away from the curb. When she stopped for a red traffic light, Ida peeked into the second box and saw a matching lamp to the one Mack has first given her. The gifts from Mack were too extravagant for the temporary bedroom in the basement. For the remainder of her drive home, she concentrated on where to make changes in her house. Ida thought for sure that Wilbur was going to have complaints about having so much work to do to prepare for her parents. Her heart swelled whenever she thought about how special and unique her husband was. He was fearless. Wilbur was waiting for his in-laws to visit and did not feel threatened by the people whose teenaged daughter he vowed to have and to hold forever. Upon her return home, she woke Wilbur up to go and remove her bedroom curtains and lamps. When he finished their master bedroom looked like a princess lived in the house. Mack's love for her was now displayed in her bedroom. She hated to get into her hot bath water and wash herself at bedtime. Mack made her feel so special. While she had been shopping, Callie was approaching Wilbur in the bathroom while he pissed. He didn't know whether to question her or remain silent. He didn't know where Rufus or Dude was. She wrapped her arms around his waist and buried her face in his chest. Wilbur sat on the toilet and buried his face behind her neck in her long curly hair while she sat on his lap facing the door. He held her swollen belly in his hands and rubbed gently. Callie thought she loved her husband, but in truth, she preferred Wilbur as the match for her sexuality. Her body felt so warm and cozy inside. Wilbur just relaxed and tried not to fight the feeling. Neither of them made a sound until they climaxed. They sounded like radiators expelling hot steam. Callie took a quick bath before Ida came back home. Wilbur stretched himself out on the sofa bed downstairs. He really did mind the work Ida asked him to do after she returned, but in view of certain circumstances, she could have asked him to walk 10 miles butt naked out in the freezing rain and he would have tried to do it. He knew that as long as he kept working, he would not have to look into her eyes. His emotions were frayed. Callie always left him listless and laden with guilt. He had an itch that Callie couldn't scratch and he was running out of reasons to keep allowing him self to long for the hot bed of deceit found only between her swollen legs. Ida knew how to satisfy him both spiritually and mentally. She could mend any ailment he had as well as he mended fences down south for the landowners. He sat lost in a daydream looking forward to a miracle that would save him from himself. Before he lost Ida he would kill Callie as dead as the president on a dollar bill.

Callie walked out to where Dude sat in the park and when he finished his card game, they walked Rufus home. He'd had a full day. The house was quiet when they entered so Dude had Callie to run Rufus's bath water. He remembered the picture of him and Wilbur holding on to Rufus's hand and it had struck a chord. When his bath was complete, Rufus put his pajamas on and played on his bedroom floor with his toy cars. Callie later sat him in a chair at the kitchen table and gave him milk and cookies before Ida showed up. Ida took a bath and she and Rufus slept together in her room. She felt she had neglected him far too long that day for him to sleep alone. Before he fell asleep he asked where his father was. When Ida told him, he insisted on sleeping with his father. Ida walked him downstairs and he scooted in bed and fell asleep.

John Jr and Effie sat wrapped in each other's arms all night to steady the reeling train ride. They were surprised to find the train pulling into the Chicago station close to the time it had been scheduled to arrive. Their bodies were tired and the both ached in their joints from sitting up all night. It was time to disembark. John reached for their carry-on luggage and Effie happened to brush against him. She felt his manhood rise. The two of them laughed so hard, it slowed down their exit from the train. Callie, Ida, Wilbur and Rufus met them at the station. When Rufus saw them he yelled, "Grandpa, Grandpa!" His hug was genuine. Rufus grabbed their bags and John Jr picked up Rufus to tell him all about the train ride. They found Chicago to be a huge place. They rode for a long time to reach the border of Indiana. It stifled John Jr and Effie to not be able to see rich green fields. In the winter months they needed to see evidence of life. Pavement showed only the replica of a hard way to go in a big city, they thought. Indiana traffic slowed down to a livable pace. Traffic lights controlled the flow of traffic so that nobody had to take chances while running for their buses. There were no tall structures that crowded the skyline. The bits of earth they saw looked diseased and malnourished. Before they came to the house, John Jr and Effie were ready to go back home. They were pleased to see their daughters healthy and happy but nothing about the north looked inviting. It looked cold, dark and dreary. Wilbur parked by the side door. Ida led them up the stairs and into the kitchen. Their father blinked and shook his head at the enormous size of it and how new everything was. His heart began to swell. He thought, "Wilbur wasn't bull shitting. He loves my baby girl." Effie reached for Ida and Callie's hands and held them to her heart. She realized that the choice they had made to allow Wilbur to marry Ida was an excellent one. His love for her was displayed all over the house. Effie wondered how one little twat could manage to rule all of what they were seeing. Dude walked in and swooped Callie off of her feet into his arms. She blushed. Effie could still see hurt when she looked deep into Callie's eyes. Ida, on the other hand, was busy fixing breakfast and told her parents to go and refresh themselves. They sat in her bedroom in awe of her possessions. Wilbur had given her everything. After breakfast, John Jr and Effie slept until nightfall. The house was warm and cozy. Callie and Ida had set the table so that they could have an intimate meal together. They ate and Wilbur sat a bottle of bourbon on the table. Effie went and unpacked the things that Mable sent the girls. Rufus had more than any one. He had clothes and toy tractors, dump trucks and earth moving vehicles. Grandpa John gave him a big book with pictures about the farm too. The women finally ran the men into the living room while they cleaned up the kitchen. Callie was busy prancing around in the comfortable clothes her grandmother Mable made for her. Wilbur put Rufus to bed after he fell asleep on the floor at ten o'clock that night. By midnight, the whole house was in the throws of lovemaking. It was a glorious two weeks that John and Effie spent with their children. Dude invited Iris and his sisters for Sunday dinner and when Ida proved to be such a good cook even Effie couldn't remember how she could have learned to cook. Ida had never hung out in the kitchen. When she went to church, she found the answer. Ida had wisely surrounded herself with middle aged women. They had the experience and she had the speed and energy. Ida's mentality was youthful. She met with the women's auxiliary once a week and had learned everything she wanted to know about cooking and keeping a budget. The women rallied around her and she listened well. What really made her abilities unique was that she always added Effie and Grandma Moore's touch to her cooking, cleaning and sewing. Iris left the house begging Ida to make her an egg plant casserole. Dude's sisters couldn't wait to tell everybody that Dude and Callie were happy. It was almost November and Effie counted silently, as she sat and watched her daughter waddle across the room. "Well," she thought to herself, if she had Dude in May, you could count from June." She couldn't wait to get to Mable so that she could talk. Dude sat thinking, "Maybe I got it the first of June." He absently stuck his finger under his nose as if a scent would bring back a memory. Wilbur and John Jr were concentrating on Rufus and his book while Ida washed dishes and waited for Monday night to roll around so that she could see Mack. The second week of John Jr and Effie's visit in Indiana sped by like greased lightning. Dude enjoyed his father-in-law and the way that he carried himself. He was proud to call John Jr an original country cool breeze. While Dude had created a swagger in his walk, Callie's father had it naturally. He kept his shoes shined and wore new shoestrings that were the proper length and neatly tied. The family spent most evenings talking around the kitchen table. Ida and Callie did the "Calico rock" that had shaken up their local school district. Dude listened to Wilbur and John Jr talk about many experiences that city life hadn't afforded him. Dude could tell that the two of them went back a long way, but for Ida to be only 14 years older than Rufus was mind boggling. He decided to put those thoughts aside to concentrate on his renewed relationship with Shirley. Since Callie's parents came to visit he had not been in touch with her. The one night he had wanted to get to her, he decided to go home. The car was gone and the lights were out so he figured they had all gone to drop Wilbur off at work. Dude had reached into his pocket for the key to unlock the door when he heard a loud cat's meow that seemed to come from inside the house. There was an alley behind the house that ran the length of the block. Before he could look behind the house, Shirley called his name from the store across the street. Dude used his coolest macho swagger to walk across the street and greet her with a smile. They toyed around and chatted until he agreed to come over the next night after work. He was flattered by her boldness. Wilbur's car passed the store while Dude and

Shirley stood and talked. When the car came to a stop, only Ida and her parents got out. Dude decided he needed a drink. He headed to his favorite hang out to hear some jive and comedy. After a couple of drinks he decided that Callie must have stayed home with Rufus and Ida had driven Wilbur to work. He stayed out until the place closed which was around two o'clock in the morning. The weather was mild, so Dude took his time getting home. When he walked in, Wilbur was walking out of the bathroom. Dude stripped and slid into bed next to Callie. He reached between her legs and fingered her wet pussy. The next morning, Dude stayed in bed until Callie got up and they walked into the kitchen together. They had shared the bathroom to wash their faces and brush their teeth. Since Callie's parents came to town, Ida had turned breakfast into a buffet. Dude had no more guilt concerning Shirley because to him it was obvious that something was going on between his wife and Wilbur. He now decided to bring out the "cat" issue because it troubled him that he hadn't been swift enough to catch Wilbur and Callie in the act. After everyone filled their plates, poured their coffee and said grace, Dude asked in a voice louder than he intended. "IS THERE A CAT IN THIS HOUSE SOMEWHERE?" Everybody besides Rufus acted as if they were caught in the act of lovemaking. Ida turned her back to the table and snickered. Her snickering brought the house down with laughter, but Dude believed that Callie and Wilbur were as guilty as hell. Rufus saw humor in the humor and hollered with the rest of them. John Jr and Effie blushed like young lovers. Wilbur wanted to put the "mutha' fucka" out of his house but he knew better than to move or act in any unusual way. He had gone to bed to prepare him self for work. By Dude playing house with Shirley, Wilbur and Callie were inventing more ways to steal moments than a Ways and Means Committee on a cruise ship. He remembered Ida coming into their bedroom downstairs and whispering to him that she was taking her parents downtown. Soon after they left Callie had come into the basement and before he could get up to make love to her elsewhere, (any room but Ida's) she had lowered her head on him. Her lips were hotter than her body. Wilbur forced his mind to return to the situation at hand. He looked at Ida and said, "Come here, Coffee." Ida snickered again. He had thrilled Ida's soul the night before. She was his main course, his princess; his soul's serenade. They all were still laughing. John Jr looked at Effie and made her squeal in memory of the way they had made love on the bedroom floor to hold down the noise that the bedsprings made. It took time for the laughter to die down. Everyone sitting at the breakfast table over ate that morning. John Jr skillfully began to talk about some of the things that had interested Dude in earlier discussions and lured him out of his state of embarrassment. Callie was first to leave the table. Wilbur stayed until Ida finished cleaning up. John and Effie were heading home the next morning so Dude took his father in law to meet some of his friends. Women came from every direction to try and entice John Jr. He found himself better able to understand why Wilbur stayed so close to home. Some of those women looked good enough to make a man leave his happy home but he meant to stick with Effie, the one he had asked the Lord for. When Callie finished venting in the bedroom, she ran a tub of warm water and crawled into the tub to relax. She rehearsed a hundred different ways to curse Dude out. Callie knew she was caught but any son of a bitch that had the nerve to point a finger at her when he hadn't caught her in the act was going to get fucked up; even if she had to poison his black ass! Her mind rambled on. "That damn no good retarded ass slow talking and slow walking Roger with the big ass dick but didn't know what to do with it is going to get the surprise of his fuckin' life when Verta's ass don't know how to fuck him. Hell! I did all the damn work and he learned how to get what he needed from my ass but it's all right now. Dude is going to take me to Calico and I'm going to show all those who laughed at me my fine man, if I don" have to kill him first." The tirade that filled her mind made her skin feel tight. She slowly took her bath and dried her body. She wanted to tell her husband more about herself but she had waited too late. Callie did not remember when she had last seen her monthly period. Her mind was blown. Rodger's wedding invitation was the last thing she remembered about Alabama. She didn't even remember writing the letter to Ida. The train ride and the sophisticated fighting woman whose husband stole money from her purse was still fresh in Callie's mind when Wilbur and Ida had met her at the train station. She heard her father's voice and knew that he and Dude had returned from their walk. Dude walked into the bedroom and told her to get dressed. They were going out for an evening stroll. Dude decided to forgive himself and forge ahead. He had a plan. They were still at the club when Wilbur went to work that night. Wilbur had a plan too. When he left the house that night, he headed in the opposite direction other than the one he usually took. Most of the time he liked to take things slowly until he could sort out the circumstances. At this point in time, Wilbur had gotten enough of both Callie and Dude. It was hard for him to refrain from being judgmental. Any wise man would have taken his wife out of a family environment. "Why didn't Dude take his wife to his mother's house," Wilbur wondered to himself. Again, he had spoken the words aloud. Every way his mind twisted the picture, he knew he had treaded into troubled waters. He had never asked Callie for sex. Something was wrong with her mind that she would take chances in her sister's house. Any other woman would have at least resisted his first pass. Callie was just as aggressive as he had been as if she had come to destroy Ida's marriage. His thoughts were in turmoil. The two of them had betrayed Ida and he knew he would lose her if she ever found out. Wilbur drove slowly down the alley. When he approached the rear door of the hangout, he switched his headlights to bright enabling him to see farther. He finally saw what he was looking for. He had traveled down the block and around the corner. He pulled the car over and stopped. Wilbur stepped from his car and picked something up. He drove back home, unlocked the door and opened it. The alley cat leaped from Wilbur's arms when it felt the warmth of the hallway. Wilbur quickly closed the door and locked it while muttering to his self, "FUCK DUDE!"

The weather was cold and rainy when John Jr and Effie headed home. Ida and Callie had not been able to convince them to buy warmer clothing for the colder climate. Their trip was towards the south where the weather was much warmer. Effie asked, "What can I do with clothes as heavy as the ones you wear in the winter time?" The girls answered her question at the same time. They said, "SUFFOCATE!" John Jr and Effie huddled together under one of Mable's comforters that Ida brought from home. Both of them hated to leave their daughters, but in truth, they were in the best of care with their loving husbands. John Jr thought about Rufus and his heart began to grow heavy at the memory of his mother, Luella. He envisioned Luella standing by her desk in the classroom. Who would have thought that his child, Ida would become mother to Luella's son? Another thing that plagued him was the fact that Wilbur had stolen his child from under his nose. Ida was so empowered and cherished by her husband that John Jr allowed his love for his daughter suppress his son in law's deed. He had shed angry, bitter tears for months after he'd allowed Ida to marry. Someone should have been made to pay for every one of his tears. He had watched Ida for two weeks skillfully govern a household filled with people coming and going. She was still a child as far as he was concerned but she depicted every aspect of womanhood. She could run circles around her mother and grandmother in a kitchen, she washed clothes three times a week, drove where she wanted or needed to go, she attended her husband's child, housed Callie and her husband and kept her husband happy. Oh well, John Jr sighed to try and change his thoughts; there were plenty of pictures and wonderful memories to take back to Alabama with them. Before he left the platform Dude looked down at John Jr's shoes and whispered a question in his ear,

"Man, what number are your shoestrings? John answered, "number-twenty, Man. Remember this. Twenty to one you've already won." He knew that Dude liked to talk jive so John Jr had toyed around with him from time to time. He and Effie boarded the train and while they all waved and blew kisses, the train pulled out of the station.

The night before John Jr and Effie left Indiana, a proud cat had strutted from behind the side door when Dude unlocked it. Callie doubled over and laughed so hard that she cried. Dude's face burned with outrage at the man that he figured was responsible for its being there. Callie was laughing too hard to see his face. She plopped down on the stairs and could not control herself. Dude helped her up for her to make it to the bathroom without wetting her panties. Callie laughed so hard that it made Dude laugh and make a joke out of it. He said, "Now girl, you know your old man was in the bedroom tearing Effie up. He probably put the cat in the hall 'cause he's a country slick anyway." Callie asked, "Well who has been waddling 'round in Iris' coochie?" Dude said, "Callie, I feel sorry for Iris. If I was anyone besides Iris' son, I would send a young man over to her house to lift her leg higher than a mug. Callie asked what man would pass up Alma or Rose. Dude had a come back. What man will pass my younger sisters up for an old lady? Callie was rolling all over the bed with laughter. Dude said, "I should have taken old Johnny down there." Callie said, "Effie got him covered. You need to hear my Grandpa and Grandma make love. The two of them neigh like horses. Callie and Dude had to cover their mouths to keep from waking up everybody in the house. Callie joked about the time she had sneaked around so that she could walk in on them and their lovemaking but they had been laying side by side when she walked in. "Dude scratched his head and said, "I bet you forgot to check out the middle of the bed. Their asses were probably tied in a knot." Laughter over took her again and Dude watched her try to compose herself before going to bed. The thought of two bodies in a knot aroused him. Once Callie quieted down in their room, Dude undressed her and examined her body. He then rubbed her stomach and kissed her navel, making little rings around it with the tip of his tongue. He sucked her breast and enjoyed the jasmine fragrance and taste of her body. Callie turned her body over and Dude took lotion and massaged her back and buttocks. He did not stop until he had done the same to her thighs, legs and feet. By the time he was done, Callie was asleep. Dude penetrated her vagina from the rear and quietly satisfied his loins. He with Callie and Mack with Ida were stifling sobs of passion at the same time. Ida had sneaked him into the basement before Dude and Callie came home. A few minutes before he'd left, Mack handed Ida a book showing numerous deposits. The balance was well over two thousand dollars. It frightened her. Ida was afraid that the large sum of money would increase her obligations to him. She could not handle that. She had been leaving Rufus sleeping to creep around with him on Monday nights. She was becoming fearful that it was only a matter of time before her luck would change if she continued to take chances. She had gotten some rest from the fandango during the time her parents were in town but Mack was hanging her ass on a string. He'd upped the ante. Mack kissed her and whispered, "Come by the store tomorrow, sweetheart, and I will explain." He then slipped out of the front basement door and walked down the street to his car. Wilbur was in good spirits when he walked into the house the next morning. On last night, everyone on his job had heard him whistling while he worked. John Jr and Effie's bags were packed. Breakfast was ready so they all sat down to eat hot biscuits and ham with red eye gravy. When Dude walked to the table, Wilbur wouldn't look up. Nobody spoke of the cat. Dude was tempted to say something but held his peace. Callie looked at him and doubled over with laughter. Dude then had to tell it to satisfy everybody's curiosity. Effie said, "This is some stuff for private eye Mable Moore." John Jr broke the table up again. He said quickly, "Now Effie, don't you talk about my mama." Somebody at the table laughed so hard that they broke wind and it broke up the breakfast feast. They all ran in different directions and opened windows. The house cooled down when the trip to the train station was at hand. Rufus made a promise to his grandfather to come and visit the farm when his Father brought him down south. Sometimes, promises turn into lyrics that can become a song. When Wilbur went to bed he remembered the promise. It put Georgia on Wilbur's mind. Ida went to Mack's dress shop the next day. Mack was glad to see her because there were customers in the shop that needed her expertise. When she finished helping the three women customers, she rang sales totaling over five hundred fifty dollars. They had been trying to decide whether to buy new suits from the rack or have them made by a dressmaker. Ida took time to figure the cost of the fabric and supplies, the quality of workmanship and cost of labor. When she presented the calculations to them, it was clear that it was better to purchase the suits from the rack if they were concerned about their budgets. Mack, who sat in awe of her ability to market his merchandise, explained to Ida that a legitimate partnership with her would validate their relationship among his peers. She could make more money on her dressmaking skills, because the store would set her cost of labor prices higher. All of the fees charged for labor would be hers, plus half of the store's profits would be hers. She promised to talk to Wilbur about his proposition. Ida walked out of the store that morning as if she were dreaming. She recounted in her head the formula of her calculations on the suits that she'd presented to the store's customers. She asked herself, "Now, how did I know how to do that?" She wondered how it came to be that she would be a business owner. Her mind skipped to over to everyone who depended on her for their needs. She would ask one of her neighbors to pick up Rufus from school. Callie's baby was due in May so she decided to wait until June to begin her business venture. Then, she would need a full time sitter through the summer months. All of these ideas were plans Ida seriously wanted to put into motion, but only if Wilbur agreed to it. Mack was excited. He wanted Ida more than he had ever wanted any other woman. Every week since he had gone into business for himself, he would play it safe and go back into the city of Chicago for missionary style, home grown liaisons. He grew tired of lukewarm old maids and young women alike whose body language were riddled with questions like, "Oh, my God, when will he finish? How will I walk naked to the toilet in front of him? Will he like my body? Why is he putting his mouth on my breast?" To Mack, fucking them felt like fishing in a commode. Nothing alive was in there. It was all shit. Ida would allow Mack to devour her with his eyes and she teased him until he had a desire to taste her with his lips. She would touch his short stubby organ and handle it with her hands as if it were a fine 24 carat golden heirloom. It was in that same manner that she would feel and examine the fine, expensive fabric in his dress shop. When he thought of the serenade that Ida's body sung to his short thick organ, his knees weakened. Ida's body never made demands and allowed him to give as much as he wanted to give of himself. She was the one and only woman he wanted in his life. If Wilbur said no to his proposition, Mack already had an alternative plan in his mind.

The holiday season was fast approaching and a jovial spirit flowed through the entire community. Neighbors and friends conspired to decorate the streets for the Christmas holiday before Thanksgiving Day arrived. Callie began to grow restless. The baby had started kicking stronger and it seemed the right time for she and her husband to move from her sister's house. The carefree days of peeking and hiding came to a close when colder weather set in. Ida stopped the short trips of running to the store for small purchases. Callie knew she was in a jam. Ida had not heard the doctor say how far along her pregnancy was and had taken for granted that she had been only two months along. In reality she was much farther. One morning Callie got up, dressed and went to find a place to move in order to get away from Ida's house. She found an apartment and left a deposit. Dude was working many hours of overtime in order to compensate for the money he'd spent on Shirley. A guy by the name of Brooks, one of his long time friends' stopped him before he reached home that day and told him that his wife, Callie had rented an apartment next door to his woman, Shirley. Dude dropped the cigarette he intended to light and said, "Man, this is November, not any damn April." Brooks, his friend said, "That's right, Dude. I wouldn't lie to you, man." Dude had been referring to April Fools Day. Brooks had understood what Dude meant to say. That was just how well they knew each other's jive way of talking. Dude looked up and saw that there wasn't a cloud in the sky. He was looking for anything positive that could rescue him from his dilemma. Dude reasoned that Callie was right about moving, because knowing that she was too far along in her pregnancy for the baby she carried to be his child, Ida was sure to put two and two together. The possibilities of that happening made it hard for him to keep quiet. He was about to blow his cool. Ida, may have been in on Callie's game only, she probably didn't suspect Wilbur, her own husband of infidelity. Dude was glad that it was almost time for him to go to work. He didn't want to look at Callie so he went to his mother's house and rested until the time to go to his job came. When he got off the next morning, he went down to the Draft Board's recruiting office and volunteered for the army.

Ida sat and watched Callie drag several cardboard boxes into her bedroom and pack each box with clothes. Dude would come home and walk around the heavy boxes as if he did not see them and go to bed. On the 15th day of the month Ennis Nelson, Jr received a notice to report to the local Draft Board. Callie had yet to talk to him about the apartment she had found. Ida tried to talk to Callie about maybe going home to their parents down in Alabama to have the baby instead of trying to go it alone. Having babies was something that neither of them knew anything about. Callie just continued to pack her clothes and would not respond to Ida's suggestions. She felt that Dude would do whatever it was that they needed to do when it came time for the child to be born. Wilbur didn't care where she went just so long as she didn't stay there. Ida managed to wear Callie's stubborn streak down when she yelled, "Callie, a hard damn head makes a soft ass! Unpack those clothes and sit your dumb mule-headed ass down somewhere!" Ida was so angry that if Callie had birthed the baby in the middle of the floor at that moment, she thought in her mind, "It would have lay there and died." Callie stopped packing and gave Ida a deadly stare. Wilbur wanted to leave the house but was afraid that Callie would spill the beans behind his back. Ida stared her sister down. She held a skillet in her hand and if Callie had said something smart, she planned to aim it at her damn head and knock her the hell out so that she could join her mind which was already out in Left Field. Rufus was in school. Ida remembered that he needed to be picked up and said to Callie, "Come and walk with me to get my child." She held her breath in hopes that Callie wouldn't add fuel to the fire. Wilbur, not wanting them to be alone, offered to walk with them. On their way out the door, he was tempted to give Callie a shove down the steps but Ida walked between them. Rufus came in from school and asked his dad if he could go down the street and visit a friend. After dinner, he was taken to his friend's house and allowed to spend the night.

Dude was scheduled to leave for boot camp on November 26, 1939. His family and friends threw a farewell party for him the night before he left town. It was held at his favorite bar called The Hangout. The party was well under way when Dude and his family arrived. "Going home tomorrow," the song blared from a jukebox in the corner. "I can't stand your ways. I'm going home tomorrow; I can't stand your evil ways. If you don't straighten up baby, I'm going home today."

Shirley stood in the middle of the dance floor and glared at Callie who walked in and immediately broke into a dance with steps that were new to everyone but Ida. Callie handed her coat to Dude and moved her hips to the beat. She stooped and brushed the floor with her right hand. As she moved her body a view of her shapely legs drew calls and comments from the men. She then threw her left hand on her hip while slowly returning to a stance and shook her hips into the shimmering dance called the "freeze." She got the dance floor hot enough to entice other women to run to the middle of the room to keep the dancing alive. Callie then strutted to the beat of the music to take her seat next to her proud husband. Dude's friends rallied around her while Shirley did her best to keep her cool. The song "Bad, bad whiskey," started dancers to step and rock to a different beat. "Bad, bad whiskey made me leave my happy home." Wilbur's glide to the dance floor caused Shirley and a few of her girl friends to swoon. He held Ida in his arms and swayed to the music. She was the youngest woman in the club. Her body was finely shaped and flexible. Ida, the little church girl did each dance step with the fresh and lively flair of youth. Wilbur was so in love with her and her ways that when he felt his temperature rise, he shouted, "Bring it on home baby!" and took a step backwards as if to present her movements to the world. Ida slowed her body down to the "cootie crawl," where she gathered her wide skirt between bowed legs and wrung her hips slowly while squatting to the floor. Wilbur stood mesmerized and watched her arise and rock to the blare of a saxophone solo. Ida began to move her feet and to fan her Mable styled, flared skirt that she continued to hold gathered between her knees that wobbled to the beat of the drums. The fanning of the skirt released the honeysuckle fragrance she wore. She stepped, fanned and twirled while Wilber held the guys back who wanted to dance with her and her fragrance. He shouted, "I'm sorry gentlemen, but everything I brought in here is going back home with me tonight." The crowd who normally frequented the hangout had never seen the likes of the two young and gorgeous women who knew how to party. Ida and Callie complimented one another's beauty and poise. The jovial group of friends and neighbors hooted and cheered. During the celebrating Callie and Ida were introduced to many of them and remembered a few names. Dude's mother and sisters sat at the table with their dates and cheered when Iris stood up and shouted, "My boy knew how to pick 'em, didn't he?" Shirley found herself in the arms of Brooks, the guy that had told Dude about the apartment Callie had rented. He had also hipped the landlord who offered Callie her money back when she apologized for being unable to move in. The landlord had said to Brooks, "Damn! Shirley probably would have blown us all to hell." Brooks had rushed over and asked Shirley to dance after Iris, Dude's mother made the comment. Shirley's trembling shoulders let him know that she was crying. He realized her heart had been broken, but Dude was his ace who had made a choice to marry the new girl in town. He held her close while she buried her face in his shoulder. After she calmed down and the music stopped, he gracefully escorted her back to her seat. That's what friends were for. He acknowledged her look of gratitude with a slight nod of his head and during the rest of the party; Shirley danced with the homeys, who, one by one made their rounds among the guest to be sure that there were no wall flowers. Those were the kinds of friends that Ennis Nelson Jr had. Ida enjoyed watching Iris cut a rug on the dance floor. Her moves were smooth and sultry like she meant to send a strong message to daring, adventurous, single men. When she got a taker, her date went and pulled her off the dance floor while her daughters and Dude brought the house down with laughter. Dude looked at Callie and winked. Wilbur was enjoying his alcohol. Alma, Dude's sister, walked over to the table where Shirley was sitting. She walked with a jiggle that made her breasts a joy for men to look at. Wilbur had slowed down pouring his drink to watch them jiggle. Ida sat and followed his gaze with amusement. She had never seen her husband watch another woman walk. Dude watched her with interest realizing that Ida did not feel threatened by her husband's attention towards Alma. He thought, "If somebody as fine as Alma was no threat to her, surely she would never suspect her own sister's betrayal." With that thought in mind, Dude turned in time to catch Wilbur watching him as he watched Ida. "Damn!" He sighed. The shit was getting too deep to stir into with a stick. He was glad to be putting some distance between he and Wilbur. Ida had to find out one day, he concluded. That settled his mind enough for him to enjoy the rest of the time that they spent at his party. Wilbur also saw how Callie didn't enjoy other women approaching the table to chat and tease with Dude. He leaned over and whispered in Dude's ear, "Hey man. It's your party. Let's boogie!" The two couples went out on the dance floor again and were joined by the rest of the dancers. Shirley even got out on the floor and celebrated like her heartbreak was a thing of the past. The mood of the party changed with the music. "Mama, he treats your daughter mean." The bee-bop tune of woe sent single women the signal to find a dance partner. It was turn-about-time on the dance floor. "He's the meanest man I've ever seen." Alma stood up. Wilbur pulled Ida onto his lap. "Mama he takes my money; makes me call him honey; mama this man is lazy; almost drives me crazy," the tune continued. Alma's date had followed Alma's eyes and found Wilbur discreetly moving his ass out of her reach by transferring Ida onto his lap. He wrapped his arms around Alma and walked her to the dance floor. The couples, Dude and Callie with Wilbur and Ida sat and had another round of drinks before leaving so that Dude could go and get a good night's rest. His mother and sisters walked him to the door and gave him hugs and kisses. Shirley watched Alma whisper something in Wilbur's ear. She sat and silently wished it were possible to exchange places with Callie for just another night. Brooks was at her side before her tears started to fall again. Wilbur made sure he limited his conversation when they all reached the house. While he had sipped on the last drink it came to mind that a good way to get away would be to visit his family in Athens, Georgia. He figured out a way to take Rufus with him by leaving early Saturday morning after the school Christmas pageant. The thought of it eased his troubled mind a little. He went to bed and slept like a baby until morning. Wilbur caught Ida completely off guard when after breakfast he said, "Baby, we need to talk." Rufus excused himself from the table and walked his plate over to the sink where Ida took it from his hands. He reminded her that it had been a long time since he visited his family and asked if she would like to go south for Christmas. When she hesitated, Wilbur decided to not react, but to give her time to answer. Ida had mixed emotions and reservations and needed desperately to get her thoughts together. When she did, she calmly asked him, "When are you thinking about going?" To which he queried, "What do you think if I was to leave Saturday morning and take Rufus with me?" We could visit for a few days and still be home for Christmas." It sounded like a good idea to Ida, but she thought of something else to ask him. "Wilbur, she asked, what if you run into bad weather." He laughed and pulled her down on his lap. "Now baby, you know can't nothing stop me from getting to you." His kisses felt good on her face. He was busy working his way down her neck planting little kisses when she jumped up remembering that Rufus was somewhere in the house playing. His wanting to go south was a greater blessing than Ida had expected. She need time to concentrate on her self and Rufus really did need to know more of his family besides his father. As much as she loved him, he was still another woman's child. She took a deep breath and exhaled. From the age of sixteen, she had been raising a child. Her love for Wilbur was just that strong and in most ways, it still was. Suddenly, her mind seemed to expand and allow her to weigh a few measures in her life. Mack, on the other hand, loved and cherished her. His love provided for her the privilege of living in a richer emotional environment. Physically both men satisfied her body but she could feel Mack's yearning to prove his love to her. Wilbur, her husband is the man she lived for. She strove to complete his world. Most women would think it strange that she did not long to become impregnated. She was busy enough taking care of the child that her husband had. Her husband built her a beautiful home but it was her responsibility to take care of its cleanliness, do the family laundry, the ironing, cooking and to avail her self to his personal needs. It certainly kept her praying. She was still a young woman who encircled herself with middle aged women who knew something about life like her Grandma Mable and knew how to reach Jesus and tell Him about her troubles. Suddenly, the dam of her emotions forced floodgates open to release pressure that had been building within her for a long time. Ida began to cry. Since the day that she and Wilbur's souls made a connection and sparks flew, a vibrant twelve year old child who, in her ignorance and freedom of expression, was swept away into a sea of emotions and rushing waters of maturity longing to flourish. The child fell instead, into a troubled, mind-boggling, abyss of scheming to take a man away from a marriage that was ordained by God. Ida had never attempted to sort out her feelings nor had she ever known how to sort them out. Wilbur heard her crying and came rushing into the kitchen. Callie rushed out of her bedroom in time to see Wilbur gather Ida up into his arms and plead for her to tell him what was wrong. She couldn't tell them for fear of sounding like a lunatic. She was mourning the loss of Luella, Wilbur's first wife and hating the things she had done to win his affections. Her memory was flooded with the secret meeting in the brush, hiding in his truck, mimicking his wife's dress and speech. It all came back and pierced her heart while she sobbed, "I am sorry. I'm so sorry. She felt that she had wreaked havoc on that marriage. Rufus ran to her and grabbed her legs saying," Mama, I'm going to stay here with you."

Callie asked, "What in the world is going on?"

Rufus tried to explain by saying, "I and Daddy were going to visit auntie but I'm not going." He held Ida's legs and would not let go. Wilbur calmed his son down by speaking softly to him. "She's alright." He spoke softly so that Rufus would stop being afraid. Ida came to herself after Wilbur sat on the sofa in the living room and held her like a baby. He had to coax Rufus to release her legs. He then looked into Ida's eyes and said, "Now baby, this is not something I have to do." Ida asked in surprise by asking, "What?" Rufus shouted, "Daddy, I don't want to leave my mama." She noted that Wilbur looked perplexed. Wilbur looked at her with a wrinkled brow asked her what she meant by "What" when she had done all of that crying. Callie handed her a tissue and Ida blew her nose and wiped her eyes. She assured them that she must have needed a good cry and would truly miss them while they are gone, but in truth, he really did need to go and visit his folks. Wilbur breathed a sigh of relief. He and Rufus went and gathered as many old photos as they could find. It was time to tell Rufus about a lady by the name of Luella who was now smiling down from heaven, happy that Ida loved her son. When Wilbur tucked Rufus in that night he told him to ask Mama didn't Luella teach her how to take good care of him. He did ask her and she replied, "Yes she did. She taught me real good." Her embrace told him the story was true. They snuggled and smiled. When Ida looked into his smiling eyes, in them she saw the vision of a mother's soul.

Dude reported to the draft in late November. There was no time for tears. After a quick embrace he was gone. When the bus he rode reached the county seat, Dude made a phone call to Shirley. He unloaded his many burdens on her heart. If all went well, a strategy that they came up with would set him free. He would have his last paycheck to go to Callie, his wife to keep down suspicion. Callie was to receive an allotment. All other mail was to be rerouted to Shirley's address. Dude's plan was to come home to live with Shirley, whose friend worked in the doctor's office where Callie went. They were going to find out just how pregnant Callie was. Dude said to Shirley, "Listen, I am not a fool for nobody. The first time she gave me some leg, it was as hollow as a log. I kept trying to get a cherry out of the box but it was empty. Somebody had baked that pie a long time ago." Shirley exhausted herself laughing at his lingo. She barely made it to the toilet seat in time to not wet her clothes. Shirley suffered the pain of rejection and heartbreak of losing him to Callie all at the same time. She drew her tub if water as warm as she could bear it and climbed into it. Hot tears streamed down her face. She tried to catch them in her hands but she splashed her hands around hitting the water so ferociously that the floor of the bathroom was wet. She screamed, "I should let the bastard just suffer like I did. Oh! Ennis! Why? You married another bitch right in my face!" Shirley was glad to be home. If she were anywhere else, people would call her insane. That thought stopped the flow of tears. She climbed out of the tub and the tears started again. She began to moan, "Ennis! Oh. Oh! Ennis, Why? Why did you hurt me so bad?" She was frustrated for allowing him back into her bed, but she could not help it. Rejection had been a big pill to swallow while the whole community watched her choke and almost perish. Her tears, like her so-called friends gave her no warning. The wet and silent tears lapped beneath her chin again and she simply wiped them gently away with a towel. Shirley finally managed to pull her emotions together and call Noreen, who was a receptionist for Callie's doctor. She found out from Noreen that the baby was due before the month of May. Shirley shouted, "Hot damn!" She thought of Dude's intimacy with Callie and started to cry again. Meanwhile Callie was writing letters to her husband and smiling.

Callie was also beginning to slow down. Ida waited for her to get dressed for Rufus's pageant. Callie hated to climb out of her warm bath water that made her body feel weightless. She was beginning to feel lonesome and missed Dude's presence and humor. Had it not been for Roger, she could have given her husband more love. Callie blamed everyone for her cold-bloodedness and calculating ways. Dude had left a note and twelve hundred dollars in the corner of the top dresser drawer. The note read, "Alright Eve, take care of little Cain. I love you now and will love you even more when I see the savings account book. He signed the note, "Love, Dude." In truth, Ida believed that if she didn't force Callie to eat, she would let the baby starve to death before it was born. She forced her to eat a bowl of soup before they went to the pageant. Wilbur and Rufus had walked to the school together. Ida and Callie walked in just as his class marched into the auditorium and took their seats. Ida and Callie enjoyed teaching Rufus his lines for the play and Christmas carols. During the play Wilbur's personality came out in the way that Rufus spoke his lines and his mannerisms. Rufus made his parents proud. Wilbur saw envy in Callie's eyes when she looked at Ida, and thought, "I'll be damned if my name ain't Wilbur 'T.' Avery 'cause 'Trouble' is following my ass around." He had to get away to search for solutions to a problem he'd tried to hand over to Dude on him and Callie's wedding day. The thing was, Dude managed to leave the mess where he'd found it. He took the soap, mop and broom with him so that no one else could clean up the mess except the one who'd made it. The lights in the auditorium came up and the children were given a standing ovation. Wilbur didn't know it but Ida was looking forward to tomorrow harder than he was.

Rufus was surprised when his class returned to the classroom after the pageant. A cake sat on the teacher's desk that read, "Merry Christmas" and Santa sat in the corner. When they returned home, Rufus undressed and put his pajamas on without being told. It had been a long day. Before Ida could get to the room to tuck him in, he was fast asleep. She pulled his covers up, kissed his forehead and went back into the kitchen. Callie complained of being chilly and went to bed. Ida had warned her about taking a bath and going out with her pores open but she would not listen. It was truly a bundle up kind of night because the temperature was low enough for snow flurries. Wilbur and Ida sat at the kitchen table together. She wanted to talk about how well the day had gone. He slid her chair over to face him. His strength displayed when he pulled the chair so easily made her temperature rise like a schoolgirl. He patted his lap for her to place her feet on him. He made her squirm and squeal with delight while he rubbed her feet. He kissed her toes and began sucking them. A sensation shot through her body and to her nipples that grew hard and stood at attention like the ears of a dog hearing the sound of his master's whistle. Ida lifted her sweater to show them off. He then teased her sweet nipples with the tip of his tongue while she tried not to squeal louder. The amorous couple still wore heavy clothing so they stopped necking and went into their bedroom. After they satisfied their passion, Wilbur stumbled out of bed to get a warm soapy towel so that Ida could continue to relax in bed. Ida was grateful for not having to think about moving until breakfast time. He went to rinse the towels and noticed Callie's door was open. He finished rinsing the towels and hung them on the towel rack to dry. Callie was shit out of luck. Ida had put his fire completely out.

PART TWO

Ida woke up the next morning with a song of joy in her heart. "Well you're the cutest thing that I've just ever seen. I really love your peaches; want to shake your tree . . . !" The upbeat tune warmed her thoughts and she felt special. Some one loved her and she knew it. She stretched her body to its full capacity and relaxed her limbs when she thought of being in bed alone at night for the next week. She wished she'd had somewhere for Callie to go for a week so that she could be in the house alone also. That way, Callie, her sister, Wilbur, her husband and Rufus, her Stepson, people for whom she normally held life together for, could create their own methods of survival skills. It would give her a chance to rest her weary bones. Wilbur and Rufus were about to embark upon an adventure that was a first for the family. Ida had never been alone in her life. She and Callie were raised together but Ida managed to choose her friends and activities separate from Callie and their brother, Lil' John. Callie had a domineering personality and would boss a person to high heaven if they would let her. Ultimately, everything she gained from a friendship or personal relationship would, more often than not, be to her satisfaction. Growing up, Ida wouldn't even walk to school with her. The idea of being bossed by Callie was an offense to Ida. During her first day at school, Ida introduced herself to Melinda who lived around the bend from her family and together they agreed to meet and walk to school each morning. Verta, the girl who married Roger, the guy who ran Callie nuts, wanted to walk with them too, but Callie had drawn Verta away. Ida reasoned that Roger must have grown tired of being manipulated. Many strategies bounced around in her head pertaining to the clothes she would pack for Rufus. Wilbur and Rufus were traveling south to the state of Georgia where normally the weather was warm. Since it was early winter, the weather was too unpredictable to take for granted. It could be cool and mild one minute and freezing cold the next minute. Ida lifted her husband's

arm and wiggled her body out of his embrace to swing her legs over the side of
the bed. Wilbur would wrap her in his arms while she slept. She stretched
again to loosen her stiff joints. On her way to the bathroom, she stopped to
check on her son, Rufus who was snuggled down in the covers of his bed with
his head barely showing. Ida washed her face and hands and smiled at her
reflection in the mirror as she remembered Wilbur and how he had sponged
her body off with warm towels the night before. She had packed enough food
to last throughout the journey, toys for Rufus, blankets, water and a comfort
bucket in case Rufus needed to relieve himself at an inconvenient time while
Wilbur drove on the highway. When the guys wandered into the kitchen they
were greeted with a hot pancake breakfast. Rufus had many questions about
the journey and Ida listened to their conversation with amusement. Wilbur
wormed his way around the ones he couldn't answer. He had had often teased
her about her ability to do the same thing. Well, she guessed she'd taught him
something. After breakfast Wilbur and Rufus retreated into the bathroom for
baths. Ida heard Rufus say, "I have to call mama so she can wash my back."
Wilbur laughed and said, "Hold up man! You don't think dads wash backs?"
Rufus laughed louder than his father and answered, "Naaawww! Who showed
you how to wash a back?" Judging from the sounds of splashing water and
laughter coming from the bathroom, Ida had the feeling that there would be
plenty to clean up whenever they came out. She busied herself packing the
suitcases and made sure that she added heavier clothing and clothes for church.
Wilbur gave her a wink and she playfully fell into his arms. He kissed her
behind her ear and whispered, "Girl, you may make me change my mind."
Callie walked by the room while Ida's face was buried beneath Wilbur's chin
and turned up her nose like an envious feline. Rufus shouted, "Ooh. Shame
on y'all! Callie stalked into the bathroom and turned on the water to fill the
bathtub. She burst into tears. She was beginning to feel sorry about her condition
and where her life was headed. The toilet sat too low, Callie's back was aching,
and the baby kicked too often and too hard and she missed her husband. She
cried until the tub was filled with enough water for her bath. One of Grandma
Mable's sayings came to mind. "The more you cry the less you pee." It made
her laugh. Callie enjoyed her bath until her appetite was whetted by the smell
of food that came from the kitchen. She was beginning to hate her self for
eating so much and sleeping at inappropriate times. She felt she had no friends
and no longer had goals set for her future. Callie stepped out of the tub and
could hear sounds coming from the kitchen so she took her time in hopes that
Ida and Wilbur would be gone into another room by the time she came out to

eat breakfast. She cleaned the tub and pulled on a robe. When everything was still she opened the door to see if the coast was clear. She found a stack of warm pancakes in the oven waiting for her to consume them. Callie was amazed at how her sister could get everything right for everyone else but did not realize that her husband was the best lover in the city. She thought of how Wilbur did everything to make Ida happy. A few minutes later, whenever the opportunity presented itself, he would satisfy himself by using her body. She tried to remember if he spoke of romance between the two of them at any time. He never had. Callie's mind went on a rampage; "He knows how to satisfy his wife but can't resist me", she thought. "He's just like Roger who begged like Samson begged Delilah. I can melt his ass at the dinner table by licking my fingers". The syrupy pancakes tantalized her taste buds and she thought, "Damn! These pancakes are good. I can make him or break him. I wonder what Verta did behind my back and when she did it. Her folks didn't let her out of the house. Why didn't I know she liked Roger? Did everyone else know that they liked each other? Did everybody hate me so much that they wanted me to get hurt? Someone could have told me something about them. I was not a terrible person, until now. Callie got up from the table and fried two slices of bacon, two sausage links, scrambled two eggs and cut a slice of Ida's freshly baked pound cake. The extra food she hoped would clear her mind and give her a burst of energy. While Rufus played in his room, Wilbur and Ida were checking the bags she had packed to see if she had left out anything. Ida chased away the thoughts that plagued Callie when she walked into the kitchen and asked if she wanted to go shopping with her and Rufus. Ida went on to explain that maybe her time with Rufus would help her to not miss him so much while he was down south. Callie did not respond to anything she said. She struggled to get up from the kitchen table and went back to bed. Ida heard her groan and watched her grab her aching back. She then sat on the side of Callie's bed and massaged her back until Callie said, "Girl, I'm not going to move." Ida laughed and said, "Shit!" Callie, your ass has eaten so damn much that you CAN'T move!" Ida gathered Rufus and headed to Mack's dress shop. She had seen some beautiful scarves that would make wonderful gifts for Ruthie and Mae Alice, Wilbur's sisters. The car was warmed by the bright morning sunshine but the weather was cold outside. Rufus busied himself fogging up the car window while Ida drove. When the coast was clear, Callie added Wilbur to her menu. Well, he reasoned that she was already pregnant so he may as well enjoy her hot action in the bed. He sat on the living room sofa while she devoured him. Wilbur then sat her on his lap and massaged her clitoris until she purred like a kitten. He sat and watched her waddle back to her room and became aroused again. After Callie sat on the side of her bed he opened her robe and used her body until he was again, satisfied. Wilbur stood and zipped his pants without making eye contact with Callie. He was grateful that she allowed him to fulfill his fantasies, but agonized over what he was going to do about the baby situation. Dude had played his hand well and set him up for the fall and flew the coup and left the hens in the hen house to lay rotten eggs. Wilbur's life lay in ruins.

Mack was elated when Ida came through the door of the shop. She had her son, Rufus with her. While Ida made her selection of gifts, she explained that Rufus would be taking them to his Aunts in Athens, Georgia and would be gone a week. She said that the gifts were indicators of how she wanted her son to be treated. Mack wanted to gather her in his arms and assure her that Rufus would be just fine. He had to laugh at him self and Ida laughed with him. She understood that he had been tempted to make a move towards her. She felt his strong love for her and it was comfort enough.

Alma entered the store just as Mack was handing Ida her bag containing the scarves. Ida spoke to her with a genuine smile on her face. She realized that if she was going into business with Mack, she had to appear professional in the eyes of the public. Wilbur had given his approval since Rufus was in school all day and she could be home by the time school dismissed. Besides, he'd said that it was time that she was paid well for her dressmaking skills. Ida started towards the door and decided to look for maternity tops that Callie might enjoy wearing. Besides, she remembered seeing Alma whispering into Wilbur's ear on the night of Dude's party. Ida heard Alma call out to Mack that she had a question. Ida left Rufus standing over by the maternity clothes and strolled over to Alma before Mack started to walk in Alma's direction. The dress was clearly marked, "Dry clean only." Ida instructed Rufus to carry the two tops up to the counter and to give them to the man who was standing there. Alma strutted to the counter to pay for her dress and Ida noticed her opened coat and jiggling breasts. Mack was watching the action, when Ida asked, "Are you sure that you have the right size?" Ida knew that it was two sizes too small when she had checked the item for the "care" instructions. What Alma wanted from the shop was Mack. When she walked out of the store, Mack held a piece of paper with her phone number written on it. As Ida checked the maternity clothes for the size, she asked Rufus to help too. He got a kick out of reading the sizes to her. Ida gave him the money to pay for the clothes and watched him proudly receive the receipt and change due back from the cost of the purchase.

When Ida and Rufus returned from their shopping, Callie had cleaned and dusted the whole house. Wilbur walked in carrying sodas and candy to take with he and Rufus on the trip. After a light dinner, Rufus was sent to his room for a nap while Wilbur and Ida loaded the car with the luggage. She was ready for them to be on their way.

The next morning Ida realized that she had no food that she had to fix for the family, no meals to plan for anyone other than herself, no child to see after and no reason to stay home. After a nice leisurely soak in the bathtub, she found a casual jersey dress and a pair of black suede pumps to slip into. The weather was cool enough for her to wear her red knitted cape trimmed in black with a matching tam for her head. Whenever she received the call that Wilbur had made it to his sister's house, she planned to walk down the street to see Iris, Dude's mother. Ida liked the way that Iris carried herself. She seemed full of fire and wisdom. She somehow reminded Ida of Grandma Moore. By the time Callie woke up, Ida had gone out. Iris was so glad to see her that she fixed coffee and said to Ida, "Sit down and drink your coffee and I'll be right out." Iris walked out of her bedroom dressed to kill. She wore a two piece green sweater set with a matching tam on her head. Soft curls surrounded her face. Her swing coat was brown mouton. The two of them got into Iris's car and headed west towards the windy city of Chicago. Ida had never been to Chicago, Illinois except for when she went directly to the train station. It was noon and the clubs were jumping with lively patrons having a good time. Iris talked to Ida as they rode down the highway about the things she missed the most since her husband passed away. When her children were young, she said, her husband had hurt her so badly by cheating with other women that by the time she stopped having babies, and working like a dog to fulfill the needs of her family, she had lost her identity. Her husband had grown slicker with his cavorting, the children stopped needing as much attention so she had to try and fill her days rediscovering what she liked and wanted for herself. Iris said that she needed a partner, who would be truthful enough to give her some encouragement and allow her to seek meaningful ways of enhancing her life. She said that she had found that special partner on the south side of Chicago. Ida was watching every turn of the car as Iris drove so she would know how to return home. Iris pulled out a pack of cigarettes and offered her one. Ida had never smoked but she was feeling game for something new. She joined Iris in a smoke and took a puff being careful to blow it out. Iris pulled the car over to the curb and parked at a club called The Living Room. She strutted in and waved her hand and was greeted by everybody in the place. Ida smiled. Iris's

popularity was very impressive. She saw couples laughing and talking; there
were tables of four that seated two couples who seemed to be enjoying
themselves and then there was the bar where singles sat and chatted among
themselves. Ida and Iris sat at a table and were soon joined by one of the finest
men Ida had ever seen in her life. Iris called him Daddy. He called her Mimi.
He ordered drinks for them because Daddy already knew what Mimi liked to
drink. The vodka and orange juice went down smoothly but Ida sipped it
sparingly. The man called Daddy soon had them laughing uncontrollably at
jokes and comments. A jazz band in the corner began to play swinging music
and many of the couples began to dance. The dark velvet draperies kept the
sunlight out and if Ida hadn't known better, she would have thought it to have
been night time. Two hours later, they left and went to another club where
they ate a variety of seafood. They left the car parked in front of the club and
caught the El Train to the Chicago Loop where Ida drank in the movement of
moments, clothing styles, beeping and tooting traffic and the rattling of dollar
bills. She watched Iris or Mimi slip in and out of dresses and shoes and strut
like a peacock. Before too long Iris had chosen an outfit complete with
accessories and stockings. The man called Daddy appeared and paid for it all,
gave Iris a wad of money and disappeared. They took the train back to the
club and drove home. Ida was determined not to ask questions. Iris said to her,
"That was Dude's real father." Ida said, "Iris, I never thought I would see
another man as fine as my husband. I got to find something wrong with him,
baby." They both had a good laugh about the words she had spoken. Iris
looked over at Ida and said, "Baby, I can tell you what's wrong with him. He's
a married man. We were both young and married when we met and we just
did what came naturally. I never saw his wife and he never saw my husband. I
made many trips to the beauty shop and would make my husband watch the
kids while I out slicked the slicker. You are my little ace boon coon today!
Girl, I didn't know how I was going to get away from my nosey daughters.
Did you ever see women who didn't have sense enough to get a man? They sit
and talk about it but if they don't be careful, their stuff will be too tough for
a man to chew!" They made it back home. When the car was pulled over to
the curb in front of Iris's house, she explained that not even Dude knew that
Ennis, Sr was not his father. Ida helped her carry her bags inside without
commenting because she had secrets of her own that she was trying to keep.
Iris's daughters asked why she never went to Marshall Fields and Carson's when
they went shopping together. Iris replied, "Because you all can't afford to shop
there, that's why!" Ida sat for a few minutes. Alma asked, "Where are your

bags?" Before Ida could answer, Iris spoke up. "We dropped them off first. I didn't know whether you were home or not so Ida came to help me carry my bags." When she walked Ida to the front gate she muttered, "None of y'all's fucking business!" After telling Iris how much she had enjoyed her company, Ida walked home and ran into Callie who sat in the parlor and had seen her with her mother in law, Iris. She greeted Callie and went into her bedroom to undress. Ida crawled into bed and slid between the cool sheets wearing her birthday suit. She'd had about as much excitement as she could handle in one day and went to sleep humming one of the tunes that she had heard the jazz band play earlier.

Callie wondered what Iris and Ida had going on. Since Dude left she was so lonely that she longed for home on the family farm. Christmas was fast approaching and she had no one to share it with so she decided to walk down the street to visit her in laws for her self. One of the maternity outfits that Grandma Mable had sent to Callie was an easy to wear, black wrap-a-round short-sleeved dress with a coordinating beige jacket trimmed in black. Since the weather had grown considerably cooler her legs and ankles were not swollen so she pulled on a pair of black stockings and pumps to match her handbag. It had been quite some time since Callie styled her hair. She made it into a French twist with a long loose curl that flowed from her right temple down to her chin. Her short walk to Iris's house was pleasant and she was glad to have thrown her wool shawl around her shoulders. Iris answered the door and gave her a big motherly hug. Gerta had cooked dinner and she hurried to set another place at the table so that Callie could join them. Marie and Alma, Dude's other sisters, walked out of the kitchen carrying hot corned beef and cabbage and sat the food on the table. Iris and Gerta added hot potato salad and lemon pound cake to the menu and pulled Callie to the table to smother her with family love. While she ate, they told her delightful stories of Dude's childhood. Iris denied that he was her favorite child but said that she'd had to protect Dude to keep his sisters from killing her baby boy. Callie was able to respond to their expressions and joined in to talk about growing up in Alabama. They had never heard of the serfs who ended up with land they had worked on during the time of slavery. They also didn't know that it had taken generation after generation to pay for the land over a long period of time. Iris was also amazed and impressed that she could go back six generations into her family's tree. During that time in history, it was exceptionally rare. Marie excused herself and came back to the table carrying five long stem glasses and a bottle of sherry. Iris looked and saw that Callie's plate was empty and filled it with another helping of everything on the table. She whispered a prayer that Callie and Dude would have a healthy baby. The rumors she'd heard about the baby not being her son's child, would have to take a back seat, she thought, because her son married the woman he loved. When her son had expressed his concerns about Wilbur, she reminded him that Wilbur loved his own wife and that she didn't believe that Wilbur would do anything to lose his wife, Ida. There was no way for Iris to agree with him in spite of his collection of suspicions. Her last words to Dude were, "Never let anyone tell you anything about your mate. Other People will have you breaking up everyday." She finished her thought and looked at her beautiful daughter in law who was laughing with her girls and enjoying the food like they all had been together from birth. Iris was satisfied that she was about to become a grandmother. Callie sat and finished her glass of red wine and pound cake while Gerta cleared the table and Alma opened a new deck of playing cards. She didn't know how to play the game of whist, so Iris pulled her chair close by her side and told Callie to watch the game until she understood it. Callie caught on quickly but grew tired. Iris talked her into taking a nap before going home which was the best thing since candy as far as Callie was concerned. She struggled to get out of her chair and went into Iris's room to lie down. Dude happened to call while she slept and was delighted that she was with his mother and sisters. When Iris's turn to talk to her son came around, he could hear the approval she had for his choice in marriage, in her voice. He was glad that his mother was pleased but his mind was made up to end the marriage as soon as she had Wilbur's child. Soon after hanging up the phone, he said, "Ain't this about a bitch?" He put his finger beneath his nostril and sniffed, remembering the first time Callie had allowed him to touch her. From the time of their first lovemaking to the baby's due date just didn't add up. He whispered, "I must go by what I know. It ain't mine."

The ringing telephone woke Ida from her nap. She had been dreaming of butterflies in a place of solitude. Each time she'd tried to catch one of the butterflies another one would appear with colors more beautiful than the one before it. She awakened reaching for the most beautiful one of all. It had yellow, brown and gold gossamer wings bordered in black and its colors shimmered in the sunlight. Ida struggled to open her eyes to find the telephone in the living room. Dude, after making small talk, had asked to speak to Callie. Ida looked all over the house but could not find her. She had no choice but to tell Dude that Callie was nowhere to be found, but when she'd taken her nap, Callie was sitting in the parlor. His mind went straight to the probability that she and Wilbur were together somewhere, because Ida had not mentioned Wilbur's whereabouts. Dude was looking forward to graduation. The ceremony was scheduled for the week after Christmas. If Callie had been home he would have shared that information with her, but since she was not, he decided to call Shirley. During the course of their conversation, Shirley brought Dude up to date on everything happening in the community. He mentioned his graduation and kept silent as she invited herself to the State of Georgia. He promised to call again before the holidays and hung up, wondering where Callie was. Finally, he'd called his mother to tell her about the graduation and the first thing out of Marie's mouth was that Callie was lying across his mother's bed taking a nap. No one including his mother wanted to wake her up because she needed her rest they said. Well, he reasoned that it was just as well since Shirley was about to come down to the graduation ceremony.

It took Wilbur fourteen hours to get to Athens, Georgia. Rufus had traveled like a trooper. He'd slept a full eight hours without stirring except for the time he had rolled over thinking he was in bed and Wilbur had stopped to get him situated and refill his gas tank. At seven in the morning, he needed to use the bathroom so Wilbur found a place to stop along the highway so that he could relieve himself. After washing his face and hands, Wilbur straightened the rear seat to make his son comfortable and fed him cold chicken and cake. The real treat was the strawberry soda that Rufus was allowed to drink all by his self. For the rest of the trip, Rufus kept his face pressed against the car window looking for and counting farm animals. Wilbur's excitement could not mask his sadness as he neared his hometown of Athens. Old memories swept over him like waters sweeping over a dam. Grief, his old enemy, reared its head but before Wilbur's tears could overflow, Rufus asked if they were almost there. He had to be strong, his mind told him. He said, "Son, we should be at the house within thirty minutes." The morning dew covered the grassy pastures like a glistening frost awaiting the warm noon day's sun. Wilbur cracked the car window of the car to smell the rich soil and clean country air. He inhaled until his lungs felt tight and then slowly exhaled to release the tightness in his chest as the result of trying hard to hold back tears. It was a long winding drive to the house from where the weeping willow stood waving in the breeze of the south winds. Mae Alice, his oldest sister met him at the door and gathered Rufus in her arms while his younger sister Ruthie Lee, ran to turn back the covers of the bed in his old bedroom. Rufus looked at the smile on her face and saw his father's smile. While she helped him out of his jacket, Mae Alice saw that Rufus still had his mother's eyes. Wilbur took a deep breath and held it a few seconds before he breathed it out. He had been exhausted before he left home but he knew that any further delay would have prevented him from making the trip at all. He simply would have lost his nerve and stayed home with Ida. There was an avocado green reclining chair that sat in the corner of his sister's spacious living room. It looked as if Wilbur's name was written all over it. After he sat down in the comfort of the chair, it felt like it too. Wilbur removed his jacket, tossed it on the sofa and while saying a prayer of thanksgiving, Wilbur kicked back in the chair as it reclined almost into a lying down position. He could hear Mae Alice and Ruthie Lee making a fuss over Rufus in the back bedroom. He thought of how Ida had packed their clothes for exactly one week but those were not enough clothes for what he'd had in mind. When she and Rufus had gone shopping a few hours before they left on the trip, he had added more clothes to the luggage. Most of the clothing in his luggage belonged to Rufus. From the way that Callie had been looking, she would be doing good to last another six weeks before having that baby. If Ida found out the truth, he speculated, he needed to have Rufus out of the way. Ruthie Lee came back into the living room to give him a big hug. Mae Alice came in and did her almighty bossing, pulled him up from the chair and ordered him into the bathroom where there was a tub of bath water awaiting him. Her hug made him almost choke on his abundance of tears. She dried them away the same as she had been doing for as long as he could remember without asking a single question. When she spoke, he spoke her favorite words with her, "Everything is going to be alright." Those were the words that she had said when each of the parents passed away. He had been devastated at the loss of Luella, his first wife, when she spoke those same words. His suffering did not cease but his mind was able to function enough to try and work his way through the many dark and dreadful hours of mourning. She spoke them again when he decided to go and ask to marry young Ida. It took a lot of courage to ask John Jr for his teen bride's hand in marriage. Since then, his allegiance had been to his wife, Ida. He felt that if the day ever came when his sister stopped saying those words to him he would just give up. He stood to lose so much and could not see himself living alone. He prayed she would never stop saying those words. The hot water in the bathtub caressed his body like a soft silk cloak of forgiveness. It was almost the evening of another day and Wilbur hadn't slept. He relaxed so long in the tub that Ruthie came in to check on him. He began to wash his hair and scrub his body with the lavender scented soap. He rinsed the soap from his body and was prepared to stand up to dry him self off, but the soft towels he held made him think of home. He stood and held them to his eyes and cried. While he sobbed into the towels, his father who always met challenges head on came to mind. One would have thought him to be a meek person, but everyone who knew Charley Avery had come to know him as a gentle giant. He had built the family house without owing anyone a dime and raised his children to be of strong character with common sense. Wilbur thought that all was well and good but totally unrelated to the circumstances that he was destined to face. His mother, Grace was a tall slender woman who tried to appear matronly but was more like a flighty princess. The clothes she would make for herself always had a flair that would make her husband, Charley Avery's day. Often during the day he would come in to eat lunch and the kids would be sent out to do some chore so that Grace could "pay him some attention." As they became older, those were the exact words that his father used. They as teens learned to use that time wisely to go places like the county fair or to visit their friends who lived nearby. Sometimes they would persuade their friends to leave the fields of the plantations to play around and eat goodies that they would sneak from the house to bring to them. Grace knew what her children were doing so when she baked teacakes she made sure that as many as two dozen would be set aside for them to sneak to their friends. They also hid jugs of water that were sweetened with sugar and cane syrup. A cool spring led to the edge of the nearest plantation. Wilbur would complain that he was designated to carry the heaviest load. Remembering how happy the boys and girls were to steal away was what stopped Wilbur's tears from flowing. "Oh yes," Wilbur whispered, "My mind is blowed fo' sho'! I'm about to loose my happy home and I sit in a tub of water thinking about damn tea cakes." He climbed out of the tub and dried himself. Wilbur's mother, Grace had such a hard time grasping the fact that Charley was gone that it had taken a year or two for her to stop talking to him. At the beginning of his ailments He'd complained of his body feeling tight and tired. In spite of the salves and tonics, the only remedies for colds and consumption at that time, he died of pneumonia when his lungs collapsed while he slept. During that particular time, there were workers who worked on the Avery farm for wages. Wilbur and the girls continued to run the farm as their father had always done until one by one the girls both married and went with their husbands. From the age of eight, Wilbur wore a tool belt and carried the tools that his father gave to him as he taught him how to maintain the property. What he came to love most was building and mending fences. Wilbur loved the calculations and the ability to measure places correctly. He liked the feel of the wooden posts, the wire, slats and boards or designing any barrier that served the purpose of the landowner. He would take measurements and design it first in his mind, draw it on paper and present his ideas to the landowner. He was twelve years old when he landed his first contract. After all those years, the fence was still standing. Grace lived another six years after Charley died. By that time, Mae Alice had moved back home. Wilbur decided to venture out after he saw that Mae Alice could handle the farm and continue to profit. Her husband could not handle farm life so he left and Mae Alice hired a fellow by the name of Pete Morgan whom she built a cabin for out back. He worked as her overseer and managed the hired help. When Ruthie's last child finished school, Mae Alice encouraged her to move back to the farm. In reality, Ruthie never married the father of her children. Everyone always thought they married but he'd always had a wife. She decided that moving back home would give her a chance to rest her mind from his mess. He and his wife had three more children to get through school and gain their independence. Cyrus Gibson bought Ruthie a house that he maintained for her and their boys but when his kids by his wife came to visit, Ruthie would come to the country and stay at Mae Alice's until they left. She loved being home and the booty calls she would make after his kids left. It seemed to keep their relationship fresh.

Wilbur finally got himself together enough to call for someone to bring him a robe. His luggage was still in the car. Ruthie walked in with a pair of pajamas with a matching robe that still had tags on them. His mouth flew open. After cleaning the tub, he walked out bare footed into the bedroom where his sisters stood with slippers and other clothes yelling, "Merry Christmas, Happy Birthday and all that other stuff!" Ruthie said, "Bro. if you had not packed a stitch, we have bought you enough clothes since you left Athens to open a men's clothing store." They could see how tired he was by the way the corners of his eyes were drooping. Rufus had fallen asleep and was in bed. They wanted Wilbur to lie in bed and rest too. Wilbur looked so good to his sisters that they felt that he was too fine for any woman to have. Ida had lucked out, they often whispered among themselves. The both of them knew women that would have paid big money for him to just pretend to want them. They were a good looking family with pearly white straight teeth, soft black eyes that at times flashed gray, coarse curly hair and like Wilbur, had their father's keen features. He was tall and slim but he had biceps that made most men envious and the women trip over their own feet looking back at him. Ruthie Lee had three sons fathered by Cyrus Gibson. He was the man that she just had to have and was willing to take him any way that she could get him. She had walked up to him shortly after Cyrus had married another girl and asked him if he knew of a special kind of seasoning to use on a rooster. It captivated him. That was all that she had wanted; his attention. When Ruthie got it, she kept it. On the other hand, Mae Alice's husband, Happy Merriweather was a man of modest means. He had grown up working as a house boy/butler in the Mississippi Delta. Happy would furnish the plantation owners with willing women and girls. He hated to hear the wailing of women that the landowners had abused from the quarters so he devised a plan to entice the wanton girls who wanted to use their bodies to be ready to satisfy the men. Sometimes the Landowners would give him a few coins if they had drank enough or if the girls used their skills to get the money they would often bring it to him. His Massa's "Mrs." (wife) was in on it too. She saved his money in her room until one fateful night things got out of hand. Two of the plantation owners got to fighting over a girl named Storia. She was freaky for the hell of it and would relate to Happy the weird things she would do to the gullible men. She'd said, "Happy, I'd just wash him and go, 'Whew' to blow a little air on it and make him wet up the bed. It makes 'em too weak to clean up his self." In the end, the two angry men decided to kill Happy instead of each other. Massa's wife, "Mrs." had used him as her toy-boy for fifteen years. She hid him away and "Mrs." put him on a train to Georgia to her widowed mother, who sent him to Charley Avery, her nephew by their nurse maid's daughter. Charley got Happy a job at the paper mill. On Sundays he would be invited to Charley's house for dinner where he was treated like one of the family. He and Wilbur would talk for hours while Mae Alice would flounce around. On her seventeenth birthday, she and Happy married and moved to town. Happy had more money in the bank than most of his bosses because he never spent any of his money. He knew how to charm people by using survival skills he'd had learned to use all of his life. It was not unusual to hear someone shout, "Hey! Happy! Come and taste this ham!" They wanted his opinion as to whether it was smoked or boiled. More often than not, he'd walk away with a portion of it. He could walk into a café and be offered something special by the cook. His opinions were respected and sometimes became a source of entertainment for his peers who wanted a little spice in their lives. Happy Merriweather had experienced things that were mixtures of fun, foolishness and sometimes wrath. Not many of his peers had the opportunity to hear a slave owner's conversation with others but he had. If he sat by the door of a café with a plate of food, it seemed to draw other patrons into the little shack where freemen often set up small businesses on their properties. Happy would eat his food real slow and when others saw him eating they would walk into the place to sit ant eat with him. Many times on the plantation, the sewing women would make shirts and trousers for him to wear when they had material left over from their family's clothes for the season. He mostly took his allotted material to have sexy outfits made for the girls he took to entertain plantation owners. He would hitch hike to Atlanta and convince a storeowner that if he would allow him to wear a shirt on Saturday that it would sell out by the next Saturday. Sure enough, when the guys would get paid, they would head to the store to buy the shirt that they had seen Happy Merriweather wear or one as close to the style that they could find. When Happy would go back with the shirt, the owner would put it on a tab because any shirt or item he gave Happy was given a higher retail price tag. His wife Mae Alice, on the other hand, loved to spend money but she made sure that her husband was comfortable and well pleased with her purchases. Wherever he went Happy would take her if she wanted to go because he loved to show her beauty to his friends. He kept her hyped up for his story telling and lovemaking antics. There were ways of love that she never imagined but that she willingly performed after he'd captivated her. One night he spanked her during their lovemaking and she was so angry that when he fell asleep she smacked his behind with her shoe. Over and over again she hit him until he finally rolled over in his sleep and flung her across his body. Later on, after she spat and brushed her teeth she swore to never hit him on the ass again as long as she lived.

The clock on the dresser showed the time of six thirty. Wilbur looked towards the window to see what the day looked like. The draperies were drawn and he could only see a little light that filtered through a crack. It was hard to tell if it was morning or evening. Just then, the phone rang and his son, Rufus was on the other end. "Daddy, can I stay?" His voice was filled with excitement and Wilbur could hear laughter in the background. Rufus had never seen so many kids called cousins in his life. Cousins were what other children had and he had always wished for. Now he felt that he had more cousins than any of his old friends had. He was anxious to play so he gave Aunt Ruthie the phone and ran to join the fun again. Ruthie told Wilbur where they were and that they had put Rufus' luggage in the trunk of the car so that he could spend some time with his cousins. Wilbur answered the question that Rufus had asked. He then said, "Ruthie, I don't mind him staying, but don't let him run wild. Make him mind his manners, now." Ruthie said, "Well you know I raised two boys myself, Wilbur. You're sounding just like your father." Wilbur had to laugh. It was the truth. He could hear the tone of his father's voice in his mind. He said, "Girl, I thought I had heard those words before." Ruthie stifled a laugh and told him that they (meaning her and Mae Alice) had called to let Ida know that he and Rufus were there and resting. He felt so relieved that when he hung up the phone he went back to sleep and forgot to call Ida concerning Rufus' longer stay in Athens. At three in the morning, Wilbur sat up in bed again but this time he knew that it was the wee hours of the morning. Old memories started up again and storm clouds that had gathered in his mind were headed back to rob him of any possible sunshine. He remembered how proud he had been of the first fence he drafted and structured. He had been twelve years old when the farmer told him of the problem he had keeping his livestock secured during the day. He said that he needed someone who would tell him what he needed to have done without trying to just focus on their own profits, but who could solve his problem. Wilbur had written down everything the old man said and set out to find a solution by drawing the proper structure. The farmer needed a new fence due to the rotting of more than two thirds of his posts. Also he'd needed to fence in a much larger space due to the increase of his herd. When he went back Wilbur showed the farmer the numbers. When he came home with money for the materials and supplies, his father was shocked. Charley, his dad reviewed the figures over and over again and finally found that Wilbur was charging the farmer more than others had been known to charge for the work. Wilbur said, "I told him that I had to charge more because of my time spent figuring out how to solve his problem." Wilbur solicited help from his plantation friends to replace the fence. He paid them more than they had ever earned in their lives. Most of them were older than he was by five years. All of his friends moved from the plantation when they finally could, but the fence was still standing. He needed someone to figure out what he could do to save his ass from the mess he'd made of his life. He noted how strange it was that he had no concern for Callie after she had given her body to him over and over again. His only emotion when he thought of her was hind sighted fear of the possibility of getting caught. It had been a game of chance. He grabbed his stomach and sank to his knees. He wailed, "Lord, PLEASE!" Wilbur's growling stomach made him remember that he had not eaten in a long time. On his way to the bathroom, he decided that the best thing for him to do was to relax and take care of him so that he would not become ill in his body. Each time he envisioned Callie pushing out a baby from between those big legs, he felt nauseous. Ida was going to leave him for sure. The scent of lavender caused him to tear up again but Wilbur fought the need to cry with every ounce of strength he had. He refused to allow his mind to take another dive into a pool of misery. He went from the bathroom into the kitchen to find food for breakfast. The doorbell rang. Wilbur thought that it was Rufus who loved to push buttons so he flung the door open to gather him in his arms. He got the surprise of his life. There stood his brother in law, Happy Merriweather. True to form, he looked as happy as hell on an oil well. Happy shouted, "GREAT LOOP DIE DO!" He grabbed Wilbur and gave him a bear hug. The two of them walked back to the kitchen where Wilbur made a pot of coffee and cooked breakfast. It felt good to be home and he found himself as comfortable in the kitchen as if he'd never been away from home. Happy confessed to Wilbur how bad he was at running the farm. It was a massive operation of supply and demand. Mae Alice had watched her parents and paid attention to the different crops and times for harvest, the slaughtering and preservation of cured and smoked meats, canning of fruits and vegetables, daily chores and maintenance of livestock and several other things too numerous to mention. They both even though separated were successful business people. They did not trust the banking industry and were debt free. They both had a good laugh when Happy confessed that he had no knowledge of where Mae Alice kept the money, but Ruthie Lee kept the books. Wilbur was impressed that Happy was the proud owner of two Men's Stores in Atlanta. He had acquired them when the owner's children had wanted no parts of the business when he'd decided to retire. The price was right and the employees had stayed put when Happy offered benefits. He would monitor operations while the world slept. The retired owner made him an offer to split the profits for ten years, but Happy paid him all of the profits for five years and after he got the title free and clear, he increased his mark up by two hundred percent. Field hands and mill workers became a thing of the past and so were cheap clothing. Happy recently retained an attorney and added an accountant to his staff. Business was booming. Finally, he asked Wilbur, "What's up with you, Bro." Wilbur got up from his chair took a deep breath and walked into the kitchen for a six pack of beer. Happy saw the slump of his shoulders when Wilbur sat down again. The two men opened a beer each and took a long guzzle before sitting their bottles down. Wilbur began to speak. He said, "Happy! Man, I am knee deep in shit that I will never be able to step out of." Wilbur kept his head down while he talked. He was more than ashamed of the things he had done. He kept seeing a baby standing facing Ida and looking like one of his sisters, in his imagination. He thought," Ida is going to leave me for sure." When he finished talking, they each reached for another cold beer and guzzled it down until they seemed breathless. Happy said, "Bro. you have to send her somewhere before she have that baby." Wilbur asked, "Where, Man? Where am I going to send her? My wife is right there too. I'm going to die a lonely man or a damn dead one just as sure as my black ass is sitting here." Happy laughed at him and said, "Your ass should have been dead if you were going to die. You shitted in the middle of the floor in your own house, man. Send her to me. Maybe to her husband or send her any damned where. You must get trouble out of your house! That's all there is to it!" Wilbur told Happy about the cat and they both howled with laughter. He talked about how Callie had rented an apartment next door to Dude's woman and how Dude had gone into the military. When Happy found that Dude was in Fort Benning, Georgia he grabbed the phone and dialed a long number. After dialing a series of extensions, he said,"Hey! Cap!" After a short pause he shouted, "Happycabee!" Happy was on the phone for twenty minutes asking questions and finally he asked for Dude's proper name and Callie's name and address. Cap, a long time friend and acquaintance of Happy Merriweather, sent for a file on Ennis Nelson. He explained that if he did not call back in an hour, it was a go. What he'd learned was that Dude, Callie's husband, would be out of boot camp on the day after Christmas, which was a week away. Ennis Nelson (Dude) was not a draftee but a volunteer who failed to disclose pertinent information. Callie Nelson was going to receive a train ticket to join her husband on the base so that proper medical care could be provided for her. Housing was being set up. In two hours time a car was scheduled to pick her up and transport her to the train station. "Wilbur, listen to me," Happy said, "Don't make any phone calls home. You must act like you don't know nothing!" Wilbur jumped up from his chair and cut a step or two shouting, "Hot damn it!" He then quickly dropped to his knees and promised God, Jesus, Mary and a few other responsible people that he would mind where he stuck his manhood from that day forth. He stood up shaking his head from side to side and wondered how something like that could have been done. He whispered to Happy, "Man, I owe you my life." To which Happy replied, "Bay Bro., we're family and we have been so for a long time." He continued to reflect on the times when he had no one but was allowed to eat and share with Charley Avery and his family. He said, "Wilbur, it was from this house that the ability to focus caused me to desire to be one of significance." Happy knew that what he was trying to accomplish for Wilbur was still in the planning stages and that it was best not to take anything for granted. So he told Wilbur to remind him to tell more about his father, Charley Avery, and his strong character. Wilbur wanted to hear it right then but the phone began to ring. It was Ida who said, "Wilbur, guess what?" Wilbur acted and sounded so surprised that Happy had to rush to the bathroom. He returned to the living room to find Wilbur in the middle of the room dancing the fox trot. Happy sat and watched for a few more seconds to give Wilbur time to come to him self enough to relate to him the whole conversation with Ida. Wilbur sat down again without saying a word until Happy inquired about the conversation between them. The way that Wilbur understood it was that a letter came by way of telegram addressed to Mrs. Callie Nelson, wife of Pvt. Ennis Nelson Jr. Included in the letter were instructions for Callie to join her husband on the base where housing would be provided along with her obstetrical and medical needs. Ida said that they had two hours to get Callie packed up for her ride to the train station.

Transportation was being provided as a courtesy from the military and the train was scheduled to leave at 8pm. She almost forgot to mention the graduation ceremony that Callie was going to be able to attend.

Wilbur slowed the conversation down to tell Ida that Rufus was having a good time. It gave Ida a chance to catch her breath. She promised to call Wilbur back before she hung up the phone. Wilbur wanted to celebrate but Happy stopped him saying, "Never celebrate when the train leaves the station. Always wait until it makes a round trip without bringing back your load." While he spoke those words, Wilbur was getting dressed to party. He sang, "Gonna have some fun tonight everything's alright."

Ida was glad that Callie had left some of the boxes packed from the time when she'd tried to move out of the house and into an apartment. In a separate box, Ida packed up all of Dude's belongings so that he and Callie would have no reason to return to her house in the future. In one hour's time Callie was all packed up. The new maternity tops that Ida had purchased for Callie were chic and the colors complimented Callie's complexion. While Callie took a quick bath, Ida made sandwiches and packed them along with other snacks and fruit for her to take with her on the train. Ida got down on her knees at Callie's bedside to thank God and to ask Him to protect her sister during her journey to Fort Benning, Georgia.

She checked beneath the bed to make sure that they had packed everything. After Callie got dressed, the two sisters called home to tell John Jr. and Effie, their parents, that Callie was joining Dude on the Army base. They were overjoyed that Callie would give birth closer to home. Grandpa and Grandma Moore hugged each other and smiled. If all things went well, they knew that fate had sealed the probability that they would behold the face of their first great grandchild. They hung up the phone. Ida went to move everything closer to the door. Callie walked up to her after she straightened up from moving the last box and said, "Ida, I need to talk to you about something!" Ida sat down and picked up a napkin to wipe perspiration from her brow. Callie sat across from her and blurted out, "Ida, I do not want this baby!" Ida sat stunned to silence while Callie continued by asking, "Will you and Wilbur raise this baby for me?" Ida kept her eyes glued to the table. Callie kept talking as if she thought that she could convince Ida to better understand her position. "Ida," she said, "I have never wanted kids," Callie said. "After what Roger did to me, I promised not to love anybody but my own self!" Ida felt her passion shift gears and she resorted to logic. Her tone of voice quivered with anger and she fought to keep the sound within the confines of her home. She said, "Girl, I hear what you're asking but I don't know how you feel because I've never been in your shoes," she paused, "but you must be crazy like a Mutha fucka to talk like you're talking!" Callie looked wide-eyed as if Ida's words were shocking. Ida continued to raise her voice. She tried to reason by saying, "I was 16 years old when I began to raise Rufus whose mother is dead. I am married to his father. How can you ask me, to raise Dude's baby, without his consent?" The implications of what Ida had spoken hit Callie's guilty conscience before Ida could weigh the matter. Callie jumped up from the table and ran to get her coat. Ida followed her into the closet and screamed, "You selfish Bitch!" Ida raised her hand to try and knock her head off but a knock at the door brought her mind back to Callie's pending transportation to the station. The driver had reservations about picking up the boxes because of what he'd heard before he knocked on the door. They hugged each other, so he proceeded. Callie thanked her sister for everything through blinding tears while Ida stood and watched the cab pull off. Her eyes were bone dry. Was the father of the baby, Roger? Could Callie have been already pregnant when she came to town? The questions that Ida asked were like wet shoestrings waiting to dry with the help of blowing breezes. She wished she had more information. Why, Ida wondered, did Callie wait until the last minute to ask her alone, to raise the baby, when she could have sat them both down together? In her wildest dreams she would have never believed her husband to be unfaithful. Ida hoped that Callie would let her know when she arrived safely. She breathed a sigh of relief. Ida suspected that she was totally alone for a reason and quickly made up her mind to enjoy her solitude to the fullest.

Callie's ride to the station was a smooth one. Every now and then the driver would check his rear view mirror to see if she was awake. To him, she looked like an angel sleeping peacefully which was a far cry from the way she had looked standing in her kitchen earlier that evening. A short time after entering downtown Chicago the crowded streets took on the holiday spirit. The traffic had all but stopped when Callie stretched her self and needed to use the toilet. The driver was the father of four children so he was aware of the routine. Normally when a pregnant woman wakes up the first thing she does is go to the bathroom. He decided to stop at a nearby restaurant so that she could empty her bladder rather than to sit in the middle of stalled traffic. The establishment was a familiar place. Callie sat in the car while he went inside to speak to the hostess. He hadn't told her where he was going but since the motor was still running she figured he would come back soon. It started to snow little flurries that kept getting bigger. They floated like tiny crochet doilies and melted into drops of water on the windshield of the car. The driver walked back to the car and asked Callie if she wanted something to eat or needed to go to the bathroom. They walked inside where the hostess led her to a small lounge and restroom. She took note of the décor and the mirrored walls none of which she had ever seen the likes of before. She relieved her bladder, washed her hands and felt rested again. After returning to the taxi Callie inquired about the restaurant and found that the driver knew the owner personally and professionally. He explained that he had regular clientele that sometimes needed special perks. He frequented certain establishments throughout the city that he encouraged his clients to patronize. Callie sat back and enjoyed some of the things that the driver talked about and soon they were easing back into the busy traffic making their way to the train station. The driver was very efficient and took care of her bags without much fan fare. Callie signed the voucher and gave the driver a sizable tip. He talked to the porter and conductor to make sure that they would remember to treat her special. While the driver watched, they each made sure she was seated on the train and made comfortable. Callie sat there and wondered just how she'd come to be on a train heading to Georgia. She had not talked to Dude at all. Her family credited him for sending for his darling wife and told her that she was privileged that he had missed her so badly and loved her so much. There were many empty seats on the train. It made for Callie, a comfortable trip all the way to Georgia. The train made several stops but Callie slept through most of them. There were three old mothering women who noticed that Callie was pregnant and alone. They followed her to the bathroom and helped her freshen up before the train pulled into the station where she was to get off. She figured that they must have thought she'd drummed up the story of having a husband waiting for her and was determined to see if anyone met her at the station. They put mum deodorant under her arms and sprinkled her with talcum powder. She washed her bottom and changed her panties and maternity top. They had sprinkled her panties with powder too. She wondered what they would have done if she hadn't had everything that she needed with her. She decided that they probably would have turned up their noses and thought that they were better than she was. When Callie exited the train, the three white hens stood in a huddle and watched her carefully like mother hens watching their chicks. Dude stood holding a bouquet of flowers. Callie smiled and waved. When she reached Dude who had a taxi waiting she waved to the hens and thought that she saw another familiar face in the crowd but she shook it off and buried her face in his chest. His heart melted with a deep feeling of love for Callie. It surpassed his understanding. She was his wife. He watched others behold her beauty while her luggage and boxes were loaded into the taxi. Still, he wondered what had transpired to enable Callie to be delivered to the base. There were thousands of new recruits in the military with tales more adverse than leaving a pregnant wife at home. He'd given her an allotment. Dude smelled a rat but was glad that he hadn't been penalized for not giving a full disclosure concerning Callie' condition. He remembered the "Cat" incident and it had "Wilbur" written all over it." Dude had been out on field maneuvers all morning. Around twelve o'clock he returned to the barracks and found orders to report to his superior officer. So far, everything had worked in his favor. He was excited about the upcoming ceremony and seeing Shirley. He had given up on his marriage and felt contented as long as Callie was not anywhere near. The day he had called her and she was nowhere to be found, he was filled with envy. After a series of calls and finding her at his mother's house asleep in his mother's room, started him to long for her again, but she had done him wrong. Dude checked himself in the mirror and liked what he saw. He was young, strong, handsome and over twenty-one. He walked into the office sporting his most masculine appearance. He listened but was mesmerized throughout the entire conversation. Dude could not believe what his superior officer was telling him. Callie was on her way to Fort Benning by compliments of the US Military. Dude stood at attention and commanded himself to look pleased that his wife was coming to join him on the base. He was told that there would be an amendment to her allotment to include their medical expenditures. When the proper time for him to speak was given, he apologized for his failure to report pertinent information to the board. The fact that he and Callie stood to gain more than he'd hoped for put a smile on Dude's face. All he needed to do then was to get in touch with Shirley before she left home. If he couldn't catch her he figured he would try to make use of guys in the barracks. Maybe someone could head her off and steer her in another direction until he could explain.

Happy Merriweather's friend called Cap was a Caucasian military officer who had been schooled in the lifestyle of slave masters. He was an older gentleman who met Happy in Atlanta, Georgia shortly after the death of his father, Brewster L. Goode who for most of his life had been an overseer on the Gridley plantation. The inhumane property owners worked their slaves to death but gave them freedom during the times when it was too dark out or too rainy to work. Cap, whose name was Caleb Goode, would order slaves back to their cabins behind his father's back so they could rest or try and cure their ills. He often took tonics and salves from his father's shack to the quarters to help with the healing of their tired and broken bodies. Caleb was an adventurous lad who often would struggle to unite broken families by reporting that one such man or woman would be profitable to buy from another plantation. His family lifestyle was just a tad better than slave life. They were free to be poor and to struggle for survival without any hindrances. Happy made Caleb admit that quite often overseers lived in conditions that were worst than the conditions of a house slave. Caleb left home at the age of seventeen when he could no longer stomach the ways of life on the plantation where work of strong, black enslaved hands were of value while his family earned a pittance for running an entire plantation. He'd watched his father carry another man's burden of guilt by mistreating those in servitude. The burden had bent his shoulders and crooked his father's neck making him resort to the same liniment the slaves used to cure their ills. Caleb left home walking. The clothes on his back were tattered and the only other shirt he owned was a hand-me-down from the Plantation owner's son. His mother who had once been a beautiful woman cooked for him three biscuits of corn pone and some meat skins. He tied the food in a bundle using his extra shirt and headed north. But for the free black people he met along the way, he would have died within a week's time. He wondered how they found it within themselves to save the likes of him. At first it seemed strange to him that of their own kind, they did not try to save. For the first time in his life, he understood the dynamics and dimension of wickedness, power and money. The thing that made a difference in whether his family either lived or died was the color of skin. It was a deep felt pain within him that must have drawn blood from the core of his being. Like a bird during a flood without a place to rest, Caleb Goode found himself wandering among the despised and rejected who had no place in society. It took five years for Caleb to turn his life around. He loved small town living and managed to find work in hardware or feed stores, barges and docks where business profits and losses were discussed and where currency exchanged hands. He vowed to never allow another human being to profit by the sweat of his brow on a farm. When he understood the ways of society better, Caleb went back to his father to try and rescue his parents from what had been a down trodden existence. It was painful to find that his father had no hope or vision of any other way of life. Upon his arrival to Atlanta Caleb set out to find a place to sleep and eat. There had been a café that was run by the folks who owned the general store down the road. He watched a young dark man who was neatly dressed in clothes that were unusual for a dark-skinned person to be wearing. The guy had walked to the back of a run down cafe oblivious to the fact that Caleb watched and followed him. There was a hole cut out of the wall of the shack where the coloreds stood to buy food. Caleb was shocked that anyone, not to mention a no account poor person would feed a dog good food. When the Happy looked at the food he was given, he'd fed it to the dog. Caleb said, "Hey, boy. What's that dog eating?" Happy replied, "Just a little something I gave him." Happy had sat and watched the dog eat and Caleb walked around to the front of the café to order. He came back with two boiled eggs, (as if to say, "I am not foolish enough to order anything else from there".) and sat beside Happy on the old rickety bench. Happy Merriweather had read Caleb like a book. When the dog finished eating and looked up, Happy got up and continued down the road. He finally found the person he was looking for. Storia had birthed three daughters, Mamie, belle and Sadie, who in the course of time followed in her footsteps. Times were better and the money was good. Happy walked with them back to the café where he had left Caleb sitting. Caleb sat and watched the men rush from the café and head down the road after talking to Happy on the side. They were filling Hap's pockets with coins. The girls stayed near Happy and three more smooth creamy chocolate complexioned girls joined them. The girls seemed to disappear but would soon be seen nearby. The white men kept coming to the rear of the café in small groups until there was a lag between the times they appeared. Happy said goodbye to the girls that were left and headed down the road in the opposite direction of the girls. Caleb followed him and saw him head off any girl that was returning to the café. Finally, he looked across the road to see the most gorgeous creature he'd ever laid eyes on. She wore a dark dress that swept the ground but one luscious leg showed through a slit that was from her upper thigh down to the ground. She held her mouth in a pout that looked like a budding rose. When she turned to walk away, he felt destined to follow her. She led him to a mansion deep in the woods that was filled with angels without wings, but they had plenty of other desirable things. Caleb stayed there for three days and two nights. When he walked down the stairs on the night of the third day, there was Happy. Happy charmed him for hours with tales of Storia and the plantation owners. They had parted promising to get together again, which they did from time to time through the years as the heavy line of servitude continued to be bold but not as brash or cruel. Caleb traveled further north and decided to join the military to try and rid himself of his feelings of degradation from the past. He had grown tired of the insecurity he felt among his peers. His choice had been wise and he found himself adaptable to obeying orders as a means to an ultimate goal. Years began to pass quickly and he found favor among his superiors who moved him swiftly up the ranks. Two or three times a year, Captain Caleb Goode would find his friend, Happy Merriweather who had shown him more in one day than the world had managed to teach him in twenty three years. In thirty years, this was the first time Happy had asked Caleb for a favor. Caleb sat back in his seat and let out a low whistle at the amount of money Happy had wired to his account. They drank one another under the table one night and in that drunken stupor, the two men, one black and the other white decided that they needed a bond stronger than their occasional visit. Blood they decided was a bit too strong. The idea of that gave them a good laugh but they both agreed that money was the next best choice. They went to the bank and each deposited five hundred dollars and asked for a book and a duplicate book in case the original book was misplaced. It was not easy to convince the banker to allow the issue of two books until he saw Caleb Goode's name, rank and serial number of the US Army. For the benefit of his brother in law, Happy deposited thirty five hundred dollars into the account for Dude and Callie's expenses. Today's equivalent is about fifteen thousand dollars. Happy knew that if Callie found things not quite up to par, Wilbur would be facing her again either in his house or at her father, John Moore Jr's house. That possibility would have created an eruption as big as creation. Happy hoped that before Wilbur went back to Indiana that he would have time to sit and listen to some of the things that his father, Charley Avery told him about. If all went well, Happy Merriweather figured, the night of Wilbur's victory celebration would be the ideal for them to sit down with time to talk.

Callie walked into a house that looked small on the outside. To her amazement the rooms were sizable and beautifully decorated in peach, mauve and green with coordinated variations of white. The living room and dining room walls were painted a dusty rose color with a hint of gold trim around the borders. The modest kitchen was painted in soft yellow trimmed in white. Green, yellow and white curtains hung at the windows. The appliances were avocado green. Her master bedroom was the color of honeysuckle and somehow, the king-size bed seemed to beckon Callie to come in and lie down. The Linen and matching bedspread was white with a hint of pastel floral around the borders and in the middle of the bed. She found enough closet space to hold all of their belongings and thought that Dude had taken care of her in that manner. He never told her otherwise. The room was even large enough for a crib, dresser and two chests. One for the baby and the other matched the over-size bed. Callie walked back into the living room and sat on her new floral sofa. She noticed that her chair was matching in style but was a soft solid peach color. She then walked over to the beige chintz recliner that sat in the corner of the dining room. The cherry wood dining room set was highly polished. Fresh flowers decorated the center of the table. Dude gave her a quick kiss and said that he had to go back to the barracks. She exhaled and was glad to be alone. She was tired and needed to get some rest and figure out how to relieve her self of the boxes stacked up in the kitchen. Dude checked out the food in the refrigerator and tipped the taxi driver on his way out. Callie tried, but she was too tired to finish unpacking. She gave her body a warm soak in the bathtub and used her honeysuckle talcum powder to give her bed a nice, fragrance, slipped between the sheets and fell asleep immediately. It was six in the morning when Callie woke up and she was hungry.

Ida busied herself and saw that Wilbur had taken many, many clothes for Rufus' one week stay in Georgia. The phone rang and it was someone from the army base wanting to know what foods Callie favored. She said that Private Ennis Nelson was on guard duty and had asked for help with shopping for his household. Ida gladly gave her the information and breathed a sigh of relief. She said, "God! I'm so glad she's gone." Callie had never shopped a day in her life! Mae Alice called next. Between the two sisters of Wilbur, Mae Alice had been designated to ask Ida if she minded Rufus staying throughout the holidays. Though a bit stunned, Ida agreed that Rufus needed more time to interact with his cousins and visit his paternal grandparents. Mae Alice had been able to tell the difference in the clothes that Ida packed and the ones that Wilbur just thrown into his luggage so she tried to cover for her brother. She said to Ida, "I wanted Wilbur to ask you if it was alright for him to stay longer before they left home but you and Rufus had gone shopping. He said that while we were talking that he would just put more clothes into the suitcase. He must have forgotten." Ida understood her perfectly. Wilbur did not forget. Wilbur felt that she had no right to be a part of the decision making process when it came to his son. Ida said, "Oh! All right, but you know I probably would have said 'no' because Rufus has never spent a night away from home in his life". Mae Alice didn't comment, but she wanted to ask Ida if she'd realized that the family considered Athens, Georgia to be Rufus's home as well. Inwardly, Ida said, "Bitch, don't you know that I can hear your ass thinking?" but outwardly she said, "Let me speak to him." Mae Alice formed an "OH" with her lips to let Ruthie know that the conversation was not going too well. She waved her hand to let Ruthie know that Ida wanted to speak to Rufus. When Ruthie pulled Rufus away from the other children, Rufus wanted to know why he had to stop playing to talk on the phone. Ida heard his protest and shouted, "IT'S YOUR MOTHER!" Rufus said, "Hi, Mama." He breathed heavily into the phone and continued, "I'm having fun. Love you. Bye." Ida said sternly, "Rufus, if you can't take the time to talk to me, I will have your daddy to bring you home tomorrow!" He put on his father's whisper and quipped, "Mama, as much as I love you, I got to come home?" He knew he had her when he heard her laughter. Rufus was too much like his father, she thought. How could she not allow him to stay? However, the conversation ended on a happy note. Mae Alice and Ruthie Lee promised to have Wilbur to call home if Ida didn't reach him at the family house.

Wilbur was sitting and drinking bottle after bottle of beer and waiting to dance. He double tied his shoestrings and put music on the turntable of the record player. The phone rang. It was Cap saying that the load had been delivered to Fort Benning, Georgia. "Crazy-little-mama—came knocking-knocking-on-my-front-door," the record crooned melodious words that made Wilbur rock with a feeling. "Crazy-little-Mama-came-knock-knock-knocking—just-like-she-did-before." The next time the phone rang, it was Ida. Wilbur and Rufus told her the exact same words. She was trying to tell him off about the way that he and his sisters had set up a scheme behind her back. The insult was greater than the crime. She asked him a question that he could not answer. Ida asked, "Now, Wilbur! Can you and your sister fix my heart break?" He knew the answer and all he could do was continue to tell his wife how much he loved her. The way that he talked could have easily turned into phone sex but her doorbell rang. They kissed goodbye. She was crushed but vowed to not dwell on it. Wilbur hung up the phone and the song continued, "But-I-didn't-want-to do-it, no-no-I-didn't-want-to-do-it. I-tried-not-to-do-it-but-she thrilled-me-so." Ida opened her door for the women's church group. At the beginning of the meeting, seven women were seated around Ida's kitchen table. Baskets for five needy families in the community were on the agenda to be packed and delivered that evening. Before they started, Mother Ellis, aged 53, sang a song and the others joined in to blend their voices in harmony with devotion to God. Another member of the group read a bible verse. Ida prayed a prayer of thanksgiving while they all joined hands. The women were satisfied that they were all on one accord which was a dominant factor in their Statement of Purpose concerning the church. The meeting's discussion led to the reasons why designated families were chosen to receive the baskets rather than others who were previously cited as being in need. Ida explained that circumstances had changed since the previous meeting. She had talked with two of the families who felt that they didn't need the basket because they knew of someone who desperately needed help. While they talked, more women came bearing turkeys, hams, fresh vegetables, corn meal, flour, sugar, eggs and cranberries. Ida had a bushel of sweet potatoes, pounds of butter and various spices in her basement. She solicited help from some of the other women to bring her bounty upstairs to the kitchen. A few of the women had questions about Callie's whereabouts and her pregnancy. They were shocked to find that Callie was indeed with Dude, her husband on the military base. Unknown to Ida, some of the women had heard that Shirley, Dude's jilted girlfriend, had gone down to spend the holidays with Dude. Ida's heart was singing "Yes Jesus loves me," on the inside while she answered their questions. After Ida told them the style by which Callie traveled, all questions ceased. The women delivered the baskets in pairs. Ida was one of the drivers. Mother Brown rode with her to deliver the food to a couple that had seven small children and had just moved into four small rooms. Sam Lane, the father, was employed but could not afford the extras for the holiday clothing and gifts. They expressed how grateful they were to be able to forgo shopping for the meal. Their Children would now receive warmer clothing and a few toys from Santa Claus. Ida took Mother Brown home and walked back into her own house, a free woman. She looked around and smiled. Ida removed and hung up her coat a few seconds before Callie called with good news. The first question Callie asked Ida was, "Remember the story about the three little hens?" Ida said, "Callie, now I know you've lost your mind." Callie said, "Girl, I met them!" Between several bouts of giddiness, Callie began to describe the ladies and told Ida the whole story in such a comical way that the two sisters laughed like children. Ida remembered to tell Callie of the last conversation she'd had with their mother, Effie about how well the family was doing. Their brother, Lil" John had wedding plans in the making and Farmer Wilson celebrated another birthday with an enormous party which was always a huge celebration because it was near Christmas time. There was something Callie meant to say to Ida while she spoken about the party, but her memory failed her so she opted to get off the phone until she and Dude could find out about the long distance charges. They ended their conversation, wished one another a Merry Christmas and hung up the phone promising to keep in touch. Ida noted that Callie never asked how Wilbur and Rufus were doing, with-her-selfish-ass.

Wilbur danced. Horns blared. "Bah DA DA DA DA DA DA Dop. Bah da da da da da da dop, ba do-ba do-ba do-ba do,-doooo-do do do do tooooo." Happy sat and watched Wilbur's movements and remembered how the slaves would find freedom in moving to rhythms created by simplistic means. They made rhythm sticks from hollow reeds and together had created patterns of rhythm. In spite of their oppressed spirits and tired bodies, a yearning within their inspired souls caused them to dance. Happy Merriweather wept and lifted a toast to Charley Avery whom he believed was smiling on his two beloved sons from above.

Alma sat contemplating whether to call Shirley or not. They had talked to Callie and found that Callie was headed to the Army base to be with Dude, her husband. A week before then, Alma noted, Shirley had planned to leave to go down to the base to attend Dude's graduation. She then looked at the calendar and realized that it was already too late to call Shirley because according to what Shirley had said during their last conversation, she was already down in Georgia. There was nothing to do but wait for Shirley call to let her know what was going on. Alma, Gerta, Marie and their mother, Iris had each invited guys over to help decorate the Christmas tree after a small brunch. Iris had someone coming that they had never met. Alma had tried to invite Mack but he said that he would not be in town. He was Jewish and celebrated in a different manner, but Alma had no way of knowing. Marie invited her friend Charles who was a playboy but loved the way that she carried herself. From time to time she would allow him to try his many charming attributes on her. One night with Charles was enough to keep her satisfied for months at a time. Gerta had someone coming who was a great storyteller and wanted to marry her. She just was not ready to mother anyone. She loved being his paramour. Charles Brown sang softly from the radio, "Merry Christmas baby, you sure did treat me nice*****," the melody was sweet . . . The table was set with small china dishes and beautifully polished silverware. The menu was smoked

salmon, steamed jumbo shrimp, hot potato salad and stuffed clamshells. The
food was just enough to whet their appetites for the meal on Christmas Day.
When Iris's guest walked in, the girls knew that he was someone special. Iris sat
and chatted with her guests and watched her daughters work the room. A few
of their neighbors came over and called others who came to celebrate and
arrived with covered dishes and bottles of wine. They did not mean to allow
Dude's first Christmas away from home to be a solemn occasion for his family.
Someone shouted, "Let's get merry, but if you can't get her, choose somebody
else!" The music changed to a jitterbug beat and the house rocked with gayety.
After the last guest left, the girls rushed to get things like the rugs on the floor
straightened out, the table cleared, dishes washed and put away and the house
back to normal. They then sat down for a final nightcap before going to bed.
This was one of the most favorite times of the year for the four women and
hosting a short and sweet cocktail party was something that they enjoyed
doing as often as their schedules allowed. During their own after party they
would serve the latest gossip and oracles on a platter. Each of them would sit
and speculate and evaluate every guest, one by one. Before they could begin
their fun conversation on that particular night, the phone rang. Alma who sat
nearby answered the phone. It was Shirley on the other end. She asked how
everyone was. Alma told her that they were fine and asked where she was
calling from. Shirley said that she had been in Georgia for two days and Dude
had arranged for her to rent a room near the base. When the time came for she
and Dude to get together, Callie had showed up at the train station. She told
about the bouquet of flowers and the white folks that cheered Callie on after
they saw Dude. Shirley took a deep breath and declared, "Somebody done put
some shit in the game!" She then asked, "Why would he tell me to meet him
at the train station if he knew that Callie was going to be there?" To defend her
brother, Alma answered, "He had to make sure that you understood what was
happening, Shirley. If he had asked anyone else to tell you, his business would
have been all over the army base." Shirley then asked, "Girl, did you know
that I was about to quit my job and move south to be closer to Dude?" Alma
covered her mouth to try not to laugh. To her, Shirley sounded like a star-
addled fool. She answered, "Naaaww, Girl. You better stay where you're able
to take care of your self. Dude has a wife, Shirley." Shirley said that someone
was at her door and put the phone down to answer it. Alma heard her brother's
voice talking bullshit to Shirley and heard simple-ass Shirley shouting, "Oh,
Baby!" The phone was hung up in Alma's face. She muttered, "Damn fool!"
and turned to her sisters with her mouth still open with surprise. Alma had

everyone's full attention while she gave the low down on what was happening on the base at Fort Benning. Iris did not feel like hearing any of it. She had suffered enough behind her husband's shenanigans. Ennis Nelson, Sr. had been a real "whipper-snapper" with his prize penis. She excused herself and went into her bedroom and closed the door. As long as her husband had been dead, there was a woman at church who had an affair with him that still, after seven long years, rolled her eyes whenever she saw her. Iris was never a dummy. She deliberately gave her life over to the care of her family only she never expected to lose her identity in the process. Ennis Sr was never obligated to anything besides going to work and paying the bills. Iris often wondered what it was that made the man decide to pretend to acquire an interest for emptying trash. Out of the blue he started to take trash to the back alley each night. The children were still in grade school and he worked during the day. After dinner, he and Iris would sit and talk while the children played before bedtime. On weekends, beginning on Friday night after dinner, Iris would sit and watch him get dressed to go out to hang with his buddies. He was free to party as long as he could stand up. Iris focused on her home and children. Only once in a while, she would allow a babysitter to come into her home after the children were asleep to watch them while she went out. Iris allowed her husband to tip around for two nights to empty the trash. On the third night, she walked out of the front door and stood on the side of the house to watch while he walked out of the back door. Iris waited until he put his arms around the woman and walked her into the shadows of the alley. The woman was too startled to react when Iris grabbed her and began to drag her back into the yard. Ennis Sr ran off and left the woman to fend for her self. He ran all the way down the alley and around the block to get back home and into his front door to sit down as if he had no knowledge of what was happening in his backyard. The children heard the woman screaming and ran out of the back door to find Iris tearing the woman's clothing off and daring the woman or any of them to cover her body with so much as a blade of grass. Iris slapped the woman and yelled, "Bitch! If you pick up a stitch, I'm gonna kick your ass again!" The woman tried to run and Iris flogged her with a shoe and yelled, "Walk your naked ass home, you cow walking hussy!" Iris's girls cried and pleaded with their mother to let the lady put her dress on but Iris was not in the mood to show mercy. Finally, the woman walked as fast as Iris allowed her to walk and a neighbor ran to cover her with a blanket. Iris yelled, "That's right, let her go and fuck your man!" The thing that enraged Iris after calming the children down was her husband sitting in the living room like he hadn't seen or heard a thing. She was completely out of breath and holding back big drops of crocodile tears when she asked him the question, why? He looked at her and asked, "What woman you talking about, Iris?" Iris was too tired and frustrated to argue and too disappointed in her husband to look him in the face. A few weeks later, she suffered with symptoms of palsy and began to take the time to sort things out concerning her husband's infidelities. For years she'd focused on his actions. She decided to focus on herself and her health. For a short while after the Daisy incident, Iris would creep down to Nolia's back bedroom at night, but little Janie had cramped her style. Nolia slept so soundly that George would have her screaming and Nolia wouldn't budge. She laughed as she remembered how glad she had been when Maggie, George's sister, took Janie out of there. She then remembered meeting her sweet "Daddy." One of the sweetest men who ever walked the earth gave her a son and allowed her to name him, Ennis Nelson, Jr., after the man of her house who had fucked his way out of the finer things of life. Iris wandered back into the room where the girls were and listened to the latest gossip. She realized that if she wanted to, she could tell them enough about their own mother to shut them up for life. Her man belonged to someone else but his heart belonged to her. If she had liked Shirley better, she would have helped her to win Dude over, but Callie had his heart. She knew that no one could mess with that. Iris prayed that he could keep the girl he wanted and loved to death.

Dude left Shirley in a rush to get back to base by eleven o'clock and he made it by a hair. His street smarts helped him to decide to keep quiet about everything until he could slow walk the shit down or until the baby was born and he then could see whom it was that the baby looked like. He loved their living arrangements and wondered when he would have to settle up. His mind began to wander and Dude remembered how his mother would find out things and worry about other women who chased his father. His father would say to her when she would interject accusation or suspicions into their conversation, "Hell Iris, Everybody goes when the wagon comes." It meant that he was the boss in that house. He was the wagon; he was the one with authority. Dude had pampered Shirley the best that he could have. Knowing how her emotional tendencies were, he coaxed her into going home to wait for him. She left Fort Benning with a smile on her face. Dude had cried while he spoke of missing her. Shirley mistook his deceit for sorrow. She was home a week before anyone knew that she was back in town. Noreen, her friend from the doctor's office passed by her house and caught the lights on so she stopped by. Within two hours there were people partying all over her house.

The guys ran to the state line for liquor while the women cooked fish and chicken. It took Shirley two days and three nights to have the privilege of being alone again. The third day brought some of her close neighbors to her house bearing gifts and the desire to hear all about her trip to Georgia. They all had a good time and applauded Shirley when she told them that all she could do was wait until Dude made up his own mind concerning his marriage. She stressed the point that it was not her intentions to continue her dedication to him. From her tip jar, she counted a little over a hundred dollars. The card games that she had hosted paid off for her.

Happy and Wilbur set the town on its heels that Sunday evening. They watched women swoon and taunt them with fine shapes and stares. Wilbur whispered to Happy, "Man, it will be a long time before my dick gets hard. I don't want a woman until I see Ida. I almost lost everything while skidding in bullshit." He still had a good time watching Happy make women beg and buy him drinks. He laughed when he imagined the look that Dude must've had on his face when Callie arrived. He then thought of something that had tried to enter into his mind but time had been of the essence and he'd had to react. The thought was, "Something was missing from the facts. Was Callie crazy enough to allow her to become pregnant by her sister's husband and not have sense enough to get from around her sister?" Something, he decided, had to be missing from the equation. Maybe it was Dude's baby, he concluded while drinking the next shot of rum.

Ida crawled between her sheets and whispered another prayer of thanksgiving. Her personal agenda was beginning to evolve and she was prepared to call the shots. She was looking forward to seeing Mack whom she knew was waiting to show her how much he cared and to give her his love.

Callie and Dude kept missing one another. When Callie was awake, he was gone. If Dude came home, she was asleep. She could tell that he was bathing and changing clothes in the house but other than that, Callie was alone and satisfied to not be bothered. Callie received a letter from the doctor's office with instructions and her appointment schedule. Each day she would walk around the complex several times to rid herself of sluggishness from the meals she had digested and slept on. On the Thursday before her scheduled doctor's appointment Dude walked in while she stood in the living room. Dude was charmed by Callie's beauty. She was wholesome looking and radiant. Most of all he was glad that she was his. Callie walked over to the sofa and sat down. Dude followed her and sat down placing her feet in his lap. While he massaged Callie's feet she fell asleep until she felt his kisses on her toes. "Baby," he whispered, I'll be back at 6:30." She got up and walked him to the door, gave him a kiss and he was gone. Callie gave a big sigh of relief. Callie really did not feel like being bothered but her common sense told her that the caliber of her present lifestyle was worth the sacrifice to keep her husband satisfied. At 6:30 she was stepping out of the bathtub where she floated and relaxed her body. She broiled pork chops, steamed some spinach and cooked wild rice for a starch. After dinner with her husband, she led Dude to the living room and turned on the radio for soft music to soothe him. They sat quietly and listened for a long time. Finally Dude spoke. "Callie," he said, "If you had it to do all over again, would you marry me?" She looked into his eyes and wanted to say something as beautiful as he had asked her but her mind went blank. He didn't try to analyze what had just happened because his heart was contented. He had a ring in his pocket that he was going to give Shirley just to make her day. He decided to use common sense and return it to the jewelry store. Whatever gift he gave to Callie, he wanted it to be special. The music continued to play and they continued to listen until Callie broke the silence. She told her husband about her experiences of surrounding herself with needy people. She decided to change some of the words concerning the needs of others. She felt that she needed people around her that she could handle. She felt safe in the company of peers who wanted her to be happy. What Callie really meant was that she was a very self-centered person. Dude was too in love to hear. He talked and for some reasons, he wanted to tell Callie about Shirley who wanted him so badly that it really was not good for her. Neither of them felt that any understanding would come out of that type of conversation had so they talked about music instead. It was fun to explore the meanings of words like, "ooh-I, hit 'em in-the-eye. I'm gonna git you sweetie-pie!" Or, "Drinkin' wine, mop-mop!" During the lighter moments of conversation, Callie made herself the third person and shared stories of episodes that had occurred around the bend of the road between classmates. Dude told of a friend of his being pursued by a woman who would not let go. After all was said, they ended the evening by dedicating themselves to each other with a strong determination to work their marriage towards the favor of God. Dude was still a might wary of the baby being his, but he had to make himself be patient in waiting to see. They slept in each other's arms that night. The daylight came too soon. Dude only had 12 hours of guard duty and he would be free to spend the day with Callie. They invited a few people over for an evening of caroling. Dude was anxious for Callie to teach the other ladies the "calico rock." The other wives came in with covered dishes and the men, bottles of booze. The men talked sports while the women swapped recipes. Callie enjoyed telling the story of train rides and the three little hens. It shifted the separation of the sexes and one by one story was told that topped the last one told. While the night was still young, they sipped on mixed drinks and lay in the middle of the floor to laugh at tall tales. Someone put on the music. "Silver Bells" rang out and started the couples dancing. "Here comes Santa Clause" and the song, "White Christmas" led into Callie dancing the "Calico Walk." Everyone left the gathering happy and singing Christmas Carols. Dude and Callie were tired but happy. They went to bed after turning out the lights and blowing out candles. The happy couple managed to talk themselves to sleep while they reviewed some of the tales.

"One early morning when I went walking, I met a woman and we started talking. I took her home to get a few nips and all I had was one mint julep. One mint julep was the cause of it all." Wilbur dreamed that he was sitting in the middle of the ocean sipping on a mint julep. When he woke up the next morning he was ready to head back to Indiana. He had watched Happy collect money all night long from his stable of women who had come into town to work. The city of Atlanta was growing at a rapid pace and Happy Merriweather had managed to keep up with most of the social activities and local politicians. A venture into a Men's store or two set many a man up for deals of a lifetime. Contracts and contacts were in the midst of exciting times and Mr. Merriweather had a handle on both. Wilbur found that he hadn't known as much about himself or his family as he thought he had. His father taught him well of business skills of his time. Wilbur needed to hear more about his heritage some of which Happy told him but were never discussed nor taught him by his parents. There were monies coming from a trust that dated back to the 1920's and handled by a firm in New York. Time would not allow him to explore the matters. Wilbur was looking forward to seeing his wife who had no idea who the man she was married to was. He was just finding out himself. He was the son of Charley Avery, a man of means and character. Wilbur could not believe the amount of money shown in the last entry of the Bank's Book that Ruthie handed to him. The book bore his name. He'd set up a trust for Rufus as it was stipulated in a copy of his father's will and he was given the names of the people listed on their family's tree. It contained the names of a State Senator and a Congressman from Mississippi. It did not make him proud.

Ida wanted to have the time of her life. She began going to the shop to situate things for her place in the business partnership. Mack helped Ida to order fabric that she foresaw as trend setting. Her mother and grandmother had taught both she and Callie to be pace setters. They ordered catalogs of patterns and accessories. When the shipments came in Ida and Mack got busy cutting swatches from the materials to keep on the sales floor with the catalogs of patterns to be viewed by the customers. It came as a surprise to her how Mack had toned down his feelings during store hours. It had been one of her concerns. She found that they indeed made a good team but she also wondered if the women kept coming to the store to see what they could make of her presence. On Christmas Eve, Mack gave her a call and asked if she would accompany him to a special family celebration. The two of them planned for her to begin to do more accounting in the store after the holiday season. Mack provided a room for all of her sewing needs and storage in one of the small apartments of his building. She went through her closets to find the outfits that would help create a wardrobe that she felt most appropriate for her new job. Ida didn't know it but Mack wanted to use her finesse to prove to his parents that the idea of him bringing in a skillful seamstress and partner could work. She broke away from what she had been doing to sit and figure out how she could go out and be home to greet her husband. The phone rang again. It was Wilbur telling her that he would be home for dinner on Christmas Day. Ida hurried to call her long distance family members to let them know that she was fine and to wish them Merry Christmas. She spent a little time grooming herself and getting dressed. Mack was on time to pick her up. He had asked her to wear one of the several dresses he'd given her and she looked gorgeous. He showed up with a tree after she told him that she could not carry a tree up the stairs alone. She got the box marked "holiday" from her storage room and threw up her usual decorations. As usual she left a few things off that Rufus always hung on the tree. Mack wanted to stay right where they were and the looks he gave Ida made her feel a little sorry for him. In small movements she taunted and teased him out of his romantic mood so that they could be on their way to the celebration. She wrinkled her nose and did silly dances to make him laugh while she put her coat on and stayed clear of his arms that reached for her. When they reached the bottom of her stairs, she leaned towards him and gave him one of her savory kisses to tide him over until the appropriate time for their lovemaking. She knew that he would not ask to climb those stairs again. Mack handed Ida the car keys for her to get into the car first while he watched to see who was watching her. When he was satisfied that it was safe enough to be undetected, he walked to the car and closed the door as quietly as he could. Ida had turned the inside lights off so that she sat in darkness and he could then enter the darkened car. They were soon headed west towards the Windy City of Chicago. Christ was the reason for the season, so Ida whispered a prayer to thank Him for coming into the world by Immaculate Conception and virgin birth to assume a personality. She looked at the bright lights on the horizon and heard jingles in the air that made her euphoric. Lakeshore Drive had a life of its own. On the outside, the weather was brisk and cold. A man walked out of the building where Mack stopped the car to open the door and park the car for them. Mack who wore a black tailored suit and black derby on his head looked distinguished and reserved as he held onto Ida as if she might disappear any minute. She watched him open a big box and thought it strange for him to leave her inside the car to open the trunk of the car. He then opened her door, and asked her to remove her coat. Mack held a fur coat that he threw around her shoulders. Ida had no idea what prestige came with the gift. He saw her smile and delighted in the fact that she made no big deal out of it. The elevator ride to the penthouse was exhilarating and Mack found it hard to refrain from petting. Ida allowed him to kiss her but warned him about messing up her makeup. The elevator door opened to reveal a magnificent view of Lake Michigan's shoreline in lights. Mack introduced her to so many people that she knew that the probability of remembering names was not on any agenda. She did remember the heavy weight champion of the world, Joe Louis. There were others too. Dorothy Dandridge, Sara Vaughn, Count Basie, Nat Cole and Pearl Bailey were sitting or standing to talk with first one person and then another. They all seemed like common folk out to have a nice time. Mack put a drink in her hand and the first sip made her a bit more aware and open to conversation. Mack suggested something to eat and made their way over to the buffet where there was food to die for. They filled their stomachs with seafood that Ida never knew existed. While they sat and relaxed over a second drink, Ida heard her name in a song that Nat Cole sang. "Ida, the girl from Carolina," was a song that had been requested so that Mack could lead her to the parquet dance floor where he planned to run into his parents. Mr. and Mrs. Joseph Nickles were impressed that Mack's choice for a business partner was young, beautiful and poised. Ida noted that his mother wore expensive jewelry and a gown that made a fashion statement. She saw a familiar cut of the fabric that was sewn against the grain to form a perfect fit for the bust line. Nat Cole began to sing, "Kitty-o" and Mack gave Ida a spin that she came out of doing the Lindy Hop. They shook the place up with their dance steps and made it come alive with celebration. Mack would turn Ida at the right times and stand poised while he allowed her to play back to him with jesters of entertainment. It made him look suave and debonair to serve her a drink after a beautiful and graceful spin. They received a standing ovation. They then took pictures with the stars. Ida and Mack were shown in a publication of the Chicago Defender Newspaper and listed as, "Partners in the Dressmaking Industry." Ida remembered a few things about the evening before, but the gift of the fur was still fresh in her memory. She and Mack had said their goodbye and she remembered being made comfortable in the car for the drive home. Her mind went to Mack and his ability to make her feel wonderful and completely satisfied. What she could not remember was the ride home and how she undressed and got into bed. Evidently, Mack had even hung up her clothes. She hoped that she was alone in the house because no one but Wilbur had that option whether to stay or go. Ida feared getting out of bed but she forced herself to get up and search the premises. She even went to the basement to look. She breathed a sigh of relief when she found no evidence of Mack being there except how she felt within. A lobster dinner sat on her stove. A bottle of champagne sat chilled in her refrigerator. Ida turned on the radio and ran a hot bath. It was noon and there were some things that she wanted to do before Wilbur arrived. Ida relaxed in the warm bath until the water began to feel cool. She scrubbed her body with lavender scented soap. After she rinsed the soap off her body, and climbed out of the tub, Ida made a pot of strong black coffee. She looked around the house to make sure that everything was in its usual place. Subliminal memories of she and Mack's passionate moments on her living room sofa sent her to dig down into the sofa's crevices to be sure that no evidence would turn up and cause Wilbur to become suspicious. The warmed over lobster in lemon butter sauce was delicious. After eating her fill, Ida ran downstairs to the alley to give the leftovers to a cat that would not leave a trace of evidence. She came back and prepared her vegetables and desert for Wilbur's dinner. A glance into the back bedroom made her remember Callie's foolish question about raising her child. She wondered if Dude had left her. "Oh, Hell Naw!" she said aloud. She wondered who the father of the baby was. Surely Callie would not have asked such a thing if the father were Dude. It was Christmas day. The doctor was not in the office. Ida wondered how she could get more information on Callie's condition. The phone rang. It was Wilbur. When she asked about Rufus, he reminded her that Rufus would stay in Athens another week. She made a remark that made him feel sorry for her. She said, "Lord, I must be losing my mind to have agreed that my child could stay away from me that long." Wilbur asked, "Should I turn around to go back and get him?" He'd wanted to give her the chance to feel in control again. Desperation caused him to betray all that he had become to her. She treated Rufus better than any mother other than his own, could have. She was fortunate enough to have used her youth to create a strong bond between her and Rufus. He felt her remorse. Ida asked, "Where are you?" He heard her voice quiver and said, "I'll be home in three to five hours, depending upon the weather." She said, "Come on home Wilbur. It's too late to turn around." He had once again played Ida like a piano. Wilbur hung up the phone and danced his way back to the car. He saw himself driving through the storms of life but knew that the strong winds were beginning to die down. Ida cried. She had been tricked.

She opened her champagne and enjoyed the song on the radio. It was Christmas time in the city so she willed herself happy and drank until the bottle was empty. She set the table for two using her holiday china and crystal glasses. Her silverware sparkled from being used during thanksgiving so she had little to do to give it a perfect shine. Wilbur entered the house loaded down with packages. He picked Ida up and carried her into the living room. She had her face buried in his chest and could feel his heartbeat. Wilbur placed a mink cape around her shoulders and handed her a gift from his sisters and Rufus. When she opened the gift from Rufus, Ida cried. It was a picture of himself with her standing watch over him, in the background. She sent Wilbur to take his bath and cried. Her tears were cut short when she remembered the mink that Mack gave her for Christmas. Ida ran to her closet and there it hung in plain sight. Fortunately she had a cloth garment bag from the store that she used to transport special items. She rushed to put the coat into the garment bag and tagged it for January 12th. It now belonged to a customer.

Before Wilbur came out of the bathroom, she hung the coat in Callie's closet. It had been such a close call that the thought of Rufus didn't bother her any more. Mae Alice and Ruthie sent her an ensemble of a satin robe, matching house shoes and bedspread. She reminded herself to look for a satin robe for her brother, Lil' John so that she could send them the ensemble. She had no use for anything that they had to offer. Wilbur came out of the bathroom and shared a beautiful and delicious meal with his wife. Her gift to him was a Stetson hat and a pair of Stacy Adams shoes. She sent him to bed and cleaned up the kitchen before she retired for the night. Old Man Winter threw a white blanket of snow over the community during the night and made it clean and cozy. Wilbur woke up and reached for Ida but her side of the bed was empty. The coffee was not brewing so he rolled over. Weariness overcame him again and he dropped off to sleep. Wilbur thought about women and saw his self on a barstool. A giant pair of red lips nipped at his penis until he tried to run. The lips smiled and showed beautiful white even teeth. He cried "No!" but the lips said, "Yes." His ejaculation was so forceful that he began to pray. When he woke up the second time, he smelled breakfast and fresh brewed coffee. Ida sat at her kitchen table and thanked God for giving her a mind to think with. The phone rang and it was Dude on the line. He was sitting at the hospital waiting for Callie to deliver. Ida asked, "Its being born a little soon isn't it?" Wilbur heard the conversation and pulled his pants on and rushed into his shirt and shoes. He turned on his heels to leave the bedroom and headed towards the kitchen. He yelled over his shoulder, "See you later, baby." Ida said, "Wait!" but he was gone. Wilbur drove off in an attempt to ease away but he was a spinning wheel. Ida tried to make small talk and ended the conversation saying, "Call me. I hope you get your boy." Dude chuckled and almost said the same thing back to her. Ida began counting on her fingers. She figured the baby would be born around Mother's Day in May. Even if she was already pregnant by Dude it couldn't have been but a month unless she fucked him the same day that she had met him. "Still, she . . . Wait . . . now! . . . One . . . . fuckin' minute." Ida decided to just wait. She reasoned that if Callie was pregnant when she came to Indiana, she would have told her or she questioned, "Would she?" Ida called home to tell her mother the news. When she and Effie began to count they began to talk about a premature baby. Ida said to her Mother," No way! Because when Callie left here she was as big as a house . . . . and she asked me the strangest thing . . . " Effie waited for her to continue but Ida's mind was trying to decipher everything. Effie said, "Ida, don't waste your time trying to figure her out. I never mentioned this before but . . . " Johnny JR walked through the door and Effie had to leave off speaking. When Ida heard the, "Hi, Honey," she knew that it was time to hang up the phone. She teased her mother and father about becoming grandparents and hung up the phone. Ida thanked God for allowing her to do the business venture. Wilbur was scheduled to return to work and she was ready to, "Do her Thaaaaang!" The sun came out and began melting the icy shards that hung from the rooftops. Dripping water from icicles made a tinkling sound. Puddles formed on the ground. The rhythmic drips from the roof echoed with harmony while tiny drops of water fell into puddles. Ida reflected upon how she'd always felt when rain interrupted her chances of seeing Wilbur working across the pasture that belonged to Farmer Wilson. She took it as a sign to focus on her personal interests and go to work. She got dressed. Wilbur flexed his muscles while lying in bed and speculated for about ten minutes before he allowed his feet to touch the floor. With desire aflame in his loins, he walked wide legged into the kitchen to find Ida completely dressed. He opened his robe and leaned against the door jam with his arms folded. Ida looked at him and used her best expression that said, "What?" Wilbur used a steady gaze for her eyes to follow his eyes straight down to his point of interest. Ida blinked and looked at herself being fully dressed. She threw back her head and laughed. Wilbur went into the bathroom to relieve himself and after washing his face and hands, he walked out stark naked heading towards Ida, who was determined to go to the shop that day. She slowly backed away from her husband who wore the same old tired ass look that captured her fast ass in the first place. Ida felt frustration at her inability to resist Wilbur's untimely advances when she melted in his arms. She followed him into the bedroom and wondered why she continued to be unable to resist his hard muscles and charming ways that set her body on fire. While she yipped he yapped. They both prayed because their bodies had minds of their own. He felt the lips. The big red lips of his dream devoured him while he tried to climb from a tall stool. The lips swallowed and he cried out even louder than he had the first time he had the dream. Wilbur slept until five o'clock that evening. Ida was in the back bedroom. When she heard him begin to stir around in the front bedroom, she ran his bath water and fixed his dinner. It was her plan to have Wilbur to take the bed downstairs so that she could make the backroom into her cutting room. He suggested that she exchange it with the smaller bed in Rufus' room so that it would give her more space and also keep the extra bedroom. During dinner Ida talked about her women's church group and the new pastor that had been voted in to replace Pastor Jack Benson. She told Wilbur of the incident with Alma when she and Rufus shopped for Mae Alice and Ruthie Lee's gifts. "Mr. Nickles really does need help in his store. Since Rufus stayed down south, I think I'll go on and start this week. I got orders from the Mother's Board for Mother's Day dresses and it's a dozen or so of them. I may as well get paid by the store while I'm making them." Wilbur sat watching her lips while she talked and wondered about something but he kept it to himself. Happy, he knew, was a true brother in every sense of the word. He thought of the dream but Happy Merriweather had pulled magic out of a hat. His arms were the longest that Wilbur had ever witnessed. He sat with a smile on his face remembering the sound of Hap's voice when he'd whispered, "Hey! Cap!" and shit started to roll a thousand miles away. It reached from Indiana all the way to Fort Benning, Georgia. He and Ida sat smiling and holding hands not knowing that they each had their separate thoughts shrouded in secrecy.

Mack's burdens were lifted by Ida's ingenuity. She'd mastered the store's routine in record time. Mack decided to venture into textiles and Ida began to get her materials dirt cheep. She also found a place to cut and sew her clothes for bulk orders. They would have her dresses made in a day or two where it took her two or three days to make one dress. Ida learned to give the clothing her personal touch with hand-stitched ornaments and accessories. Instructions were given for the manufacturer to leave hems and certain seams undone so that her handiwork would be recognized. Ida only had to sew her tag on the inside and press the orders for delivery. When the extra week was ended and the time for Rufus to return to Indiana was at hand, Wilbur pretended that he couldn't get off work. Ida simply waited until he decided to tell her the truth. In her heart she already knew that they had taken Rufus away from her. Wilbur tried to calm the storm by switching to the day shift so that Ida would never be home alone. It was not really because he'd cared so much for her, but Ida was moving a little too fast for him. She had always been the perfect homemaker but lately. Her little ass was just too perfect. Well, Ida figured that she was a free woman. She told herself that her son and husband belonged to a family who was not her family. A letter had come from the school telling her that her request for Rufus' school records was forwarded to Claremont Elementary School in Athens Georgia. She put it in the back bedroom with her other business papers and waited for Wilbur to tell her. That night she went to bed and received a call from Mack to meet him at the store. Wilbur was done with nights but had filled in for one of the supervisors. Mack and Ida made love over and over throughout the night and Ida knew that she was going to stay home the next day. She walked into the door and Wilbur stood there asking to know what time she'd left. She asked him when he was going to bring Rufus home. She told him that she had went back to finish some things at the store in order to keep a doctor's appointment for that day. Wilbur doubled back for the day shift and called home every hour on the hour to try and keep up with Ida. Mae Alice had told him that the child had too many relatives to be raised without them. She simply had not considered Ida's feelings. Athens became Rufus' home. He loved it. Down in Athens, Georgia the children returned to school the Monday after Christmas. Rufus was taken to school with his cousin, Fredrick, who was one of Ruthie Lee's stepsons. The teacher acted as if he had been there all the time. Mae Alice had called Happy who called a school board member to get the registration process moving. Cecelia Morgan, the teacher of the class was given information that she used to request records from Indiana. All of the necessary arrangements had been taken care of before Christmas Day. Rufus scouted around with his cousins and fascinated them with his knowledge of trucks and tractors. His grandparents loved to spend time with him and were grateful to God for having him around. They had bonded quickly because he saw his own features on their faces. Ida began to call him weekly and promised to visit. She wondered how anyone could break her heart without having any regard for her feelings. Rufus had given her enough responsibility in her life to help her mature at a normal pace. The two of them had grown into mother and son. She saw that she was going to have to teach a few people a lesson.

Dude and Callie lost themselves in each other. Graduation was over and they both gave a sigh of relief when it was over. Callie continued to be her husband's pride and joy while he prayed to God for strength to accept whatever came out of their situation. Dude was so in love with his wife that his platoon members wondered how he could take their teasing so well. From time to time when they would begin to tease him, he would pull her picture out and show it. They knew that she was a knockout. Some of them would whistle and shake their heads. While they swooned he would laugh. Callie treated him like he was her Prince Charming within the confines of their home. The house was always neat and clean and he began notice some of Callie's actions. Dude saw the Ida in her personality. Another time he wondered if he saw traces of Effie in the way she acted. Often times when she made him "holler" in ecstasy, Dude wondered if it was Grandma Mable's antics that she had laid on him. During the month of January, Callie increased her walking. She tried hard to follow doctor's orders. Many of their neighbors began walking with Callie to keep her encouraged. On Valentine's Day, her water broke. Dude was out in the field and was scheduled to be gone a week. Callie got dressed and went to the hospital alone. Since her pains had not started, the trip was not stressful in any way. There were so many things running through her mind that was positive that Callie decided to make her mind up concerning the baby's future. If it looked like Wilbur, she would go home and leave it with her mother. In a week, she figured to be down in Alabama. Dude was the person who had to obey military orders, but not her, she thought to herself. The first painful pressure gripped Callie around one o'clock in the afternoon. She lay and watched the movement of her stomach with interest until the pains began to come more often. Callie's unbearable pain caused her to become nauseated and she finally yelled for help. There was a flurry of activity that she totally ignored to concentrate on relieving her body from its trauma. She felt the searing hot tearing of her vagina and something felt like hot rubber tumbling out on the table. Many hands seemed to pummel and knead her abdomen while she lay resting. She awakened at six o'clock that evening and Dude sat at her bedside. She had no idea how long he had been there. The baby weighed six pounds and was 18 inches long. It was a girl. Dude had many questions. The doctor told him that the baby was full term but that any birth weight over five pounds was considered full term. Doctor Samuel had seen families torn apart by suspicions. The army was no place to add to a man's stressful situation. He and Callie had talked and she had shed tears. That being the care that she needed, he promised to fix it so that childbirth would not be a burden. Dr. Samuel kept his promise. Dude sat smiling with a beautiful bouquet of flowers in his hand. He had already seen the baby. She did not favor Wilbur. To him, she looked like his sisters, who favored his father, Ennis Nelson Sr. Since Dude identified with his sisters, he took it for granted that the child was his. He kissed Callie and wished that they could do it all over again. As beautiful and wholesome as she was, Callie had chosen to be his wife and the mother of his children. He remembered calling out to Callie, "Hey, Breeze, what's shaking?" She answered, "Ain't nothing shaking but the leaves on the trees." Laughingly he had finished the rhyme, "and they wouldn't be shaking if it wasn't for the breeze." Dude asked Callie if he could name the baby. Callie didn't remember seeing the baby but smiled and asked him if he was sure that he wanted to take the task upon himself. He reminded her of their first conversation and said," My mother is named after a flower. I've always loved it. There is a tiny flower that grows from a cool green tree that gives off a sweet fragrance throughout the year. The name of the flower is called myrtle. In reality, Callie cared less. She gave him one of her impish smiles and nodded her head to agree with him to name the baby Myrtlennis Nelson. Callie saw the baby when feeding time came around and saw the features of her baby's true father. Dude stayed by her side for as long as he could and when he left, he called home to shout out the good news. After the baby's visit Callie received another visitor. Happy Merriweather posed as a grandparent and was allowed to see the baby through the glass window of the nursery. Captain had been notified of Callie's labor and relayed the message to Happy who had been only a few miles away. Credentials for him had been sent to the guarded gate. He walked into Callie's room and introduced himself to her as one of the instructors on the base. Callie did not smile, but nodded her head and shook his hand. A spark hit Happy and to hide himself from her eyes that drew him in, he bent and gave her a slight kiss on the forehead that smelled of jasmine. He offered congratulations, turned on his heel and marched from the room. The woman was almost too beautiful to have been real. Wilbur would've had to be a punk riding on the spinning wheels of a bicycle to have turned that woman's advances down. Happy wiped his brow after he got into his car and said, "Whew! Great God from Zion!" He called Mae Alice so that she would deliver to Wilbur a message. The words were, "Its time to start a family of your own. You are running behind." When Mae Alice called Wilbur, he was at work. She asked Ida to give him a message. Ida hung up the phone in her face and did her wash. It took his sister two days to get through to him but Ida got a call from Dude. He said that the baby was a beautiful girl who favored his sisters. Ida's mind resorted to shuffling as if it were a deck of cards. She pictured Roger who did not have features of Alma's. Dude's features were mixed between "Daddy" and Iris's good looks. She and Callie's parents or grandparents had no features belonging to Dude's family. Suddenly, Ida received a vision of someone who did favor them and she screamed. Callie had said to her that a lot of things did not make sense. She knew that they needed to talk in a bad way. When she finished her wash, she went to the store to finish ordering a shipment of robes for a church choir. There were Thirty-seven church choir members who had to be measured for robes. Ida solicited her women's church group to help her measure each member. In turn, she made a contribution into the group's treasury. They were ecstatic. It was more than they would have made from their usual selling of chicken dinners having and a social fish fry. It was only six days past the middle of the month of February but March winds had begun to blow. Ida stopped at Iris's house to congratulate her on becoming a grandmother. Iris handed her a picture of the baby that she had received only hours ago from her son. She invited Ida into her bedroom where there were dozens of baby outfits sprawled over the bed in varied sizes. Ida sat down and laughed until she cried, but when she tried to stop crying she couldn't. Iris sat and listened while she talked about Rufus and the way that Wilbur and his family had hurt her. The community all thought that Rufus was Ida's natural child and had not known of Wilbur being a widower. Iris held Ida in her arms until she quieted down and told her how proud she was of her for being strong enough to move forward with her own life. She said, "Ida, you are a young woman. If you wanted to, you could have babies of your own. There are many women who don't have courage enough to mother their own children, not to mention someone else's child. Rufus' deceased mother could not have given Rufus any better care than you have given him. So, Ida, be proud. Be strong. Decide whether you want to have a baby for yourself." The words that Iris spoke felt like a balm that soothed Ida's trampled heartstrings. She realized that she had done a lot of living in a short span of time. She decided to make herself a baby out of her God given talents. Business was booming and she had time on her side. She started reminiscing while she continued her drive to work. Grandma Mable had often made her laugh by using circumstances to add and subtract. Ida decided to try it out on her situation. She gave Wilbur what he'd needed. She was providing Mack Nickles with what he wanted. Rufus was within his rights to be raised by his own people. She whispered, "Three times one equals three." She felt her heartstrings slowly release them in order to fulfill the obligations that she had to herself. At the day's end, Ida had ordered the church robes, given the Mother's Day dress order most of the detail and ornaments and taken in three more orders for church choirs. Wilbur had reheated a meal for dinner and ran her bath water. She smiled but really considered it to be too little too late. While she sat in the tub and washed her body, the phone rang. From Wilbur's tone of voice, she knew that it was one of his sisters. He walked into the kitchen and sat at the table to await Ida's exit from the bathroom. When she stepped from the tub, she turned around to open the drain for the water to go out. Ida felt strong arms hold her and encircle her with a towel. Wilbur's shoulder shook while he cried and begged her to forgive him for hurting her so badly. He came close to confessing everything but he could not bring himself to cancel all of the hard work that had gone into clearing out his house. Ida had no more tears. She allowed him to hold her until he finished crying and watched him dry his eyes. She didn't have any babies. Ida put on underwear and a casual dress and left Wilbur in the bathroom to go and put dinner on the table. After dinner, they sat and talked and made love. Ida felt like she was playing with a brand new toy. She read his face and analyzed his emotions until she decided to go to sleep. Before that night she had not realized that he had been the recipient of what was owed to Rufus. His mother was dead too, she thought. Maybe he needed to be shipped to his family. Ida laughed so hard that she slid from the bed to keep from waking up Wilbur. Her mother called. Ida looked at the clock before answering the phone and was surprised that it was still early in the evening. Effie was excited about the baby and wanted to know how her family was getting along. Ida could hear Grandma Mable's voice in the background of their conversation. She asked to speak to her after she told Effie that she had her own a business. She then had to talk about Rufus. Effie could hear sorrow in her voice and knew that it would take Mable to console her. When Grandma Mable came to the phone, Ida told her about the business. She whooped! And shouted, "Baby, I knew that you would do it one day I wondered what you would do with all of that talent." When Ida described the manufacturing parts of it, Mable said, "Send me five hundred dollars." Ida quipped, "Is that all?" They laughed until Grandma Mable's voice took on a tone of secrecy. She asked, "Did you see your niece's picture, Honey?" Ida answered, "Yes," and covered her mouth. Grandma Mable whispered, "Child, your sister has given birth to something that is not welcome to come home." She continued, "Dora Mae will kill her and Farmer too!" Ida had seen Farmer Wilson's features on the baby's picture also. So Callie had been pregnant when she got to Indiana. Grandma Mable said that she had to get off the phone to console Effie. They said their good-byes and Ida stood with her mouth open. She wondered how many others Callie had screwed before she got to Indiana. Old Farmer Wilson was as ancient as hell and probably had moths in his drawers. Surely Callie did lose her mind. Ida wondered if Roger knew.

In truth, Callie thought that the baby was Wilbur's. She had forgotten about how she had climaxed so long and hard when she allowed old Farmer Wilson to enter her. He had been so long and thick that he'd told her not to move so that it would not hurt so much. She remembered how she'd wiggled from beneath him and ran home with her panties in her hand. She did not remember until she saw Myrtlennis, her baby daughter. Dude had taken over from that point. Myrtle was three years old before Callie's parents saw her. Dude was being shipped overseas and Callie went to Alabama to wait until he sent for them. Farmer Wilson got wind of Callie's arrival and made his way to the Moore farm. Mable sat the baby in his lap. Effie put on her boots and left to get a little fresh air. She was glad that the men had gone into town. Callie walked out of the kitchen and stood behind the old man's chair while he beamed at his daughter. When Mable could take no more, she went into her room and closed the door. Callie took pictures and promised to meet Farmer Wilson later in the day. He gave her five hundred dollars and went home to ravish Dora. It never happened. Dora sat on the porch and was in the middle of a sick spell when he went home. Farmer Wilson heated some water and cleaned his wife up and put her to bed. He was quite slow but he put some meat for soup and took a bath himself. Each time his wife woke up he would either feed her or give her medicine. She said that she felt better and from four in the evening until eight that night, she sat up in a chair and listened to the radio. Callie came over a little before she went to bed and told her adventurous stories and about her comical experiences. When the time for her medication rolled around again, she took it and fell asleep. Callie and Farmer Wilson stood in the shadows of his back yard. He could not keep his hands off of her body. In his barn, they made love by moonlight that filtered in through cracks. Callie could not believe it. Farmer Wilson was the only man to get it right. Her body responded to his slow grinding and opened her spirit like rose petals. He asked her to leave his child there in Atlanta. Callie promised to give it some thought. When Dude sent her the money to travel back to Germany, she went, leaving her daughter, Myrtlennis behind. Ida wanted to kill her. A few months later, Callie wrote that she and Dude were expecting another child and that Dude was just as excited as he had been before. Wilbur and Ida both were glad that they were in Germany.

Ida was making money hand over fist. Wilbur thought that she sewed each day for eight hours straight. During lunchtime, she would take care of Mack's needs and most afternoons, she was in Chicago or some other city attending fashion tradeshows. Mack bought her a home in Atlanta where she would stay for two weeks out of the year. Wilbur would send her to Alabama to visit her parents. She then would drive to Atlanta so that she could visit Rufus who was crazy about Ida, his gorgeous mother. Three days she would give to Rufus. They shopped for school clothes and attended the County Fair faithfully each year. Those three nights she spent in a boarding house. She would round up all of his cousins and treat them to whatever Rufus wanted to enjoy doing with them. Then Mack would Wisk her away to their home hidden in the hills of Atlanta. Any extra time that she took, Wilbur thought that she was buying for the store. He became tired of thinking. His change to the day shift seemed to only complicate things. He felt better when he worked nights and during the day he knew where everyone was that he cared about. His family had split in the blink of an eye and he needed them to be together again. Wilbur began to train his men to do his job. He knew how to complete his supervisor's job in fifteen minutes and get paid for eight hours on the clock. He saw the labels in the back bedroom that read, "Fashions by Miss Ida" or "Around the Bend Fashions." Whenever he would drop by the store, there was Mack and another sales clerk working like beavers but no Ida. He wondered how she managed to do all of that sewing when she was hardly there. Her answer had been simple enough. When she was at the store, Mack was gone. They had different field positions. She and Mack held on to their Monday nights for as long as they could. Ida told Wilbur that she used Monday nights at the shop for alterations and Laid a Way purchases. On Tuesdays she turned in her report and got paid. One Wednesday night, Wilbur left home at 9:30 at night to go to work. There were many trains running and he wanted to give himself plenty of time to get to work. At 2:00 in the morning he went home. He found her bed empty. Ida came rushing through the door at six o'clock in the morning. Wilbur grabbed her and took off his belt. She allowed him to draw back his hand before she made her voice sound as chilling as ice. "Wilbur, if you let it down, you are going to go down with it. I declare before God!" He asked her in a high pitched quivering tone of voice, "Where the hell have you been, woman?" Ida had seen the car when she turned the corner so she doubled back to Iris's house and woke her up to use her telephone to call Mother Brown. Iris had just made it in herself from George's back bedroom down the street. When she answered the door, Ida scooted in pass her and asked, "Girl, where is the phone?" While Ida used the phone, Iris washed up and came back into the living room. Ida whispered, "Mother Brown, you were sick last night and I just left your house. Girl, you were sick!" Ida listened for a second or two and said, "Around midnight. You called me around midnight. Bye!" Iris let Ida out of her back door and whispered, "Keep your cool, now." Ida answered Wilbur with a question of her own. "Now where could I have gone but to sit with somebody sick, Wilbur?" She asked in a stronger voice, "Who the hell is sick?" Ida shrugged out of her coat and headed towards the bathroom as she answered, "Mother Brown. Remember how I had to stay until her daughter got there before?" He asked quickly, "What's her number?" Ida rattled it off as she climbed into the bathtub. She swooshed warm water up her ass and scrubbed her body with the honeysuckle fragrance ivory soap that she has spruced up herself. When her bath was finished, she got out of the tub and wrapped a towel around her body and flung the door open so hard that it hit the wall. Wilbur grabbed her and she flung her fists like a mad woman because he was trying to stick his finger into her vagina. He did it and she tried to slap his face but her hand hit his shoulder instead. He began laughing and trying to hold her while she swung at him. He whispered, "I'm sorry, baby." Ida pretended to be out of breath and went limp in his arms. Wilbur carried her into the bedroom where he laid her in bed and rocked her to sleep. Her last thought before going to sleep was, "Damn, I'm good!" Around the Bend Fashions created the Chemise dress and Wrap around skirt. Grandma Moore called Ida and said, "Girl, send me my money." Ida was putting all of her creations on the racks. She turned the swag of material from the Calico dancer's skirt into a double kick pleat. Her sheik designs were labeled "Miss Ida." Wilbur did not realize who she had become nor did she really know the man she'd married.

  Wilbur and Ida received an invitation to Lil' John's wedding and John and Mable Moore's 50th anniversary Celebration. The dates were two weeks apart.

They planned it that way so that everyone from out of town could plan to be on a two-week vacation. Wilbur was not too keen on it but he didn't want Ida out of his sight for so long. She had too much energy for him. She knew how to put his lights out and have the evenings to herself. The one thing that stayed constant in their lives was her damn honeysuckle. He once thought that she had voo doo'd him with it. One night he took her soap that she'd made and hid it in his car under the front seat. Now his car smelled like honeysuckle and when he went to work, his coworkers accused him of playing around with a sweet smelling young thing. He tried hard to keep Ida hid from the world. Wilbur did increase his poker nights though. Alma tried hard to become a part of his life but he just didn't want to be that close to Dude. One night Wilbur stayed out all night with her and went to work to sleep. She opened every avenue but he just didn't want Alma. They both got drunk and he took her home, helped her drunken ass up the steps to her door and rang the bell. When he saw lights come on in the house, he ran back to his car and took off before anyone could see him. He saw his own house lights on and figured that he had finally caught Ida, with her little slick ass. He'd often had the feeling that she was letting someone fuck her all night. His liquor kept talking. The same Mother damn Brown was the one that only got sick on Monday nights and always at midnight. He almost caught her hot ass but that damn phone call tripped him up. Aloud, he said, "Um Huh!" If he had just felt her pussy at the door, he would have caught her and she would have fainted for real, the liquor said. Wilbur eased into his own house but only found Ida asleep on the couch waiting for him to come home from his poker game. The telephone was in her hand so he hung it up and switched the lights off and went to work. He had a hard time convincing Ida that he had been home. She asked him why he hadn't gotten into bed and he remarked, "I could ask your sweet little ass the same (thaang.) Who do you think hung up the phone?" Wilbur was on a roll. "If I didn't come in, how did the lights get turned off?" He shouted, "Why didn't you tell me about this?" He shoved the old newspaper under her nose that showed her all chic and as fine as hell standing with Nat King Cole, Sarah Vaughn and Dorothy Dandridge at a Christmas Eve Ball. He almost laid his finger on her nose and said, "Ida, I want to trust you 'til I die, but if I ever stick my finger in your little tight pussy and come out with water again, I'm gone. I should 'a whipped you like you'd stole something' that morning!" He ran out of breath and when Wilbur could he continued, "Rather than hurt you girl, I'll leave you and go back to mending fences." Ida tried to get a word in edgewise but he would not stop talking. She grabbed his hand and tried to make him feel or touch her anywhere so that he would come to himself but he had already snapped. The only thing that stopped his tirade was when Ida said, "I was waiting to hear from Callie. Dude called and said that it's a girl and it looks like his side of the family." Wilbur said through his gritted teeth, "I don't give a good damn about no Dude and Callie, Ida. All I care about is you! But you, girl you, you, comin' mighty damn close to hanging on a shoestring." Ida asked him a question that snapped his head back. She calmly asked, "And just what da fuck do you think you're getting close to?" With her head moving from side to side Ida wagged her finger and lowered her voice so that he had no choice but to shut his mouth and listen closely. She said, "You and your family got together against me and took my boy. If his mother is dead and I got the damned daddy, why can't I have his child too?" She asked, "When was the last time a dead person asked you anything" Huh"? Tell me, Wilbur! When you look around this mutha fucka, what do you see? Huh, Wilbur? Ida was so angry that she answered her own question. "You see damned fool like me standing in the middle of this 'got-damned floor, that's what! I was a baby myself when you came and asked my father fu' me. I was given to you to love and cherish and not be mistreated!" Wilbur was so ashamed that he had hurt her that he had hurt her that he walked away. He did not know what else to say. His wife had spoken the truth and that settled it. Ida stood flat footed and dry-eyed waiting for her husband to say another word so that she could chop his ass up into little pieces. Wilbur poured a shot of Old Granddad liquor and opened a can of beer. Ida went to the cupboard and took out a shot glass for herself and sat directly across from him. She filled it with whiskey and threw her head back to drink it straight down. Wilbur chuckled when he saw her down another one. After she drank the second shot, Ida felt better. She said, "Wil-bur, I sucked-y-o-u-r-DICK!-YOU-CALLED-ME!-your-WIFE!-IDA!-Wilbur, yo' called me CALLIE! Yu duddy-mutha fucka!—you." She took another drink, and another and another. Wilbur sat waiting for her to pass out and when she did, he undressed her. He went to turn the bed covers back and returned with her gown. A rent receipt lay by the bed. After he laid her down, Wilbur crawled into bed beside her, picked up the paper and saw where Ida had rented an apartment. He shook his head. Wilber remembered his first encounter with Callie. Stolen moments had been sweet to him. He spread Ida's legs and let his imagination run wild. When he entered her his mind came alive with descriptions, "the shit is good and tight and hot," it said. Wilbur knew that he was a-b-o-u-t—to lose it so he slowed down his stroke when he felt her open up a little. She grunted and he lifted some of his weight off of her and deepened his stroke until Ida shouted, "Oh!—sh-sh-shiiit!" Wilbur lost it as Ida cried out—"MMMAAACCKK!" Her little tight ass pulled him deeper into her body and he began to laugh. Wilbur got out of bed and put her rent receipt into her wallet and vowed that Mack had lost the battle. He felt vindicated and planned to start all over with his wife. His question to himself was, "How would he do it?

Wilbur and Ida Avery traveled south together for the first time. It had been many years since their marriage. Wilbur made sure that they traveled back to Alabama in style. They planned to pick up Rufus in Athens and head to her grandparent's farm in Alabama. Ida asked Wilbur to stop so that she could check into the boarding house before they went for Rufus. He knew and understood why she requested it but Wilbur felt that she had been given enough time to heal. Everyone had gotten hurt in the process of Rufus' transfer to the south. Ida freshened up and changed clothes at the boarding house but Wilbur hadn't seen her bring a bag of clothing in. He asked, "Baby, you wouldn't mind if I looked around, would you?" Ida answered, "Not at all." Wilbur opened the doors of the closet to find enough clothes for Ida to have stayed for six months. He noted the evening gowns that matched fabulous shoes and handbags. A fluffy cotton bath—robe and shoes and matching underwear in a clear container sat on the closet shelf. Wilbur realized that he had peeked into another world that belonged to his wife alone. She stood and watched him look around with a smile on her face and a twinkle in her eyes. Wilbur said, "Girl, do you think that I came all the way down here and am not going to show off my prize?" Like lightning, Ida fell into her "bend" personality. She wondered if she would ever be able to untie herself. She felt him gather her in his arms and whispered, "Wilbur, do you know how to play a piano?" He was flattered and asked, "Baby, am I getting the song right?" Wilbur wanted to remain like that forever. For once, he did not need her clothes off to feel the life of their love. He wondered how many closets she had that made things easier for her. She had weathered a storm and had somehow come through it. The two of them walked back to the car after locking the door of the boarding house and headed towards the Avery Estate in Athens, Georgia.

Rufus sat with his cousin Fredrick and waited for his mother and dad to arrive. Mae Alice and Ruthie Lee were in the kitchen pretending to be busy preparing lunch. They did not feel guilty of anything, but thought that Ida's youth governed her feelings. Their lineage governed how they felt. Rufus was in line along with Ruthie Lee's three sons to inherit the sum total of a prosperous estate. They both felt that they had rights too. Rufus saw them pull in front of the house and ran to the door to open it. He watched them in fascination how Wilbur walked around the car to open the door for her. Rufus had yet to see another woman or girl whom he thought was as pretty as his stepmother was, Ida Avery was. Wilbur had not seen Rufus in three years and was surprised how tall he had become. Rufus held the door for Ida and Wilbur to enter the house. Ida strolled in like a peacock. Rufus led her to the sofa and sat beside her to interlock his arm to hers. Wilbur stood in the middle of the room and threw both hands up in jest. Mae Alice and Ruthie Lee saw him look at Rufus and laugh. He said, "Man, you just going to take my woman. Huh?" Freddie doubled over and said, "Uncle Wilbur! All he talks about is his wanting to see his mama. I thought maybe you had died or something." Wilbur playfully tugged at Ida and asked, "Where is your own lady at, man?" Rufus gave Ida a big hug and got up. While everyone laughed, he and Freddie went down the road and came back with another boy and three girls who were waiting in the wings. When the young people finished pleading, another car was going to Alabama for the wedding. Ida saw that "all for the asking"; Wilbur's sisters had their hands full. She would have never allowed Rufus to expect her to appease his friends like that. After lunch, they gave everyone time to throw a few clothes into their luggage and headed south. Rufus' friends had already packed. Ida clenched her teeth to refrain from straightening out a few things. The girls rode with Ruthie and Mae Alice. The boys rode with Wilbur and Ida. Pregnant Callie greeted them at the door. When Wilbur saw her he exclaimed, "No Shit!" Ida whispered, "Lawd have Mercy." Rufus could hardly wait for the car to stop rolling. He jumped out and gave Callie a big hug and was glad that he wasn't dreaming. Wilbur laughed out loud and wondered what Dude was up to this time. What really happened was quite simple. Callie had longed for Farmer Wilson. Dude thought that it was depression and recommended that she return to Myrtlennis, their child that she had left with her mother, Effie in Alabama, and greatly missed. She agreed. The Moore's were glad to have her back so that she could take care of her daughter. Farmer Wilson was getting younger by the day and Dora got the personal care that she needed. Callie cared for her like she was their daughter. Wilbur saw Myrtlennis and picked her up. He felt giddy. Never in his wildest imagination would he have believed Farmer Wilson to be able to handle Callie. Mable eased up beside him before he knew that she was there and whispered. She said, "Listen. You can take the child up this way," she pointed in the direction of the bend in the road. She turned to point towards Farmer Wilson's place and finished her sentence by saying, "but you can't take her over there." Wilbur began to laugh so hard that everyone wanted to know what Grandma Mable had said. He and the child walked over to the front steps and he sat down to wipe his eyes. His laughter was infectious. Ida began to laugh because she and Mable had shared strings of comedy from the time she was a toddler. She walked over to Wilbur and invited him inside to see something special. Wilbur dried his eyes again and when they walked inside, every room in the house looked bigger than he'd remembered. Effie had turned the sewing room into two equally divided spaces with a hallway down the middle. On one side was a large bathroom. On the other side was a linen Closet. At the end of the hallway was a door that Wilbur thought was the back door. When he opened it, he and Ida walked into a room as large as the house. It was decorated for the wedding. John JR, Ida's father, walked in and the men rushed towards one another to embrace. John was glad that Ida still had the twinkle in her eyes when she looked at her husband. He said, "Boy, I see you still got your cat." Wilbur danced while they laughed. Ida left them jiving and playing like boys and returned to give Ruthie Lee and Mae Alice a tour of the house. The boys were given Lil' John's room to sleep in. Wilbur's sisters and the girls were given the master bedroom where John and Effie slept. It was large enough for a full sized bed and a sofa bed. An extra Roll a Way Bed was tucked into the closet. She showed them where the linen was before they reached her old bedroom that she had redecorated the year before with a larger bed, new carpeting with matching bedspread and draperies. Effie and John moved into the living room to sleep on the sofa bed. Callie and Myrtle slept together in her old bedroom. Grandpa and Grandma Moore were the only ones in the house that did not make a change. Lil" John came in and greeted everyone and took the young people with him. He and Rufus and Freddie were like peas in a pod. Before they left, the women and girls had a good talk. Mable summed it up saying, "Don't y'all do nothing that you can't wash off, you hear?" Mable pretended to dislike the kisses they each planted on her cheeks before they headed to the car. You could hear them laughing all the way to the car. They heard the women laugh too. Mable stood up and headed to the bathroom saying, "And I know I better wash this bullshit off my face." Grandpa Moore yelled, "Who is that messing with you, Mable?" She strutted into the living room and sat in her Rocker beside him. He pinched her cheek and winked. Callie shouted, "Hey now! Now that's how I want to be." Ida thought, "Shit, Callie. Farting around with Farmer Wilson already got your dumb ass in the chair." Wilbur's two sisters didn't have a clue as to what had transpired between Callie and Farmer Wilson. They agreed and laughed with Callie and continued to chat while Ida served them lemonade. Towards evening, Ida and Wilbur headed to the bend of the road walking hand in hand. They walked to the schoolhouse and sat on the steps. Ida saw memories come alive in his facial expressions. They looked down the road and saw Rufus and his gang approaching. The kids circled the school and played around. Ida showed them the place where one could peek through a crack and see the classrooms and talked to them about education and beginning maturity. Wilbur and the boys left to check out a few fences while Ida answered questions that the girls had about makeup and clothing styles. She asked them to remember the most important parts of their conversation concerning style. Ida explained that it was wise not to deviate from the style that looked good on their bodies. She said," When you finish with the fad, you need a style that looks good on your own body to return to. Your style defines your personality which is what people are usually impressed by." She wanted to go a little deeper but they were not quite old enough. Wilbur came back with the boys who asked him many questions. While he continued to talk, they all walked back around the bend to the house together. The Wedding was the next day at 2 o'clock in the evening. The men and boys sat out in the barn and talked late into the night. John had added another twelve feet of space onto the back wall of the barn and had it fixed up like a bar room. Wilbur almost became envious until he remembered how different Indiana was compared to the south. In Indiana a place like that would have sent everyone to jail.

Lil' John sat and listened to the men talk. He kept his eyes on his father who was the sharpest farmer he knew. Growing up around his Grandfather and father turned out to be rewarding in more ways than one. During his high school years, Lil' John would come home to what many of his classmates considered a boring atmosphere. He'd enjoyed every moment of it. He would eat a snack, do his homework, change his clothes and find his father somewhere on the grounds or out in the pasture. Effie and John JR made farming look easy but he'd found it hard and grueling work. Lil' John watched his parents set goals that sometimes fell short due to unforeseen circumstances. One could lose a whole crop overnight and force a lucrative contract to dwindle down to nothing. He'd watched his grandfather issue alternative recommendations that did not make sense to anyone but himself. Father and son would disagree and tempers sometimes flared between the two men. Grandpa Moore was known to nip things in the bud. At the very first sign of trouble he would pay the workers as if they had completed the failed crop, and then have them plow it up. The field would be planted over again with new seeds and most times yield double or triple the beans or corn. The workers made more for the year, but the farm would still come out with a profit. Lil' John heard Grandpa Moore say at different times, "Hell, a poor man's got to win sometimes. Why the hell else would he keep on working?" His parents and grandparents kept the house lively and the farm profitable. After Callie left home, Lil' John was able to ask a few questions that had plagued him. While his sisters were home, he could not bring himself to ask questions about girls while he'd watched them play dangerous games. He would have spilled the beans in order to stop them in their tracks. For a short period of time, he was disappointed in them both. Then he met Estelle. The girl had a mind. She could tell him off and make him feel like a dog but when he barked, she'd come running like a fool. Estelle was original and no one else could make him feel like making himself a better person. She loved him and he knew it. He had brought several girls home to meet the family. Effie dared him to bring anyone else to the house to meet her because each one felt that they were special. Lil" John would drop them within two weeks. In a week's time while he ignored Estelle, she would have the time of her life being a teenager. She'd make him try to find her.

Estelle desired to be left alone, but her family was large and she was always needed for something. When it was time for her to attend school at age 6, she felt that there were other important things to do at home because from her older siblings she'd already mastered academics. By the time she was 10, she was able to turn her sister's old skirts and blouses into a new look. Most often it was simply the way that she chose to wear the clothes. Skirts were worn backwards and given a sash through the hem that she tied in a bow. She then matched the bow with another one on the opposite side, did the same with the blouse and flounced around enough to attract attention. For weeks, she would see others quickly follow the style. Lil" John would laugh at everything that she wore but his laughter was a cover-up for his admiration. Once she realized it she knew what to do. Estelle toned down her outrageous appearance and watched him find all kinds of reasons to talk to her. She forced herself to become a good listener and concluded that Lil' John had been deprived of speaking because of his talkative sisters. He talked her right into having sex by describing the interactions of the farm animals and teased her when she'd declared that she did not enjoy it. The joke was on him when she refused to ever do it again until marriage. She explained that she would have a reason for trying to enjoy it if it was to make a husband happy. Estelle watch Lil' John throw temper tantrums, date other girls, totally ignore her for sometimes weeks and finally return to apologize and promise to never pressure her again. They became each other's puppet and held onto the strings until they became musical instruments in tune with the rhythm of their hearts. When they turned 17, Lil' John took Estelle to meet his family. They had dinner and talked at the table about daily chores. Effie and Grandma Moore sat and watched Lil' John give Estelle Ida's old garden boots so that she could walk with him to the barn. When she put them on her feet the two women blinked and looked at each other. Lil' John then asked his mother and grandmother to join them while he showed Estelle the baby calf that had been born two days earlier. Neither of them had seen the calf and was delighted that he had asked. Effie whispered to her mother in law, "She's the one." Effie, Lil' John's mother, had seen the look in her son's eyes when he handed Estelle the boots. They held a look of adoration. When Estelle took the boots and put them on her feet, she looked up at Lil' John with eyes so bright that it was as if he had given her a ring. The four of them stood and watched the calf for a while and then headed back to the house. The young couple stopped at the front steps and sat down while the women went inside. A few minutes later, Lil' John and Estelle came inside and sat down at the table where Effie and Grandma sat drawing a pattern. Lil' John looked at Grandma Moore and asked, "Grandma, did you make Mama's wedding dress when she and daddy got married?" She answered, "Yeah, but this is not a dress I'm drawing." He said, "I know, but did daddy ask you to make it?" Effie said, while looking puzzled, "And he will never let me forget it. It was a beautiful dress. I still have it." Lil' John sat up a little straighter and pushed his chair away from the table to stand up. He excused himself saying, "I'll be right back." He returned to the room with a bouquet of flowers and a small box. Estelle was enjoying watching Grandma's drawings and didn't see the flowers or the box. When he proposed, "Estelle, will you marry me?" She jumped up and ran to Effie and gave her a big hug. Then she ran to Grandma Moore and hugged her. Lil' John stood laughing and said, "Girl, is you gonna answer me?" Estelle looked at Grandmother Moore and looked back at Lil' John. Lil' John sighed and said, "Wait a minute." I got it backwards." Effie nodded her head, "Yes you do. Get it right now." He then turned to Grandma Moore and asked her if she would make Estelle's wedding dress. When she answered, "Yes," Estelle held out her hand for Lil' John to slip the ring on her finger. When it was time to take her home, Lil' John drove her home in his father's truck. He opened the door for her to get into the truck and went into the barn where the men were and asked his father for a tape measure because he couldn't ask his mother for it. The women did not know that he had heard about the pussy paper. He then returned to the truck armed with a pencil, paper and a tape measurer. He did not leave Estelle until three o'clock in the morning and went straight to bed. Lil' John planned to get up early the next morning to give Grandmother Moore Estelle's Blake's measurements.

The Blake family was held together by Hazel, wife of Ulesee. She and Ule had come together only once and she found herself pregnant. Since that time, only after childbirth was she ever free from submitting to her husband. Every night like "clock work" sex was his sleeping pill. Each time she'd had a baby, he gave her until her body had a chance to complete the cycle of drainage and would go back to his routine. She had each child thirteen months apart. Hazel taught her girls to be reliable and able to care for themselves as soon as they could comprehend enough to follow instructions. Estelle was the youngest of the children and caught on to most things quickly. She was the first to marry. Hazel had all kinds of help preparing for the wedding. She had not liked the idea of Lil' John's Grandmother making Estelle's wedding dress but she said nothing. Also she frowned on the fact that her daughter would be married in her in law's house. The parents of the bride received an invite to dinner from Lil' John and when they arrived, she was impressed by the family. Grandpa and Grandmother Moore had Hazel and Ule in stitches. When they went home and told the rest of the family about the good time the families had together, she relaxed and felt a little better about the plans that Estelle and her husband to be, had made. She knew that whatever Estelle wanted, she was going to get and from the looks of her drawers that she wore on her engagement night, Lil' John was her twin trooper. Effie could see Hazel's look of anxiety when she and her husband entered the door on the night of the dinner party. She remembered how she'd felt about her own family on her wedding day. Fortunately, they fitted right in because the Moore's enjoyed people for who they were and encouraged them to be themselves and join the celebrating. Since John Jr and Effie's marriage, her sisters had found other mates and her older brothers left Alabama and migrated north to Muskegon, Michigan where they married and sired other children. Effie and Mable had made curtains and slip covers for her parents the year before and had them over for dinner on Christmas Day. She was deep in thought when she felt Hazel's eyes upon her. Effie smiled and began to talk to her about her family and how Mable had made her dress. As she talked, she saw some of the tension leave Hazel's face. After dinner, Mable showed her the pattern she and Effie designed for the dress and gave her a chance to share her ideas with Estelle while they sat and listened. Grandma Mable took note of the differences in the three generations. She and Grandpa were stronger and felt secure in their faith. The following generations wavered in faith and procrastinated. When all was said and done, the original pattern was selected. Grandma and Effie had later called Ida who ordered the sequins and beads for the dress and designed a matching veil. The wedding was short and sweet but was far from being simple. It was planned to be a family affair but Lil' John and Estelle's whole High School class, all of Calico and surrounding neighbors showed up. Every family brought food and many included beverages and wine enough to share. Estelle's family alone had fried enough chicken to cover a table. The women congregated in the huge hall near tables of food to serve and replenish the bowls of various salads, fruit pies and platters of ham and chicken. The vegetables were kept hot and the lemonade cold. Extra tables were hurriedly built and set behind the barn that sat with its huge and wide doors open from the men's Hide a Way in the back. The young people were gathered on the front porch and in the parlor until they could eat no more. They all wandered to the rear of the barn and began to expend their energy by dancing the latest dances. The bride and groom took charge and made everyone join in. Lil' John sent Rufus and his friends to get a move on and usher the women outside. The young men carried chairs outside and made it convenient for everyone. Small children were free to roam around until they needed naps. Myrtlennis and the lot were put to bed after they fell asleep in their mother's arms. Wilbur sat where he could keep an eye on Ida as much as he could because after the Callie and Farmer Wilson deal, he didn't trust any of the men. Things finally slowed down after the bride and groom left for their honeymoon. Two hours later, the Moore's said goodnight to the last of their guests. Mae Alice and Ruthie Lee sat in the parlor talking to men that they had met. The young men of Lil' John's high school class brought chairs into the house and stored tables in the barn. Estelle's sisters were putting platters and kitchen items away while Ida and Rufus' friends did whatever else needed to be done. Callie was nowhere to be found. Ida and Wilbur stood on the front porch and waved as Rufus headed back to Athens with his two aunts and his friends. They themselves were leaving out the next morning to return to Indiana. Callie was in her room when Ida awoke the next morning. Effie sat on the side of her bed wiping tears from her eyes. Ida walked in and was shocked to see her mother crying and before she could ask what was happening, Callie shouted, "Why don't you mind your own business?" Effie said, "Farmer Wilson" and before she could finish the sentence, Callie looked at Ida and said, "Just be glad that your man ain't the damn daddy!" Ida grabbed her sister and dragged her from the bed. Wilbur came running but before he could stop his wife, she wrapped the sheet around Callie's neck and put her foot on one end while she pulled it on the other side with her hands. Callie's face turned "Beet" red. Callie's eyeballs bulged from their sockets like they were ready to pop out. Their father and Wilbur had a hard time prying her fingers loose from the sheet so Wilbur picked her up. When Ida's foot moved, John Jr and Effie were able to loosen the sheet where Ida's foot had held it down tightly. Callie had fainted. Effie shook her and while continuing to call her name. She fanned until her arms gave out. Grandma Mable came with a cold towel and laid it on the back of Callie's neck while waving smelling salts beneath her nose. Ida sat in the kitchen hoping that she had killed her sister and was disappointed when she heard her voice. She ran to the door to see Wilbur holding Myrtlennis who was looking at him as if she wanted him to explain to her what was happening. Effie and her father was busy picking Callie up from the floor. Effie realized that Ida was trying to get near her sister again and placed herself between them. Ida saw the move and said, "Oh! Mama! If you knew why I wanted to kill this bitch, you would help me!" Ida managed to reach around her mother and grab a handful of Callie's hair. Someone yelled, "Ida! The baby is in here!" Ida was already pulling and could not control herself. Wilbur put the baby down and grabbed Ida in his arms. Her strength gave away to cries into his chest. Wilbur held her until he walked her out of the bedroom and Effie led Mable to a chair. Grandpa Moore never went into the bedroom. He figured that whatever Callie got, she had it coming. She had caused him to lose a dear friend by fooling around with his neighbor. He couldn't look Dora, Farmer Wilson's wife, in the eye anymore. He wished with all of his heart that Callie's husband would come and take her with him again. Ida and Wilbur stayed in Alabama another day. Ida sat and made Dora three sack dresses. When she took them to her, Dora was delighted. Wilbur drove them to town to look for accessories. By it being a Sunday, every thing was closed except for the gas station and a small pharmacy. While they drove back to the farm, the three of them laughed and talked about the days of hard times and work in the fields. Wilbur and Dora laughed about the similarities of their former lifestyles on the farm and feeding kids from the quarters. Suddenly, Dora doubled over in pain and called it another sick spell. Wilbur pulled his car into the yard of a couple that he saw sitting on the porch watching their children play. The woman took one look at Dora and sent one of her big boys to run down the road to get Dutchie Lee Mills. The tall dark woman came running. She carried a big bundle. Wilbur helped the woman's husband who sat on the porch to lay Dora on the ground beneath a big tree. The children were taken inside the house where Ida was told to keep them. Wilbur stayed close by his wife's side and wondered if they were going to have to tell the old Farmer that his wife was dead. Someone sent for Farmer Wilson who went and asked his neighbor and friend to go with him. John Jr was not about to send his father out alone so he and Grandpa Moore followed Farmer Wilson down the rood about two and a half miles. They drove their own truck. Dora was asleep under the tree when they arrived. Farmer Wilson's face was broken into sorrowful frowns when he began to yelp like a dog. He fell from his truck and started crawling on all fours. "Dora-Dora Dora, Dora. LORD! Dora! Dora!" Dora answered, "What?" Farmer fell on his face and began to scamper backwards. Dust flew as his toes scraped deep trenches into the ground. He was trying to lift himself but his muscles were weak. Two women walked out of the house carrying the babies. Dora Wilson had given birth to twin boys. Ida and Wilbur inspected their car for blood but there was nothing there. Ida later learned that Dora had padded herself heavily because she'd had a very heavy discharge. In all of her forty-six years of living, Dora had never conceived. For months she thought that she had an ailment that she would die from. When her water broke, she thought it to be part of the illness she suffered. Wilbur and Ida rushed back to town to find soft fabric to make some clothes for the babies. Wilbur could hardly drive for laughing and Ida was in tears. They wanted to pull off the road but they had to keep going to reach town before the store closed. Before they reached town, an Indian Squaw sat by the side of the road and sold blankets. Ida swore that she was heaven sent. There was nobody there earlier and when Wilbur told the story, no one had ever seen any Indians around the area. Ida was able to find soft blankets and an assortment of soft woolen fabrics for small mattresses. She, her mother and grandmother were still sewing when Grandpa and John JR returned home. They gathered Wilbur and slipped out to the barn where they laughed until the beer ran out. Wilbur thought about Happy Merriweather and laughed thinking, I'd have bet anybody that he wouldn't have been able to fix that shit!" Farmer Wilson drove his family home with his dick shriveled up in his drawers. He'd had to leave Dora in the truck to take his babies in the house. He walked Dora in and helped her to undress and get into bed. She lay and waited while he brought the newborn babies to her and placed them on her breasts. When they began to suck, he felt himself to see if he was stirred. He felt nothing but felt his pants leg and whispered, "Thank You, Lawdy!" Before he went to bed himself, Farmer Wilson heard a knock on the back door. When he opened it, Mable and Effie walked in with everything they needed for the babies and included food for him and Dora. He sat down and cried. When he finished wiping his eyes, Grandpa Moore, who had driven his family back to Farmer's house asked him, "Man, where the hell were you trying to take your whorish ass when Dora answered you?" He countered, "I'll be damned if I know. Hell! I thought she had come back from the dead, man. It scared the shit out of me." John Jr showed him how he was moving backwards while Effie warmed Farmer Wilson and Dora some dinner. Satisfied that the family was comfortable, the Mores went home to help Ida and Wilbur prepare for their journey.

By the time Wilbur reached Highway 31, he had begun to tell Ida the story of who his father, Charley Avery was. He said that, "At an early age, Charley Avery had known that he was special. He and his sister Millicent were born to a young girl by the name of Lilly who was the daughter of Suddy. Charley Avery's grandmother Suddy, was a nurse on the Clinton Avery Plantation. His other grandmother was Mrs. Millicent Brannard Avery, wife of the plantation owner and mother of Clint Jr., his father. Mrs. Avery had Suddy to nurse her first child, Missy, at her breast until she was all of three years old. It had kept Missy from being under foot while her mother attended various tea parties and while she traveled with her husband. When Clint as an infant he was nursed by Suddy. Suddy would feed Lilly from one breast and Clint from the other. Suddy already had three sons who were much older than Lilly. They were in charge of harvesting the annual crops on the plantation. The overseers would oversee the planting of the crops. Old man Clinton Avery had solved the inhumane treatment of his workers by limiting the activities of the overseers. After his annual planting was finished, the overseers were free to go and plant crops for themselves. There was Bernard aged 22; Joe aged 26 and Wallace who was 28 years old. They were the trusted sons of Suddy. From age 12, they had all worked the fields while their mother nursed babies. At the age of forty, Suddy found out that she was pregnant and nine months later, on the same night that Mrs. birthed Clint, Suddy delivered Lilly and was sent from the quarters to nurse the newborn baby boy while she nursed Lillie. When Lillie grew old enough to fend for herself, she would hide from young Clint who thought she was his pet. Suddy would make the cook's fire in the early mornings so that Laura the Plantation's Cook, would have a little more time with her family. Suddy had been at the plantation through three generations. Her Great grandfather and grandfather were strong, black muscular men who had died from being trampled by a team of horses. She saw her father get sold to another plantation and never heard tell of him again. Suddy did not know her mother, for she and her father were sent to the Avery plantation with a group of women who mothered her. Fortunately, it was the place where his father had longed to be. They had pointed out her great grandfather and grandfather shortly before his joy turned to sorrow. From her father Suddy learned how to work around the rules and how to make herself invisible to white folk. She tried to keep her girl child close by her side because Lilly loved to wander off to explore their surroundings. Young Clint loved Lilly as one would love a pet. As soon as he learned what sex was, and the power he had over she and Suddy, he began to have sex with Lilly. One morning she hid in the loft above the big kitchen of the mansion and watched her mother build the fire in the big fireplace so that Laura, the mansion's cook, could begin cooking as soon as she came in. Suddy looked for Lilly when it was time to go but Lilly deliberately stayed hidden away and watched her mother stroll across the yard to the cabin where fieldworker's young children were left each morning. Laura was a short, dumpy and dark complexioned, round butted, woman who looked like a Cupid doll with cut bangs on her forehead. From her hideout in the loft Lilly lay and peeked between the boards. She watched Laura with great interest as she bustled around the kitchen gathering ingredients to make biscuits. She saw Theo the Houseboy, ease himself behind the chimney corner while Laura's back was turned. He was a short caramel colored man with a thin moustache and pearly white, straight and strong teeth. His features were in the likeness of a proud pony. Theo cleared his throat and sneaked up behind Laura and teased her by touching her crouch and grinding against her buttocks. She responded when he began to kiss her neck and kiss her on the lips. Lilly was as quiet as a mouse until she saw Theo unbuttoned Laura's dress to make her breasts spill out of her clothing. When he began to give suck, Lilly closed her eyes. "Yuck!" She had to cover her mouth and hold her breath for fear of being caught snooping. When she dared to look again she saw Laura spread eagle on the floor and Theo holding what resembled a pole in his hand. He lay and poked her between her legs and made her whine like a hungry puppy. Lilly watched them shimmy like a chicken with its head cut off. She saw a difference in the way that Theo did it to Laura and how Clint did things to her.

Clinton was a mild mannered young man who wished to follow in his father's footsteps. He and his sister Missy, short for Melissa, had grown to love the land. He would sometimes work side by side with Lilly's older brothers to learn what they knew about the planting and harvesting. He watched them order the workers to weed when it was necessary and to spread the growing bounty in order to increase the yield of the grain. They mentored him and he mastered them. It was sometime in the fall of the year when Young Clint found out that his endeared Lilly was pregnant. She had become ill and threw up down by the spring. Her heaves were so strong that they had made her cry. Before she became ill and started heaving, he had made love to her. He had already noticed how fast her heart had been beating. He had also kissed her on the neck and her neck had felt alive with a strong forceful throb that seemed to have an echo. Clint dipped his handkerchief into the cool spring water and washed her face. He remembered when his favorite mare had been mated and its strong heartbeat after it had conceived. Clint asked Lilly if she was going to have a baby. The tears started again and he sat and wiped them away until she stopped crying. Young Clint coaxed her further into the woods and led Lilly to a chinaberry tree that provided better shade and where the water ran cooler. Lilly watched him take his shirt off and spread it on the ground over the tree's roots that lay above ground. While she continued to sniff and hiccup, he walked away and crouched down about five feet from her and began to mimic the cheetah and jaguar's hunches. He peeked beneath her skirt while she squealed with laughter at his comedy. He growled and kissed her knees, her thighs and did not stop until he felt body give in to ecstasy and heard her familiar sounds of satisfaction. Clint raised himself to look into her eyes and whispered against her lips, "I'm gonna see to you, Lilly." Lilly did not know what he meant but she kept her eyes cast downward and believed that everything was going to be all right. Clint left her by the tree and walked a half-mile to the fields to find Lilly's brothers. When he found them he gave them instructions to place certain workers so as to cover their work and to meet him at the house. The three of them were troubled as to why they were being uprooted from their chores. They wondered if something had happened to Suddy. The three of them still slept in the cabin where Suddy was housed in spite of the fact that they each had children who lived with their mothers in other cabins. No provisions had ever been made for families in bondage to live in unity. The slave owners were free to separate and sell them at will. From what living had taught the enslaved was, where a slave was born was where he died if he was lucky. Clint led the three of them to the back door of the mansion where they entered by way of the kitchen door. He instructed Laura and a tall woman named Jenny to show them where they could bathe. Jenny pointed to a trough out back and gave them rags and lye soap. The sunshine had warmed the water. The all removed their tattered shirts and scrubbed their bodies, dried their bodies off and went back to the kitchen where Theo beckoned for them to follow him. He gave them clean clothes and led them to the chimney corner to pull off their dirty ones. They hesitated to follow Theo into the other parts of the house but he begged them saying that if they didn't follow him, he would be punished for not doing as he had been instructed to do. After much reasoning and discussion, he was able to lead them into the library where Clint sat waiting for them. Laura sent for Suddy and told her what had happened as far as she knew and gave her the clothes that her sons had pulled off. Suddy became weak with fear. She wondered if Clint had decided to sell her sons. She prayed until blinding tears began to flow down her face and lap under her chin. Suddy remembered how Old Master Clinton had worked her man to death. She watched helplessly as the old man broke her man's spirit down to a whisper and demanded that a song be sung to the top of his voice. She also remembered how his father before him had sold her father because of his sorrow. Having lost his father and grandfather from the one accident had caused her father to grieve himself into a stupor. He was sold outright. In anger she washed her three son's sweaty clothes until she saw them come out of the mansion and head back towards the fields. With relief, Suddy rinsed and hung the wet clothes to dry. Before she could calm her nerves, she cleaned her cabin from corner to corner, making her surroundings as pleasant as it could have been. The first thing young Clint had wanted to know were the names of Joe, Wallace and Bernard's children and their children's mother's names. Joe, Suddy's oldest son was the father of four boys ages 7, 10, 13, and 9 mothered by Berta on the Byron Plantation. Wallace, the middle son had five boys and two girls by Josie Lee, daughter of Laura the cook. Bernard had a boy 6 and two girls ages 2 and 4 by Berta's sister Dot on the Byron plantation. Clinton finished gathering the information and sent them back to work in the fields. Next, he went to talk to his father about a business venture. First he talked to his father about becoming a landowner and then about purchasing slaves. They discussed the possibility of legalities that could hinder the transfer of land ownership at the demise of the original owner. When they finished, Old Massa Clinton understood some his son's concerns. His wife, Millicent Brannard Avery who knew nothing about business, would be subject to make costly decisions which could easily cause Clint and his sister, Missy to lose their inheritance. There were 18 acres that ran from the border of the fields past the creek and surrounding wooded area where the trees grew for lumber. Young Clint asked for that land. He wanted to cut the trees down to make room for his vision to come to fruition. He'd waited three months for his father to make a decision because his mother was against it. Millicent Brannard had married Clinton to further her father's interests. She had made her father proud by marrying a prosperous plantation owner and she wanted to make him prouder by one day giving him all that she had. Her children meant nothing to her except to please her husband who adored them. There was another six acres behind the mansion that young Clint was watching but he decided to wait before asking to buy it from his father. He had looked over the boundaries and knew how he planned to situate Lilly. Clint had the trees cut down forty feet from the spring and left the big Chinaberry tree standing. After selling some of the lumber, he offered his father money to buy Suddy and her family. He promised that Joe, Wallace and Bernard would continue to work the fields. By Suddy having been young Clint's nurse, his father agreed to sell her and her family. Her value had diminished but her sons were of great value. Old Massa and Clint had haggled over the price of Suddy's sons, and finally Clint said, "If I have to buy them, I will make you pay for the work that they do in the fields. Sign them over to me and things can continue as always." His father smiled at his son and was proud. Between the two of them, they had solved many of the problems that had plagued the old man. He had gone through list after lists of his own kind that were trustworthy and had found none. He knew what Millicent's plan was too. She loved satisfying her father and it was fine with him as long as he had someone who satisfied him. He did.

At sundown, Suddy saw Lillie walking from a wooded area towards the house. She had a sparkle in her eyes and threw her hips from side to side like she was tying a bow. Suddy began to pray. She said, "Well Sir Jesus! What's da likes o' us gonna do wit' dis kind o' chil' dat is carryin' a load?" Though she had known how young Clint had begun to use her daughter's body for his pleasure, Suddy was helpless to change matters. When Lilly hid from him, Suddy was content not knowing where she was due to her powerless state. On the other hand, Joe, Wallace and Bernard, Lilly's brothers were glad that it was young Massa Clint who pestered their sister instead of some poor helpless man in bondage. The three boys had hated watching how Old Massa Clint's wife, Mrs. Millicent would make their mother nurse her pasty faced baby. When guests came to the mansion, Suddy would stay at the mansion leaving Lilly behind to be cared for by them. The best thing that they could do was to feed her clabbered or sour milk when she hungered. Once when the guests had stayed for a week, Suddy recruited Laura the cook, to hide Lilly in the loft so that she could sneak away from the nursery and feed her. Laura would leave the mansion and take Lilly back to the cabin at night with a little fresh milk from the kitchen. Suddy fashioned a nipple for her baby girl by using a hog casing pulled over the mouth of a jar. That way, the boys could feed the baby in her absence. Lilly was weaned long before young Clint was. He nursed until he too was three and Suddy had a hard time keeping her milk flowing. She had tried to give him to suck with another woman but he refused and weaned himself by sucking on a casing that Suddy fashioned by putting it on the wide mouth of a jar. Young Clint found favor with his father. He was given the land behind the mansion so he had three cabins built over near the side of the fields. From money left over from the sale of left over lumber, he went to the Byron Plantation to purchase Berta Dot and their children who were fathered by Suddy's sons, Joe and Bernard. Before doing so, he instructed them to wait for him at the cabins. Inside of the cabins were three huge beds with mattresses made from straw and corn shucks. A fireplace with a mantle was built on the end wall and a table with four chairs were built and sat near the door. Joe looked and Suddy was coming down the road with his family when Clint pulled up with Berta and Dot. Anyone would have thought that someone had died when they began to cry and howl. Young Clint tried to escape their emotions and yelled, "Y'all git this stuff out of my wagon. Come on! Hurry up and go inside and y'all go to bed! Joe, yours is the first one. Give the one with the most chullins the one wid' the most beds." He took off like a shot with tears streaming down his face and wondered what his ancestors had been thinking about to have treated people worst that dogs. Another wagon pulled up bearing the belongings of Berta and Dot's family. Master Byron had instructed the others on the plantation to load up the wagon and not touch so much as a nappy string of hair. Suddy and Josie Lee with the help of Joe's children had walked all of their belongings from up the road.

On the deeds, Clint named the occupants as Joseph, Wallace and Bernard Averyson. He as owner of the land named them beneficiary of the individual plots. Everything that they produced on their sites was theirs and if they found a way to profit, he told them that they could keep the money. He had a plan to free every slave that the plantation owned when the time was right. His mother and her family stood between time and the goal post. He prayed that for Lilly's sake, he had the time. Early the next morning, Clint saw Suddy's family head towards the fields. With precision they gave the other workers orders and worked along with them. Clinton knew he had it right and hoped that God would show him how pleased he was with what he was trying to accomplish.

The next day young Clint waited until the sun was high before sending Suddy and Lilly to the spring. Lilly had not been near it since the day that she had gotten ill. The sun was warm but the fall of the year blew cool breezes in the shaded woodlands. Suddy threw a shawl around her shoulders and wrapped Lilly in a muslin sheet. The chinaberry tree stood tall and laden with berries that had dropped to the ground and smelled like a sweet evergreen twig. There also sat a house that looked small and newly built. Lilly showed no surprise and had not been told to go inside so she and Suddy stood there and looked at the small porch in the front of a parlor. Clint came from the back and told them to go inside. The two women walked inside and showed no sign of expectations. He left them standing and came back with a load of furniture. Clinton instructed them to put it anywhere they wanted to. When they finished the three bedrooms were filled with beds, dressers and a commode for the pee pots. Cabinets for the wash basins were built into the corners of the rooms. It was a shotgun house only each room was larger than the one before it. The front door led you to the parlor and an archway led to a larger and then another and yet a room that was as wide as the house and then a hallway that was nine across and six feet long. The door at the end of the hall led to a kitchen as large as a cabin. A pump had been sunk on the side of the house. There were porches on each side of the hallway with stairs that led to entrances into the house. There was another porch attached to the rear of the house that you could only enter from the kitchen. The house had plenty of windows with shutters. Another load of furniture and other items were brought in by workers and sat in the middle of the floor. Suddy and Lilly waited until the men left before they began to look through it. There were wash basins and pitcher sets for each room, pee pots, lanterns and dishes, pots and pans. Young Clint returned with another load of furniture. With the linens he brought Lilly and her mother made the beds and noticed that they were given pillows which they had never owned. He put a small sofa in each room and a plush velvet chair in the parlor. Three men brought in a big potbelly stove and set it up in the kitchen near the fireplace. A smaller one was set up in the parlor. Every room had its own fireplace on the outside wall. They fastened a big safe for food storage to the kitchen wall that had bins for flour, sugar, dried beans, dried peas, onions, potatoes and corn meal at the bottom. A screened section had three shelves for cakes and pies and breads and canned fruits and vegetables. The higher shelves were used for storing the canned foods for the winter months and dishes. Next a long wooden table large enough to seat a dozen people with benches and two chairs was brought in. When a high backed stool was brought in, Suddy looked at Lillie's belly and expected to see jubilation. There was none. A chiffonier and dressing table was put into her bedroom and still no sign of joy showed on her face. Lillie was clearly worn out and needed rest. Finally young Clint walked in carrying a crib and Lilly began to dance around in a circle holding both hands over her mouth. He placed it in the largest room and showed them how to lock the doors. Before he left, they walked to the front of the house into the parlor where they found all of their belongings from their cabin. Clint looked Lilly in her face and whispered, "I'll always see after you, gal. This is you and Suddy's place to stay. Go to bed now, you hear?" He led her to the largest bedroom that sat by the hallway and told her again to go to bed. Before Suddy could lock the door, Lilly was fast asleep. Suddy drew water and filled the pitchers and kettle. She hung the big iron pot in the fireplace and made a small fire in the stove. After she reheated dinner, she woke Lilly up so that she could eat her supper. Lilly was almost too tired to eat. When she finished she went and gathered her old corn-shuck mattress and placed it on top of her new mattress, lay down and went back to sleep. Suddy smiled and shook her head and whispered, "Da gal must got a good one, hah!" Young Massa Clint hadn't told her where to sleep so she slept in the smallest bedroom and reminded her self to ask him in the morning. The sons of Suddy had settled into their cabins with ease. Their mates had brought everything they had in this world with them. There were pans and cooking pots and foods like potatoes, onions, salted pork, meal rice, dried beans, peas, flour, sugar, vinegar, soda, lard, pepper, salt, turnip roots, rutabagas and lye soap. The children were happy to be with their fathers and tried to stay as close as they could by attempting to sleep in one bed. For the first time in their lives they felt live strings of adoration that completed the loose ends of their existence. They saw living strength of a strong and vibrant man who begot them once and again. When the men went into the fields the next morning, their reasons for going took on a new meaning. They truly had something to harvest.

Suddy was up at dawn. She had an extra half of a mile to walk but she didn't mind doing it. It had been invigorating to bathe in private for the first time in her life without watching the door for intruders. She had walked out of the house using the side entrance and discovered what the area was designed for. There was a gutter where rainwater could water the hedges and also it was a place where she could dash her bath water. She knew where she would plant her garden. It just made sense. She and Laura glanced with glee when they saw one another. There was no music playing but somehow they moved to the same beat of joyous rhythm. Suddy's old cabin in the quarters became a church. Clint's mother, Mrs. Millicent Brannard Avery helped to set up a replica of her family's traditional Sunday service. Ten feet were added to the front of the cabin for the altar and another ten feet to the rear of the cabin for extra benches. She sent a wagon to her father's plantation and an old piano was brought back. The carpenters were kept busy building benches while strong muscular men cut down big, tall trees. On Sunday mornings Mrs. Avery would drag Old Massa Clinton to church with her and Mistress Missy, Clint's sister who would play the piano while they sang. Old Massa Clinton was the one to deliver the sermon that always told his chattel where they belonged and who's rules to obey in order to please God. When they would sing "I Am 'Bound For Canaan Land," many tears for their homeland were shed. Those in bondage identified with the children of Israel and their exodus. They enjoyed bible stories of victory and were able to envision a God who bore a person's suffering and pain. It caused them to step lively and to believe that endurance was no longer an issue because surely, they trusted God that righteousness would prevail. Suddy would sit on the backbencher by the door and look at the window that she had once sat and prayed in while waiting for her man to return from the hard labor in the field. In each corner of the cabin were memories and tales of woe but the Lord God seen fit to take her to a mansion where she could rest. She sat with her head bowed down and would not look into the eyes of the Avery family and asked God to bless others as he had blessed her. After church was finished she hurried out of the door to keep away from idle talking and rushed to her daughter Lilly who thought it best not to mingle. It was nigh Christmas and they had not seen hide or hair of young Clint since the night he had moved them into the house. Lilly knew that he was not in town because when Suddy brought home the laundry from the mansion, none of his clothes were there to be washed. She came to love the solitude and the feel of the life that grew inside her. During the day sleep would often shroud her like a soft blanket and she would lie down and rest peacefully. Suddy and Laura kept her with an assortment of sweet cakes from the mansion. Lilly had twice received loose and flowing cotton dresses that made her smile knowing that they were from young Clint. Her brothers would bring their families to visit and they all would sit in the kitchen and talk over cups of tea and eat crackers that Suddy had baked. Josie Lee, Berta and Dot would tip around from room to room and whisper while they secretly longed for Lilly's lifestyle. She looked cared for and adored. She looked calm and sweet whereas they remembered pregnancies that were harsh and sometimes brutal. Joe, Wallace and Bernard would josh around and enjoy seeing their mother looking majestic in her much deserved surroundings. They would leave by moonlight and return to their cabins to refrain from drawing attention to Suddy and Lilly. It happened to be the best thing to do because Suddy and Lilly had their hands full enough with getting ready for the childbirth. Suddy collected old rags and sewed them together in layers. She used bits of wire strung and tied together for a brush to prick the muslin or heavy denim fabrics to make it soft enough for a baby's skin. From the mansion's laundry Suddy found rags that were used for dusting and turned them into soft diapers. She did not ask others to participate and did everything for her daughter in order to keep the birth a secret. On the last day of the year, Lilly's water broke. Lilly did not know why she had kept having the need to stay on the commode. Her mother saved everything until the proper time came around for its use. When it was time for dinner, Suddy gave her a plate of food while she sat there but it seemed hard for Lilly to swallow. She sat the plate on the bed. Suddy, who knew everything, said nothing. She felt that since the girl was going to have the baby, nothing else mattered. There were two things to do. One thing was to shut her mouth and the other thing to do was wait until the baby was born. Suddy sat nearby and listened to her daughter's complaint of the misery in her stomach and pain in her back. She placed a chair in front of Lilly and a pan of water within her reach. When the pain became what Lillie described as "too hard to bear," Suddy instructed her to bend over the chair and push. Brown paper and clean rags lined the floor beneath Lillie and Suddy knelt holding a sizeable piece of material to catch the baby with. He tumbled out of his mother's womb with the loudest groan that Suddy had ever heard anyone bearing a child make. Charley took his first breath and hollered. Suddy yelled, "You got a boy chil', Lilly." Suddy tied two bows and cut the cord between the strings about three inches from Charley's tiny stomach. She instructed Lilly to continue to bear down so that she could rid herself of the last pains. After the baby had been bathed and wrapped, she laid it beneath the covers of Lilly's bed and attended to Lilly who had dispelled the placenta. Suddy immediately picked it up and wrapped it up in the brown paper and cloth. She then tied it in a bundle to take and bury beneath the roots of the chinaberry tree. Lilly was washed and soft towels placed between her trembling loins. Her body was so sore that Suddy had to help her into her padded bed and lay the infant upon her breast to suck. Dark haired greenish blue eyed Charley was in the image of his father. Lilly felt the world release her into an abyss where the pain no longer mattered. All she continued to feel were the tiny lips pulling her nipples for her rich life sustaining substance. She slept. Suddy walked outside through the side door and went to the big chinaberry tree over by the spring to bury the cauls deep into the earth. The sound of singing reached her ears in a low tone of bass and continued until it took on a rhythmic tenor and alto chord. As she searched the sky for a sign, she remembered that it was watch night. Millions of slaves were praying around the world out of fear that their loved ones would be sold. There had not been a sale of chattel from the Avery plantation to another for years so Suddy was comforted in feeling that all she'd heard was a celebration of wellness. She walked back to the house with her eyes brimming with tears and wondered what was going to happen to "dat white young 'un in da house." She wondered if Old Massa Clinton would find out about the birth and move the child out of the house that young Massa Clint had built. Surely, they would sell him to another. Lilly and Suddy did everything that they could do to keep Charley's birth a secret. Her sons agreed to keep their families away so that their wives would not be tempted to talk. Lilly did not attend church and grew to enjoy being alone with her baby on Sunday mornings as well as when Suddy would go to the mansion. In the mansion's kitchen was where Suddy let the cat out of the bag while she and Laura talked. That early morning when Suddy arrived at the mansion and the fire was already made. Laura, the cook sat by the huge fireplace wiping tears. She told Suddy that she was fearful of birthing another child since the midwife of her other children had passed away. Suddy had never helped bring a child into the world before Charley was born, but she had known that the situation of her daughter called for perseverance. She simply did what she had to do. In an attempt to console Laura, Suddy used the phrase, "like when my gal birthed her boy." Suddy stood stoking the fire and did not see Laura peek at her through the fingers that covered her eyes. She turned around when Laura began to cry louder and began to remind her that she would start others talking if she didn't quiet down. Satisfied that she had put a lid on Suddy's memory, Laura began to rush around to gather ingredients for her biscuits. Suddy went to gather the wash and headed back home. The weather was cold but many conveniences now lay before her and she had warm water that she no longer had to carry far for the wash. The nearby spring furnished her with water and the fire built beside it heated more water than she had ever hoped for., young Clinton Avery was having the time of his life. He was sowing wild oats in Atlanta, Georgia. For years his father had been selling grain and Clint needed to find the best markets. Things were changing and business was booming. He wanted to get into the trading loop before the knot was tied. He found that freight trains were the best mode of shipment and that Duluth, Chicago and Minneapolis had biggest storage facilities. After making a lucrative deal, he'd headed home but became sidetracked by ladies seeking gentleman husbands. He was baited and herded into a society that moved quickly and made it hard for a man to loosen the ties. From Atlanta, he wired his father to ask for help. Old man Clint wired him back. "STAY PUT UNTIL YOU GET PAID." The old Massa went to work. Tons and tons of wheat, corn, oats, barley and rice filled boxcar after boxcar and were delivered to Duluth Minnesota. Every hand on the plantation that could be spared was sent to the fields. Another shipment was sent to Chicago. Young Clint stayed put until he received his money but had seen open land in Athens, Georgia that was loaded with young cedar saplings. He was mindful of a young lady who'd gone all out to win his affections but marriage was not on his mind, only business. A young man by the name of Jesse Burkes was looking to marry but was a shy fellow. Their paths crossed one evening during a party at the Peach Orchard Hotel where ladies were more plentiful than booze. Clint talked to the young man about Miss Blanche Crenshaw until he was blue in the face in hopes that he would approach her. She was gorgeous but desperately looking for a husband as well as needed one. She had climaxed before Clint could enter her good and he hurriedly had pulled himself out to save himself plenty of trouble. In case he'd left a seed or two he needed someone to marry her. He already had his sights set on Delpheen Eugenia Byron who was the daughter of Millwright Byron whose plantation was adjacent to the Avery's land. She was young, raw, gorgeous and untouched. Clint's talking with Jesse changed into coaching the young man whose confidence had shown some improvement. When the opportunity presented it's self, Clint introduced gentleman Burkes to the Crenshaws and politely made his escape. What he found in Athens was a lightly populated wooded area. It hadn't taken Clint long to find the owner of the property that he was interested in but legalities depicted that he remain nearby until the property was cleared for sale. The owner was heavily indebted and fortunately for young Clint, they were willing to sell the land to him that grew timber needing another ten years or so to grow into profitability. Clint used the time wisely and visited the landowners in the surrounding areas. It seemed the perfect place to settle and build a proper estate. In his mind he viewed the sale of cedar for millions of dollars and a mansion for Delpheen.

Wilbur talked while he drove. Ida listened while he talked. When they would stop the car to eat and relax, Ida made sure that the conversation was diverted to their personal lives instead of the story that Wilbur heard from his relatives. She had found herself tense during Wilbur's storytelling and wanted to release it before she heard more. Ida also wondered how Mack was and longed for home. Wilbur was about to bite down on a fried chicken leg when he noticed the wistful look on her face. Ida's mouth was filled with chicken and cake but he kissed her anyway making her laugh. Ida heard the sound of his zipper and looked into his eyes and pleaded, "Wilbur, No!" She was melting on the inside as he slid her onto his lap. Skillfully, he slid her panties to the side and entered her. They sat in an alcove of trees near the highway and forgot everything except their need for one another. As always, Wilbur helped her to get straight by brushing her hair and straightening her clothes. As usual, they had a hard time staying untangled enough to continue their journey. Ida teased him when he finally removed his lips from her mouth saying, "Wilbur, you've already played the piano. Are you going to sing too?" She stuck a piece of fried chicken in his mouth and laughed when he had tried to sing. They had only four more hours of driving to do, so they brushed chicken and cake crumbs from the car's seat and drove back to the highway and headed home.

In the throws of ecstasy, Laura screamed for Theo to stop before he hurt the baby. He struggled hard to maintain an erection behind her outburst because to his knowledge, he'd never sired a child. He conjured a fantasy as fast as he could to complete his business with her and spun her around asking, "What is you talkin' 'bout, Laura?" He continued, "I ain't got no chil' by you and nobody." It made her burst into tears and scowl at him. She pouted and began to strut with her hand on her hip. She gyrated with her other hand and said, "since yo' livin' is so easy in dis big house' ya thank ya is a Massa but cha ain't! He gotta boy chil' at Suddy's an' you is gonna have young 'un ret' here." Theo countered, "Suddy ain't got a baby!" Laura said, "But her Lilly do!" Theo had been taught to show no emotions. His first day in the big house took him to the Massa's room to build a fire. He was eleven years old and had walked in on old Massa Clinton boning the big sewing woman named Elsie. He'd made her lay crossways the bed on her belly and while he stroked she was making grunting sounds of ""uh hu, uh hu." Theo could not move his feet to turn and run from what he saw. Old Massa turned to see him and with his eyes, willed him to stand still. Massa growled between his teeth, "Elsie, don't you move gal! Ya hear?" Lay here 'til I come back!" He'd kept pumping until he finished and got up. He then led Theo out of the room and to the kitchen where he instructed the cook to feed him. From that day, Theo played the game and his expression never changed. He finished eating and asked the cook for a pitcher of iced tea. He took it into the library and sat it on a table before scurrying off to listen at Mrs.'s door. Theo listened at the door to see if he could hear her maid bustling around. What he heard instead was the sound of her plea to her husband saying, "You promised to never ask me to do it again!" He heard smacks and kisses amid Massa's groans. She cried, "Aaah!" while he yelled, "For gawd sake woman, swallow! Hurry!" She sobbed in protest while he cursed her. At his young age, all Theo could do was masturbate but Annie, Mrs.'s maid saw him and whispered, "Boy don't waste that!" She took him into a closet and allowed the young man to use her for his release. When Theo groaned, she'd laughed but was surprised herself when she climaxed. They both knew that Massa would go back to his room so they sneaked into the library and shared glasses of iced tea while Theo explored the rest of Annie' body. When the two or them figured that they had given Mrs. and Massa enough time, Theo and Annie showed up with basins of water for baths. Theo had told Annie of the baby's birth and while she bathed Mrs., Annie mentioned that Suddy had a new baby at her house. The tide changed. She rushed to dry herself off and to get dressed. Mrs. had known about Lilly and how young Clint had followed her around so much that she'd hid from him. She was also dead set against his decision to buy the family and to build the cabins for them to live in. Mrs. had begged her husband to keep the land because she secretly hoped that everything would eventually end up being a windfall for her side of the family. To please her daddy, she'd married Clinton Avery for his wealth and had hoped that he would eventually work himself to death. Young Clint, their son had foiled her plan and now her husband was beginning to not go to the quarters for satisfaction but to demoralize her standards with freaky acts during what should have been lovemaking. Although it was not a long ride to the spring, without consulting anyone, Mrs. had the carriage brought to the front door and ordered Annie and Theo to load it with several packages wrapped in brown paper and tied with string. She then sent the driver back to the stables. Mrs. walked the two servants back inside and whispered while wagging her finger in their faces saying, "Y'all do not know whar' I'm a goin' an' whar ever ya think I'm a goin' ya betta fo' git! Or else I'm a gonna see to ya!" Mrs. Millicent Ruth Alice Brannard Avery stalked out of her house and hopped onto the carriage to drive herself down by the spring. She wanted to be alone to see what her bastard of a husband had allowed young Clint to do. She stopped the carriage near the chinaberry tree. Nestled in hedges sat a little shotgun looking cabin. Millicent faced the parlor that was the smallest room. She approached what looked like a rose petal structure as the rooms appeared to jut out with one being wider than the other until a screened in porch on the right side of it resembled the rounded leaf of a flower's stem. Suddy opened the door before Mrs. got to it. Lilly had finished the ironing from the big house after Suddy left to make the fire for the cook. Mrs. walked in and saw the freshly ironed clothes by the door. It infuriated her that a house had been built for the likes of Suddy. Young Clinton had given them the impression that he was having quarters built for Suddy's sons, not a house good enough for "the likes of me," as she put it. While Mrs. strolled through the house, Lilly sat rocking her baby by the kitchen window. When she had finished her ironing, she had taken a bath and slipped on one of the first dresses young Clint had given her. Suddy was grateful that her dress was one made from flour sacks. She was certain that if Mrs. had seen a dress that looked better, she would have torn it from Lilly's body while she sat with her eyes cast downward. Millicent had only to see the child's hair to feel her battle of lifetimes begin to press its way into her life. She stomped to the front of the house and yelled to the top of her lung's capacity, "SUDDY! GO "N GIT DA PACKAGES FROM DA CARRIAGE." and "hurry up, gal!" Suddy ran like a frightened animal the twenty or more feet to the carriage and began grabbing and pulling to put the items anywhere she could get them so that she could get them into the house. She tied as many bundles as she could and put them in her skirt's tail and discovered that if she tucked it in the front, more room formed at the sides for her to fit the rest of it in to be tied up in a great big balloon. Suddy tied the skirt and waddled towards the house. Mrs. was so angry that she slammed the door shut before Suddy could reach for it. Suddy did not flinch but turned slowly to ease herself around the house to the side door. Mrs. hadn't seen the walkway so to her Suddy had simply vanished. She felt her strength completely leave her when she heard Suddy's voice come from the back bedroom. Whipped, she drug what felt like the weight of the world to the carriage and used the little strength that she had left to try to whip the horses to death. The field hands saw the clouds of dust and wondered why Mrs. was alone in her carriage. She pulled up in front of the mansion and sat trying to control her breathing. Theo and Annie were afraid to touch her after she waved them off before stepping from the carriage. Annie saw her limp towards the office and sent Theo to find old Massa Clinton. Annie watched Mrs. have trouble opening the door to the study but continued to wait for instructions. She then sneaked around to the library and entered the study herself. The next time she heard Mrs. touch the knob, Annie opened the door and stood behind it. Mrs. picked up papers from her husband's desk and began growling like a wounded hound dog. Her face felt twisted against her will. Frightened Annie stepped from behind the door as old Massa and Theo came running in time to catch Mrs. when she fell. Urine covered the floor where she lay with one eye opened. Her other eye remained closed on the side where her mouth twisted. Massa tried to pick her up but she was dead weight. He sent Theo to send someone for a doctor. He and Annie tried to lift her to a chair but her joints were as stiff as a board. Annie ran for a mop and towels. Theo sent for the doctor and kept running and ended up in the kitchen where Laura managed to get enough information from him to fix hot tea and to send smelling salts to old Massa. Suddy's daughter in law, Dot was in the kitchen helping out when Theo ran in and calmly took off her cook's apron and donned a maid's cap and apron, put the tea in a silver pot, the smelling salts in her pocket and strolled into Massa Clinton's office. It was a mess. Massa was trying to get his wife to speak while everyone else huddled in a corner. She sent Annie for two strong women, sheets, a pillow, warm soapy water, clean towels and a gown for Mrs. Avery. She saw that Massa was in shock so she ordered Theo to pour him a shot of liquor. After he choked the liquor down, Massa came to himself enough to ask Theo again to send for a doctor. He gathered his fallen papers while the floor was being cleaned up and wondered what it was that Millicent was after. He put the papers into his safe and locked it. Dot and the two big women finished cleaning Mrs. up and lifted her in the clean sheets to carry her to bed. Essie was one of the big strong women that Annie had brought in to help with Mrs. Avery. By tucking her chin Essie had tried to dodge Massa when it was time to leave but he knew that walk and called her back. She almost resorted to tears. The man would suck her breasts so hard that the soreness would wake her up in the middle of the night. After making her cry, he would sit his nasty butt on her stomach and fold her sore breasts around his penis and squeeze. When she thought about that and more acts that he made her do, she could not hold back the tears. He said, "Hush gal, and go to my room!" He locked her in and went into his wife's bedroom with the doctor. When the doctor left, old Massa Clint played in Essie's big purple vagina until she purred like a kitten. Theo rushed back into the kitchen and told Laura to take food to Essie's children and to tell them that she had to sit with Mrs. who was sick. Laura was a wee bit jealous until Theo explained to her how Essie was tortured. Annie sat with her hands folded and prayed that Mrs. didn't die. She said, "My ass will be sent straight to the damn field if Mrs. leaves dis earth, Lawd." Laura left Massa two plates of food on the stove with a pitcher of iced tea and two slices of apple pie. She took the rest of the food to Essie's children who had never had it so good. Essie was the mother of four half grown children. Their father lived on the Pritchard plantation about five miles down the road. He had stolen away before supper to be with Essie and would make it back to the Pritchard place by dawn. That was the routine. Laura covered for Essie and took her man a plate of food too. When Massa went to sleep, Essie tipped through Mrs.'s room butt naked and cracked the door. Theo saw the light and came running. He told her that all was well and sent her back to Massa's bed smiling. Old Massa Clinton arose early the next morning and ate Elsie's pussy like it was fresh fruit. He then penetrated her until she pumped him to sleep again. In preparations to leave she gave a small cough and made his withered member slip out of her vagina but he had her trapped beneath him and she was afraid to move. At dawn he finally rolled over and she scampered from beneath him and rolled to the floor. That maneuver made her able to crawl through his wife's room and on into the linen closet to find something to cover her naked body. Essie fashioned a skirt and top from a piece of worn muslin and went through the kitchen. Suddy was just getting the fire started. She had not heard anything about Mrs. Avery's illness and rushed to get the laundry before she stirred. Before Laura came in to cook, Suddy was back home.

She nor did Lilly have any idea that young Clint had sent clothes for the baby until they opened the several bundles that Mrs. had ordered Suddy to bring from the carriage. Millicent had no idea what was in the bundles that she delivered. She had only wanted to punish Suddy for living in such a place as the new house. Mrs. wanted to have her daughter who was 6 years older than her brother, young Clint was, to deliver the bundles to Suddy but her daughter would have nothing to do with the workers. At a young age she had been admonished for wanting to play with the children her age. She'd cried when her brother could fondle and play with Lilly and she was not allowed to mingle with anyone. Young Missy's focus was on one day leaving the plantation to find another life for her self besides people watching. Their faces were too pasty she thought and their lifestyles were devious and controlling. She secretly had a crush on Theo but he would never have guessed it.

Bernard and Dot walked the two miles along the spring to see Lillie and Suddy. Everyone in the field had seen Mrs. Avery riding roughshod in her carriage. That was unusual for the members of Massa's household. Sometimes the drivers sneaked to show off by making clouds of dust but Millicent had been the driver. Over supper, Dot talked about Mrs. getting ill soon after arriving home that afternoon. Bernard jumped up from the table and rushed out of the door without sharing his concerns with his wife who loved to gossip. He had whipped her about talking so much in the short time that they lived together because he learned early on that talking could get one killed. Young Massa had done a good thing to put them under one roof and it was his intent to teach his children how to survive. He took long steady strides as he walked and could hear his wife's short quick steps as she tried to keep up. He kept what he knew about Mrs. to himself and was relieved to see a lantern's light flickering in Suddy's window. He knew it was a signal for the shutter was slightly opened. He picked up a pebble and threw it to hit one of the kitchen windows where no light was. While he and Dot stood in the shadows the light went out. A few moments went by before Bernard stood in the moonlight for Suddy to see who he was. He then gave her time to unlock the door for them to enter the house. They walked in and Bernard embraced his mother in the dark. He asked no questions so that he would have no answers. His father had told them to work steady, eat hearty and rest. He'd say, "And leave business to the white folk because they have plenty to lose." A few whispers in the dark that Dot couldn't hear was all he needed before heading back to his cabin. Joe and Wallace would be told in the morning that all was well.

Young Massa Clint received the news of his mother's illness before he left Athens. The baby clothes that Mrs. had taken to Suddy was part of what should have been taken to the cabin with the crib but had been left out. Since leaving the plantation his concerns were towards the business dealings to enhance the holdings of his family. Suddy's boys knew where he was but they never breathed a word. For himself, he purchased another 200 acres of timberland in Athens, Georgia for a steal. One week later, he was home and found his mother doing better. Theo furnished him with bath water and plenty of soap to bathe with. He went to see Suddy's sons and gave them each the same money he paid the overseers and their papers of freedom. The three men had made the family quite wealthy and had carried out every order that he gave them. He did not want them to ever leave the Avery plantation and had tried to take away every reason for them to leave. They owned their cabins and the land that went with it, their families were together and he planned to pay them decently. His only request was that they'd never tell. Young Clint's next stop was down by the spring to the place he now planned to call "The Creek Settlement." It pleased him to see that the draperies had been hung and the curtains were in place. He had ordered them special. Lilly had bathed her son who was almost four months old and ruddy like young Massa Clint. The child's eyes had changed from blue-green to greenish gray. Clint stood in the doorway and watched him devour the milk from Lilly's breast. Baby Charley pulled away from his mother's breast to look at the man standing in the doorway and let out a loud burp. He smiled and gurgled trying to talk to Clint. Lilly kept her head lowered. She saw someone's boots but fear had gripped her to the point where she felt faint. Lilly had always known that what had happened to her family would come to an end. Her thoughts were that Mrs. had sent her son to take the baby and get rid of the whole lot of them. Clint kneeled down to look into her eyes. He spoke in the softest tone of voice he could muster to ask Lilly if he could hold her baby. Lilly clung to the child. Clint called out to Suddy and she came running. He told her to take the baby and when she did, Clint kissed him on the head and instructed Suddy to take him into the kitchen and to cook. Lilly had run to the parlor and began to wail. By the time Clint found her hiding in a corner, she'd crouched in a corner like a caged animal. With one hand he grabbed her tiny wrist and with the other, he lifted her gown. She struggled against being led to the settee but was no match for his strength. She felt her natural instincts kick in and soften her emotions. She knew how to please Clint because she had done it all of her life. Lilly lay down on the floor and lifted her own skirts. The smell of cinnamon and vanilla teased Clint's senses when she fanned her skirt. As much as he'd wanted to enter her, the feelings in his heart overpowered the feelings in his loins. Clint made his swollen member wait until he held Lilly until his heartbeat eased up. He remembered that she'd given birth and wondered if what he'd wanted to do with her would be painful, so he rolled on his back to situate her on top of his body. Lilly smiled and came to herself. She kissed his hairy chest, his neck and his face. He held her head still and planted a kiss on her lips that made her wanton. Suddy heard her yelping like a litter of pups. Lilly's body had engulfed Clint's erection and throbbed. He felt hot and cool pulsation and could not contain himself. Suddy had armed herself to peek and see what they were doing. She found young Clint with his head beneath her skirts. When Lilly moaned in ecstasy, he lifted himself and penetrated her again and called her name over and over until he began praying, "my gawd, help me." Suddy ran back into the kitchen to put her firewood away that she had grabbed to defend Lilly with. She smiled and hunched her shoulders. Clint went into the kitchen when he could again walk and sat down to eat the food that Suddy prepared. Lilly washed herself and changed her dress. Clint left taking baby Charley with him with no complaints from Lilly who now had no doubts of his being returned to her. He walked into the mansion shouting, "Look y'all! Here's Charley." Missy and old Massa Clinton reached for the gurgling child at the same time. The three of them went into Millicent's bedroom and sat the happy little fellow on her bed. She dared not protest for fear of having another stroke. Before Charley had his first birthday, Lilly was expecting her second child. Young Clint started working in the fields to clear his head. He adored his son and wanted to live forever between Lilly's legs but he knew that his secret longing had to take a back seat to reality. Every morning he would have breakfast with Lilly and play with his son. He loved the smell of cinnamon and vanilla and wondered if he had the strength to leave Lilly to marry properly. Secretly, Lilly wanted him to go. He would rock Charley to sleep and force her body to yield to him every single morning. She had already decided that he needed a wife so that she could get some rest. One day when Lilly was in her seventh month of pregnancy, Clint failed to show up and headed to the Byron Plantation. The evening before he left, he instructed Suddy to stay home. He had a plan to bring her laundry from the surrounding plantations so that she could begin to make money. His plan was to provide her sons with a mule and wagon. They would pick up the laundry, Suddy would wash and iron it, the sons would deliver and he himself would collect her money and pay her each week. Everything he touched seemed to turn to gold. Clint saw no reason why Suddy shouldn't be paid. He had a smokehouse and a barn built for Lilly so that he could live in comfort. He gave them a milk cow, five laying hens and two roosters. Suddy loved it. She was finally contented to attend to things that mattered to her and have money. It didn't matter that she had no reason to spend it but she felt alive with esteem. One day Clint went to collect Suddy's money from Millwright Byron. He saw Delpheen who wore a sundress and climbed a pecan tree to shake a limb and make the nuts fall to the ground. Her mouth looked like a ripening peach and his imagination took over envisioning a bursting pit on the inside that housed a soft seed that he desired to fertilize. Clint collected the money that was left for him at the back door with the maid and walked around to the front of the house to request a visit with Millwright Byron. Delpheen came running into her daddy's office while they talked and sat with her legs open so wide that Clint could see her panties. The old man thanked him for the laundry service that gave his old gal a chance to catch up on mending. Clint's mind was elsewhere and the old man saw his daughter open and close her legs with a rhythm that made Clint break out in a sweat. He said, "Clint, as you can see, I desperately need a deal of another kind." They made small talk until his wife found Delpheen and forced her leave her father alone with his company. The old man had quite a story to tell and it made Clint begin to rethink his plan. It was the money that Millwright Byron offered him that closed the deal. He explained to Clint that his father in law had made him an offer when his daughter had set her sights on him. Millwright said that he was enjoying older women who loved a good time but the young girl who later became his wife, was so freaky that he'd looked for her father to kill him any day. Instead her father had made him an offer. Young Clint stifled a laugh because he'd had every intention to ask for Delpheen and it would not have cost the old man a dime. Millwright ended the conversation by saying, "Just remember one thing. If she's anything like her mother, you may become tempted, but I'm gonna trust you not to hurt her." They were married that Christmas day and Clint moved into the Byron Mansion. Only his family knew. Nothing changed between him and Lilly except that he refrained from penetrating her. The day that Lilly gave birth to their daughter, Clint was busy in Athens building a cabin for himself in the woods to protect his holdings. The rest of the story was too long for Wilbur to finish for he and Ida had made it home.

From the time they arrived home Wilbur began to watch Ida like a hawk. The only time that she found to see Mack was on Wilbur's poker nights which was every Monday and Friday night. Since he'd switched to the day shift, Wilbur came home before midnight on Mondays but on Fridays he was subject to stay out all night depending on whether his money was tied up in a game or not. Ida's two weeks down south without seeing Mack had put a strain on their relationship but had not affected the business. There was work waiting for her that she had known about and on her first day back, she busied herself taking new orders while Mack's cashier rang sales and handled the establishment's flow of customers. Ida called Mother Brown who gathered the women's church group for a meeting that concerned the upcoming appointments she'd scheduled to measure two wedding parties. One session was for the bridal gown and six bride's maid dresses. The second session was scheduled prematurely for a bridal gown, six men's shirts and four bride's maid dresses. It would give Ida a little space to breathe in case of a cancellation. A choir wanted new robes and needed their orders filled first so the meeting lasted a bit longer than Norman and Wilbur was able to sit and listen to them conduct their meeting and marveled at how concise and professional Ida was when it came to business matters. After the women concluded their meeting, Ida served them tea and sandwiches. Some of them opted for a stronger beverage and it answered a question that had plagued Wilbur for some time. He had sometimes wondered where his beer had disappeared to. Now he could stop looking for a few signs of Ida's indiscretions; however, some signs remained.

Mack had waited for a call during the two weeks that Ida had taken off work. The call had never come. He busied himself at the shop and took long lunch hours with other business owners on the block. Together, they formed a citizen's organization comprised of businessmen in the downtown district. After listening to their plans and calculations he found it to be a good thing and was able to network and increase his buying power through the organization. Ida had set things up so well before she left that he breezed through the time without much of a problem but he had missed her terribly. The day Ida had walked through the door of the store again, was the day that Mack felt alive again. It was mind over matter but Mack could not tell the difference. While Ida was away he had languished and pined. Ida had carried her panties to work in her purse because she knew that every chance Mack got, he would find his way beneath her clothes. When the cashier prepared to go out for her lunch break, Ida asked her to run an errand before she returned to the store. Ida wanted Mack to make love to her. She locked the front door and allowed him to ravish her in the sewing room while they watched the door through a mirror to see if anyone approached it to come in and shop. They were happy that no one did. Ida gave him more hugs and kisses than she wanted to but she knew he needed them. After their hot maternal liaisons Ida sent Mack to lunch. She was sewing when the clerk returned to work. Before he left, Ida instructed Mack to purposely be seen at the lunch counter where the clerk was asked to pick up her meal. Mack had walked in to wave at the clerk and then paid for her lunch as well as paying for Ida's food before he went to his citizen's meeting. After she finished eating, Ida washed up, put on her clean panties and worked closely with the clerk. That night, she ravished Wilbur the way that Mack had made love to her. It so impressed Wilbur that he gave her a little more space. He reasoned that there was no way that the girl could have given him loving like that and lay in the arms of another man. But Ida did. She and Mack offered the clerk a position with the industry that did the sewing for Ida. In less than six months, through her clerk, Ida's personal touch was transferred to an establishment that used real people to do the detailing after the final pressing of the clothing. Ida's shipments came in by the truckloads on hangers. She increased her prices by the costs of her personal touch, for shipping and handling and for pressing to further increased the store profits. It gave her less sewing to do at the store and more time for Mack who was beginning to spend much more time with members of the newly founded citizen's organization than Ida wanted him to.

In mid November Ida received a call from Effie telling her that Callie had given birth to a baby boy and that Dude was there for the birth. Ida asked, "Who does the precious little boy look like?" Effie whispered, "He looks just like his sister and I'm trying to get them away from here before Farmer Wilson comes running." She then asked Ida something that rocked her world. Ida had been upset with Mack earlier in the day for deciding to pay dues to an organization that he had not invited her to become a part of. She suggested that Mack leave the value of her shares of stock out of his calculations. The value of the business had increased by a profit margin of 95% after she had gone in with her skills. She had no intention of allowing Mack to give it all away. Ida had hurried to the bank to sell her shares without Mack's knowledge and gone home. Her mind was made up to sell out and stay at home with Wilbur. When Effie had asked the question, Ida's mind went blank. She told her mother that she would have to call her back later and hung up the phone. Wilbur came home that night to a brawling wife and a cold meal. Ida was on the telephone saying, "The cash is in the account for operations. The stock is in the store to be sold. The orders have been filled and the bills are paid. Now Mack you can keep the business going, hire you some help, or you can stick it all in a check and give it to your citizen's group. It makes me no never mind. She hung up the phone and ran to Wilbur to cry. He turned her tears into laughter when he asked, "Baby, who do you want me to kill?" Ida blew her nose and told him what had happened and Wilbur almost danced. He had his wife back. He called Effie and asked why she needed them to come to get Callie's children. Effie explained that Callie was determined to leave the children in Alabama and go back to Germany with her husband. Dude was too in love to resist her decision to do so. She and John Jr had to work the farm and it was not fair to Grandpa and Grandma Moore to be obligated to care for the children at their ages. Wilbur knew that the children were the offspring of Farmer Wilson. He promised to make arrangements to get the children and bring them to Indiana until something could be figured out. While Wilbur and Ida were trying to figure how or when to travel back to Alabama, Mack was trying to figure out how to win Ida's affections again. He was at a loss as to why she chose to defy his judgment call concerning the business. He also wondered if she had ever truly loved him. During the next few months Ida was just sick over what had transpired to cause the conflict between her and Mack. She had gotten used to carrying a heavy load of cooking and house cleaning not to mention the excitement of having a busy schedule concerning her and Mack's business venture. She went into mourning as if there were deaths in the family and indeed there was. Her relationship with her sister, Callie had died. Her relationship with Mack and all of his adoration towards her was dead. Her Career was now dead and every day, she received calls for her to please breathe the life back into it. Rather than face the turmoil, each morning Ida would get up and get Wilbur off to work, remove her phone from the cradle and return to her soft bed to cry until she fell asleep. Wilbur began to work hard to try and root her out of her turmoil but was unsuccessful. The place where Ida was mentally could not be reached until early one morning she felt a tiny flutter in her stomach that surprised her. A bitter taste rose quickly to her pallet that made her run to the toilet to wash her mouth but instead, she threw up and gagged until she felt empty inside. Wilbur heard her gagging and rushed to her side to see how he could help. She gagged while he cried and pleaded for her not to die. Ida almost cursed him out for adding to her discomfort by whining like a bitch; but remembered his old traumatic bout with grief. She allowed him to wash her face and help her to her feet. His eyes were smiling but Wilbur's mouth was grim. He helped her as much as he could have under the circumstances. After Wilbur sat Ida down at the kitchen table, he went back into the bathroom and filled the tub with warm water. "It's for you, baby," he whispered. He said, "I didn't put any scent in the water. I can't tell whether it will make you sick or not." Ida was a bit puzzled at his comment because Wilbur knew that she'd always scented her bath water. She climbed into the tub and began to lather her wash cloth when another bout of nausea hit her. Wilbur who watched her with interest with the same smiling eyes took the perfumed soap out of her hands and gave her bar of Ivory soap from the linen closet. He left her side for a few minutes to call off work and was able to solicit a co-worker to go in on his off day to fill in for him so that none of his own time would be lost. When Wilbur returned to the bathroom, Ida sat motionless. He added more hot water to the bath, and lathered Ida's back until she moaned with delight. Gently, he washed every inch of her body and almost laughed when he remembered the morning that her little ass had jumped into the tub to try and outsmart him. In his mind he saw the young girl slide a sheet of paper from her notebook to regain her composure after sending sparks his way. He had straightened her skirt and brushed dried grass from her curly locks, retied her ribbons and waited until she was safely home after their lovemaking. Wilbur's emotions got the best of him and tears began to flow. As he helped Ida from the tub, he said to her, "Ida baby, you know what's wrong, don't you?" She said, "I know I'm good and tired but I'll be alright. Just let me get my nap out." Wilbur wiped his eyes and laughed at his self. He had fallen in love with her innocence and each day his love for Ida grew stronger. While she slept, he sorted the wash and dusted every nook and cranny of the house. He had a taste for bacon and eggs but something reminded him that the bacon was not a good idea. Instead he fixed oatmeal, scrambled eggs and toast. Ida's nap lasted for four hours but her delight at how her husband cared for her on that morning was to last a lifetime. When she finished her breakfast, she asked, "Wilbur, where is the coffee?" Wilbur chose not to answer but sat a thick vanilla milk shake in front of her instead and said, "See if you like it."

The two of them sat in the kitchen and talked for another hour. Trusting his instincts, Wilbur asked her to get dressed so that they could take a walk along Lake Michigan before the cold weather set in. He wanted her to wear something chic and comfortable because he realized that in a few months, she was not going to be able to fit her clothes. Ida still did not have a clue that she was expecting a child. Wilbur didn't want to be the one to tell Ida, he wanted God to tell her. To him, it was just too sweet a gift for him to step out in front of the giver. Ida was beginning to feel like her old self while she sorted out the clothes she would sport for her husband. They had not walked together since their trip to Alabama. She chose a rust colored cotton ensemble that had a short olive green blouse and a long knee length coat. Around her neck, Ida tied a calico colored scarf of olive, rust and gold. When she walked out of the bedroom Wilbur whispered, "Shhhiiit! Girl, you're gonna make me quit my damn job and stay home with you everyday." Ida didn't know how she glowed. When she had tried to apply her makeup, her stomach flopped so she had hurried to take it off. She looked wholesome and angelic. Wilbur helped her into the car and wanted to rush with her to the doctor's office to make sure that she was ok. He wanted to shout something into the air so that all of nature would hail his pregnant wife. But instead he began to tell another story. It made Ida laugh to hear about how he had viewed her actions when her hormones raged. In a million years, she never would have thought that it was he who had gone to her father to make her stop following his truck around town. Ida had forgotten the night that she'd hid in the bed of his truck and popped her head up when he neared home. Wilbur made her laugh until she cried. Nearing the beach, Ida felt vibrant and free. Wilbur parked the car and opened the door to get out. He'd wanted to open the door for her but she was already out of the car and rushing to take off her shoes to walk in the sand. The air off of the lake was warm but the winds were high and blew as if sacred secrets were being told. Wilbur took her hand and began to walk along the shore until they came to an old dried and hollowed log that had probably washed ashore many years before. He pulled Ida into his arms and sat her on his knee. Ida whispered, "Down boy, I'm hungry." Wilbur said, "Girl, I'm going to make you remember this day." Ida jumped from his lap and ran back to the car. Wilbur yelled, "Girl, if I knew you were going to act like this, I wouldn't have married you." It took a while for them to finish laughing but when they could manage to stop; they kissed long and mellow as if their hearts were binding them together in a melody. They ate seafood dinners on the waterfront before returning home. While lying in the comfort of her husband's arms Ida received the message from the giver of gifts that she was indeed pregnant. When she had arched her body in surprise, Wilbur thought that Ida was having a climax and was surprised when her body enveloped him when he had tried to pull out. He had a hard time getting up the next morning but Ida had his breakfast ready and his lunch packed for she needed him out of the way so that she could get on with her plans. There were patterns to be purchased and sewing to be done. Wilbur thought, "God, you must have said something. Thank you."

It was not long before Ida found that she had more work on her hands than she'd ever imagined. Her creativity was at an all-time high. Her women's church group headed by Mother Brown jumped on the bandwagon to promote everything that Ida worked at. Around The Bend Fashions became a designer line of children's clothes. Ida was simply sewing for her own satisfaction when she showed the group a few of the sets that she had made from soft fabrics that were not necessarily flannel. Mother Brown offered to buy all of the clothes for a project to raise funds for the church. The autumn leaves were falling and thanksgiving was right around the corner. Wilbur and Ida were looking forward to the birth of their baby and the birth of a business venture had snaked its way into their mix. Without consulting Wilbur, Ida called upon Mack to do her a favor. With every fiber of his being, Mack wanted to refuse to have anything to do with her but his heart felt as if it moved into another realm of reality and spoke on its own. He heard it say in a tender voice, "Come in and talk to me, Ida." Ida waited another week before she went to the shop on Main Street. Mack had hired another person for shipping and receiving and was busy taking inventory when she walked in the door wearing a simple navy colored chemise dress with matching wedge heels and purse. For warmth, Ida had hugged her shoulders with a gray cashmere wool shawl. Mack looked at her and smiled but had to quickly lower his head to keep his tears from becoming evident. The cashier knew who Ida was and ran to her with outstretched arms. Mack asked her from a distance, "How long do you have for a meeting, Mrs. Avery?" She answered, "My next appointment is scheduled for a 1:30 luncheon. Will that give us enough time for the details we need to cover?" He cleared his throat and answered, "I think so." As soon as Mack closed his office door he said, "Ida, you look marvelous. Tell me what it is that you need." Ida removed her shawl while Mack watched her eyes glow. He also observed how her hips carried her weight. His jaw dropped and Mack could not close his mouth. Ida broke into a smile and her eyes twinkled so brightly that Mack had to look elsewhere. He said, "I'll be damned if that Wilbur Avery isn't the luckiest bastard in the world." After hearing her proposal Mack agreed to allow Ida to order everything she needed through the store and to hold on to her trademark and pattern copyrights. They reviewed the necessary accounting costs for fabric, shipping and handling and storage fees, which was only one forth of what he would have asked any other company to pay. Mack once again connected her to a manufacturer for outsourcing and the meeting ended. Before she left he asked Ida when the baby was due. Ida slipped out of her shawl and walked over to him and straddled his lap. Mack buried his face between her breasts and cried. When he loosed his grip on her, she stood up and removed her panties and allowed him to make love to her. She knew that it could do no harm for she was already pregnant. She sat there as long as he needed her to and whispered her appreciation of his adoration and inspiration while he struggled to make the time stand still. Mack exploded so intensely that he stood up while Ida held on to him for fear of falling. Fortunately they did not turn the chair over and Mack was able to sit down easily so that she could rise from his lap. After he zipped his fly, Mack reached for Ida again. The clock on the wall said twelve fifty. Ida needed to get home to fix Wilbur's dinner. Mack led her to a small sofa and coaxed her into lying down with her head in his lap. He then lowered his head to kiss her lips while massaging her clitoris until she moaned and cried against his lips saying, "Mack, why do you love me so?" And then she cried, "Ooh," when his fingers found the pulse deep inside her body. With his lips, Mack pulled Ida's tongue into his mouth where it tasted sweet with satisfaction. Ida rested for a few minutes and stood up to clean herself up and to put her panties back on. While she straightened her clothes, Mack washed his face and hands. Next he drew up an agreement containing the terms that they had discussed. He realized that the fire that was blazing between them and would never go out. Wilbur had her wrapped up in a beautiful package that was a gift from the heavens and neatly tied with a bow. Mack loved Ida and was willing to take any portion of her that he could get. He reasoned that maybe it was time for him to look towards finding a mate and starting a family for himself. The fact that Ida had become pregnant by Wilbur and not him had cleared his mind enough to think of his own needs and best interests. Ida had just finished putting on a fresh supply of lipstick and a dab of cologne behind her ears when there was a knock on the door. She scooted back into the chair across the desk from Mack. That's when she'd heard Wilbur's voice saying to someone, "Meeting or not, I need to see him." While the cashier was trying to stop Wilbur from entering Mack's office, the shipping clerk rang his phone yelling, "I'll get him for you sir." Mack hurriedly pulled a pine scented cover from a closet shelf and shook it hard enough for the sharp scent of pine to fill the room. Ida pulled a slip of paper from her purse and began to write. Before the pine scent filled the room, she quickly put her pen and paper away and closed her purse. She had plans for the note and the scent of pine was not part of the plan. Mack answered the phone in a tone that said, "Speak up! I'm busy!" His employee said, "Mr. Nickles, there is a Mr. Avery to see you. Are you still in your meeting?" Mack answered, "Ah, yes, but it's alright. He's my client's husband." The pine scent had mellowed out a bit and the room smelled like a cedar closet. Wilbur stalked into the office and Mack jumped up to shake his hand but Wilbur's eyes were on Ida who smiled and said, "I see that you got the note." Wilbur asked, "What note?" Ida looked puzzled and said, "If you didn't see the note on the kitchen table, then why are you here?" Now Wilbur was puzzled. He said, "I haven't been home. I just saw the car." Ida hunched her shoulders and gave him a big smile and handed him the contract saying, "Look at this. I need you to go over this with me so that I can decide if a line of baby clothes might work. It is not the same as a partnership, but a lot of money can be made without my spending a lot of time away from home." Wilbur took the contract but he could not read a single word for seeing the color of red. He stared in hopes that his vision would clear up but it didn't. The words on the paper that Wilbur's angry eyes could not focus on was being read to him by Mack and Wilbur's mind was able to zero in on what Mack was saying. He looked over at Ida and asked, "How will you be able to pick up your shipments and make the clothes sell without a store, and how can you market from the church's basement without them being liable for taxes?" Ida looked at Mack and said, "Ok. So I think that these things need to be taken into consideration before I sign this, Mack. Since this is no longer a partnership things may need to be handled differently." Wilbur interjected, "And she's pregnant and I'm not going to have her coming here in the cold and snowy weather. Did she tell you that she's pregnant and that the baby is due in April?" Mack said, "Well, you guys let me know what you all come up with. Like your wife says, 'There's plenty of money to be made' and just maybe you should consider that, Mr. Avery." Ida needed to beat Wilbur home to put the note down. Wilbur needed some air. An image had formed in his mind of Ida's legs upon Mack's shoulders with her shouting, "MMAAACCCK!" He had never told her what she had screamed in her drunken stupor while he had made love to her. The two of them walked to their cars together. Ida told him that she needed to stop by Mother Brown's house to review what had transpired but what she really wanted to do was slow him down from rushing home so that her note would be situated for him to see. He shocked Ida when he countered, "Leave the car here at the store. I'll take you by Mother Brown's house and then we can go to lunch." While Wilbur drove Ida was devising a plan to send someone to her house to place the note on the kitchen table. A very surprised Mother Brown opened the door to let Wilbur and Ida into her house. While the two women talked, Wilbur dozed off to sleep to the sounds of words like "key issues" and "contracts on the table" that sounded about right for the reason why they were there. Mother Brown's daughter came in to get money for her mother's prescriptions so that when they left the room, it gave Ida a chance to toy with her husband. Ida stuck her tongue in his ear and whispered, "I love you, darling." She watched his groin swell. Instinctively, his hand covered it and he never woke up. Shortly thereafter, Mother Brown took Ida and Wilbur into her basement and showed them where the clothes could be kept, where the orders could be filled and explained how they would use their tax write off to profit the church. Everything was put into a neat little package but Wilbur wondered why his wife's name had to go on the contract alone. Mother Brown promised to carry it to the committee. Mother Brown then worked at stalling them by offering a cup of tea. Her daughter had been sent to Ida's house to place the note on the kitchen table and had not returned with Ida's keys. Ida went to the bathroom and was able to wash her ass to rid her body of Mack and sprinkle a little talc onto the seat of her panties. When she came out of the bathroom, Ida suggested that Wilbur go in so that when they got to the restaurant, they would already be prepared to eat without using a public toilet. Ida was handed her keys and Mother brown was handed a wet wash cloth from Ida's handbag, and whispered, "Mercy. Child you got to slow down." Her daughter who was about ten years older than Ida was anxiously covering her mouth to keep from laughing aloud. Neither Ida nor Faye Brown's mother knew the reason why Faye had laughed. She had seen Wilbur with Alma shucking and jiving a few times. Though Alma had seemed the aggressor, Wilbur had left the club with her twice on a Friday night. It appeared to her that whatever it was that Ida was hiding should have been considered fair play.

Wilbur drove to pick up Ida's car from the store in silence. He decided to drive separate cars to the restaurant and to allow Ida to get home first. He had too many questions and very few answers about the events of the day. He watched her stroll to her car without turning her head in the direction of the store. His calculating mind surmised that it was a dead give-a-way. If her ass weren't guilty of anything she would have looked towards the store to wave or

something, he thought bitterly. After finding two parking places side by side
he followed her into the restaurant and when they were seated Wilbur ordered
a shot of scotch and told Ida to order a meal for him too. She knew what he
wanted. Wilbur was on his third shot by the time they were served. He sat
chillingly and sipped his drink while Ida ate like a starving refugee. When she
finished Wilbur sweetly asked, "Can I order anything else for you, baby?" He
ordered another fish platter for Ida to carry home and after walking her to her
car, he told her to go on home. He said that he had a stop to make. The
suggestion made Ida's day. He drove to the liquor store for a bottle of bourbon
and took his time driving home. When Wilbur arrived home, the note was on
the table just like she said she'd left it. He questioned her motive for leaving it
on the table if not to further prove him to be a sucker. Her favorite fragrance
of honeysuckle permeated the air like Voo-Doo, but he had a plan to Who
Doo her damn Voo-Doo to give it a lasting effect. Wilbur found Ida stretched
out in bed. Nice move, he thought. He began to remove his leather belt while
Ida lay smiling like a damn cherub. When the leather cut through her flesh,
Ida grabbed her butt and screamed bloody murder. Wilbur wound her gown
tightly in his hand until she could not move. He sat on the side of the bed and
held her face down while she screamed into her pillow. He said, "Ida, I'm
going to break your ass . . . (WHAAAP!) Sounded the leather as it repeatedly
connected with flesh. Or I'm going to send you back . . . (WHACK) to your
damn daddy." Between words, he whipped her ass until it bruised. Ida's cries
of, "Wilbur please!" Turned into, "Somebody help me." Wilbur snatched Ida
up to look into her face and said, "Why would you try to play me for a fool?
I am not your daddy. He is some kin to you. I ain't! Do you understand that
I can kill you, girl?" Wilbur put a death grip on Ida's cheeks and she tasted
blood. His eyes bore through her until she closed her eyes to shield her mind
from the chilling thought of dying. When Wilbur saw her tears, he returned
to his right mind and sat on the floor but he still held Ida's face in his hand.
She had no choice but to match his movements or he could have easily broken
her neck. Ida sat whimpering and waiting for a chance to get away from her
husband, the man who had cherished her so damn much that he now wanted
to kill her. She slapped him in the mouth and hissed, "Hey Baby, you have
done it now! Kill me then, Mr. Fuck up. I didn't come cheap and I'm not
going to leave this world broke, busted and disgusted. Ida ran to the closet and
pulled out a small handgun that Mack had given to her for protection while
working in the store. One look into Wilbur's eyes made her wish that she had
left it where it had been but she couldn't turn back. "Wilbur said, "Ida, you

already killed me. You did it today when you let that sawed off Jew boy touch you again." Surprised, Ida asked, "What do you mean, touch you again?" Wilbur snatched a drawer from the dresser and dumped it out on the bed. He said in resolve, "Check it out. I've been your fool for quite a few years now. I was waiting for you to grow up. You are carrying my child, Ida. Do you think I'm going to let you be a stomp down whore after I've given you my best?" Wilbur reached for Ida and she pulled the trigger that sent a bullet through the closet door barely missing his head. When Wilbur came to himself, he walked out of the bedroom to find that Ida had left the house wide open and disappeared.

Iris sat and allowed Ida to pour her heart out to her. A few moments before then, Iris had heard what sounded like scratches on her front door and peeked out of a window to see Ida who fell into her arms when she opened the door. She had heard an echoing gun shot and wondered which direction the sound had come from. Ida still held the pistol in her hand. Iris carefully took Ida's gun out of her hand and pleaded with Ida to tell her anything that she could. Being impatient, Iris ran to the phone and called Ida's house. Wilbur answered the telephone. Iris breathed a sigh of relief. Wilbur told her to come and get anything that Ida needed but he thought it best that she stay away because the way that he felt at the moment might cause him to fuck an elephant up. Iris hung up the phone and told Ida to stay put until she returned with some of her clothes. She walked down the street letting her imagination run wild thinking that the house would be in shambles. The house was as neat as a pin. The stuff on the bed along with the drawer that the papers had been thrown from was all Iris saw that was out of place. Wilbur let her in and sat alone in the parlor while Iris gathered some of Ida's things. When she showed Wilbur what she planned to take to Ida, he pulled a piece of luggage from the hall closet and began to match each outfit with matching undergarments and shoes. He packed her bathrobe and slippers, her toiletries, comb and brush. Iris laughed and asked, "Now who's going to carry all this shit?" Like a good little boy he answered, "I will." He then said, "Tell her to call me when she gets ready to come home. I don't want to have to kill her, Iris. I got to cool down." Wilbur walked Iris back home and sat the luggage at her front door and went home. Three drinks later, he crawled into bed and slept until morning.

Ida sat in a state of shock at Iris' dining room table. She knew that she was wrong and was too humiliated and embarrassed to sort it all out in her head. For the first time in her life she was at a loss for words and stood to lose the love of her life just when the ultimate blessing of finally being pregnant had come to fruition. Iris used her key to open her front door so as not to startle

Ida by the sound of knocking. Gerta, Marie and Alma each went into their rooms after the initial commotion to give their mother a chance to understand what Ida's problem was. Iris had taught them well. When she called them into the dining room they entered with chattering and greetings to Ida as if nothing was wrong. Marie sat a bottle of red wine on the table while Gerta brewed a pot of tea. Iris handed Ida her robe and slippers to cover her gown and wiped her face with a warm cloth. A cup of tea with cream suddenly appeared on the table. Ida took a sip of it and it seemed to loosen her taut nerves. Iris then poured a glass of wine and took a sip of it. Ida began to tell her side of the story that brought the house down when she said that she was pregnant. Iris sarcastically asked, "Hell is that why you shot at the man? Oh Damn!" Of course the story of Crazy Miss Daisy came up but Iris didn't mind the girls sharing it with her friend, Ida who laughed her self to tears. They even shared a story about Mother Brown of Ida's church group who had one night run naked from the back door of the church in the wee hours of the morning some years ago. She and the pastor had gotten caught with their clothes off when the pastor's wife found his car parked behind the church. They had entered the church through the cellar door and so had the pastor's wife. The naked woman had been so swift that the pastor's wife and the community only saw a naked lady running down the street with her clothes but Iris had picked up her scarf and taken it to her the next day. Then there was the story told of another devout church going lady that would sneak the worst looking man in the community in her back door whenever her husband worked the night shift. Her name was Ingrid. Old man Gilbert and his wife lived across the alley from Ingrid and her husband. For years Gilbert who was well endowed and Ingrid had been lovers until a nineteen-year-old young man by the name of Jesse became attracted to her. When Ingrid began to slight Gilbert, he became enraged. He had gone to her back door for three nights in a row without getting a response. Ingrid's husband had only one more night to go for the night shift before he'd be switched to the next shift and Gilbert was determined to get the loving that he had become addicted to. The problem was this. Jesse was young and well endowed. Ingrid could not taper her needs enough to return to the old man's lovemaking. With him she'd had to work at it, but Jesse knew how to give as well as he got. Gilbert stood to lose everything that he had but still he went and kicked Ingrid's door in to gain entrance into her house. When the police came Gilbert insisted that the two people inside had stolen his money. Jesse managed to escape without Gilbert knowing who he was but Ingrid stood naked in her backyard where Gilbert had dragged her by her hair. Gilbert earned a weekly paycheck that paid his way back home. Outwitted Ingrid lost everything she owned which included her husband. Ida sat and listened to tale after tale until Iris suggested that she get some rest. Iris led her to the bedroom and turned back the covers of the bed. Ida did not object to being helped into bed and fell asleep soon after the covers were pulled up to her shoulders. Alma gave her bed to Iris and slept in her brother's room that still smelled of his cologne. It was a nice scent that made her long to exchange places with Ida.

Early the next morning, Wilbur stretched himself and got up to make a fresh pot of coffee. He acted as if he did not have a care in the world. His anger had subsided in the manner of a father who had to punish his child before the child came to harm. A thought came to his mind that he knew was from heaven because it came in the form of a scripture. 'Obedience is better than sacrifice'. Then into his thoughts came other words that warmed his soul and gave him comfort. 'Train up a child the way he should go and when he is old he will not depart from it'. Ida had been a child when he married her and he realized that the rules of the script changed regarding the man and woman's relationship. He now wished that he'd given her time to mature before satisfying his senseless selfish sexual appetite during her youth. Being his wife, his duty now was to love her as Christ loved the church. Wilbur poured himself a cup of coffee and packed his lunch. Between sips of the strong dark caffeine laced liquid he dressed and headed to work. For years Wilbur had watched his peers go in and out of restaurants and had taken pride in the fact that his wife cooked hearty meals for him every day that God had sent since their marriage. That morning, he'd had to swallow his pride and walk into the restaurant to sit beside them. When breakfast was over he'd left with many things to think about. Those guys had many tales of woe that was simply hilarious. Somehow Wilbur allowed them to talk him into having them over for his initiation into the "ODB" Club. The party was set for the following Saturday night at nine o'clock sharp. When his shift was over a group of co-workers rallied around Wilbur and encouraged him to meet them for dinner at six o'clock that evening. A place called The Chicken Shack served down home meals. The guys had often treated themselves to it and knew that it was the best place to eat meals when wives refused to cook. Wilbur went home to bathe and change clothes. He noticed a note lying on the floor that must have been slid beneath the door. He ignored it and left note where it lay. After his bath, Wilbur slipped into a pair of gray slacks, gray cashmere sweater and a short black leather jacket. When one looked at him from the feet up, he looked like a prince. If they looked from the head down, a woman could never get pass his eyes that made them trip over themselves. On his way out of the door after picking up his keys from the kitchen table, he walked into the bathroom to tip his hat to his reflection. Courage seemed to smile and wink back at him by his reflection. Driving to the restaurant was a feat by itself. One young lady saw him stop for a red light and struck up a pose in front of his car. When the light changed, Wilbur had to ease his way around her to keep going. He watched another man slap his companion because she was staring at him while he drove. He said to his ego, "Get a grip. It's the same shit warmed over. A bird in the hand is worth two in the bush." He continued on and refused to remember any parts of his troubles except the big appetite that clamored for the food he wanted for dinner. During dinner Wilbur tried to tone down his presence by looking serious and a little annoyed. It did not work. The waitresses made such a big deal over him that he ordered a coke and asked one of the other guys to order a meal for him. He didn't need anyone playing in his food and wanted to discourage any notes being passed his way. His co-workers were laughing at the antics of women as they vied for Wilbur's attention. When his food arrived and the waitress saw it being slid in front of Wilbur, she snapped her fingers as if to say, "Why didn't I realize that?" She whirled around and slid her note to him with a smile on her face that appeared to say, 'I just can't help myself.' Wilbur had to smile at the way that she moved while walking away. An old veteran sitting at the next table posed a wise question. He allowed, "Hey, fellows. Why don't you guys pick up his slack? Don't let 'em all get away." One by one the guys finished eating; they began to tease the waitresses enough for Wilbur to finish his food which was delicious. He sent the veteran a shot and a beer to show his gratitude. Wilbur was taking his last bite of peach cobbler when Iris, Ida, Gerta, Marie and Alma strutted in the door. Alma had watched Wilbur leave his house looking too good to be trusted. As fast as she could, she went home and told Iris. Having finally gotten the whole truth out of Ida while her daughters were at work, Iris knew that Ida needed to move quickly. Men minded their egos being bruised. Pregnant or not, she knew that Ida was in grave danger of losing her husband. Iris also knew the psyche of the women who worked at the Chicken Shack. They loved the street life and weekly paychecks that rolled up in the restaurant. Iris rushed to tell everyone in the house to get dress. They were going out to dinner. She was so geared towards the excitement that Marie would not let her drive. Rose, Iris' other daughter took a rain check on the action. Lately she had been working around the clock and wanted to rest. Iris got a rush when it came to squashing bullshit

and reuniting lovers. When the four beautiful ladies climbed out of the car at
the restaurant, Iris said, "Come on ladies, let's strut!" Iris wanted them to
really impress everyone in the restaurant. They did. The guy sitting next to
Wilbur whistled and said, "Man! My dick just got hard as hell!" Wilbur doubled
over with laughter when his brother-in-law Happy came to mind. Someone
put money in a jukebox that sat in the corner by the door and the music
blared. "Its something you got baby and you ought to know. It makes me say
my, my, oh, oh I love you so." Ida's movements caught the rhythm. Wilbur
smiled and his eyes traveled from one face to another of the men who sat at his
table. The old veteran laughed out loud and said, "Boys, don't you let no
secrets slip by you now." He had watched Wilbur's eyes and already knew
what was up. The veteran left his seat and gave Wilbur a high-five. He said, "If
I had just a little of what you look at everyday, whew!" Wilbur reached for Ida
when she walked past and gently pulled her to sit down on his knee. Her eyes
glistened as he introduced her to his co-workers. Wilbur then called the other
ladies over and asked the staff for another table to be added to accommodate
the rest of party. The waitress that had written the note walked boldly to the
table and smiled at Ida as if to say, 'You go girl!' Iris said, "See what mother
meant?" Within five minutes Iris was seated with the older gentleman at the
next table. While the music played they shared memories of the past and
surprised each other when they found out that their paths had crossed years
earlier. In another five minutes, Iris' daughters had so much conversation and
jive going on at the table that the restaurant owner began to pass out business
cards and thank the guys for giving him some play. The patrons were staying
put and joining the merriment. There was a line of patrons on the outside of
the restaurant but people were buying drinks on the inside. The sat and nursed
their drinks while they chatted. Orders-to-go caused a flurry of activity and
the owner sent another round of drinks to Wilbur and his friends. He didn't
want the night to end but because the Men had to work the next morning,
they downed their drinks quickly and stood up to leave. Iris and her gang took
their dinners as a carry-out because they were going to protect Ida if circumstances
called for it. Ida rode back with the women that she had arrived with and
Wilbur drove home alone. Wilbur's co-workers walked him to his car like
soldiers and warned him to keep his cool. They reasoned that if Ida had shot at
him once, the second time would be easier. He took their advice and did not
say anything to Ida but goodnight. The next morning Wilbur was man of the
hour among his coworkers. One of them said, "Man, if I had a woman that
fine I would let her put a bullet in my ass every day!" Another said, "Man tell

the truth! She caught you fuckin' didn't she?" Wilbur quipped, "If I got to sit here and listen to all of this shit, I want every one of you broke ass Muff's to put me a dollar on this table." Dollar bills landed on the table from every direction. Wilbur was glad when the time came to go to work.

Gerta got wind of the ODB gathering and alerted Iris who took Ida shopping for food to prepare for Wilbur's party. She said, "We are simply going to crash it. Alma, call Brooks and them and tell them to show up around ten o'clock at Wilbur's house." Those that Iris mentioned were all of Dude's friends who would party at the drop of a hat. Ida was enjoying Iris' exciting outlook on life. She had never ventured out socially except for church activities. There had been the one Christmas party with the stars that she had enjoyed but a party in her home was something new. When she mentioned cleaning up for the party, Iris said, "That's what's wrong. You are just too damn clean for your own good. Your house is already clean enough to eat off of the floors." They spent the rest of the day cooking baked ham, potato salad, fried chicken livers, dirty rice and clam cakes. Iris set up the ingredients to make dinner rolls before answering a knock at the door. Ida saw Wilbur walk into the kitchen and kept her cool. He stopped and leaned against the door and folded his arms. Wilbur cleared his throat before he began to speak. He said to Ida, "If you going to be doing all of this cooking, why don't you come home and do it." She answered, "Don't worry. It's for your party." Wilbur frowned and asked, "Girl, who have you been talking to?" All Wilbur had planned to serve was chips and beer during a few hands of poker. Iris' counter held enough food to serve at least fifty people. Ida said, "Nobody in particular but I just want your first event to be nice, Wilbur. You've made our home too nice to half step. Wilbur asked her what she would have done if he hadn't stopped by. Ida tucked her chin and looked up at him like a mischievous child. Wilbur laughed and reminded her of the time that she'd come into the barn wearing the boots with her skirt tucked at the waistband of her skirt. The two of them howled and hooted with laughter until Iris walked into the kitchen and told Wilbur to go and get his car since the cat was out of the bag. Ida also asked him to break down the bed in the basement and set up for his poker games down there. Much of the community had never seen their home and they were in for a real treat. Ida and Wilbur had more room to party in than most of the nearby night spots and party they did. The poker started downstairs and when the men tired of swapping lies and drinking to the success of Wilbur's marriage

They went home and returned with their significant others. Between Iris and her daughters working the party and Wilbur being a great host, it was a fun evening. Wilbur made a toast to Iris and presented her with the tip jars from the bar and food tables in hopes that everyone would leave while a very tired Ida slept in her bed. After being introduced to the wives of Wilbur's coworkers, Ida had crawled into bed. She had never been as tired in her life. It was daylight Sunday morning before the house cleared out. Iris sat at the kitchen table while Wilbur checked the basement to make sure that there were no stragglers. Wilbur read her mind when he returned to the living room. He asked with concern showing in his tone of voice, "Iris do you see how peacefully she is sleeping? Could you sleep that well after shooting at someone's head?" He said, "If I let her go, the world would eat her alive within a month. I've planted this garden so I may as well finish the job until the harvest." Iris coaxed Wilbur into taking a drink with her so that she could take the time to gauge where his head really was. Her fear and concern for Ida was genuine. Ida was guilty of doing what Wilbur had accused her of. She asked Ida to make a promise to never ever admit it, no matter the circumstance or she would be guilty of committing suicide. Iris asked Wilbur for a pillow and a blanket. She felt better sleeping on the sofa. Wilbur, like a son did just that. He gave Ida the covers and bunked out in the middle bedroom. When Iris awakened around noon that Sunday morning Ida had crawled into bed with Wilbur in his inebriated state and wrapped her body in his arms. Iris went home to count her tips.

For the birth of baby Charles Wilbur Avery, both families traveled north to Indiana from Alabama and Georgia. Dude and Callie flew in from Germany with their third born child to visit with Iris. Johnny Sr and Mable were finally persuaded by John Jr and Effie to travel north. Lil' John and Estelle led the pack to accompany the two generations. Rufus who followed his uncle Dude into the armed forces was able to take a two-week leave to drive to Indiana with Wilbur's sisters, Ruthie Lee and Mae Alice. It was nearing the end of April and the weather was dry and warm with an air of melancholy that sent young hearts scampering around looking for love. Ida kept the family in stitches showing old pictures and clowning around with Myrtlennis who had just turned nine years old. In an attempt to make her backbone slip like Mae West, Ida went into labor. Mable moved Wilbur out of her way and rubbed Ida's back until she was hit with a bout of nausea. Mable, who could barely walk shouted to Wilbur, "Pick your wife up and get her out of here." Effie and John Jr. grabbed her packed bag and headed with Wilbur to the hospital. Two hours later, a curly haired green-eyed chubby baby was born who was the spitting image of Rufus and Wilbur combined. When Effie saw how much

infant Charley favored Rufus she looked at Wilbur and asked him if he and
Ida had pulled a fast one on the family. Wilbur wanted to remind her that they
had visited him and Luella after Rufus was born but he thought better of it.
This was Ida's finest hour and he couldn't bring himself to mention Luella's
name. Wilbur felt that he owed a debt to Ida that he could never repay because
of all they had gone through together. The doctor happened to walk up to
Wilbur in order to congratulate him and Effie blurted out a question in the
middle of his telling Wilbur that all was well. The doctor looked at Wilbur
and asked, "Should I answer her question?" Wilbur swelled with pride and
said, "Go ahead, Doc." He already knew the answer to her question. "Yes
Ma'am, this is the only pregnancy Mrs. Avery has ever had," he answered with
a smile. John Jr spoke up and said, "Effie, this is not so hard to figure out you
know. Evidently Rufus, the baby, Wilbur and his father Charley looks
like." . . . When John Jr hesitated Wilbur finished the sentence saying,
"Grandpa Clinton Avery." While Ida was in the hospital, Wilbur stayed by her
side as much as he could and thanked God for the family support. The families
rejoiced to be able to all be together and Dude was so happy to see Wilbur
again that he'd struggled to keep tears from falling. Wilbur hugged him in
spite of his guilt and hoped that Dude was not destined for heartbreak. He felt
a dreaded that one day Callie's infidelity would surface and cause a calamity.
Myrtlennis and Calvin really and truly looked like Dude's sisters. If it weren't
for the fact that Wilbur knew Farmer Wilson he would have believed the
children to have been Dude's offspring also. Iris tried to hoard the children
and promised Dude and Callie that she would help to take care of the children
that were being left with Wilbur and Ida. Grandma Moore wanted to take the
little baby home to Alabama and pitched a fit until Grandpa Moore agreed to
allow it. Dude took Mae Alice and Ruthie to meet his circle of friends. They
fell in love with Shirley and invited her to Athens. Shirley knew a lot of
playboys and debonair gentlemen. She also gave them juicy gossip of the life
and times of their envied sister in law, Ida. Ruthie and Mae Alice both shook
their heads and marveled at the love that their brother bestowed upon Ida. Lil'
John and Estelle enjoyed Dude's crowd so much that Lil' John copped Brooks'
pimp walk. Estelle did the "Shirley" and had the crowd falling off of their
chairs. When it was time for the families to return home, the community
rallied around Ida and Wilbur. They had shared their family with everyone
and caused many of their neighbors to draw closer to one another as if they
were being drawn by a chord. Rufus stayed at home until the last possible
minute and took a flight back to the army base where he was stationed. He'd
had good reason to stay around a bit longer. Lizzie heard of his arrival and

called him shortly thereafter. She informed him that there was someone who desperately needed to meet him. He waited until Nash, Lizzie's husband, left for work and carefully groomed himself for a special event. Rufus had not seen his son before leaving for the armed forces. The child was like him in so many ways that the community was in awe and waited for a showdown between Lizzie and her husband that never happened publicly. Lizzie's husband had accepted the child as his own but behind closed doors Lizzie paid dearly. She chose to work nights while her husband worked the evening shift as a way to continue to provide a peaceful environment for their children. They barely saw one another. The day that Rufus was introduced to his son, Edwin, Lizzie's daughter was sent to play with a neighbor that lived a few doors down the street. Edwin was two and a half years old and growing into quite a handsome specimen. While Rufus held him on his knee he noticed that Lizzie was pregnant again. Pregnant or not, he could not resist making love to her after rocking Edwin to sleep. The neighbors that had seen Rufus go into the house never saw him leave and worried that Nash would catch he and Lizzie in a compromising position but by the time Nash came home from work that night, Rufus had left by the back door and cut through the alley to visit friends on the next street. His head was swimming when he returned to the house later that evening. Brooks, Dude's friend had pulled his coat tail about the carryings on of Nash and Lizzie. They had become swingers and the baby that Lizzie carried was fathered by someone other than Nash. Rufus decided to spend as much time with his son as he could before he left town again. His future seemed to have become uncertain. He realized that between Georgia and Chicago, Athens would make the better place for him to call his permanent home. He had for years hoped that he and Lizzie would build a future together but there was too much between them now that had upset the balance in his life. Rufus partied hearty until the days of his leave dwindled down to the last moment. His flight was ready to leave O'Hara Field when he arrived at the airport. When the plane rose above the clouds he didn't know when he would see his son again but had promised Lizzie that he would keep in touch. Callie and Dude drove Ruthie and Mae Alice back to Athens, Georgia and took a flight to Germany from Atlanta.

Dude kept his whole heart entwined in ways to please his wife. His mind was wrapped in his career. His children were what Callie seemed most pleased with and anything that she did concerning them was alright with him. Dude lived to make her happy. Somehow Farmer Wilson managed to disappear whenever Dude went to Alabama. Dude never saw him. Callie would breeze into town in May each year for Mother's Day. She would arrive on the Friday before and Farmer Wilson always met her at the airport. They spent Friday nights and Saturday together and on Sunday morning, Farmer would take her back to the airport for her father to pick up and drive her to the farm to celebrate with Mable and Effie. One year Dora foiled their plans when she'd insisted on riding with her husband that fateful Friday night. Dora refused to let him out of her sight. He took her to visit everyone they knew that evening including the Moore family. Callie had waited stranded at the airport until midnight before calling her father for a ride. She insisted that he take her to the hotel so that she could arrive on mother's day but John Jr took her to the farm instead. Callie acted like a junkie with a bad habit. Effie asked if she was pregnant again. They all had a good laugh before everyone went back to bed that night. Farmer Wilson and Dora sat on their porch most of the night. He finally heard the engine of John Jr's truck start up and knew that Callie had found a way to get home. Dora heard it too. Actually, she had heard much more. But she never heard her husband leave her bed and walk to the barn before dawn. Callie waited for him in the dark where they made love until the rooster crowed on Saturday morning. Dora went into a rage after finding Farmer Wilson's side of the bed empty. She threw on a house dress to cover her night gown and headed towards the back door only to see her husband walk in with an innocent expression on his face. If she had stayed in bed and looked through the window, she would have seen Callie making her way into the foliage and tall grass at the bend of the road. Wilbur and Ida hired limousine service to the Chicago Railways for the Moore families. After a tour of the city they boarded the train headed towards the Mason Dixie Line. The generations had a glorious time all the way home. Iris kept Myrtlennis, Callie and Dude's newborn baby and their brother, Calvin while Mother Brown sat with Baby Charley at home. Nobody reminded Mable that the baby was not on the train. He remained with Ida until it was time for him to begin kindergarten. That summer he, Calvin and Myrtlennis met four siblings and visited with Callie and their father, Ennis Nelson. Farmer Wilson dropped had his set of twins off with the Moore family and picked them up before Dora returned from church. John Jr took Dude to Birmingham which was four hours away. Callie had crossed so many avenues that he learned to shelter Dude as if he were his son. Dude never saw the twin boys who looked like his sisters just as much as Myrtlennis and Calvin did. Callie spent time with all of the children. Farmer Wilson picked up his boys when he was on the way to get Dora. When Dude returned, him, Callie and the other children went to the county fair. He never laid eyes on Callie's lover. The only other person in the world besides Iris and her lover who knew Dude's real father and that Dude looked just like him was Ida. She hid it in her heart with the many things that she deemed unfruitful so that it could whither away in time. Wilbur and Ida took their time returning home from the Chicago Railway. The two of them had finally gotten enough of family ties. They stopped for a few moments to overlook the Chicago Skyline on Lakeshore Drive. Ida felt his arms encircle her and she lay her head on his chest while the winds blew softly in whispers of dreams that came true and words of contentment that made one desire to live forever in cool breezes. The bend of the road was embedded in her memory like the smell of sweet honeysuckle in the summer sun or dew that gather upon sweet smelling roses. She and Wilbur were one in life, love and consciousness. Just as she concluded her thoughts Wilbur whispered in her ear, "Hey, Baby. This is tight." Ida giggled like a school girl while he tightened his hug and nibbled her ear lobes. She winked at her husband and said, "I'll show you tight later."

The final tonality seems to have become the end of a string of melodies played in chords both light in harmony and sweet in memories that will continue in the rhythm of the creator of the original musical score. Many years later, Myrtle asked Thera a question during one of her visits. She queried, "Now you know I was adopted, don't you?" Thera truthfully answered saying "No, I only knew that you lived with your Aunt Ida and Uncle Wilbur." Myrtle, who was as dramatic as ever, strutted across the room and picked up an old photo that sat on the tall piano that she'd played during her high school years,. After taking a long look at it, she handed to Thera the enlarged picture. In the picture, Myrtle stood beside a man whom she was the spitting image of and said, "Thera, that's my father, Farmer Adonias Wilson." She continued to speak while Thera sat with her mouth opened in total shock at the words that were being spoken. Myrtle continued to speak boastfully. "I have a lot of brothers and sisters in Alabama and most of them live on our father's farm. A few of them live in a place called Calico that's tied to a huge plantation where we meet every year for a reunion. They all come to see me when they pass through here from time to time." She said that her Aunt Ida had allowed her brothers go back to Alabama to live with their grandparents but she hadn't let her stay. Thera understood that Myrtlennis probably would have headed straight to Farmer Wilson's farm and demanded to see her father. Her Aunt Ida and Uncle Wilbur would take her for a short visit and bring her back to Indiana. Myrtle didn't seem to realize the confusion her presence could have caused between Dora Wilson and her husband. No one had been able to stop the affair between Callie and Farmer Wilson. She added that most of her rage and defiance had been caused by comments that her Aunt Ida sometimes made to

Grandmothers Effie and Mable about her mother. Thera noticed something about the photo of Farmer Wilson that was another shock because it had been taken by the piano. She then remembered seeing the old man who, for a short time one summer, had sat in the hot car on sunny days while Wilbur tinkered around under the hood. So Adonias Wilson had traveled north to visit his first born child and had taken the picture before going home. She summarized that Dora Wilson must have been a strong woman to have not committed the crime of premeditated murder. With the twins that Dora Wilson birthed, Myrtle's family tree showed eight siblings. Callie Nelson gave birth to six children and Dora Wilson gave birth to the set of twin boys. Callie's children mingled with their brothers in school but until they became independent, they were not allowed to frequent Farmer Wilson's home. Thera wondered how Callie had been able to keep her husband Dude in the blind all of those years while she had babies by a man older than she was by two generations. When she shared those thoughts with Myrtle, she'd said, "I guess she used a taut string to keep her man tied to the rhythm of her heartbeat so that she could swing back with a song she'd play just for him." Thera responded, "Girl, I kind of like rhythm your words just played." Myrtle began to sway saying, "Me too. Listen. A taut string can make bells ring, hearts sing, men kings, women queens, winter spring, and people that dream to do damn near anything." Thera remembered the phrase of a rhyme that read, if it's tight, its right!

The two women finished their laugher. Myrtle whispered in Thera's ear like they were kids again. She said, "If you really want to hear some really tight shit, go down the street and talk to Dude's mother, Iris Nelson. Thera took a rain check.

      And got the heck
      Out of looped strings
      And the many things
      That tied her mind
      In a passionate bind
      To Taut Strings of Calico

THE END

12/16/2005